GypsyAngel-T~~
"Biker
The Black Book Files
T.S. DeWalt © 2023

*Taken from real life events and near death experiences
Without being too graphic in nature*

Copyright © GypsyAngel-Twisted Steel Publications 2023

First Edition

Kindle Desktop Publishing

First published in Great Britain

All Rights Reserved

*We are simply creatures of a mindless repetition, caught-up in a wave of distinct possibility
Which has been deliberately, slowly, and perhaps even painfully played out?
Over the course of a great deal of space and time, that doesn't really exist
But we do what we do regardless, and that's what makes us who we are*

Without limiting the rights under the copyright reserved for this book, no part of this publication is to be re-produced, or transmitted, in any way, shape or form, including photocopying and recording.

No part of this publication may be stored on a retrieval system, altered or transcribed, in any way, shape or form, by any other means, without the copyright owner's specific permission.

The named Author (T.S. DeWalt) asserts his moral, legal and God given rights, to be identified as the "Sole Creator," of this work, from start to finish, including editing, spelling, typesetting, punctuation, language and publishing.

The words within, either written or expressed are merely the author's opinions and/or interpretations of such opinions, unless otherwise stated. The sole purpose of this book is to tell the story, or stories, for entertainment purposes only, regardless of those who may, or may not agree with any of its contents.

The greatest care has been taken in compiling of this book, however, no responsibility can be accepted by the writer, publisher, or any other compiler, for the truth and accuracy of the information provided, therefore, based upon true events and providing certain names, times, dates and places that have been strategically altered, hopefully beyond any and all recognition, this work should only be considered as historical, adult fiction, and any similarities regarding any person or persons, living or dead, is purely coincidental, accept for the author himself.

© *T.S. DeWalt* 2023

For more information on how to order a signed hard copy of this book,
Please email
Gypsyangel@mail.com.

Contents
Book one: A Nomads Tale

Chapter 01: In the Blood.
Chapter 02: Home is where?
Chapter 03: P.P.P.
Chapter 04: Heaven or Hell.
Chapter 05: The Edge of an Abyss.
Chapter 06: Dead Man Riding.
Chapter 07: Control.
Chapter 08: Crowded Trains.
Chapter 09: Deneneka MoogStraffen.
Chapter 10: The Mechanic.
Chapter 11: The Hotel.
Chapter 12: Another Trip to the Past.
Chapter 13: A Different Club.
Chapter 14: The Emerald City.
Chapter 15: A Strange kind of Wickedness.
Chapter 16: Outside El Paso.
Chapter 17: Twenty-Six Minutes.
Chapter 18: The Big Sky.
Chapter 19: Time.
Chapter 20: My Last Fall.

****

Dedications

*To **Sharon**, the love of my life and my very own **Angel**, without whom, none of this, would have ever come about. You've made me want to be a better man and I've lived my life for that, I've lived for you, I've lived for ours, and I live for what we are together.*

And to all friends and acquaintances, both known and unknown, who have accompanied me on this journey, in one way or another?

Not least of which, are those of you who are actually reading these words right now.

I thank you all and I wish you the best in everything that you do.

Prologue

Let me just start out by saying this. I'm old school; I treat everyone as I'd like to be treated. If they're good to me, I'm usually better, and I always have been. Respect is a key issue, as Controversial as that seems to be these days. Morality goes a long ways as well, because the older I get, the less I find of that, and I'm sure that that's not a good thing. A man's word should be his bond, and his obligation is to stick to it regardless of the outcome.

Too many people don't seem to understand that, and they lie, steal and cheat their way through life, as if there were no consequence to their actions at all. That needs to change, before this world can step into its future.

People need to be held accountable. Leaders need to lead and quit ripping people off. Liars need to be exposed, and the people that wage war, need to have that war, brought right to their own doorstep.

The world is ready to change; all we have to do is be that change.

But that's not what this book is about, although some of it might be?

I've lived my life to the Hilt, with Honest, Integrity, Loyalty and Trust. But I'm also a biker born and bred, and I will be until the day I die. It's in the blood, so I won't apologise for that.

I am who I am, and I'm exactly what this world has made me out to be. So if you don't like that, or bikers, or even the machines that they ride, then I'd suggest that this book really isn't for you at all. But if you do like bikers, then what I'm about to tell you, is as straight-up as it gets.

So enjoy what's written here. Relax and spend a little time in my world, knowing full well that you can always leave it whenever you want to, whereas I can't, because this is who I am, and writing these stories, is just a view of the past that I've already lived through.

You on the other hand, could easily throw this book out the window, if you don't like what's written in it. Just don't be an asshole about it, because there's too many of those in the world, in-fact everyone has one, so what would be the point? They all spew shit and none of its sweet. If you don't believe me, chomp on down.

If you do like it though, tell your friends about it. Put it up on your media pages and help a poor boy out. Spread the word and wish me well at the same time, give me a five star rating on Amazon, and I'll write another one, maybe even better next time?

Because there's no point to any of this, if no-one wants to read it. If you don't like it, then just do what I suggested and throw it out the window, it's pretty damn simple really. After all, it's only a book and there are billions of them out there.

Either way, what you're about to read, has already been written, already been lived through, already been put into stone, soaked in blood, sweat and fucking tears etc and there aint no going back on any of it. It's done and dusted. So Enjoy.

1
In the Blood

I was brought into this world just before mid-night, with a large amount of blood on the ground, fire in the sky, heavy smoke rising-up through the air, and a lone wolf howling, somewhere off in the distance.

There was also a dark, shadowy, silent-type of figure that was probably a large bird of prey, silhouetted across a full moon, which was raised-up high into the midnight sky at the time, far above the haze and way beyond the stench of a fading desert, during its pre-dawn, early summer's flight.

It was bound to be a troubled life, right from the get-go, as they pulled me out of my dying mother, and then laid me down in the cool night air, perched on a raggedy ole bedroll, and wrapped-up in a crusty used blanket, right next to an old motorcycle that had definitely seen better days before it was driven down south, along a large empty span of desert highway, that had taken us to the wrong side of nowhere, and would eventually lead me straight through a living hell, before I hit a dead-end that is, and no matter how many miles I had to travel first, or which way, I ended up going?

I had a head full of dark and mysterious secrets back then, that have haunted me, for far longer than I can remember now, along with past-life memories, and some curiously tainted, but colourful delusions, that usually came to me, from right out of the blue, and left me just as quick.

There were some abnormally intensive nightmares as well, which consisted of a somewhat twisted, yet unknown future that never quite seemed to come about as I expected, but they certainly have come close at times, I can tell you that.

My father was a biker, lost to the freedom of the life he chose, and the course that he plotted on that fateful night. His father had been a cowboy, who had owned one of the largest ranches in the State of Texas at the time, and my mother? Well, she was a full-blooded **Cherokee Indian**, who had always told me that she wished they had dropped me instead of that damned motorcycle, which I've never argued with, because I know now, that I've been on one hell of a ride ever since.

Of course, as a newborn child, I wouldn't have remembered any of that shit, but in less than a year, my memories kicked-in, my world turned up-side down, my brain started to engage, and then I began to realize, that my future was being written out in ways that I had no control over, nor did I have any say so in the matter what-so-ever.

I didn't like that, in-fact I still don't, but no matter how hard I've tried to change things, I've had to live with it. So I reckon it's time that I wrote about it, just to set the record straight. This is part of that story; you can take whatever you want from it?

****

2
Home is where?

I live in a house with an incredibly grande, palatial type of view that spans at least fourteen miles, across an amazingly long and low valley, which slowly drifts into a cool, crisp, shallow and almost lazy kind of sea, that most people refer to, as the English Channel.

On a good day, when the sun is up and shining bright, and the weather is cool, crisp and clear, I can sit outside on a self-made, wooden-deck, drinking a glass of lightly spiced, sun-baked, lemon tea, curiously watching, as the ships sail by in the distance, mentally taking notes of their shape, size and speed, while at the same time, silently wondering, where it is, that they might be headed to next.

Of course, there's an app for that these days, telling me exactly what I want to know about them in the first place. Where they've been, where they're going, how big they are and whom it is, that actually owns them etc. But somehow, that information, just takes away the magic of the moment, so I seldom use it.

There's also an app for airplanes that fly overhead as well, which are usually on their way to or from Gatwick airport, or perhaps one of the smaller airports in the area, but it's the same story for them, I still prefer to use my imagination, or at least, what's left of it, anyway.

Far from being a palace though, my home is just a simple one bedroom bungalow, sitting on top of a hill, close to the end of a cul-de-sac, right next to what used to be a Bed and Breakfast that some really good friends of mine once owned and it's slightly above a little town called Heathfield, which is comfortably nestled into the hillside of the Wealden district, which is an area of natural beauty, or so they say, deep in the heart of East Sussex, in the southeast of England.

The house is a little older than I am, it's a little run down to be honest, a little worn out, a little crooked, broken and bent, but it's a house that's lived in, and it's filled with the love of a generation, that I simply wouldn't have traded for the world.

People have asked me, "Where you from Mate?" What are you doing here? Why? And I generally tell them that this is my home, and that there is no other place that I would rather be.

They usually leave a little miffed, slightly curious, and totally confused, because I don't sound like I'm from here at all. I certainly don't look like I would be, and I guess that I don't act like I am neither, at least some of the time anyway. But to me, home has always been where the heart is, and this place along with its people, have certainly taken mine.

It's been that way for decades now and I've loved every minute of it, but before that, I spent most of my time travelling the world, endlessly searching for something that I never found. Wasting so much of my life on trivial pursuits that were never too close to my heart to begin with, and constantly chasing that power, fame and fortune thing, along with all the broken dreams, that I may have held back then, like the ones that most of us find, never come true anyway, no matter how hard we try.

I've come pretty close though; I'll have to admit that. In-fact, I've succeeded in more things, than most people will ever get to try and do in the first place, and I know, that I've had my share of some really good times doing it, but I also know, that I've had a lot of bad times as well.

I've climbed some of the highest mountains, in some of the strangest places and I've seen what life was like on the other side, but I've also been to the bottom of some of the lowest valleys and pits, that you could ever imagine and trust me, I didn't like what I saw there. Not one bit.

I'm guessing that that part of my life is almost over now, but you never really know what's around the corner these days. After all, things do have a habit of going bump in the middle of the night, and the what was, or what is, suddenly becomes, the what could've, would've, should've been, and there's very little that anyone can do about that. Besides that, I'm nowhere near as young as I used to be, nowhere near as strong, healthy, or as restless as I once was, and I suppose that, in the grande scheme of things, there aren't that many dreams left for me to even try to make come true anymore, at least, for myself anyway. But I guess that's alright, because I've already done my time. I've played the game and I know, deep down inside, that I played it, just about as well as anyone could.

I didn't win anything of course, but then again, I guess no-one ever does, because that's really not the point to begin with, but I gave it my best shot, and we all know that you can't ask for anything more than that now, can ya?

So now, I sit here, trying to remember the stories of my youth, along with different parts of the life and times that I've lived, for as long as I'm able to and hopefully, I'll be able to invest whatever time, effort and income that I might have left, into this old house and it's amazing surroundings, for future generations that will want to feel the love, comfort, compassion and warmth, that this building, house and home, has brought to me and then of course, I will also keep on supporting my wife, family and whatever friends I have left, as well as the local community, in whatever ways that I possibly can, and who knows, maybe one day, I'll be able make someone else's dreams come true, or at least, help them along their way?

Oh sure, I'll still travel, but it probably won't be around the world anymore, because there's really no need for that now. I've been there and done that, and to tell you the truth, apart from private, corporate or even military travel, I've had a gut full of all those high-occupancy, low-altitude, so-called commercial flights, with their nervous and sedated, or completely inebriated, self-centred passengers, that usually end up, very loudly, regurgitating in their seats, and then throwing-up their liquid breakfast, lunch or dinner, into an already used, plastic lined, paper sack, which they inevitably try to hide, somewhere deep in the pocket, that's located on the back of the chair, that sits directly in front of them, usually, without a single thought or a care in the world, for whom it would be, that actually has to fish it out, at the end of the flight.

While at the same time, their darling little angels, are creating havoc by running up and down the aisles, yelling and screaming at the top of their lungs, dodging all the passengers that would surely like to wring their pretty little necks, if they could only get away with it, until finally and quite abruptly, they too, suddenly start to spasm, shake and vomit, which quite unnecessarily, ends up spraying everyone else around them at the same time.

And I certainly won't miss any of those tired, worn-out, over-worked, under-sexed, ill-tempered, hosts and hostesses, that simply can't be bothered to do their jobs right on a good day, let alone in the middle of the night, because of jet-lag and a 24 hour party that they attended to, right before they boarded the flight in the first place.

Nor will I miss those funky headphones, micro-shots, magazines and travel books, along with other personal and duty-free items, that usually get themselves, strewn about, here, there and everywhere, that they shouldn't be, because of high turbulence, bad weather, and a piss poor choice of route to begin with, causing the half drunk, half-stoned, or completely half-witted pilots, along with their crew, to carefully manoeuvre their way around them, much like an obstacle course, as they slowly lumber by, forwards and backwards down the aisle.

Then there's all of those incredibly boring queues, with mile after mile of carry-on luggage, accompanied by what seems to be, so many more wasted hours, filled with the noise of a big-top circus, complete with clowns and animals, all waiting for their passport stamps, along with a slew of extra questions, that you know, you have already answered, on all those bloody forms, that you really couldn't see to read in the first place and last but not least, there's all those cranky, high-nosed, inquisitive, stuck-up, so-called customs officials, that truly believe they have every god given right to detain and harass you, simply because you might look or act a little different than the rest of the people that live in the country that you're visiting to begin with.

And all of that was on a pre-booked flight that you inevitably paid way too much for in the first place, hoping to avoid the exact same situations that I've just described.

But it sure beats the hell out of sailing, where you still have the queues, the kids, the clowns and the baggage, and of course, the wasted boarding time, just so you can spend the first week clinging to your bed, because you can't find your sea legs and your head won't stop spinning.

The second week, simply bores you out of your ever loving mind, with old movies, bad food, too many stupid people, not enough space, and a lack of good entertainment, and then the third week, is usually spent, with most of your time, simply wondering why in the hell you hadn't taken that bloody airplane flight to begin with?

Besides that, with the way that computers are these days, I can easily trip around the world and see what I want to see, without ever having to leave the comfort of my own home. Who would've thought?

Now, don't get me wrong here, because I do love to fly. It's just that I prefer the comfort of a private jet, or a personal plane, or even a helicopter, for some of those short in-land excursions that we all have to take from time to time, and of course, I've flown down many a highway in the past, sitting on top of my favourite V-twin engine or perhaps even a few Japanese four or six cylinders, from time to time, with two bits of rubber barely touching the ground and the wind screaming past my ears, as I cranked up the throttle just as far as it would turn and to be honest, I'd really like to think that one of these days, I'd be able to do all of that again, before I shuffle off this mortal coil, but to tell you the truth, it's highly unlikely now, because it looks like those days are over for me as well, but the memories live on.

The SST (Concorde) was a great plane to fly on, over the ocean of course, not quite as good as a Blackbird SR71, but that's another kind of plane altogether.

London to New York, in just under four hours, and then back to Paris in less than five, having breakfast, just north of Tiffany's on fifty seventh and fifth, and then a fine steak dinner, somewhere south of the Champs-Elysees.

Yeah, that was the life alright, but until they bring back Super Sonic Transport, or perhaps something even better, then I reckon I'll just stay on the ground and eat my food in the comfort of my own home and it's truly beautiful, but slightly less than majestic surroundings.

After all, I have a lifetime full of memories, that need to be written down, which is going to take me years to complete, if I can complete them at all that is, especially as slow as I write.

Some of those times were pretty damn good, but a lot of them weren't, and some of them were simply out of this world, but at the end of the day, they are what they are, and they are, all mine.

I can only hope that you'll enjoy the ones that I share with you and that you'll want to read more of them, as they're written out, because to be perfectly honest with you, that's what this is all about anyway, after all, what good are memories, if you're the only one that can actually use them?

So, where to start? That's always the question, isn't it? No matter what the answer is and I suppose, that it really doesn't matter in the long run, because the stories are already here; I just have to bring them all out of their hiding places and then put them down on paper for you to read. But, it's never been that easy for me, because I've lived my life, as a pretty private individual, most of the time anyway, and I suppose that that has suited me over the years, however, when you're writing a book about the people you've known, along with the things that you've done in your life, then all of it changes in a heartbeat, and what was once always private, suddenly becomes very public indeed.

3
Paedophiles, Perverts and Pretty women

I wasn't born with a silver-spoon in my mouth, and I definitely didn't have a little gold bar, or a crumpled-up gift certificate, shoved-up my back-side, or hidden away somewhere else, just as deep, dark, damp, and mysterious. But I sure had a lust for the life that I was given, and that's just a plain and simple fact.

I was born a fighter, from the get-go, and I reckon that's what really counts in the end, because this life is always worth fighting for, no matter what you have to go through, or what you have to do, to actually live it?

I didn't have a highly-paid, smooth-talking, good-looking, slick, executive type, as a father figure, and I wasn't fortunate enough to have a young, attentive, attractive and affluent socialite, or an extremely elevated, professional, or government minister, as a loving mother, and I'm almost positive, that I wasn't born a royal neither, although it certainly wouldn't have been much of a surprise, if I had ever found out, that that was truly the case.

I was never going to be a movie star, or some sort of super-athlete, or any kind of a high-born society type at all, and I definitely wasn't brought into this world to be a liar, criminal, beggar or thief.

I wasn't that kind of person, and I never have been. But I've certainly lived through some pretty fucking wild, crazy, dangerous, and extraordinary times in my life, and I aim to write about those eventually.

I've been a lot of places, I've known a lot of people, and I've done some incredible of things with my life, but I've always refused to judge, or be judged, by any wealth, property, possessions or labels, that I may or may not have acquired along the way, because let's face it, it's never been the suit and tie that makes the man in the first place, it's always been the way that he wears it, if he wears one at all that is?

Which I seldom do, and to be honest, none of that's gonna last for any length of time anyway, because there's always going to be someone around the corner, that thinks they want it more than you do.

Someone who believes that they deserve it more than you, regardless of the cost or the sacrifices that you've already made, especially your own government, a disgruntled employee, a wife, a husband, your kids, or an ex-business partner for that matter?

Someone's always around, waiting to take what you have, not even realising, that there's always someone else, who's been waiting to take it from them as well.

Never mind, that's just the way things are these days. They say it's a dog eat dog world that we live in, and eventually everyone gets eaten, one way or another. But the truth of the matter is, dogs don't actually eat dogs, they have more fucking sense than that.

My life took on a pretty strange set of un-explained circumstances right at the get go. Complete with a lot of twists and turns in it that appeared to be more than just a little coincidental at times, especially when all the pieces have been put together. Which I suppose, became the catalysts to writing this book in the first place, as well as having the kind of life, where I was always wondering, whether or not, any of it was truly coincidental, or if coincidence really exists? But hey, I'll let you be the judge of that.

The woman, who took care of me after my birth, couldn't afford to keep me in the first place, and like so many other kids, I was eventually placed into a children's home, to be adopted out by not so perfect strangers.

It didn't matter that it was eight thousand miles away from where I was supposedly born. It didn't matter that it was a different country. It didn't matter that the man who essentially ran the children's home, was the uncle of the man who adopted me and it didn't matter at all, that my real relatives, never even signed the paperwork, which isn't legal in any court of law these days. So I hope you understand why, I might have questioned all of that?

Of course, nothing's perfect as we all know, and I wouldn't hold anyone accountable or responsible for any of that today, and to be completely honest, I never knew what happened back then anyway, because I wasn't three-years-old at the time of my adoption.

But I know that I went through hell afterwards, and that's something that I'll never forget.

Apart from being born premature, with a small hole in my heart, undeveloped lungs and a complete inability to move around, I also struggled with different kinds of sicknesses, like Polio, tuberculosis, pneumonia and whooping cough, for the first few years of my life as well, which I've always assumed was actually brought on by the cold, damp, living conditions, that I had to endure back then.

I certainly wasn't alone with that; after all, it was the early nineteen-fifties, and no-one had quite figured out, how to heat-up a house properly yet, apart from a central fire place, and a stove in the kitchen, of course.

I was constantly ill, in and out of the hospital for several months at a time, suffering with bouts of pleurisy, colic and gout, asthma, arrhythmia, mini-migraines that would last two or three days at a time, along with major migraines that would last a week to ten days, or more, allergies, drug reactions and never-ending diarrhoea, along with night-time sweats, bed-wetting, the occasional sleepwalking, and some pretty strange and lucid dreams, that never seemed to leave me alone, as well as a large amount of intense, and crazy nightmares, that I still remember to this day, amongst some of the other things that I truly wish to forget.

I was less than a year old, when I had my first major event, which seared me down to the bone, and literally changed my life forever. Caused by a simple pot of cooking oil that was left unattended, and boiling away on the top of a stove, while an incredibly curious, but slightly frail, baby-boy with blonde hair and blue eyes, and nothing on but a diaper, quickly reached-up for its handle without another thought in his head, pulling it downwards and spilling its contents all over himself.

That was a pretty rude awakening to say the least. A baptism of fire, as some would describe it. Quite possibly the work of the Devil himself, with the mark of the beast, left on a throw-away child, that was never going to amount to much anyway, which was the belief of far too many people back then, especially afterwards.

Something that would never be forgotten, or forgiven, I can tell you that, etched into the deepest, darkest, memories that I have of this life, along with all of the scars that came right along with it, both inside and out.

That was only the beginning of my journey, and I had already lost my voice, the use of one of my hands, most of my senses, and almost an eye as well, which I certainly wasn't too impressed with, but I soldiered on anyway, as we all do in the end.

I lost whoever it was that was taking care of me after that; No-one ever told me, what actually happened to her? It's assumed that the bills from my accident were probably way too much to for her to handle, but maybe it was something far more sinister?

What I do know, is that I'd been told too many lies about it all through the years, and I never have found the truth, so I've resigned myself to the fact, that I probably never will.

I can only go by what I remember, which, wasn't a lot at that age, but I sure did have my visions back then, along with some extremely violent, and intensive dreams, or nightmares at times, as I've already said.

Suffering from broken nose, two black-eyes, a cracked-skull, and a pierced eardrum, along with a concussion, at the age of three, through a deliberate act of cruelty and violence, by the hands of a deranged woman, who claimed to be my adopted mother, but had no idea of how to raise a child in the first place, let alone, actually want to raise one, wasn't easy let me tell you.

A year after that, it was a completely fucked-up tonsillectomy at the age of four that had me lying on an operating table with a sheet over my head for the next twenty-six minutes. Just about as dead as dead can be.

That wasn't the first of many near death experiences that I've had in this life, but it was one of the longest. I was gone from this world, at that particular moment in time, and I really didn't want to come back to it, not for love nor money, especially back to such a horrifying existence that I'd been living through in the first place. But it just wasn't meant to be.

At five years old, my adopted parents got divorced and shortly after that, a friend of mine was raped and murdered, in front of my eyes.

We had taken off to explore the Hollywood hills sign, which we did, and then we were snatched-up by some bad people, who took us into a house, and fed us candy. But it wasn't really candy, in-fact it wasn't any kind of sweets at all.

It was pills that we were told was candy, and I think that my friend probably ate too many of them at the time. I don't remember much about it though, I've been told that I repressed those memories from the back of my mind decades ago, but I can still remember the cops kicking in the front door a few days later, along with gunshots, and the ambulance people taking my friend away.

I also remember my new adopted father, walking past the cop cars, as he came to get me, and I've had too many dreams or nightmares about it, but fortunately, they've subsided over time.

Later that year; I got bitten by a rabid dog of all things, accidently of course, but it also meant spending a long and painful week, lying in another hospital bed, having a variety of different tubes and needles, shoved into my stomach on an almost hourly basis. Naturally, I was sick for months after that.

At the age of six, I was hit by a car that didn't stop, while I was out riding a bicycle in the parking lot of a motel, that we were staying in.

I can still remember that quite clearly, it was an old black, large, skinny tired, sedan convertible, with two people in the front seat. One was an older man, while the other was a woman, and both of them were in their forties or early fifties.

The car itself, was just like what they had in the movies, an old roller type or maybe a German car with the big front end?

I was lucky that they had used that, because basically, it just ran right over the top of me, after they knocked me off my bicycle first.

Of course the cops decided that it was just an accident, but cars don't hit kids on bikes, stop, deliberately run them over and then speed-up and away, like nothing had happened in the first place, especially in a parking lot, where they veered into me as soon as they came off the main road to begin with.

I remember the woman's laughter as well, and I swear that I heard her say, "That'll teach him for being a fucking rat", a chilling memory to say the least.

We were gone from California after that, and I doubt whether my friend's family got any justice for their loss. No witnesses, no crime they say, pretty sad really.

At the age of seven; it was all of those childhood diseases that got to me, one after the other, like scarlet fever, chicken pox, measles, mumps, meningitis and rubella etc. Of course, I was already jabbed-up to the hilt by then, being a military brat and all of that, but it didn't help. I suffered from high blood pressure, fevers, migraines, heart-palpitations and jaundice, all at the same time.

There were other moments during that time as well, other Incidences and illnesses that really aren't worth mentioning, or even remembering at all, while some of them were simply ones that I've tried hard to forget.

Needless to say, there were too many times that my young body wanted to quit this world for good, but every time that happened, there was always something that just wouldn't let it go.

It's been that way from the beginning, but sooner or later it'll end. After all, nothing lasts forever and I suppose when you get down to it, that's just another reason that I finally decided to tell my story, so to speak.

Now I know, that I'm only one of many in this world, and that everyone has a story to tell. I'm no different than anyone else in that aspect. We all live the lives we live, regardless, and I'm not making any excuses here.

I'm not looking for any sympathy, forgiveness, understanding or retribution, for that matter. I'm just laying it out as I lived it. You can make what you will of that.

I was picking potatoes out of a farmer's field, when I was seven years old, lugging those hundred pound sacks, to the roadside, as I filled them up to the brim, sleeping in an old, abandoned wooden-shack, that had dirt and mud as a floor, and sharing the space, with a variety of bugs, spiders and snakes, along with certain other creatures, that were always lurking around the corner, somewhere in the shadows.

Emptying out buckets of pond scum every time it rained, using whatever dirty old rags, dried-up cow-dung, old newspapers and semi-fresh straw, if I could find it, to plug-up the holes that were in both, the roof and the walls.

It wasn't easy and it sure wasn't sweet, but I didn't have a choice in the matter, it was the life that I was living, and to be perfectly honest with you, it was a whole lot better than what I had already been through, so I didn't complain too much about it. I just did what I was told to do, and that was all there was to that.

I was given a dog, for my eighth birthday. It was actually a gift from my first adopted father, who had recently re-joined me, after being absent since the car incident in California, for the last couple of years or so?

Who knows where he had gotten to at the time? Probably stationed overseas maybe? But I really don't know for sure?

The man had left the military by then and hired on as a farm-hand, spending most of his days mending fences, fixing machines, running errands and whatever else they could throw at him, while I still worked out in the fields.

He spent most of his nights in town, down at a local bike club and a couple of titty bars, chasing women, smoking dope and drinking way too many whiskies, which is probably where, how and why, he got the dog in the first place.

It was a miniature, Doberman Pincher, which I fell in love with, but as fate would have it, and in less than a month or so later, the landowner's son, who really didn't like me, or maybe he liked me a little too much, turned eighteen, and he was given a 12-guage shot-gun for his birthday.

No-one knows why exactly, but one of the first things that he did with that gun, was to shoot my little dog, right in front of my eyes.

I can't tell you what happened next? I was in a state of shock, filled with anger, hate and rage, splattered in blood, and completely insane with it all by then, but somehow, I ran and got a straight razor from somewhere, and then I ran back to the landowner's son, who was still showing off to the group of boys that he had been with earlier when he shot my dog.

I walked up to him without a word spoken, and then I tried to cut his throat, but fortunately, the landowners son was a lot taller than what I was at the time, so instead of cutting his throat, I ended-up cutting him all the way down his chest, from his collar-bone, down to his belly-button, giving him a nice, deep gash, that took over a hundred-and-eighty-five stitches to close, and hopefully, the scar it created, served as a lasting reminder to never to shoot anyone's dog, nor anything else, for that matter.

I remember that look on his face, as he dropped the gun and grabbed his chest. I remember him saying "What have you done now boy?"

I also remember picking the gun up and pulling the trigger at the same time, as I pointed it towards his face, but fortunately, both barrels were empty by then.

I guess we were both lucky for that?

Afterwards, I ran back into the shack with the gun in my hand, not having made any escape plans of course, trying hard to hide myself away in the dirt and the mud, and forget about what I had just done, along with the death of my little dog, that was still laying out in the field, but it wasn't long before they found me, and after getting my ass beaten by them, and the boys older sister, who had joined them on the search.

I spent the next few days, locked in a local jail cell, battered, scraped, and bruised, which I figured I deserved, and then the following months at "Boys Town" for my troubles, which I really didn't deserve at all.

Boys Town was like a boarding school, set-up for convicted juvenile offenders, kind of like the American version, of what a Borstal was here in England.

I was lucky though, I could have been locked away for years for what I'd done, but I quickly convinced the Dr's, that it was a one-off incident, that I wasn't likely to repeat, after all, who could really blame me anyway, it was my dog that the boy had shot, and to me, that was like shooting family, in-fact, that dog was probably my only family at the time, if you really think about it?

Of course my adopted father, disappeared again after that, automatically fired from his job I suppose, and presumably too damn embarrassed, to stick around for me anyway, which suited me fine at the time, especially under the circumstances.

Needless to say, my eighth year on this planet, was literally hell in a basket, and there was nothing that I could do about it, even if it was my fault, as they kept telling me.

Now, there were two types of foster parents back then, as far as I knew? Those who wanted sex and those that wanted slaves, and all too often, the two would conveniently merge into one, especially during the middle of a long, dark night.

It didn't matter if it was a man or a woman, I had already been through both of them by that time and sometimes, it was both at once.

After Boy's Town; I was thrown back into it again, but there wasn't much difference being there really, because boys can be cruel at any stage of their lives and they'll always steal, fight, or fuck in a heartbeat, depending on what they think they can get away with at the time. It's just the nature of the beast, but the fact is, there's too many sick and twisted fuckers, in this world, that don't give a damn about how old you are, who or what you are, or what your situation is, just as long as you can get them off, and I reckon that I was about two years old when I realized that for the first time, no more than three, that's for sure.

Paedophiles, Perverts and Pretty women, I've survived them all sure enough, but that's just another thing that's haunted me for most of my life, along with the people who became such a disappointment to me, because of that in the first place, and trust me, there were too damn many of them.

Relatives, teachers, neighbours and friends, and the list goes on. But let me tell you something here and now, there's no excuse for an adult to be fucking around with a child, and it doesn't matter how small your dick is, or how much you twitch, because children, have the right to be children, for just as long as they can be, and the only right you have to that, is to leave them the fuck alone, plain and simple.

This world is sick enough, without putting any of that shit on a child and I don't care who you think you are or what your fucking religion is, it's just wrong, with a capitol W-R-O-N-G.

I was out packing, lugging, and selling fruit and vegetables, along the side of an open road, at the age of nine, and after that I worked in a bakery for a little while.

I helped deliver milk in the mornings, and I had a paper route as well, by the time I turned ten. When I reached eleven, I stayed with some bikers for awhile and started working on a building site, as a carpenter's helper, which eventually became one of my main forms of income through the years, but there was a lot of other jobs that I did along the way, and to be perfectly honest with you, there were probably too many of them at the time, especially back then, but still, I always did what I had to do, no matter what that actually was? I also got myself into a world of trouble back then as well.

Now apart from time in the Military, being a patch-holder for a motorcycle club, and owning my own Roof Consultancy and General Contracting business, I've chased storms for a living, worked for travelling fairs, spent time as a roadie when I was younger, was a bouncer, a doorman, body-guard, and a part-time bounty-hunter as well, and yes, I had to shoot a couple of people during that time, in self-defence of course, but that was my life back then, and I had to live it, to the best of my abilities.

I was young, cold, hard, loveless, and probably heartless, during those years as well, toughened by the life that I was forced to live and what I had to do with it, but I took no quarter, and it didn't matter who or what it was, it was always my way or the fucking highway, and if people didn't like that, then they had best be moving on, just as quickly as they could, because I didn't suffer any fools gladly, as the saying goes. I never have and I never would?

I don't regret any of that, it's just the way that I had to live, but I also know that I might have been a little too hard on certain people, other than what I should've been, and I realise now that I'll have to live with those decisions, regardless of the way that things actually turned out?

I've collected old cars, bikes, dirt-machines, and a variety of scrap-metal for a living. I worked on farms, ranches, mining fields, and so many building sites through the years, that I could never remember them all.

I've also worked on seismic monitors, and different oil rigs in the Arctic. Lumber mills and logging camps in the Pacific North West, bars, restaurants, truck-stops, and gas-stations, not only from coast to coast, north to south, east to west, but also around the world at times, and I could never even count all the factory jobs that I've had in-between, which almost drove me completely insane with their incessant little noises, mindless repetitions and never-ending bloody split-shifts.

I hated those times with a passion, and I guess I always will. But along with all of that, I managed to hold a few positions with some fairly prominent and high-profile corporations, like Boeing, the Southland Corporation, Black-Rock and Enron for awhile, which also included some national-defence contractors, eventually becoming a sub-contractor of choice, to most of them.

There was even a time between all of that, when I was the personal body-guard of a certain VIP, which I may tell about, at some point in the future, just not yet.

My military experience, being a biker, and knowing some fairly interesting people, certainly got me that gig, but then again, I was probably just in the right place, at the right time.

Anyway, as a Contractor and then later on as a Consultant, I was at the top of my field and all of that eventually took me to the top of some of America's largest and tallest buildings, like the 747 hanger, in Everett Washington, or the Mall of America in Minnesota. One Union Square, and the Vance buildings in Seattle, the Sears Tower in Chicago, the CN Tower in Toronto, and both of the Twin Towers in New York City, just to name a few. In-fact, I may have been one of the last roofers on top of those buildings before 9/11, but that's another story altogether.

I spent a lot of time chasing storms through the States and Canada, as I said, which provided me with an extremely good living through the years, while at the same time, it simply trashed any real hope of living a so-called normal kind of life, that I may have wanted, and of course, I played guitars, wrote a lot of songs, and rode motorcycles through-out those times as well, if not every day, then every chance that I could get.

I've worked from daylight to midnight, seven days a week, doing what I had to do to survive. I've worked four hours on, and two hours off, twenty-four hours a day, seven days a week, for months at a time, and I even took on three fulltime jobs at the same time, at one point in my life, which really did drive me mad, through a lack of sleep, if nothing else?

And all of that, was because I had to keep a roof over my head, put food on the table, pay the bills, and try to get ahead in this life, the best ways that I could, and yet sometimes, especially when I think about it now, I realize that I'm no further ahead now, than what I was when I first started out all those years ago, feeling like a Hamster, left on a treadmill, endlessly running its life away. Who would've thought?

Now I suppose that some people might think, that was a pretty charmed life, and I'm sure that I wouldn't argue much about it, because I know just how lucky I was, to have been able to live it. But there were other times in my life, when I was homeless, jobless, helpless, and completely hopeless, not ever knowing what the next minute would bring, let alone another day, and you can bet that I've prayed to the Angels, to never be there again, because I had already lost most of my mind, half of my senses, all of my family, most of my friends and acquaintances, and sometimes I had even lost every bit of meaning, and desire that I had for life itself, but I was still here, and I would be for awhile.

And through it all, I've heard the voices of the dead egging me on, and I've seen that proverbial light that shines so bright at times, at the end of a very long, dark, tunnel and you can believe me when I say, that there was more than just once or twice in my life, that I've had to travel up and down its entire length.

I've also been told by some of those that have left this earth before me, that there is definitely more to life than what we will ever know?

Hell, I've even talked to God, or at least what my idea of God really is, and I believe that he or she has answered me back on more than one occasion, and maybe even the Devil himself, has had a few things to whisper in my ear as well, if I would only stop to listen that is?

Of course if you don't believe in any of that, then you could just say that I lost my fucking mind for awhile, and that maybe this entire book is simply an insane effort to justify all of that to begin with, written by the insane, for the insane? Who knows?

I've was never materialistic, or even interested in a lot of money as far as that goes, although I've owned several different types of businesses through the years, a few houses and properties etc, but unfortunately, I could never seem to plan for much along the way, because I found out too early in life, that plans, like promises, get broken, and then all that you're left with, is an incredible amount of heartache and pain.

So, I've tried to avoid situations like that whenever I could, although I realized that it wasn't a possibility in the first place, because there was always going to be those "ties that bind," that everyone seems to collect and gets attached to, just like my little dog "Red," when I was only eight-years-old, and it's the same for everyone else, no matter who you are, where you come from, or where it is that you think you're going to in the first place?

From the time that I was four years old, lying dead on an operating table, for those long, suffocating, twenty-six minutes, right-up to my latest accident, that stopped my heart from beating for a few seconds, something has been here for me, something has been looking out for me, something has been watching over me, something has been keeping me moving along, and I believe it's still here.

I'm sure it exists, but I have no way of proving it. In-fact, I don't even know what it is, but it's always been here. I can feel it, I can taste it, but it's only when I get close to it, that I actually get to see it, which is a shame really, but in the end, I know that's the way it has to be, because let's face it, everyone wants to go to heaven at some point in time, if there is such a place? But nobody wants to die to get there, and who could blame them for that?

Of course I may be insane, but then again, maybe it's true that only a few people will ever get to feel what I've felt? It's a feeling that I've had for most of my life, and it's a belief that's never changed, no matter where I've been, or what I've had to go through. But don't get me wrong here, because that aint what this book is all about either.

There's things going on in this world that no-one will ever know, but all I can do is write about what I do know. What you're reading is only the beginning of what I'm going to write about, because I'm hoping to write at least five books in this series altogether, not all of them will be the same subject though, because I have different stories for different occasions, but it all depends on how well this one goes down?

Each one will be a book on its own though, with different characters and places etc. After all, I bore myself to tears most of the time, so I'll write about others, that's for sure. Anyway, enjoy.

****

4
Heaven or Hell

There was a time when I lived like some kind of jacked-up, modern-day cowboy, out riding the range, on a slick little, dark-painted, one-trick pony, that was always filled with liquid magic, surrounded by polished chrome, soft rubber tires, decorated Italian leather, and a large V-twin motor, sitting way down low, humming between my legs, while resting on a hard and rigid, American made steel frame. Back in the days when America still made steel that is.

I fell in love with motorcycles before I could ever ride them, and once I learned that, I expected to keep em up-right, straight, and in-between the lines, as I effectively and efficiently, manoeuvred them in and around all of the traffic, that was out there with me, somewhere, no matter where that somewhere was at the time?

I learned to avoid every seen, and sometimes un-seen obstacle that flew my way, for literally decades by then, which always appeared to be waiting for me, like some sort of mad, or insanely demented demon from hell, or perhaps it was simply a stone-cold, murderous assassin, who was usually looking for the right opportunity, and the exact moment to strike.

In-fact, there were years on-end, when I'd practically fly through all of those tight, little corners, long drawn-out curves, and sudden lane changes, that were consistently being thrown-up along the way, catching the wind for days at a time, riding at eighty-five plus miles an hour, just about every chance that I could get and always trying to find that succulent little sweet-spot, on my American-made V-Twin motor, while at the same time, enjoying the vibrations that came right along with it, that usually put me somewhere in the middle of a "Mental Zone" that I could never truly explain, or even start to understand?

And if I was lucky, which to be honest, I usually was, it was with the wind and the rain, falling somewhere else, way off in the distance perhaps, with the sun beating down upon my back, or the moon, high-up above, softly illuminating, my way back home, no matter where that was at the time?

Sometimes, I'd travel like that for days, scooting from one part of the country to another, with nothing more than a smile on my face, and the love of freedom, etched somewhere, deep inside my still beating heart, but most of the time, it was usually around the area that I was living in, or visiting, and perhaps a few of the other towns that were scattered up and down the highway, north, south, east or west.

A lot of that time, was spent with some pretty close friends and associates, who were riding alongside me, or slightly behind, in a well-known formation that was establish almost a half-century before. But there were other times that I can still remember, when I was out there on my own, flying down a road that I never knew existed, let alone, where it would take me to in the end?

Normally, I'd carry a set of handmade, richly-embossed, Italian-leather, saddle-bags, along with a few small but necessary hand tools, a fairly large hunting knife, and at certain times of the year, a somewhat bulky, but still soft and comfortable bed-roll, just in-case I had a reason to pull up along the way. And then of course, there was my favourite little chrome-plated snub-nosed, three-fifty-seven magnum, which was small, light and hammerless.

It was a Smith and Wesson, with a smooth, black hand-carved, wooden handle that had the word *Gypsy* etched into the bottom left-hand corner of it, which I carried with me on most of my rides.

It was a gift from a good friend of mine, whose life I had saved one night, from a group of street thugs that were literally kicking the shit out him in an alley way at the time, in a case of mistaken identity I might add, as we both found out at a later date. But it didn't matter about that, he was a friend that needed help, and I just happened to be in the right place, at the right time. They picked on the wrong man that night and it was the wrong time to be messing around like that anyway.

Or perhaps, it was a plain and simple Army issued Glock, or my old Desert Eagle, that was strapped to my side for good measure, covered-up or concealed, with a tight, smooth, soft leather vest, accompanied by a well-worn, road-beaten jacket, that had two rockers, both above and below a certain well-known, and extremely hard to miss patch, that was centrally located on the back of it, along with tags on the front and down the sides of it as well.

I was the kind of man that usually got his way back then, and I always made damn sure that it showed every chance that I could get. It didn't matter where it was or who I was with at the time. I walked tall, pulled my own weight, had my eyes wide open, kept my back up against the wall, and continuously held my head up high, no matter what? I was living my life to the Hilt. And that was about all there was to that.

I owned some reasonably lucrative businesses at the time, which employed dozens of people, on a full-time basis and a few more, on a part-time one as well. I also owned a couple of dozen motorcycles, some pretty fast cars, a few old pick-up trucks and a couple of great RV's, along with several private properties, and some prime commercial real-estate, that were all rented out or leased, and securely handled by a management company that I had also bought shares in, at one time or another.

I owned a restaurant, a night-club, a couple of bars and a gas-station, at one point in time, and I managed to acquire several shares in other corporations that were either up and coming or already established in the world of business and down on Wall Street, but don't get me wrong here, because I certainly wasn't rich by any means, I just had it going on, and I was always hungry for more.

After all, I was fairly intelligent and knowledgeable with it as well. I was young, quick, decisive, intuitive, strong, not bad looking and usually healthy back then, but more to the point, I had always held on to my own no matter what, or where?

Of course, I had partners to contend with as well; who always had their own agendas going on, which usually didn't include mine at all, but that was the price of doing business back then. It's something that you get use to eventually, something that you truly can't avoid even today, if you really want to get ahead in this life, that is? But all in all, my heart and soul belonged to the open road long before any of that other stuff ever came about.

I was born to it, made from it, carved into and out of it, and I've always sworn that I had at least a million pieces of it, shoved-up underneath my skin, jammed at the back of my throat, crawling up and down both of my legs, and running through every single one of my veins.

It was my main addiction, and I always made sure that I owned it, lock, stock and double-barrelled at times.

It had been the air that I breathed, from the moment that I came into this world. It's been the water that I drank, the food that I ate, and the life that I lived, for about as long as I can remember, and there was never any doubt about that. It didn't matter what I was doing at the time, where I was going to, or even who I was with? I was a Nomad and that was undeniably through and through, into the blood, down to the bone, and lived to the Hilt.

I never thought that any of that would change, no matter what I did? But in the end, I was wrong in so many ways. ***Dead wrong in-fact.***

****

I'd been the kind of biker that was used to riding up-front and centre, with the rest of the club, riding not too far behind. Plotting the course and setting the pace, for all of the others to keep up with, staying at least two steps ahead of the storms, three, maybe even four steps ahead of our rivals, and then of course, it was five, six, and seven steps ahead of the law, most of the time anyway, but not necessarily in that order, and not always out of harm's way neither, because let's face it, I rode like God looking for Satan most of the time, or at the very least, I rode like Hell looking for Heaven, and I loved every minute of it, maybe even more than I loved life itself?

It was the kind of life, that not many people get to live, and I knew that only too well, in-fact; I was often reminded of it, on a daily basis, by one person or another. Usually, it was some kind of an idiot of course, some brain-dead little parasite with a death-wish that simply didn't have a fucking clue about much of anything to begin with, thinking the world revolves around them so to speak, and believing that everyone else should cater to that. You know the type of people that I'm talking about? They come in every shape and size that you can think of. But I was a man caught up in a man's world back then, and most men that I knew, accepted that for what it was, however, there was more than just a few fools that didn't, and they paid a heavy price for their mistakes in one way or another?

It had been one hell of a journey though, that's for sure, wherever it took me and whether or not I had actually wanted to go there in the first place? But it was also the kind of life that most people wouldn't want to live, even if they could, because it was never quite as simple, safe, or secure, as it should have been and at certain points in time, it was always full of problems in one way or another, no matter what I did or what others did along the way. And I know now, that there were too many times, that it should have taken a much better man than me, to actually sort things out. But hey, I've always done what I've had to do, and you definitely can't fault me for that. Or can ya?

I suppose that's why we surround ourselves with people that we know in the first place? People that will always have our backs, and then live their lives, the same ways that we live ours, to the Hilt, plain and simple. People, who believe in the club and the some of the same things that we do, like Honour, Integrity, Loyalty and Trust. Because when the shit hits the fan, you're not the only one that's going to catch that splatter, and the more hands that you have with you at the time, the quicker you'll be able to clean up the mess, and then hopefully, move on to better things.

At least that's what you tell yourself, and for awhile, it may be true, but we all know that when it gets right down to it, it's going to be our life that counts the most, to us anyway, no-one else's, and then you'll have to do, whatever you have to do, no matter what the consequences are.

That's just the nature of the beast really, or the name of the game if you'd like? It doesn't matter about the people that you may have helped along the way, or how many of them have actually turned around and helped others, if and when they could of course, or even the ones that you've had to hurt in-between times, because that's just the life you live, and you'll need to get your head around that sooner or later, otherwise it'll just drive you mad in the end.

Now, the very nature of being a patch-holding biker, such as an Angel or an Outlaw, a Profit, Joker, or a Priest, or any number of the so-called one-percenters that are out there at any given moment in time, could quickly bring on a whole slew of negative imagery, combined with some pretty hefty metaphors, to some people's minds at least, that live in today's society, unless they themselves are actually bikers, or at the very minimum, they've known a few bikers in the past.

Usually, the word thug, gang, greaser and criminal, quickly enters into the minds of a lot of people that don't actually ride a motorcycle to begin with, or have never had any real interest in motorcycles in the first place.

However, that's a wrong use of the terminology, and it goes against the very definition of what being a "Real Biker" is all about. Which to be honest; has always been too negative and unjustly promoted as such, through a variety of bought and paid for media outlets, and throughout the course of time.

Fake news, is what it is, and we've all seen it before, no matter what it's about, or even when for that matter? But don't take my word for it. Check it out for yourself.

The fact is; that in a majority of countries and cultures around the world today, you'll find a huge percent of the population, quite familiar with most motorcycles and their riders, and they've all supported that lifestyle, in an assortment of different ways.

Motorcycle Racing for instance, has taken on a phenomenal up-turn, in recent years, with a heavy onslaught of super-bikes, and e-bikes, that have been created by various manufacturers, and the industries behind them.

Every motorcycle out there, has had a team of not only riders, but designers and engineers, architects, manufacturers, sales personnel, assembly-workers and painters, then there's mechanics, truck-drivers, transport-managers, cooks, cleaners, hotel chains, along with a variety of clothing accessories etc, all of which, include the general population that's surrounds them, and then goes on to support an even larger lifestyle, that spans from the lowest, to the highest levels, in every society.

Of course, there's the off-road bikes, the scramblers, climbers, field and track racers and the tricksters etc, who's owners, simply live for and love to do what they do, always spending huge amounts of time, money and energy doing it.

Motorcycles have taken on the world by storm and stealth, growing more popular, on a yearly basis, with lighter, faster, and larger machines, than ever thought possible before and of course, amongst all of those riders, and all of those workers, there's bound to be a few bad apples kicking around, so to speak, but that's hardly the norm, unless you're a member of an outlaw motorcycle club that is.

Now I'm not saying that all outlaws are bad neither, because you know yourself that we're not. In-fact, you could say that most members of an O.M.C are simply your average type of citizen, underneath their denim and leathers, which typically works from dawn until dusk, raising a family, supporting their lifestyle, and enjoying their freedoms, while being part of the community that they live in as a whole, and that's usually in a good way, but you have to remember that being a member of an O.M.C, also comes with a lot of responsibilities and some of them, won't always be legal, moral, or even righteous at times. No matter how hard we try?

It's the nature of the beast really; and it generally comes with the territory, after all, if you're going to be labelled as an "Outlaw Biker" then you damn well, best be acting like one. Anything less, is just not good enough.

Now, if there's one thing that you need to know about this life, then it has to be this. It takes a different kind of person to be a real biker these days, and I reckon that it always has. After all, you don't wake-up early one morning and say, "Hey, I must be a biker" and then run out the door and buy yourself a full-dresser, or some sort of a manic, speed machine, that you can simply scoot on down the road with, faster than stink on shit. And you definitely, don't decide that today of all days, is going to be "the very day" that you're going to change your life forever, no matter what it takes, or what anyone else, has to say about it.

That just aint a reality my friend, but don't get me wrong here, because we all know that there's a lot of people out there, that really would like to change their lives in some way, shape or form, regardless of how it's done, however, becoming a biker, isn't an option for most of them. In-fact, being a real biker, isn't an option at all.

You don't get to pick and choose this life, instead, it's a life that will always pick and choose you, one way, or another, regardless of whether you like it, or not.

It doesn't matter how much money you have, or even the lack of it, or how much you think you really want this way of life to begin with, or perhaps, you think, that you even deserve it, in some "special" kind of way? But that's not how it is at all, because you simply can't buy this life. It's the one thing that's not for sale. It never has been, and it never will be.

Oh sure, you could always buy the best of the best, if you really think you're rich enough, that is? You could spend a million dollars, or a million pounds, on just the right machine, sitting way-up high, or down so low that your backside is only twenty-plus inches off the ground, mounted on a truly large, quilted, hand-made, Italian leather-saddle, propelled down the road, by an even larger, American made, V-twin engine, with some of the fanciest chromed alloyed wheels that anyone has ever tried to put rubber on. Sporting all of the latest technology, complete with twenty-first century gadgets and some of that fancy Kevlar clothing, right along with some of the best bells and whistles in the whole damn world, but that just aint where it's at my friend, no, not at all. That's not a real biker, in-fact, it's nowhere near.

That's more like a Klingon, Poser, or a simple Weekend Warrior type, that's always been just another Wannabee, no matter what they've done with their lives, or what they think they'd want to do with it?

A Wannabee is someone who wants to be something, which they'll usually never be, regardless of what that something, truly is.

They'll try to dress the part, and act the part, and they'll try to convince everyone around them that that's what they really are, but it's easy enough to see through, if you know what to look for, and besides that, if you're a real biker, then you just live the life, twenty-four-seven and three-sixty-five, regardless of what it means, or what other people think it means, at the time.

You throw yourself into it, consistently and constantly, on a daily basis, hour by hour and minute by minute, like a baptism of fire, or perhaps even one that was performed in a Jewish or a Catholic church somewhere, while at the same time, you'll have to remember that real bikers, don't actually do religion in the first place, because their only God, is the club itself, and its church, is a meeting-room somewhere, that's usually located, deep inside the clubhouse walls.

The congregation, if you'd ever want to call them that, is strictly composed of club members, and they are your family members now as well, and the "Word of God" is the ways of the road, the oath to your brotherhood, and the rules of the club itself, no matter what they might be?

It's pretty much, as straightforward as that, because most bikers know what they are, right from the get-go. They know it every single day of their lives, and they simply live it that way, to the Hilt, into the blood and down to the bone. They don't have a choice in the matter, it's already in their character, it's in their make-up, and there's nothing more that they would ever want, except for that, and maybe, just to be left alone to be who and what they already are.

A Klingon, poser or a wannabee, is just another one of those great pretenders of the world, that almost everyone knows and frequently sees, but don't try to kid yourself for a minute, because there's too many of them out there these days, just take a good look around you, especially when the sun is shining, and the weather is warm. But don't get me wrong here, because we all love those weekend-warrior types. They're what truly makes this world go round, and most of them are fairly harmless anyway.

They're the ones, that fire-up their painted steel, highly polished, chromed, rubber mounted, lean machines, early on a Saturday morning, frequently pissing off their neighbours, just in time to scoot on out into the country, far away from all of the hustle and bustle, of their daily little "Straight Citizen" types of lives. But by the end of a Sunday evening, and usually long before the sun goes down, that slick little painted sled, is headed back into the shadows, to be covered in cloth, and bound-up in chains, never to see the light of day again, or at least not until the next Saturday morning that comes around, and only then, if the sun is truly shining.

****

I've wasn't that kind of biker though, so this definitely aint going to be that kind of story. I already knew what I was, long before I ever learned to ride. I grew up with motorcycles, and I got to know some of the men that rode them, at a fairly young and impressionable age.

Most of them were my uncles, cousins, brothers and friends, and whether I was related to them or not, didn't matter at the time and it certainly didn't hurt me any, in the long run.

They were some hard men with soft names, like Mother, Preacher, English, La-Bonk, and Del-Le-Rue. Cowboy, Spider, Wolf, Waz, Snake, Bear and Rabbit, and then of course there was Sonny, who just happened to be one of my favourites to begin with, and in-fact; as it turned out, I was actually related to him in a certain kind of way.

There were others of course, like Ted Cotton and Ted Bird, who were definitely brothers from a different mother, and yet they acted like a pair of demented twins when they rode out together, always set on some sort of death and destruction, or hellfire and damnation, for much of the time anyway.

Little-Ginge, Brian Abrahms, Bobby Bolton, Pete the fish, and then of course, there were the dozen or so Dubois brothers, amongst so many of the others, with normal sounding names, that I could never remember them all. But they were just as tough and just as ready as the rest, including my own adopted father way back when, whom they all looked up to at the time, and were only too happy because of him, to take a kid under their wings and teach him everything that they knew, about anything at all.

What I learned from them, was a helluv a lot, and there's not much doubt about that, although, what I've managed to retain through the years, is probably debatable, but hey, I guess I'll just have to keep on living with that.

They all rode hard and fast, they worked hard and long, and they always fought hard, and played even harder, living each moment, day by day and minute by minute, to its fullest, never worrying about tomorrow or what it was, that might just never come, let alone thinking about what the consequences might be, that we'll all have to face in our lives eventually.

Live-free, love-hard, ride-fast, get-rich, or simply die-trying, was pretty much spoken from every man's lips back then, and we continuously took all of that, to the Hilt, with Honesty, Integrity, Loyalty and Trust, and that my friend, was about the way it was when I was coming up in this life, but things change, people change, and the world, well, it keeps on turning, one way or another.

****

To Hell and Back

Somewhere out there in the darkness, *far beyond those neon lights. Riding hard out in the country and no-one else was in my sights. Just another lonely Angel, didn't have no place to be. Always running from the Devil, and he was slowly catching me.*

Now I came across a woman, *who was out there on her own? Her eyes were blue and bright as fire, but her heart was made of stone. She was standing at a cross-road, in the middle of the night. I slowed down and she jumped on, and asked if I could ride?*

So I cranked up that ole throttle, *past a hundred miles an hour. She could hear that motor purring and she could really feel its power. The moon was up there high above us, as the sky was turning black. We were headed down that road to hell, and we were never coming back.*

Now, I really don't remember, *just how long we rode like that. It might have been a million miles, with her sat there on the back, but somewhere after my sweet Texas, before that lonesome Georgia tide. I swear I heard her saying; you just took this devil, for a long, long ride.*

And now you might just see me riding, *out there every now and then, an Angel running with his Demons, riding high upon the wind. I never know just where I'm going, but I sure know where I've been.*

You see, I rode that road, right straight to Heaven, down to Hell, and back again.

****

5
The edge of the abyss

I've been a man on a mission for most of my life, but I could never tell you why that was, or what that mission was truly about?

It was constantly changing, ebbing with the tide, cresting with the moon, dropping in and out of my crazy world, like a fresh fallen snow that was scattered on a hill-top somewhere, high-up in the Rocky Mountains perhaps, near Denver, Boulder, or Colorado Springs, or maybe it was down low along that California coast, somewhere between Salinas and Monterey, out near the Fort Ord military base, where I did my initial basic training, all those years ago.

Or perhaps, it was like some of the people that I've known who were simply here today and gone tomorrow, never to return to what could've, would've, and should've been, in the first place? Who Knows?

It doesn't matter now though, because what's done is done, and what's gone, is gone, and there ain't no going back on any of it, even if you wanted to? But I can assure you this, day in and day out, year after year, here, there, or anywhere, I was doing my thing as usual, and I always did that to the best of my abilities, and you could bet your bottom dollar, that it was continuously to the Hilt.

Then I woke-up one morning and found myself in a completely bizarre situation, that I could never fully explain, nor even start to understand, no matter how hard I tried, and I soon began to realize that it was all over anyway, and whatever the mission had been in the past, really didn't mean a thing to me anymore. In-fact, none of it did. Who would've thought?

People say that time, fate and the elements, along with the natural laws of science and physics, all have their ways of catching us up in the end. But I'd been riding that highway to hell and back, from the moment that I took my first breath, long before I could ever walk or talk, and you might just say that there's been some pretty strange, weird, and maybe even wonderful, un-expected and un-natural laws, that were riding right along with me at times, or perhaps, it was one of them, that was driving me along in the first place?

I may never know for sure, because time has a way of doing that, but this is a part of that story, seen through various bits and pieces, of a life that was going places and doing things that not many others, have even dared to dream about.

It was a life, lived to the hilt, with honesty, integrity, loyalty and trust, which is pretty damn important to me as you could probably tell, but more than that, there has been some pretty wild, crazy, and even insane times along the way, and I suppose, if I think about it long enough, there was a lot of dumb-assed luck involved as well.

But I don't want to get ahead of myself here, because this entire story has so many twists and turns in it, that it's going to take some time to weave our way through it.

Now it's an incredible sensation, waking-up alone, along the side of an open road, not knowing where you are, or where you've been, at any particular moment in time. Especially during the middle of the night, and in the middle of a work-week as well, but there I was anyway, and all that I could really do, was to ask myself, ***"What in the hell is going on?"***

As soon as I opened-up my eyes, I was able to take a quick look around, and then realized that I was propped-up against an old guard-rail that was running alongside of what appeared to be a very long, dark and lonely stretch, of empty desert highway.

How I got there? Where it was? Or why I was out there to begin with? Didn't even register at the time, and so I just assumed, that I'd been down that road before, and for whatever reasons, I was bound to be down that road again.

Only this time, the trip itself was a lot different to what I'd been used to before, and I know now, that it was one of the most significant turning points of my entire life, up until then at least. In-fact, it was one that I could never have imagined, planned for, or even dreamt about, for that matter.

To start with, I was lost, which was unusual for me, because I had taught myself how to read a map when I was seven years old, and ever since that time, I've made sure to know exactly where I'm at, at any particular moment and in any given situation. I had also spent years in the military, as an M.P. at first, attached to the Airborne Rangers, and then as a Reconnaissance Specialist, in the Special Forces, or the Green Berets, as they were known back then.

There were a few other things as well, including military intelligence for awhile, jumping out of some perfectly good airplanes at the time, usually just for fun, and only a few thousand feet above the ground, over the jungles of South East Asia at first, and then down to South America afterwards, but hey, that was then and this was now, and to be honest, I hadn't been through any jungles in the last fifteen years or more, except for maybe a concrete jungle that is?

But there I was, alone, dazed, totally confused, somewhat damaged, and completely fucking soaked from a bitter, freezing rain. Who would've thought?

Now, blood had been oozing out of an open wound, that was located somewhere at the back of my head, which had trickled itself downwards, eventually sticking to the shirt, jeans and the leather vest, that I was wearing at the time, and then of course, it finally rested into a thick, dark, semi-circle, down along the ground, where I'd been sitting, for who knows how long?

One of my arms felt like it was broken, completely swollen, awkward to move, numb to the touch, and the hand was totally numb as well. My arms, legs and chest, were extremely bruised, cut, scraped and painfully sore, and it felt as if I had cracked some ribs on the right hand side of my chest, making it pretty damn difficult, for me to breathe at the time.

My left thumb was swelled-up to at least two, or even three times its normal size, the skin had split around it, in several different places, and it was still bleeding. The fingers on the hand, felt as if they had been broken in two, although not nearly as bad as the thumb.

My legs felt like they were on fire, but at the same time, they were as cold as ice, cramping, painful, and it felt like I'd twisted my ankle somehow, making it difficult to use. The foot was swollen, and it was filled with pins and needles, that simply wouldn't quit.

So, I was in a right fucking mess, to put it bluntly, barely alive, hardly aware of my surroundings, and completely caught-up in-between the here and now, and what was obviously becoming a very different, darker and distant future.

My thoughts were running rampant, my heart was racing faster than I had ever known it to race before, my eyes were thick and heavy, and my head was pounding like an incessant bloody jack-hammer, that I was sure I could hear somewhere, way-off in the distance.

I began to question everything that I had ever thought about, or even imagined, while at the same time, I was filled–up with more pain and emotion, than I could ever remember, and at the end of it all, I still couldn't figure out why I was out there in the first place? It was an absolute mystery to me?

In-fact, my mind was blank, as if it had been shut-down, erased, or maybe something worse, and yet somehow, I knew, deep-down inside, that I had spent my entire life, up to that point anyway, trying to avoid scenarios like this, but I didn't know how, and I didn't know why? Still, there I was anyway, and all I could do, was assume that at some point in the not too distant past, I must have lost touch with my sanity, or whatever reality, I may have previously known, for whatever reasons, only I simply hadn't realized it yet, nor had I even seen it coming.

I didn't feel that I was prone to that sort of thing though, at least as far as I could tell? After all, they say that insanity runs in families, but I've never had a family to begin with, so that just couldn't be the case.

There had to be another reason behind it all, and what I had to do now, was to find out what that reason was, if I ever got the chance that is?

I had travelled the world by then, going places and doing things, meeting different types of people, from all walks of life, and then getting to know some of them well enough, to call them my friends, and yet, I had always known where I was, at any given moment in time. In-fact, I had never been lost before, not unless I had really wanted to be lost in the first place, that is.

After all, I had been doing that for years, travelling here, there and everywhere, even going into places where most people would never go, no matter what? Hell, I stowed away on the SS France at twelve years old, not once, but three fucking times.

It was my life, it was in the blood, it was in my heart and soul, so to speak, and I was pretty damn good at doing what I did, even if I did say so myself.

I was born to it, at least that's what I've always told myself, but somehow, after all of that, after all the places that I'd been to, and all of the people that I had known in this life, I still found myself out there on that fucking highway, wondering what in the world, had really gone wrong?

Piss poor planning, you might just say. Reckless behaviour, sudden, or prolonged stupidity, with a capitol S, along with a complete lack of respect, for my own well being, as well as that of any others, that I may have known along the way? Or was it all, actually done by some sort of pre-conceived thought, or design?

Had somebody actually orchestrated all of this? Had I been that stupid to have become the victim of a crime? Or had I simply had an accident that I could no longer remember?

Those answers, were completely absent from my mind, at that point and all that I could do, was hope that time would eventually, tell me the tale.

Now, it appeared that the last of my possessions, as meagre as they seemed, had been carelessly, stuffed into a small set of leather saddle bags, that were lying on the ground, spread out, near the bottom of my feet.

Clothing basically, a set of blue denim jeans, an extra long-sleeved Pendleton-type of shirt, some pretty standard black underwear, and a thick pair of winter socks, along with a small cloth bag, that had a few bits of blue coloured stone and some papers in it, which I could barely read at the time.

Apart from that, it seemed like everything else, was simply gone, everything that I could have ever wanted, hoped for or even dreamt of, had simply disappeared, and there was nothing left anymore, not even the memories of a lifetime, that I knew, I must have previously known?

Homeless, penniless and alone, I began searching for the answers to questions that I never even knew existed, and if I did, I didn't remember them. Where, when, how and why, became too insignificant to even contemplate, and whatever it was that I needed to search for now, seemed to exist somewhere far beyond the realms of any imagination, reality or comprehension, that I may have had, and yet somehow I knew that it was there, none the less, if I could only find it?

Then, as I sat there watching the rain, slowly turn itself into snow, I started to feel as if I was slipping towards the edge of an unknown abyss, about to be dropped into its dark, frozen, depths, and I suddenly realized, that it didn't matter about the choices that I'd made in this life, whether they were good, bad, or completely indifferent to what any other person would actually choose? Because the fact was, knowingly or not, those choices had already been made, regardless of who it was that might have actually made them, and the consequences of those choices, had led me up to that moment, a moment that was unlike any other moment that I've ever experienced before, or at least, that's what I thought, as I sat there shivering from a bitter cold, harsh and howling winters storm.

Now most people would probably tell you, that I was suffering from some sort of shock and concussion, along with some extreme exposure to the elements, and with a certain amount of damage that was done to the back of my head, which basically, had caused my brain to swell, and in turn, triggered several distinct, and very colourful delusions, that I couldn't control, nor could I have ever imagined, or even started to understand them. And I wouldn't argue too much about that, because in reality, I was simply sitting there alone, at the edge of a long, dark and empty stretch of highway, watching what was left of my shattered life, quietly fade away, possibly faster than it had ever done before.

However, what I was feeling at that particular moment, and what I was truly going through, were completely different things, and that alone gave me reason to reinforce the belief that I've always had, that there is something more to this life, than what any of us, actually realizes? But don't just take my word for that, because it may be the path that I alone have had to take and your own path, as well as any others, might actually lead you towards a different destination altogether, who knows?

What I can say, is this. That Abyss, has always been there, lingering, somewhere far beyond the depths of my imagination, or the lack of one, and the real question wasn't whether I was about to fall into it?

No, the real question was more like, "Was I finally making my way out of it?"

The answer remains the same. The truth can never be changed, but I believe it's the perception of that truth, that I learned to recognize, and perhaps, even more than that, I may have actually come to accept it for what it really is.

What to do with it though? Well, that's just another question, that's been running through my mind ever since. A question that I've been trying to find the right answer to, especially after all these years. Writing about these things and telling the world my story, might hold the key, but who really knows, in the end, all I can do is try.

You see, I never realized, just how far that road would take me, or how many years would fly by afterwards, or even where it was that I had already been to in this life, long before that moment ever came about. After all, I was dead to the world at that point in time, and I guess in some ways, ***I've been dead to it ever since.***

****

6
Dead man Riding

When you're dead, you're dead; it's as simple as that. You don't know what's up or down, in or out, here, there or anywhere and you really don't care anymore, because nothing seems to matter now, if it ever did? You don't feel, you can't hear, and you definitely won't speak.

Life goes on without you, as if you were never there in the first place and there's nothing you can do about that, even if you wanted to or if you really tried, because the dead are dead. They don't tell tales. They don't lie, they can't steal and they definitely won't cheat.

At least that's what we've all been told in the past, but I can assure you this, that ain't always the way it works, because sometimes, there are those clever little clues, along with certain signs and signals, that the dead use to communicate with, and then of course, there are those other times, when the dead, will actually rise-up again, and return to the land of the living and usually, that's with one helluva vengeance.

I know this for a fact, because I've been dead before.

****

But let me back up for a minute, and I'll tell you how I got into this mess in the first place.

It was another time, another place, and a different kind of life, compared to what most people were living back then, but it was never gonna be the way that I thought it should have been, no matter how hard I tried to change it.

It was all that I had ever known though, and I had lived with those thoughts on a daily basis, for too many years by then, secretly hoping that things would eventually change themselves. But nothing was ever as simple as that; in-fact, nothing was ever quite the way that I thought it should have been in the first place.

There was always some sort of outside influence, some kind of un-seen, or unknown presence, with a hidden agenda, or maybe it was a dark ominous cloud, that was descending over my head, along with an inevitable course of action that I'd have to take, no matter what it cost me and regardless of what I wanted or at least what I thought I wanted at the time?

After all, it had been that way for my entire life, and I guess that I just figured that that's what had gotten me down the road this far to begin with. So, I wasn't about to stop it now, even if I could?

I took a long look around, as I left the club that night. Almost as if I was looking at it, for the very last time.

I remember seeing a young heavy-set prospect, with a shaved-head, a dangly earring, tight, worn-out, old blue jeans, and some sort of crazy looking tattoo that appeared to be travelling up and down the side of his face, then rapidly disappearing underneath his collar, that I had never noticed before.

A newbie I quickly assumed, that was standing outside, smoking a cigarette, alone in the shadows, near the end of the building, watching over the motorcycles that were all lined-up in a row, with their heavy ass-ends, tucked-up tightly against the wall.

The kid had nodded his head in my direction, as I finally made it through the door, so I just assumed that he knew who I was, although thinking back on it later, I wasn't so sure? After all, he could have been anybody really?

He was a single, dark, solitary figure, out there on his own, standing underneath a moonlit sky, watching over a half-a million dollars worth of G.A.M.C. machinery, as if his very life depended on it, which to be quite honest, it probably did?

Let's face it; bikers can be pretty damn precious about their machines. I know this to be a fact, because I always have been and I guess I always will be.

I also noticed a couple of love-birds that were sitting in the cab of their pick-up truck, that was parked-up near the corner of the lot, with its engine still running, sucking face with each other, entangled in naked arms and legs at the time, totally oblivious to the outside world, and without a care or even a worry, about who could actually see them sitting there.

Then I noticed the two tractor-trailers, which were parked-up just outside the hotel rooms which were further across the lot, one was a dark-red, bull-nosed Peterbuilt, and the other some kind of fancy KW cab-over, if I remember right?

There were three more without their trailers, parked head to toe further out on the road as well; all five of the hotel rooms were booked as usual. Business was good.

It was easy money really, and the girls who worked it, they were always kept happy, healthy, safe, and secure. After all, the restaurant was open twenty-four-seven, three-sixty-five, and every one of the hotel rooms, had a hidden panic button, that went straight to security, if trouble ever happened?

I had always run a tight ship, and I've never liked stupid people, so if any punter got out of hand, they got tossed quicker than what they knew had hit em, and if they didn't like that, or if they were simply too much trouble to begin with, then they were quickly eighty-sixed for life, never to return.

Anyway, all of that was before I started-up my bike, kicked it into gear, twisted the throttle, and then finally roared off, out of the parking lot and into the middle of the night, like a mad-man on a mission, out for one last and final ride.

Of course I didn't know that yet, but I swear that I could feel it coming anyway, like a bad omen hanging around your neck, pounding you to the ground, tearing you up inside, and then trying to smash the life right out of you.

It was a moment caught-up between what was already and what was yet to come. But again, I didn't know that? I didn't know that I was a dead-man riding that night, nor did I ever think it would happen so fast?

I suppose that we never do in the grande scheme of things, not until it hits you in the face that is, like some bloody random brick, that's been thrown off an overpass in the middle of nowhere, and by then it's too late to do anything about it anyway, because the damage has already been done.

Assassins, they're always out to get ya, and it doesn't matter who you think you are, or where you're at, at the time? They're out there anyway, especially when you least expect em, when you can't out run em, or hide from em, and usually when you don't even know where you or they're at?

That's when they like to strike though and that's just the plain and simple truth of it all. I've had my run-ins with them before, and it aint too funny I can tell ya, but they haven't got the best of me yet, and hopefully they never will.

It was raining that night, who would've thought? Bloody winter showers and all of that, but I really didn't mind the rain that much, I never have.

A little bit of rain has typically kept me more alert, even more alive, than what I usually felt, besides that, the rain has always cleaned-up the air around me, as well as the roads that were laid out in front of me, but most of all, I loved the smell of it, especially when I was scooting down the highway without a care in the world, alone, relaxed and usually, deep into some sort of restful, or maybe even peaceful thought process at the time.

Now, the meeting that I had just come from had ended fairly abruptly, leaving me with a strong, sharp, twisted, type of feeling that was sitting there, like a lump of hot coal, searing me down to the bone, somewhere near the pit of my stomach.

Something was wrong, that's for sure, but I couldn't quite put my finger on it and I couldn't quite get my head around it neither, which is fairly unusual for me, because I've always been the kind of guy to stay focused, especially when others couldn't. I suppose that my Army days might have taught me that?

There was a war about to take place, and I was caught-up in the middle of it, no matter what I had to say about it, or what I could actually do to try and prevent it from happening to begin with. And I certainly didn't like that much, not one bit. But I also knew that I didn't have a choice in the matter. Too many things had happened for any of it, to stop now. Blood had been spilt, sides had been chosen, and the life that I've always known, was about to come to a sudden, final and fatal conclusion.

Something that no-one would've seen coming, in a month of Sundays. Or maybe I did, but I just didn't want to think about it at the time.

Normally, a meeting at the Desert Rose Inn was a little more relaxed, even laid back most of the time. After all, it was an amazing bar to go to, with great food, good looking waitresses, intelligent bar-keeps, and some pretty good entertainment from time to time as well, world class even, if I do say so myself. But that night had been strictly business, and as usual, business was booming.

Twenty-five or thirty puppets, five strikers, an accountant, a couple of sergeants, three captains, a half-dozen associates, a V.P. (vice-president) and another twenty-five plus, so-called, friends of friends, along with yours truly of course. All meeting over what was yet to come, what was already, and what should and shouldn't be, at least to their way of thinking, but not necessarily mine.

It wasn't bad for the middle of the week though, but I also knew that it was all going to hell in a bucket, no matter what was said or done, and that really isn't a good feeling let me tell ya, no matter who you think you are?

Now, it didn't take a genius to know, that once gambling was opened up to the public, serious money, and even more serious players, would be crawling out of the wood-work, looking for their piece of that proverbial pie, so to speak. And with the new hi-tech machines, that were brought into play, at all the local establishments, it was only a matter of time really, to see who controlled the most, and then to figure out, who it was that was actually, the most in control.

Drugs, prostitution, loan-sharking, certain goods and services, and of course, several different kinds of personal protection, has always been the main stay for most bikers through-out the years, and investing those funds into a so-called, legitimate business, wasn't an easy thing to do, but the talent had always been there for me and I had managed to do quite well, for what seemed to be a fairly long period of time.

Change was coming though, in the form of legalized gambling, Government backed and sponsored, and of course, it was opened-up to just about anyone that had the coin to compete, and you could bet, that there were way too many of those.

Rich kids mostly, with their Daddies trust-fund accounts, that really didn't know their asses from a hole in the ground to begin with, and they certainly had no idea about what to spend that money on. But there were others as well, and some of them were pretty serious players, with old style finances, along with older family traditions and beliefs, as well as numerous connections, that were already well protected, with a lot of old style muscle, and the right kind of modern day machinery behind them.

People like the Irish, Mexicans or the Italians, or the Chinese/Japanese types, which were old school, old families, old friends and definitely old money.

The machines weren't cheap to begin with, because the government controlled that aspect of things. You could easily say goodbye to thirty-five percent of your money, right then and there.

Licensing wasn't cheap, and the location rental was never cheap either, unless you already owned the property of course, which was always in demand, and it was all too limited as well. Federal regulations saw to that.

You could put three or four machines in here and there, but you couldn't have seven in the same place, or you could have a whole building full of machines, just as long as the payouts were only a quarter of what the regular payouts were.

Payouts were maxed at a thousand dollars in this State, which was hardly worth the effort, or so I thought. After all, you could ride down to Vegas in less than twenty four hours and win yourself a cool million dollars with the single flip of a coin there. If you were lucky enough, that is?

But the way the "Man" wanted this to work, was definitely penny on the dollar stuff, and it would take a lot of hard graft to make any real profit from it, even if the larger payouts, were only an average of one, in every three or four thousand.

I didn't like any of it and I argued through the night about it all. On the one side, I could see the long-term investment that was being laid out. Sure, five or ten years down the road, and maybe it would pay for itself, eventually. If everything went well enough that is? But on the other side of the coin, there was also that immediate little cash crunch, or should I say, five million little cash crunches to be exact, and each one of them, with its own name, rank, and serial number, but the worst part about the whole deal, was the locations.

The best locations for something like this, was going to be with the "Neveau Riche." Up-town, five-star establishments, places of the rich and famous etc. Places that were already held by more money, than you could ever shake a stick at and a hell of a lot more influence than what most bikers had ever dared to dream about, and of course, above and beyond all of that, was the absolute power aspect, a power, that could never be bought or sold, for neither love nor money, because it was already owned, operated and controlled, by a certain select and shall we say, nameless few.

People, that could make you disappear forever, without a single trace, and wipe your very existence off the face of the planet at the same time, as if you had never been born in the first place.

Definitely not the biker bars, titty clubs, or even whorehouses, but hey, the "friends of friends" didn't quite see it the same way as I did and all I could do, was wonder why that was?

It wasn't like they were stupid, ignorant, or even asking for a hand out, in-fact, nothing even close to that, because they already had the cash to splash, and they were always looking to invest their money into something new. That's just what they did and there was never any doubt about that. But what they were after this time around was a double-up. Matching funds, along with an equal partnership in the club itself, which of course, was something that I'd never consider doing in the first place, and as it happens, the anti for all of that on my side, was over Two and a half million dollars, which to them was merely peanuts at the time, but certainly not to me.

Right now, was definitely not the time for any of this to happen, to say the least? The **"Bandaleros"** were on the move as usual, and they were pushing the **"Road Kings"** right along with them.

They were two of the largest motorcycle clubs in the world now, and of course, each one had to be bigger, better, badder, and a lot stronger, than the other one had ever thought about being, and they weren't messing around with that.

The war in the east had turned bloody, and it had been going on for far too long now. Regular citizens were being affected; innocent people were getting in the way, some of them had been maimed or even killed at times, and of course, the media was involved, pushing it out on the nightly news, squawking about it on the radio, and then writing it down in the daily papers.

So it was no surprise that the governments on both sides of both borders, started drafting new laws to outright ban, or at least stop motorcycle clubs altogether.

Business was slowing down in the east, which had a knock-on effect for the rest of the country, and eventually, the rest of the world. In-fact, whole industries were drying up, and people were running scared, the federal noose was tightening around them and it certainly didn't feel good to anyone at the time.

I'd seen it happen before, back in the late seventies, and the early eighties. Entire clubs had been wiped out; Montreal was one of the worst with over a hundred and fifty bikers from the Satan's Soldiers Motorcycle Club, that were kidnapped, killed, jailed, hospitalized, or had simply disappeared in one way or another. Who knows what really happened to them all?

It was even rumoured at the time that "Mother Meckuen," the president of the main chapter, had had his head cut off and then delivered to his wife in a pretty little, plastic lined, cardboard box, complete with a bow, and a greeting card, just in time for Valentine's Day.

Now, I ask you, who in the hell does that kind of shit? Nobody in their right mind, surely? No-one could be that sick, twisted, demented or fucking depraved.

Anyway, it was a mess to say the least. No-one knew which way to go from there, or even whom to trust after that, for way too many years afterwards, and it affected far too many people, including some of those that I personally knew at the time.

It was business sure enough, but at that particular point in time, it wasn't any of my business, so I never let it bother me, although I'll always remember it, like it was yesterday and for me, yesterday was bad enough.

In the south, one of my chapters, **Rebel's Crew**, had just got hit pretty badly, and the reasons behind it, wasn't really known yet.

Rebel was all right, but three of his younger sergeants were dead, a half-a-dozen righteous rides were completely trashed and of course, the clubhouse, which they had only just rebuilt that spring, had been blown-up again, and as you would imagine, business there, had stopped altogether, thanks to the local constabulary and the feds of course, even though they weren't so sure who was involved at the moment neither, since no-one was really talking and again, no-one saw anything anyway, because they never do, and who could blame them for that?

I had an idea about it though and I knew that it wouldn't be too long before the truth came out. Shit like that never stays a secret for long anyway. It was only a matter of time really, and I had lots of that.

I had also made a call as soon as I found out about it, and I knew that if there was one thing that the guy on the other end of that telephone line was really good at doing, it was hunting people like this, just as quickly as he could. Which was never too long in the grande scheme of things? No matter where they ran, or where they tried to hide.

Still, things had been pretty good for a long time by then; there hadn't been a killing in my ranks for the last three or four years, up until that point in time anyway, and I was pretty damn proud of that, after all, my boys were well-known to be the best of the best, but it had been a long time coming and like a slow moving storm, it would carry on out of control, and probably for a long time to come. Unfortunately, things like that, usually do.

So no, it didn't make any sense to me, to invest into this new agenda that they'd been talking about. That money was needed for other things, and that was the way that it had to be. It didn't matter who liked it or not, because this was business plain and simple and this particular business was mine. I just had to hold on to it, and then stand my ground as usual. Who would've thought?

It didn't take me long to find the highway home that night. After all, I had made the same trip on a regular basis for the last couple of years or maybe more.

It was my M.C. as well as my nightclub, which I owned outright, lock, stock, and barrel as they say, along with a few personal investors, and the bank of course, and I had always made sure that things were running just as smoothly as possible, even if that meant making several daily visits, or the odd night-time one as well, like the one that I had just made. It didn't matter which one it was, it had to be done regardless, and I was the only one that could really do that.

The rain had finally stopped falling, just a few miles into my ride, and the throttle was cranked wide open by then.

The roads were drying out, and I loved the feel of the wind rushing towards my face. That's what I lived for most of the time, the simple thrill of the ride. The rest of it didn't matter at all, but out there, I could fly and that's exactly what I needed to do right now, I needed to fly. I needed to fly as high and as far, and as fast, as I could possibly go, because time wasn't waiting for me, or anyone else for that matter. It never does, it never has, and it never will.

The wind screamed in my ears, when I reached that hundred-mile an hour mark. One-ten, one-twenty, and if I could, I'd make time slow right down, stop it, or even spin it around awhile, and what was yesterday, would now become tomorrow.

But of course, I knew that I couldn't do that sort of thing, not a chance in hell.

I really don't know why, but for some reason, I started thinking back through all of the years, remembering the good times and some of the bad, as I gently pushed my custom painted, fairly new, modern day, steel horse, in and out of the curves that were consistently laid out in front of me.

Someone had done an amazing job designing that highway, putting all the right cambers in all the right places, cutting through the scenery at the right time, taking it down through the valley along the river, and then a gentle climb back-up to the top, with a few hair pin turns, and the odd ridgeback thrown in along the way.

It was a good ride; it always had been, almost as good as that coastal highway, down in Southern California, which is still one of my all time favourites.

The sun, the sea and the sand, along with a great biker's bar, that was called the Silver Moon, back in the day. You couldn't beat that, no matter where you went.

In-fact, that's one of the reasons that I bought the Desert Rose to begin with; it had the same sort of feel about it. Almost like coming home, not just for me, but for everyone else as well. It was a great place to be, that's for sure.

My mind drifted backwards even further in time. I hated it, but I couldn't stop it. Those memories were rearing their ugly head, and there wasn't much that I could do about it.

Growing up in the fifties hadn't been that bad really. Sure, I lived through a lot of heartache and pain back then, but who hadn't?

I got through it, as we all do. I survived it in the best ways that I knew how and whatever it was that might have hurt me in the past, had just become part of the fabric that had made me stronger in the long run.

It was the iron in my armour, so to speak; a little rusty now perhaps, slightly bent and out of shape in places, possibly even non-existent in others, but still, it was that, that was keeping me protected, even after all these years.

I remember the Chevy's and the Hot-rod Lincoln's of my youth. The fancy Ford coupe's and those crazy-assed, low-riding Cadillac's along with the pretty bottom Mercury's that cruised up and down the strip, half-way out on main street, almost every Friday and Saturday night, with their horns honking, their lights flashing and their radios blaring out just as loud as they could get.

All of them with young assed drivers, that were out to pick-up every good looking woman in sight, as they slowly drove past them, travelling at no more than five or six miles an hour, consistently watching all the girls who were huddled together down on the street corners, that were always talking amongst themselves, and usually about what they were wearing at the time, or who's boyfriend had the finest car, the most money, the fanciest house and probably the biggest dick.

I also remembered watching those girls myself, as they waited around for the Cadillac's to drive by, with their brushed velvet seats, fancy paint jobs, chromed wire rims, and convertible rag tops, which of course, only the richest boys in town could actually afford to drive in the first place.

But the best of the best, was that powdered blue and white, fifty-five T-bird, and of course, the red and white, nineteen fifty-three Corvette, that one of my uncles, happened to own.

They were both kept in perfect showroom condition, all the way up from Flint Michigan and Chicago Illinois originally, but they were hardly driven anywhere else, unless of course, it was out on a clear summer's evening, with the moon shining bright and some gorgeous young, big breasted, little honey, sitting in the passenger seat, with her pretty long legs, slightly opened and her skirt, pulled-up high, and you just knew that she was definitely not into driving too far away from where those cars were actually stored to begin with.

Yeah, my uncle was a pretty lucky guy back then, until the war took him that is. He made it home alright, but he could never drive those cars again, a chopper crash near the DMZ, and then a sniper round that took out the lower part of his spine, making his legs completely useless.

In the end, he sold those cars, wheeled himself out to the garage afterwards, and then put a bullet into his own head. Shame really, he was such a sweet guy, one of my favourites.

I still remember the Bobby socks and the pigtails that some of the girls wore back then, with their super tight, button-down blouses, extra large breasts, hard, lengthy nipples, and smooth, three-quarter length, pleated skirts, while at the same time, they'd be wearing that dark, glossy red, Marilyn Monroe, type of lipstick, with a heavy blush and foundation, green or blue eye shadow, and of course, they all had a smile for every good looking guy that came their way, including me most of the time, even though I was still a baby compared to the rest of them. Well maybe not all the rest, but you know what I mean?

You weren't anyone, unless you had three or four of those sweet babes, riding right along with you, in your brand new Cadillac convertible, driving it just as slowly as you could, around the circuit throughout the night.

Bikers had never been counted for much with that crowd back then, and in-fact, they still aren't. Four wheels are usually considered to be much better than two and a whole lot safer to most people anyway. But that had never put me off, after all, I was more than just a biker, I had a little bit of class going on, at least that's what I always told myself.

I remember burger joints and the drive-in movie theatres, root-beer and roller-skates, street-rods, raisers, and ice-cream parlours, and then of course, I'll always remember my love for the motorcycles.

American made, American strong, with a machine like that, you could never go wrong. Which even back then, was just your typical, mindless, commercial bullshit of the times? It was thrown out on the telly and in the theatres, which I suppose, is no different than today really? Never mind, it definitely worked, that's for sure.

I remember the blue jeans and black leather jackets that I still wear even now, after all these years, as well as the smell of burning rubber in the air, and high octane gasoline, which usually got splashed onto my boots, jeans or leather jacket.

I remember long roads, clear-skies, and mile after mile of used-up old Tar-Mac that always took me to where I wanted to go and a lot of the time, where I had never been to before, but that was the way it was back then, Heaven on Earth, you might just say, at least for a biker anyway.

So yeah, growing up in fifties was just as good as any other time I figured, maybe even better than the rest, but you never know that for sure? Because things change, people change and before you know it, we've gotten a whole lot little older, if we're lucky that is?

I began thinking about what it was, that actually made me the way I am? What was it that led me down this road to begin with, and what had really brought me through it all? Was it my birth mother, or the woman who was gone before I turned three, or my father, who had died at my birth?

Maybe it was my adopted parents that split up when I was five, forcing me to go through children's homes and foster parents, with sick and twisted, wannabe mother and father types, which led me to the streets, and then eventually the jails that I found myself in, right before they shipped me off to Viet-Nam?

Of course, some people say, that it was the war itself, or that it was the memories of seeing a few of my closest friends at the time, shot, stabbed or completely blown to pieces right in front of my eyes, or maybe it was the twenty-plus years of constant, bloody turmoil, that I'd been living through ever since?

Some people say I was a hero back then, apparently more than a few times during my tours over there.

Gaining a Bronze Star, a Purple Heart, and a couple of other medals for some sort of bravery, or so-called exceptional distinction? But who really knows for sure?

I can barely remember it now, three frigging tours over there, and they're all just a bloody blur really? It's pretty strange how the mind works, and it's not really funny how that time has been simply been blanked out. Oh well.

To be honest here, I was just doing what I had to do to keep myself alive, which is something that soldiers, aren't supposed to do in the first place?

They're supposed to die for their country and all of that. So you can believe me when I say, that I was more than a little surprised, when I finally did return back home. But now, I felt nothing really, in-fact less than nothing most of the time, if that was even possible?

Instead of feeling like some sort of a hero, I felt more like a villain. One that was stuck-out somewhere, in another dimension perhaps, or another place in time, and there was always another endless bloody war, no matter where or what?

I didn't like that feeling at all, not one fucking bit. But hey, that was my life, take it or leave it, it was all that I had, whether I wanted it or not, never mattered?

In-fact, that's all that we ever have, so we make the most of it, because when it's over, it's just fucking over, and there aint no coming back from that, at least that's what I used to think?

Never mind though, life has never been too easy to begin with, and if it ever was, it probably wouldn't be worth living it anyway.

Too damn boring I'd have to say, and let's face, what doesn't kill ya, just makes you stronger, or so they say? Whoever they really are?

I was lucky with that kind of thing, because I was never bored for very long; I just wasn't that type of guy. I always had something going on, something that I needed to do, or some place that I needed to go, and there was always someone else to see, day or night, week after week, it didn't matter when, or where it was.

If I was needed, I was there. That's just the way things were, and you can bet that I loved every minute of it, at least most of the minutes that I didn't actually hate.

So, none of the past mattered to me now, because it was all just slivers of some distant, faded, memories, that were comprised of way too much bullshit, that I had to go through, and didn't want to keep in the first place.

In-fact, the sooner they disappeared, the better off I'd be, as far as I was concerned, because everything that I've ever lived through, had only made me stronger.

Everything that I've ever been through, had simply become a part of what I was, who I was, how I was, and how I'd always be, even though, it was never by choice, you understand, because most of the time, it was like sheer fucking necessity, or perhaps some sort of providence, or maybe even karma, built-up from another life?

I was a soldier, a prophet, an engine poet and a brother to the sun, but more than that, I was an Angel, forever and always, and there was no doubt about that, because I was born to it, brought-up in it, lived with it, and I'd probably die from it in the end.

I guess that I figured, that that was about all there was to that, whether I ever wanted it or not, never became a question in my mind. It was all that I had, all that I had ever had, and I held on to it, no matter what.

My life had been lived on the edge of some unknown abyss, standing at a point, that was fixed somewhere between a colourful, yet somewhat ghostly sort of light, and some really dark, powerful forces, that were always more than what anyone truly knew?

One day, I'd fall to one side of it or the other, but the next day, I'd get back up again, and then I'd jump to the opposite side, which is not much more than what a mountain climber does really, at least that's what I had always told myself.

Every day was different, that's the way it was. That's the way it had always been and that's the way I liked it. After all, I was pretty much used to that, and perhaps I figured that it was the only way to be, for me anyway? Regardless of what I wanted, or what I thought I wanted at the time?

It was right about then, that all of a sudden, and out of the darkness, a massive bright flash appeared on both sides of my mirrors, at exactly the same point in time, almost blinding me on my ride. It was like the heavens had opened-up, turning the night into the day, in less than a heart-beat, and sending a shiver up and down my spine that I couldn't possibly begin to describe.

Something had exploded into a massive fireball, something, somewhere, way-off into the distance that was far behind me now, way-back from where I had just come from. I couldn't tell what it was yet, but whatever it was, it was huge and it had lit up the sky like a tomahawk cruise missile that had just hit a fuel depot, somewhere near the southern border of Iraq and Kuwait. Somewhere, around the Persian gulf, as you might imagine?

My first thought was a plane crash, or that a meteorite that had fallen out of the sky, but of course, I know better now, in-fact, it was something completely different to any of that. I also know that I should have stopped right then and there, but I didn't, and I should have slowed down a bit, and maybe even turned around to check it all out properly, but I didn't.

I was in the zone by then; really enjoying my nights ride out, scooting along, into the country, without a care in the world, and let's face it; it wasn't any of my business anyway, so it wasn't any of my concern, or was it?

Oh shit, who put that fucking truck there?

****

Postscript

If you ever hit something on a motorcycle, with the throttle wide open, and you just happen to be up and over that hundred mile an hour mark at the time, then you could pretty well guarantee that you're screwed and about as close to being dead as dead can get, which is undoubtedly the best word to use in that kind of situation. Dead that is.

After all, the bike you were riding is suddenly trashed so far beyond recognition that it would be impossible to salvage any of its parts, or even identify the ones that were left. It would be completely broken, bent-up and twisted, so far out of shape that you could never use any part of it again, with its bits and pieces, thrown here, there and everywhere, which would take days and weeks to finally find, let alone, sort them all out.

Some of which, may have even become a part of what it was that you actually hit to begin with and some of those other bits and pieces, might have even become part of you, turning you into a form of twisted steel, in every aspect of the word and its meaning.

But regardless of that, everything about that bike and you, has suddenly been wrenched in ways that you could never imagine, let alone describe, and every little bone inside your body, suddenly feels as if it's just been smashed into a million pieces, whether it has or not? And if you're lucky, and I do mean lucky, then nothing works at all. Your mind, your body, infact your entire being just stops, and then it starts to go numb as you find yourself drifting into that big black hole that's been filled-up with nothing more than emptiness.

Before any of that happens though, you'll remember everything you've ever said, done and lived through in life, the good, the bad, and every bit of the fucking ugly that you've ever known, or tried to know, or imagined, no matter how small, and insignificant it may have been at the time. And no matter who you think you are, or who you were, and there aint no getting out of it, trust me.

It's a feeling that we'll all have, at some point in our lives, I can guarantee it, but some of us, will get there a little faster than others, and then some of us, might even come back to tell the tale.

****

Addendum

They would've propped-up the open coffin, with me in it of course, somewhere near the corner of the clubhouse walls, leaning it in a fairly up-right and secure position, with a cigarette in my mouth, along with an extra-large schooner of wine, whiskey, vodka, or one of my favourite beers, duck-taped to my cold, dead, lifeless hand.

I'd have a pretty good pair of sunglasses on, wrapped-up tight over my eyes, a soft leather skull-cap, or a great looking, cotton bandana tied around my head and I'd also be wearing, my favourite long sleeved, Pendleton shirt, Levi-jeans, black-leather vest and comfortable riders, all dressed to the nines and going out in style.

Of course, there'd be a couple of young, voluptuous, long-legged, good-looking, scantily-dressed little honeys, standing by my side, attending to my every need, while overseen by the Sergeant of Arms and couple of pumped-up prospects.

My colours would be resting on the back of a chair, sitting close to my feet, with my favourite skid-lid, wallet and gloves, layed out on the top of it all, while one by one, the band of brothers, sisters, relatives, and friends, would slowly toast to my passing, shot after shot, after shot.

A couple of hours later, depending on the mood of course, and when the family was truly ready, they'd finally close the coffin lid, carry me out to old Willies side-car rig and cautiously strap me into it, before we headed down the highway, towards that ancient non-denominational churchyard, with its crowded and overgrown cemetery, where, like many of my brothers and sisters that had gone before me, I'd be carefully laid into my final resting place, within a grave that was already dug out and waiting.

It wouldn't that much different to a poker-run on a sunny afternoon really, with all the rank and file carefully lined-up behind us, travelling two by two, on their trusted, American made, V-twin machines, riding at close quarters of course, each one vying for their own position, to help place the coffin into its final resting place, and lord have mercy on anyone, that tried to squeeze themselves into the procession that didn't belong, because that would have been a big mistake on their part, huge in-fact, but hey, this just ain't the old days anymore. In-fact, it's nowhere fucking near.

****

7
Control

Back in the days when men were men and women just didn't want to be. You know what I'm saying, maybe sixty or seventy years ago now, long before the science and some of its deranged geniuses, started screwing around with the human genome, trying to turn us all into a new version of a "Long Pig" two-point-fucking-zero and then some, most men did whatever they wanted, or whatever they had to do at the time, and just as long as it didn't hurt anyone else, no-one ever questioned it.

They didn't ask for permission and they definitely didn't need a fancy piece of high-priced paper, that was bought through years of mindless indoctrination and countless hours of sleep-deprivation, along with a slave-labour mentality, extracted by some so-called higher educational institution, just to let everyone know, that they could do what they wanted to do, whenever they wanted to do it. Instead, they just went out and did it, and it was as simple as that.

If they screwed-up whatever they were doing at the time, then they'd fix it, or they'd hire someone else that could fix it, and then they'd move on to something else and do whatever that was, in the best ways that they could.

In the end, they'd perfect whatever it was that they were doing, and they'd be damn good at it. Proud of their accomplishments even, and perhaps in time, they'd become the best of best, real experts of their trade, so to speak, and then maybe, they would eventually hand that knowledge down to the next generation.

That's how Business was built. That's how Kingdoms were ruled, that's how the world was run and that's the way it's always been, since the beginning. Just do it.

I've known that in my lifetime, perfecting so many careers, that it might make some people's heads spin, learning most of those skills, from the very best of the best, but nowadays, most people will never know that kind of life at all, because it's been tragically altered, changed with the onslaught of personal Computers.

Let's face it; you can't even take a piss these days, without someone else knowing about it. They monitor your water, your electricity, your gas, the foods that you eat, the drinks you drink, the clothes you wear, the places that you visit, even the blood, sugar, and alcohol levels, that run through your veins, all done with computers.

They control everything, from the World Wide Web, to the satellites up in the sky.
From the family automobile, to every boat, dingy and ship, that's out on the ocean.

They control the planes, the trains, the busses, coaches, and every tank, weapon and bullet, utilized in the fields of war. Hell, they even control the soldiers that occupy those fields, and they always have.

They control all communication, news, phones, radio, television, movies and advertising. They control the schools that your kids are in, the hospitals that are needed for the sick and the injured, and the graveyards that are filled with the quick and the dead.

There's nothing that isn't computerised now, and whether you know it or not, your name is somewhere on their list, tucked away inside a machine, that's connected to a million other machines that they have control as well. But they can't control your mind, not yet anyway. Not unless you want them to?

Don't get me wrong though, because they really are trying to do that. Without your knowledge of course, or your consent, and there's no doubt about it.

They've actually been at it for decades, maybe even centuries, and for some people, they've already succeeded and for others, well, I guess they'll just die out eventually, becoming some kind of faded memory, in a sea of faded memories, lost to the grande delusion of things yet to come, and someone, somewhere, will consider that to be a win-win situation. You can bet your bottom dollar on it.

Simply put, they want control over every aspect of your life, and their ability to do such a thing, is rapidly approaching the 100% mark, whether you know it or not, or whether you want it or not, and it appears that no-one can stop it, or so they say, whoever "They" are that is?

They've taken what was once a living world, and turned it into a dying planet, and the sad part about that is, it's bound to be some sort of computerised, artificial-intelligence machine, that out-lasts us all.

Call me crazy, but I for one, don't think that that's such a great idea, but at the same time, I've also wondered whether it's happened before? Could it be that where we are today, is not really a matter of what "They" call evolution at all, but more like a straight-up, manmade, or maybe some kind of a machine made manipulation?

It doesn't make sense that humans supposedly walked out of Africa a half-a-million years ago, and then all of a sudden, within the last twelve-thousand-years or so, they became domesticated?

How and why that happened, should probably be the subject of everyone's conversation at least once or twice in their lives.

After all, they want you to believe that for 490,000 years, mankind was nothing more than a mass of nomadic tribes, scattered around the earth, living in trees, caves or portable tepees, hunting and gathering what they needed to survive, but somehow, during the last 12,000 years or so, after a lengthy Ice-age, and numerous world-wide, cataclysmic events that saw fire, rain down from the heavens, earthquakes, floods, and repeated volcanic reactions, that surrounded the earth and almost destroyed the atmosphere, they suddenly became aware of a different lifestyle and decided to plant crops, corral their wild animals, and then build roads on difficult terrains to travel on, along with brick-houses en mass, laid out in huge cities to live in. Yeah right?

What really happened during those first 490,000 years and before that time? Where did we really come from, why are we here, and how many times have we been here before, sitting on the eve of destruction, letting these fools rule over us, and letting these machines rule over them?

Is it perpetual? Or do these machines eventually break-down and die themselves? Are we living inside of one? Are we one of them ourselves? Are we living at all?

As you can probably tell, I don't believe a word of it, there's too many questions that remain un-answered, and too many other things that remain hidden from us all.

Too many things that don't add up, and for someone who loves his math, two plus two, must always equal four, not three or five, as some are trying to make us believe.

Darwin wrote a book in the eighteen hundreds called the "Theory of Evolution." With "Theory" being the operative word here.

He was paid a lot of money, by some very powerful and influential people that were out to crush religion at the time, which to be honest, had a stranglehold on society for too damn long. It worked out well and his book became extremely successful, as we all know. Of course those powerful people made sure of that.

Now-a-days, people try to convince you that his "THEORY" actually meant FACT, when we all know, especially in that particular case, that there are no facts. The math simply doesn't add up.

There are no studies, no empirical evidence, and no way to recreate anything of the sort in any scientific environment, and there's certainly no way to monitor thousands upon thousands of years that have already past. Unless they have a time machine of course, but they certainly haven't told us about that yet.

Now you can speculate about it, if you want? You can debate about it until the cows come home. You can theorize it, and you can believe what your so-called higher educational institutions have programmed you to believe, for their acceptance of course, but the fact is, for the last 12,000 years at least, man hasn't evolved at all. In-fact we're just the same as we ever were, maybe even less.

Oh sure, we have the technology of sorts, we've got machines and computers, along with the ability to live like Gods and Kings, but we haven't evolved into anything, in-fact, it's pretty much the opposite. We can't even replicate what the people of the past built during their time, like the pyramids or mega structures that used hundred ton blocks of stone that were hoisted up four or five stories in the air. Structures like the Sphinx or Stonehenge, or some of the temples around the world that have been carved out of pure granite, perhaps on some of the highest mountains in their area, like Machu-Picu?

How about the fact, that there was electricity long before Edison, flying machines before the Wright bros, electric cars in the eighteen hundreds, and electronic robots before that? Don't take my word for any of this, just look it up. I ain't lying.

Einstein explained it all, when he wrote "The laws of Thermal-Dynamics" Which basically states, that everything and everyone, will fall into chaos eventually? No ifs, ands or buts about it.

Yeah, I know he was paid to do that as well, but let's face it, Order out of chaos, simply doesn't happen, without a driving force behind it, and every living thing on this planet, eventually falls into chaos.

It's born, it grows, it gets sustained by others, it sustains itself, and then it grows old, gets sick, withers away, and finally dies. Complexed order, maybe the most complicated on the planet, turned into complete chaos, that's the natural selection of things. That's the survival of the fittest, that's the way it's always been, and that theory has been proven, time and time again.

You can produce it, manipulate it, speed it up, or even slow it down, but you can never stop it, and why would you? It's been that way since the universe began, however many billions of years ago?

It's the opposite of evolution, something that I like to call Devolution, although that word has already been used to mean something entirely different, which makes me wonder why that is? But it's a proven fact regardless. Replicated time after time, year after year, century after century, and you don't have to be a paid shill, or have a piece of paper to know the difference, you just have to open-up your eyes.

****

But that's not what this book is about. That's just an opinion of mine, to show you where I'm coming from so to speak, and it doesn't matter whether you agree with it or not, or whether you can even see the same side of things? I'm not trying to argue with anyone here and I'm not trying prove or disprove anything, I'm just telling a story the way I see it, and as a writer, that's about all that I can do.

My opinions don't matter, any more than anyone else's; I've just written them down for the world to read and I'll stand by them regardless.

I have another opinion before we start on the next part of this book, that I've decided to add to all of this as well, just to let you know where I'm at, and what I believe may or may not be happening on the world's stage today. But again, it's just an opinion, right or wrong, it doesn't really matter. You can agree with it, or disagree; it won't affect what's been written.

It's simply a brief synopsis of the life that I've lived, up until a few years ago anyway, and once you've read this book through, then maybe, you'll know why I think the way I do. And let me just say this, I aint special in any way, shape or form, because there's millions of others that have lived their lives like I have, and millions more that are going to, in one way or another. That's just the nature of the beast that we all deal with.

****

8
Crowded Trains

Crowded trains and over-booked planes, football, basketball and baseball stadiums, over-packed, and over-stacked, with the mindless, arrogant, self-centred masses that are out for themselves, regardless of the reason, the season, or even the weather? And the amount of garbage, misery and debris that they leave behind is overwhelming.

Indoor hockey rinks, and outdoor rock concerts, packed-up pubs, and stacked-up clubs, that are continuously filled with inebriated little fools that can barely spit out a complete sentence, or even stand-up straight, most of the time, including yours truly, when I was too damn young to know any better, or just too stupid to care.

Private parties, movie theatres, mass demonstrations, and some pretty irate, even intense rush-hour traffic, while standing-still in the middle of the gruelling heat, on a long summer's day, located somewhere just outside of Mobile Alabama or Memphis Tennessee, Tulsa Oklahoma, Dallas, El Paso, Huston or Phoenix Arizona, while sitting on top of a large V-twin motorcycle, with no particular place to go, and no real need or even a good reason, to be there in the first place.

Sturgis and Miami spring breaks, New Orleans Mardi-Gra, Cinco de Mayo and the day of the dead (Dia De Los Muertos) somewhere south of the border?

New-York in the middle of its longest winter, watching the ball drop in Central Park, with over a million other people at the time, who were all wrapped-up in their Parkas and blankets, huddled together in three feet of snow, waiting for the frostbite to set in and then it was off to California for an even longer, hotter summer, while running mindless through the streets, with the Watts riots going on, or the ones that were brought on by the injustices of the Rodney King scandal a decade or two later.

"Why can't we all just get along?" He said at the time, still battered, bloodied and bruised from being beaten by the Law enforcement of the day. It was a great question back then, and an even better question now.

Vegas, Laughlin, Reno, Portland, Seattle, Vancouver, Boston, Chicago, London, Paris, Rome and Madrid.

Hong Kong in the middle of the night, for an unexpected layover and then on to Kobe Japan after the earthquake in "94"

Sitting in a Café in Amsterdam, Luxemburg or Istanbul, Military service of course, in Viet-Nam, Laos, Cambodia, Germany and then down in South America afterwards.

Alaska to Bimini, Vancouver to Saint John's Newfoundland. Greenland, Iceland, Australia, New Zealand, the South Pacific and of course, a beautiful little Island that I call home, that's stuck out in the middle of the North Atlantic.

Altogether, I've travelled to a lot of different countries, including every State and Province, both north and south of the US borders.

That's a few billion people that I've shared airspace with, at one time or another, and all of that, was during some kind of outbreak, epidemic, or so-called pandemic. But I've never seen the amount of lies, deceit and so-called misinformation, or anything near the likes of what's been happening today, and I truly hoped that I never would?

Now I'm no Dr, and I've never claimed to be. And I'm sure that people will argue over this until they're blue in the face, but we do live in controversial times, so I'm going to put my two pennies in here as well, because I've never seen the world shut down, with everyone forced to wear a mask, stand six feet apart, ignore the sick, the elderly and the dying, and then be coerced, or even forced into taking a new kind of Mandated Synthetic Injection, en mass, regardless of whether they wanted it or not? And regardless of what's actually in it, or what it does to them for that matter?

I've never seen disease disappear, only to be replaced with another one that has the same set of symptoms, and then have certain people blame the ineffectiveness of that supposed new medication, prescribed and mandated, on those that wouldn't take it in the first place. I've never seen so many Dr's, Nurses and other hospital staff fired from their jobs, because they wouldn't accept a treatment that had no track record, which was brought out for emergency use only. AT THE SPEED OF SCIENCE, or so one representative of big Pharma said at the time.

I've never seen Hospital Protocols changed; diagnostics and prognostics manipulated in ways that certain drugs and treatments were dropped or simply refused altogether. End of life medication, given to patients that might have otherwise survived. DNR's given out and performed, without any prior consent or knowledge. Relatives refused admission to be with their loved ones. Autopsies refused, Ambulances deliberately held back for hours at a time, inaccurate and flat out lying news reporting, and now Sudden Adult Death Syndrome, which in my opinion is SIDS on a larger scale.

I've never seen so many people, who have basically given up on their hopes and dreams, and their lifetime ambitions, just to join the ranks of the unemployed, simply because they were told to do so, by some bat shit, crazy little fascist fool, that thinks that he or she, actually has that kind of power and authority over them to begin with.

I've never seen so many farmers forced to give up their lands, kill off their stock, and plough over their fields, because of a bureaucracy, that should never have come about in the first place. I've never seen so many shop-keepers, and small business owners, simply give up their livelihoods, and then lock-up their doors forever.

I've never seen so many suicides, or children turn on their parents, grandparents, and older siblings, wishing for their early demise, and I've never seen so many homeless people, living on the streets of Seattle, Portland, New York and L.A. not to mention every other so-called Woke/liberal/democrat/WEF/UN city located in the western hemisphere, like London, Paris, Amsterdam and Rome etc.

It wasn't a virus that did that; it was actually a New World agenda. The so-called Great Reset, or Agenda 21/30, sponsored by rich and powerful elites just like Darwin was, and if you haven't heard of it by now, then you better look it up, because it's coming to you, whether you know it or not? In-fact, it's already here, and it was planned decades ago or maybe even centuries? But don't take my word for it.

Go online and search for the W.E.F. and Davos, because every head of government around the world now is controlled by them, and it's that simple. They don't hide it. They think that they're better than everyone else. They think that they rule us all.

Now, I could be wrong about all of this and I'd be the first to admit it, if that is the truth, but it strikes me that a hundred years ago, the same thing was going on, only they called that time, "The Great Leap Forward." Look it up sometime, you might be surprised? Stranger things have happened I can tell you that.

Now I've climbed to the top of a lot of mountains in my life, and I've been to the bottom of some of the deepest and darkest valleys that you could ever imagine.

I've travelled through jungles and sailed a few seas. I've stayed in five-star hotels, eating caviar for breakfast and drinking over-priced champagne for lunch, but I've also been homeless, helpless and pretty damn hopeless at times, sleeping underneath the stars, with nothing to eat, nowhere to go, and not a lot to live for.

I grew up on the streets, and I learned all about this life, from an early age. I was thrown into it right from the get-go, and I've had to deal with that ever since.

It wasn't easy, and it was never fucking sweet, but all in all, it was still my life just the same and I was content with living it, up until now anyway.

I've owned property, cars, RV's, motorcycles and trucks. I've owned businesses, had partners, and several different careers at the same time, and I've been to the top of some of the tallest buildings in the world, as well as at the bottom of some of the largest. I've owned just about everything that I've ever wanted to own, at one time or another, but I've also owned nothing at all, and not once did I ever listen to anyone that told me that I couldn't do, what I wanted to do, when I wanted to do it.

Not once, did I let someone tell me, that I couldn't have what I wanted to have, when I wanted to have it, and not once did I let someone tell me, that I couldn't go to where I wanted to go, when I wanted to go there.

But don't get me wrong here, because there's been too many times my hopes and dreams have been shattered along the way, and I've always been lied to, by those that think they're better than me. Told that I only have myself to blame for that? But that is simply not the truth, because they've written the rules, that we can only learn as we go along, and if we break those rules, then we're thrown right back down to the bottom of that abyss again, time after time.

And sure, there's been millions of things that I haven't been able to do, when I've wanted to do them, just like everyone else in this world, but that's the life we live and no-one said it was gonna be easy. However, the one thing you never do is give up. You don't give up on any of it. Not now, not ever, no way.

You don't listen to people that tell you, that you can't do something, when you know damn well that you can and you probably already have. You don't listen to people that tell you lies, and break their promises in less than a heartbeat, and you certainly don't listen to anyone that doesn't care about you to begin with, which to be honest, is going to be about ninety-nine percent of the time, and ninety-nine percent of the people that you know anyway, and it doesn't matter who you are, who you think you are, or who you wannabee in the long run? They don't care and that's a fact of life.

I started out with nothing in this life, as we all do, and in the end, I'll have nothing to show for it when they burn my body to a crisp. They'll make sure of that. But I'll leave these words behind regardless.

We'll all get there in the end, that's the inevitable part of this life, so why in the hell should we be worried about any of it now, just because someone else tells us to do so? I don't think so. This is my life and I'm gonna live it the best ways that I can.

If anyone disagrees with that, they can go fuck themselves. They don't pay my bills, they don't put any money in my pockets, and they certainly don't care if I'm able to put food on the table, or keep a roof over my head, and I know that I'm not alone with that.

They want everyone like me to simply drop dead, and they want everyone else that's under fifty years old, to become slaves to their new world horror system.

Well, I have a problem with all of that, but if I'm lucky, I'll get to write more about it when I can. I just hope that people like you, will stick around to read it and whether you learn anything from it or not, will be up to you, not them, whoever they are?

Anyway, thank-you for joining me on this journey, it means a lot. I hope that you've enjoyed what's been written here so far, and that you will continue to read the rest of this book and then be on look out for the next one that I hope to publish in the not too distant future.

****

Back on Track

Last night, the Desert Rose Inn, a popular nightclub, bar and grill, and motel, that was located on the outskirts of the city, was completely blown to smithereens, in what appears to be the beginning of a bikers new turf war.

The police estimate, is that around ninety or more members of the "GypsyAngels" motorcycle club, were eliminated during the blast, which completely destroyed the nightclub, the restaurant, all of its motel rooms, and most of its parking lots.

Included in the list of casualties, were at least fifteen regular staff members, along with several part-time employees, at least five long-distance truck-drivers, along with numerous ladies of the night, and the Owner/Founder/President of the nightclub, as well as the motorcycle club "Gypsy Justice Freedom."

Police suspect that as many as sixty or more regular patrons could have been there at the time, bringing the entire death-toll up to over a hundred and ninety-five people, who have now tragically lost their lives.
Investigations are ongoing and all of the traffic is being re-directed for several blocks in the area.

Investigators are looking for any witnesses to come forward and have set up a new hot-line for any information that may be pertinent to the case, no matter how small or trivial it may seem to be.

The number to call is 1-800-555-7171 and of course all calls are and will be treated with the strictest confidentiality, as much as possible.

****

9
Deneneka MoogStraffen

Deneneka MoogStraffen had fallen in love with the boy, long before he ever became the man on a Harley, and years before she finally figured out who it was that he'd grow-up to be.

To her, he was a husband, partner and provider, the absolute true love of her life, but to the rest of the world, he was known as the President and Owner of the "***GypsyAngels Motorcycle Club***", a motorcycle club, based in the north-west.

Gypsy Justice Freedom was a talented man, and he used his talents well. He got his "***Angels***" involved with everything that he could think of, including certain political agendas. He even got the club ceded into the State, so that no other clubs could legally come in to his territory and set up shop. He channelled club funds into whatever was profitable and he was good at it. It wasn't the largest or the richest club in the world, but it was well known, and it was all his.

Deneneka MoogStraffen didn't care about any of that though. Together, they lived in a nice house, at the end of a cull-de-sack, on a fairly quiet street, in a pretty good area of the city, and they even had a few cops for neighbours.

The kid went to an interesting school, they always had what they needed and more, and she got to drive around in her husband's sweet little corvette, a mint cherry-black, 1969 Corvette Stingray with **GYPSY** on the license plate.

She loved that car, more than any of the others that she had had in her life and she looked damn good driving it as well. Apart from riding on the back of her husband's motorcycle once in awhile, for charity events and the odd Poker runs, there was no way that she would ever let herself be thought of, as a "Biker Bitch" and that was about as simple as it gets.

"Let the boy's play with their toys" she always said, and of course that's just what she thought they did.

She was at home with her son that night, just about to go to bed, when one of the neighbourhood cops that lived across the street, knocked on the door with the news.

****

"Hey Dee, I've just heard that the ***Desert Rose Inn*** has just been blown sky fucking high, he said, nobody got out of there alive. It's the craziest thing I've ever seen, the blast even took out the parking lots, hell, our boys have got at least five blocks in all directions cordoned off as we speak and oh, I'm really sorry Dee."

She hadn't heard the last part all, her heart had been racing and her head was pounding so hard that she had simply passed out in his arms. It couldn't be true! *Gypsy* can't be dead.

Time passed way too slowly for her over the next few months.

The funerals came and went like clockwork, and there were too many of them.

The doctors, relatives and so-called friends of friends, came and went as well and the kid, well he just kept on growing as kids always do.

Selling off everything was the worst part of it all.

The life insurance would pay for the house and the funeral, but still, the bills would be piling up, and she didn't have a job. In-fact she hadn't worked in years; she didn't need to work with *Gypsy* alive. He did it all for her, he took great care of her, maybe too much so, because now she'll have to do it alone. But she knew nothing of business. Big business, small business, it didn't matter to her, not even her husband's business.

She never had an interest in that; in fact she didn't even know how many businesses he actually had. She only knew of one besides the nightclub, and that was **"Eagle Construction,"** it was a renovation company that was located somewhere in the heart of the city. But where it actually was or who ran it, she had no idea. She had never been there before.

She just knew that *Gypsy* owned it, and she also knew that whoever was running it now, wasn't putting anything into her accounts, *Gypsy's* accounts that is.

So eventually she hired a lawyer to find out more about it and whatever else he could find out about of course. It never entered into her thoughts, that the "*GypsyAngels*" motorcycle club was a business in itself; it never crossed her mind, not even once.

****

"I've got a little news for you Ms. Freedom, the voice of the Lawyer on other end of the line said; "***Eagle Construction***" is actually owned by the "***GypsyAngel Corporation***" which your husband owned at least sixty percent of. So to be brief here, there are about seventeen separate companies that the corporation owns and if we liquefy sixty percent of those assets, then you are probably looking at about seven-million-dollars coming your way. Of course there are my fees to be considered in all of that."

"Excuse me *Deneneka* said, did you just say seven-million-dollars?"

"Yes Ms Freedom, the lawyer said, but if we work at it for a couple more years, we could probably come out with a little more than ten million dollars.

Now the down side of this; is that your husband owned a couple of other businesses that didn't do too well, and there are actual court orders, for accounts receivable etc.

Fortunately, these only add up to a hundred-thousand-dollars or so, and shouldn't be of any major problem. I'll be sending you all of the information on the corporation in the mail within the next few days. Let me know which way you want to go on this and we will get you there as soon as we can.

Have a good day Ms Freedom; I'm sure we'll talk again soon. Bye" (Click).

Deneneka was floored by that; she always knew that her husband had been a talented man; because to her he was the man with the golden thumb, a bread winner, a real money-maker, a man that always had something going on, no matter what?

She knew that, but apparently, so did others, and that she didn't know. *Gypsy* had owned a corporation not just a business.

A Corporation that was worth millions, a corporation that owned other businesses, maybe even other corporations? Shit, she thought, she needed to think carefully about all of this. This wasn't just a walk in the park. This was some serious money and now it belonged to her.

What the lawyer didn't tell her was better than that. It wasn't that he was deceiving her; it was just that he hadn't found out all of the information yet.

The investments of the **GypsyAngel Corporation** had spanned the continent, and then spilled into the world beyond. The GA Corporation had made money in the U.S., Mexico, South America, Japan, the Middle East, Europe and Australia.

Seven-million-dollars, was nothing really; Seven-billion-dollars was more like it and that was probably cheap.

Deneneka Freedom wasn't the only one that was out of her league, the lawyer was out of his as well, infact way out. Of course, one of his major problems was the fact that he didn't know her husband, or the fact that her husband had been the President of the "**GypsyAngels Motorcycle Club.**"

****

Now, "**Eagle Techtronic's**" was actually one of the greatest money makers of the Corporation. It was tied into a major computer company back in the early seventies through friends of friends.

Eagle-Tech quickly became a leading, up front, yet distant, and almost invisible player in the software industry. Supply and demand, whatever that company needed, *Gypsy* produced and the combination was nothing short of brilliance.

From a small warehouse, into three massive office buildings and a large factory three or four years later, *Gypsy* was right there doing what he did best.

His company had even helped with the building of the personal underground home of "Mr & Mrs Big" in the 1990's, a project that was originally slated for several million dollars, but eventually cost well over a hundred million dollars to complete. Not bad for a single dwelling?

With computers gaining a foothold in almost everything that's relative in today's world, it wasn't long before "*Eagle-Tech*" was investing in other technologies, and reaping the benefits of their achievements as well.

Multiple Shares were bought up in Harley Davidson Group of course, The Boeing Aeroplane Group, Ford and General Motors, along with a few start-up companies like Egg-head software, and a little known company called Yahoo.

A major investment at the time; was spent on a medical facility in Northern Canada, which was slated to research stem cell materials, genetics and DNA. manipulations, as well as microscopic computer bits and pieces, which were all high on *Gypsy's* list of personal investments for the future of friends, family and possibly all of mankind?

He believed in the facility, and its proposed research, so much so, that he had bought-up the land and had it built, before the Canadian government actually realised what he was up to.

At the end of all the bureaucratic bullshit and red tape that he had to jump through just to build it, the U.S. government stepped in, and had the facility declared as an "American outpost" and although *Gypsy* still owned it outright, the U.S. Government would officially run it from there on out.

That just pissed the Canadians right off, so they froze all the traffic to and from the facility on Canadian soil and in Canadian air space. This was anything outside of the 400 acres of ground that *Gypsy* owned and the U.S. controlled around the facility.

In the end the U.S. agreed, that some Canadian Scientists, as well as their own American Scientists, should and would have equal rights to use the facility, if and as long as everyone could work together. And so it was that **"*Wolf Manor*"** (not the actual/technical name), was brought into existence.

All of that led to the birth of "***Eagle Transport***" Two hundred of the newest and sharpest Tractor/trailers that money could buy, Kenworths, Peterbuilts, Internationals and Mac's etc. Homes on wheels for up to 400 drivers, crossing the great divide and both U.S. borders, north and south, day in, and day out, with them transporting anything and everything, and every single truck and trailer, had to have the ***Eagle*** logo on its side. An image of a huge golden eagle that was painted in mid-flight, with "***Eagle Transport***" painted underneath it.

Each truck averaged about a half million miles a year, and with only four miles to the gallon as a normal fuel expense, it was more than just wise to invest in oil stocks, in-fact it was a real necessity as well.

The next company on the list was the ***Eagle Import/Export*** Company. It operated by importing various bits and pieces, like goods and vehicles for so-called rest and recreational purposes, and then it exported small weapons, pharmaceuticals, grains and fruits, or just about anything else, for basically the same reasons.

Everything was purchased from the manufacturer and shipped to the customer within a matter of days. Most imports were acquired from Mexico, South America, China, Japan, Taiwan and Korea.

Exports were sent to Canada, Europe, Africa, India and Australia although there were also others and the best part about this business, was the motorcycle parts that were being brought in from Japan, China and Taiwan.

For a motorcycle club, this was a necessity, although those parts were never used on club property, but they were great value for the wannabees, the hang-arounds and all of those the week-end warrior types of course.

Business was booming and the import/export part of it helped it to go global.

"***Eagle Oil***" was probably one of the most interesting of all of the companies. It was started in the mid-eighties with junk bonds, club money, personal funds, and a few financial friends as backers as well.

Gypsy had hooked-up with some real heavy weights, like Shell, Chevron, BP, Exxon and Enron. So the next thing that you knew, the company had quickly become a very minor player in some major stakes in

South America, the Mexican/American Gulf, and the Middle East of course.

His time in Nam had really helped him out there. He had met some bigwigs while he was over there, and they were already into oil at that time. So when the opportunity actually came up, sometime during the Savings and Loan scandals of the 80s, he jumped in with both feet.

These guys had shuffled the so-called losses of the day, into a little known country called Kuwait, on the southern tip of Iraq, buying up considerable amounts of oil, mineral and natural gas rights, along with the rights to farm it all.

It didn't matter much to *Gypsy* at the time, that he was becoming partners with the future president of the United State's eldest son, who in turn would become president himself. To him, it was just another business venture to get into, simple as that.

He almost lost money on it all though. People had forgotten that Iraq had actually owned Kuwait, at one point in time, and for its freedom, Kuwait paid royalties, Annual taxes and certain other financial obligations, back to Iraq.

The Princes of Kuwait however, conveniently reneged on these obligations from time to time. Infact they had done so at least five times in the last one-hundred years and each time this happened, the Iraqi military was sent into Kuwait, to force the issues and each time Kuwait and its royal highnesses of course, would, could and did eventually pay up.

So when the current King, Saddam Hussein, gave a call to Madelyn Albright one bleak and cheery afternoon, while she was stationed at the U.S. consulate in Kuwait in 1990 and asked her what the American policy would be about the country at that moment, considering that they had purchased so many of the oil and mineral rights, she simply told him that there wasn't one.

Of course once she realized what his intentions were, she was on the phone to her boss, who after being involved with, and eventually running the C.I.A. for twenty-five or thirty years, had finally made President of the United Sates.

Not that it made any difference to the way the U.S. was run, but not wanting any more scandal added to his namesake, namely by the older son that got him involved with this mess to begin with, by channelling those ill-gotten funds gained through the Savings and Loan scandals into the oil and mineral rights of Kuwait, a new policy on Kuwait was quickly drafted-up and the rest is as they say history.

They started-up the gulf war, and a couple of hundred thousand Iraqi people died fighting for the rights to rule their own country, plain and simple.

Of course, no-one remembered that Saddam Hussein had fought Iran before all of this, and that he was backed by the U.S. government and its policies etc. More to the point, they were the policies of the C.I.A.

No-one seemed to remember that Saddam Hussein was put into power in his country with the help of George Bush Senor via the C.I.A. to begin with, and that Saddam Hussein had the entire American financing and backing that he needed, from that moment right through to the present.

No-one remembered the bloody Iraq/Iran conflict that saw the Shaw of Iran deposed as a leader, allowing religious zealots more than ample opportunity to wage war on Israel, Palestine, India and Afghanistan, just to name a few.

That activity eventually led to the so-called terrorist camps, and other activities of the modern age, and then it gave birth to some of the same people that we are at war with, at this very moment in time. What's more than that though, is the fact that no one really cared.

When you sit down and think about it for awhile, it seems that the entire world accept for maybe China, Russia and North Korea, has been run by the Bush family for over half a century or more, and of course it's really not over yet, because they're still fucking breathing.

The Fifth Company was "*Eagle Construction*"

It wasn't just a renovation company as *Deneneka* had originally thought. No, **Eagle Construction** was into a lot more than that.

Sure it started out as a small roofing company, after all, that's what the man was back then, a roofer, carpenter, painter, decorator, and a demolition man, but he built on to all of that. He came up with a company that would do anything at anytime, and they were good at whatever they did.

It didn't matter what it was, **Eagle Co**. was into it. Concrete? No problem, Steel? Not a problem. Demolition? No problems at all. **Eagle Construction** got the job done. Simple, quick and efficient, and it worked really well.

The best part about it was that it didn't matter to *Gypsy* at all; it was just a game to play, another aspect of the life that he lived. It didn't matter whether it made money or not, it was only a company after all. It wasn't meant to be forever, nothing ever is. The fact is though, it made a lot of money through the years, and it was still making money now.

Eagle Construction had started buying up properties for renovations in the eighties. Then those properties were sold on for some extremely large profits.

Some of the largest projects; were quickly converted into retail rental units and leased for years at a time by customers such as the Boeing Airplane Group, the Sears Corporation, Bennaroya, and Pacific Northwest

Bell Communications etc, providing an exceedingly good cash flow for the corporation, which was always used in other investments of course.

Even a small Island was eventually bought. It was big enough to house a whole town if it was developed properly, but instead it was used as a holiday resort for certain company employees, along with their families, and members of the **"G.A.M.C."** *GypsyAngels motorcycle club*.

Of course the other companies were making money as well, but nothing like these first five. If you put the rest of them all together, you might come up with a half-a-million dollars in profit every year, and simply put, that was pretty small potatoes. They were more for show than anything else, a tax write-off maybe, and to keep some of the club members gainfully employed and looking fairly legit.

One of them was a small motorcycle shop, run by a well-known and well-trusted lifetime friend of *Gypsy's*.

Hunters Cycle was the name on the plaque on the front door and on the sign in the parking lot as well, but in reality, it belonged to the ***Gypsy Angels Motorcycle Club.*** It did its business for **G.A.M.C.** members only, usually anyway, but there were also friends and relatives, that were allowed to bring their bikes there for work as well.

The wrench that ran the place was known by practically every Harley dealer in the world and was considered to be one of the best of the best. Tough as nails, with a heart of gold, and as honest as the day was long, if he couldn't find it and fix the problem that your bike had, then you knew you had to scrap it and build, or buy a new one. It was as simple as that.

Another business that *Gypsy* owned was a small grocery store, with a two-bedroom flat attached above it. It was run by an ex **G.A.M.C**. member and his wife.

The man had been involved in a near fatal accident while on a road trip with the boys and when he got out of hospital he found that *Gypsy* had bought the shop for him to run, even though he had never done anything like it before in his life.

Gypsy was like that though; he took care of his own no matter what?

Another business was an appliance repair shop. It fixed refrigerators, stoves, washers and dryers etc. Nothing too major really, and sometimes the guys that ran it did scrap metal runs for the club and the bike shop as well. It was penny on the dollar stuff, but it was good for club members.

A couple of gas stations, and a paint shop were last on the list. They were simple investments really, not a lot of profit. *Gypsy* knew this though; he was never a greedy man. He wasn't any "Robin Hood" type either, but where he really made the money work, was with the club. No-one could touch that, not even his wife. If she had ever thought about it that is.

Which she definitely hadn't yet, in fact no-one had, or had they?

****

10
The Mechanic

Harold Herbert Hunter, who was also known as *H*, *triple H* or simply *Trip,* was out of town the night that the **Desert Rose Inn** was blown up. But even if he hadn't been, he wouldn't have been there anyway. He had long since settled his accounts with the club and was quite content on being "just a friend."

He and *Gypsy* had gone back as far together as anyone could have, back to the early years when they both were kids. They had always been fairly close back then, almost like brothers, but *Gypsy* had a strange sort of darkness about him that *Hunter* never liked, so eventually he chose to distance himself from all that, as much as possible.

Nowadays he ran the bike shop for the club and he loved being around to do custom work for the boys. He was a good wrench, who knew all of his motors inside and out, flatheads, 45's, knuckles, pans, and evolutions, it didn't matter what it was, if he couldn't fix it, no-one could and it was about as simple as that.

His love though, was collections, human collections that is. Hunter had become a skip-tracer over the years, a tracker or bounty hunter, whichever one you preferred?

When someone skipped out on their bail, he was right there bringing them back and it didn't matter where he brought them back from?

He did it for the thrill, like a cat and mouse game, but the club made a lot of money at it and he was as good at doing it, just as good as he was at wrenching, probably better, if the truth were known?

He was down in L.A. at the time when he heard the news about the bombing. It came in over the vans radio. He had tracked a skip to a seedy little hotel on the East Side of Burbank. Nothing big really, no one famous, just another poor, black, neighbourhood crack-cocaine dealer with ties to the Crips, the Bloods and/or some Jamaican posse?

The guy liked to rock the world though, he even had his own brand of crack pipes that he sold on side, but his real problem with the law, was that he was also caught carrying an Uzi at the time of his arrest, so his bail was set at just over a ½ million dollars. And what that meant for *Hunter,* was easy pickings and a cool fifty-grand for the club.

Of course after hearing the news about the bombing, he was secretly hoping that when he kicked in the door, the little shit would be waiting for him with another Uzi in his hands. Then he could just shoot him dead, catch a plane back to Seattle and come back at a later date to collect his van and the skips death certificate.

Fat chance of that though, he found the skip totally naked, too drugged-up, half asleep and too damn accommodating. So he just threw him in the back of his van and after driving another seventeen hours or so, he made it back into town.

The first place he went was the *Desert Rose Inn*, even before he dropped the skip off. The cops already had the place tied up in knots, but they all knew him, and they let him go on through.

The first thing that he noticed was the parking lot. There were about two dozen cars out there along with at least fifty or sixty bikes all burnt to a crisp. The front wall of the club was gone, the roof had collapsed and all of the windows and doors were blown out. He'd seen this shit before and his blood was boiling.

Was and/or even Sonny, would never have done this he thought, they wouldn't fuck-over their own cousin like that and that's a fact. Blood is always thicker than water, especially for an Angel.

So it wasn't the "Road Kings" of the north or the south, no matter what the cops might have had to say. And it wasn't any Jamaican Posse either, they would have just shot the place up and stole all the cars, and you could definitely guarantee that it wasn't any street gang neither, because they simply wouldn't have had the balls to do such a thing.

No, a quick deduction would suggest that it was those spick loving, half-bred mother fucking "Bandaleros", a real personal favourite of his (not), and if they didn't know by now that they were on the wrong side of the fucking tracks, they soon would, believe you me. They soon will, he thought to himself again.

By then, he had seen enough, it was time to get the skip buttoned down and collect his bounty. Once that was done, he was headed over to the house, *Gypsy's* house that is.

****

"Harry, I'm so glad you're here, *Deneneka* said, as she opened up the door, I haven't seen you in awhile, have you been all right?"

She was the only woman in the whole world that could get away with calling him that. Harry, god he hated that name.

Gypsy used to kid him about it when they were younger, *Harold Herbert Hunter*, what a fucking name, he used to say, instead of the KKK it's now the fucking HHH and then he'd laugh, he always use to laugh when they were young. But then life just got too damn serious for him, too serious for everyone really, through all the years anyway?

"I'm sorry Dee, I would have been here sooner, but I was in L. A. at the time. I had to bring a crack dealer back to town. He skipped out on a half a million or so. You know how it is Dee, just taking care of business, TCB all the way.

Anyway, are you all right? This shit's gotten pretty damn heavy, way too quick, who would have ever seen this coming, definitely not me?

Do you know who all was there? Do you know whose left? Tell me what you know girl and maybe we can figure out what really happened?"

"Oh Harry, she said, I don't even want to think about it right now, *Gypsy's* gone, he's fucking gone, and I don't know what I'm going to do without him. Do you understand that? Do you know what I'm fucking saying here? *Gypsy* is gone!"

Yeah, he knew perfectly well what she was saying, but he still couldn't believe it himself. It didn't make any sense to him because there was no real reason as to why it would have ever happened in the first place. *Gypsy* was one of the good guys; he didn't deserve this kind of shit.

Hunter spent the night with *Deneneka*, trying to comfort her, but she was in a world of her own.

Gypsy had put her up on a pedestal, protecting her from anything that might have been a problem, but somehow this didn't quite fit the bill.

She was lost to the moment and would probably be lost for quite awhile. It's too bad really, Hunter thought, she should have been a Biker bitch, but she wasn't. She was more like a solitary rose caught-up in the middle of her own twisted thorns now.

He stayed with her until the sun rose and then left. Not that he wanted to leave, just that he had to. It was up to him now, to see where the business was and to find out who all was left to deal with it. It was a new day on the horizon and perhaps it was time for a new start.

He started thinking back to the first time he met *Gypsy*. They were about nine or ten years old at the time. They went to the same school, lived in the same little town and had some of the same friends and acquaintances.

The town was a little shit hole, called Huntington.

Gypsy acted like a king, even back then, full of fire, full of life and boy did he ever have some dreams. In his dreams, he would conquer the world, and *Hunter* was always there with him, right by his side.

It was *Gypsy's* idea to take off in the first place. Let's just go see the rest of the world, he said, and they did. They saw it all, God did they ever.

Europe, Mexico, South America, North America and all of Canada of course, Japan, Korea, Viet-Nam, Cambodia, Laos, Hong Kong and even some parts of China.

Now it wasn't all done in one trip that's for sure, because it took years and it wasn't like it was always meant to be neither, because sometimes it was more like butting your head against the wall, a solid brick wall that is. So yeah, sometimes it was pretty damn painful. But it sure was fun at the beginning of it all, and it had been quite the adventure through the years as well.

****

Hunter pulled into his own driveway at about seven am. He pressed the button on the dashboard and watched the gates swing open. The wolf was already out in the yard, laying on the grass verge waiting for him.

It seemed like that damned mutt, actually knew him better than anyone else at times, anyone but *Gypsy* that is. It was a huge animal, a pure arctic wolf, only it had a jet-black coat and piercing blue eyes, a one of a kind type of animal.

Gypsy had brought him back from Alaska when he was a cub or a pup, or whatever they called baby wolves? He pulled-up on his bike after the trip, completely covered in dirt, dust and road rash, grinning from ear to ear, while *Hunter* was out in the yard and then reaching inside his coat he pulled out this little black ball of fur.

"Here you go *Hunter*, he said, this is you. Treat him better than you treat yourself and you'll never be alone."

"You mean "yours" don't you *Gypsy*?" *Hunter* replied,

"No *Hunter*, I meant, you."

The big *H* didn't get it, and what's more was the fact that he had always hated dogs. *Gypsy* knew that, but of course this wasn't a dog, it was a fucking wolf, it must be different right? But just how was it supposed to be him?

Gypsy said, "I'm going to tell you the story about that damn mutt *Hunter*, but let's go crack open a beer first, I don't want to have to start it and then get thirsty halfway in between."

So into the kitchen and straight into the fridge they went. They opened a couple of bottles and he started telling his tale.

"I was scooting down the Al-Can (Alaskan Hwy) about a hundred miles into nothing, when I heard a tinkle hit the road. I looked down and saw a puff of smoke coming off the motor so I pull over real quick. Shit I thought, I've thrown a rod, or I had blown a gasket out or something similar?

Then I saw oil pouring out of the bottom-end, and that's when I realized that I had just lost the exchange nut on the crankcase. So I stuffed the open hole with a rag and scooted back to where I thought the nut may be lying. You know somewhere around where I heard that Tinkle sound in the first place? And hey, sure enough, I found it pretty quick, even if I do say so myself.

Anyway, I screwed it back in as far as I could get it, when I realized that I didn't actually have a wrench to tighten it up with and of course, I thought to myself right there and then, Damn, if only *Hunter* was here, he'd have all the wrenches that I'd need.

It was about then that I heard a voice off in the distance. At first I thought it was just the wind, but then, there it was again, only this time it was kind of like a baby crying, you know? A little sad really, anyway I looked around and saw a hole in the side of the hill, kind of like a small cave or a dugout type of thing, so I walked over to it and that was where this mutt was laying.

I was just going to leave him there, because you can never own a wolf, they're like an endangered species right? Anyway I was just about to turn around when I noticed what it was that he was laying on. It was a wrench pack. Can you believe that?

You know, all wrapped up in plastic, tied-up with some dusters handkerchief and this mutt was lying right on the top of it.

So I picked him up, grabbed the wrenches and then realized that I had just put my scent all over him. I knew his momma wouldn't be too pleased about that, in-fact I hear that she would have just killed him on the spot, so I put him inside my jacket and eventually brought him all the way back home with me. And that *Hunter* my man, is why he's you, crazy shit or what?"

"Yeah man, that's pretty wild all right, so like, what am I going to call him *Gypsy*? Hunter, Harold or Herbert" he said with a half-assed smile.

"No man, I've already name him for you," *Gypsy* said.

"Oh I see, so what did you call him then *Gypsy*, Mutt?"

"No *H*, much better than that, I named him "Chief" he said, laughing as he walked away.

That had been over seven years ago. Chief had grown so big since then, standing on his hind legs, he stood over 6ft tall and weighed in at well over 250 lbs and *Gypsy* had been dead right about him, he had never left *Hunter* for any reason and *Hunter* would never leave him.

That's the one thing that *Hunter* never did like, or even understand about *Gypsy*, it was part of his dark side and when he was dark he was black, blacker than the fur on Chiefs back. He was usually right with it as well. He'd been that way his entire life.

It was like he knew of the future before it happened, uncanny really, or maybe, it was something that had been watching out over him, whatever it was, sure could shake the earth at times, and yet it still charmed the birds right out of the sky.

Hunter never knew what it was, but over the years he had seen that darkness come and go, and each time it came, it grew progressively stronger. *Hunter* couldn't handle it in the end; it was as if *Gypsy* was losing himself to it, like he was fighting some great battle between the dark and the light, good and evil.

That's why he left *Gypsy* when he did. He needed some distance from him, a little peace of mind and perhaps, a little bit of sanity to go right along with it. Too many things were getting out of hand, too many so-called coincidences were happening and too many times *Gypsy* would see them coming and then dodge the bullet so to speak. But that's over now he thought; *Gypsy's* dead and the clubs gone up in flames.

Then he remembered that *Gypsy* had said that all of this would happen about three years back, but he didn't pay much attention to him at the time. He didn't want to know about it anyway. He was happy doing what he did now and that's about all that he wanted to do. He didn't want to be bothered with any club business anymore, so he basically closed his ears about it.

Too late to worry about that now though, it's been done and dusted and there ain't no going back on any of it, even if he wanted to.

1990 was the Anniversary of the agreement between the State of Washington and the *GypsyAngels Motorcycle Club*. The so-called big wigs back then, had decided not to renew the agreement. They said there wasn't any need to anymore.

They said that "Bikers" were a thing of the past, just another dying breed that was heading for extinction. They said, that new laws were coming into effect, that would prohibit motorcycle-clubs altogether, they said that motorcycles would eventually be band anyway, unless they were electric and that their insurance companies would be make it way too costly to ride them.

They said the future wasn't going to stand for any non-conformist groups and bikers were the first on their list.

So "they" basically told *Gypsy* to close up shop, the gig was up, the game was over etc. But of course, he said, "Fuck that, he didn't need the State's permission to stay in business and as long as that's what it was, that's what he'd fucking do."

They didn't like that much, but what could they really say? They couldn't be seen involving themselves in anyone's private agenda back then, without some kind of backlash from the feds, so they had to let him play the game out.

They left him hung out to dry really, and as it turned out, hung out to die in the end. It's funny how some things change, when others never do? Never mind, it's a dog eat dog world that's for sure.

****

11
The Hotel

I was barely nineteen at the time, going on fifty, and feeling every bit of it, when I stepped down from the dark-side of a murky-grey, un-marked military jet, sometime in the summer of the early Seventies, feeling totally ratted, tattered, frazzled and fried. Psychologically damaged, but temporarily reprieved, from fighting in a war that was nobody's business in the first place, let alone mine.

Laos, Cambodia, and Viet-Nam, were thousands of miles away from where I grew-up and about a million miles away from where I really wanted to be, but it was their time to shine in the spotlight of the Worlds Stage, and I was just another actor, that had been sucked into playing his part in that particular movie. I just didn't realize it would turn out to be such a bloody horror story.

Now don't get me wrong here, I wasn't complaining about any of it. I know that we do whatever we have to do in this life, and I was pretty damn good at doing what I did. In-fact, I figured that I was one of the best of the best at the time, and if the truth were ever known, I loved every minute of it anyway and I definitely wouldn't have traded it for the world.

There's something about a war that brakes you as you once were, and then it makes you as you need to be, and there's no in-between any of that, no going back on it neither. Because when it's done, it's definitely done and dusted.

Hell, I had even signed up for it all to begin with, grabbing the bull by the horns so to speak, riding high upon its crooked back, instead of being stomped into the ground by one of its heavy, cloven-hooves, or maybe pinned to the wall by one of its horns?

And let's face it; I had trained long and hard for that fucking privilege and for every mission that I was ever on, making damn sure that I got the highest marks available, out every bit of Intel, testing, training and prep, that they could throw at me in the first place, while at the same time, I always tried to keep myself at a distance, slightly above and a little beyond, the rest of the rank and file, doing whatever it took, to get to wherever it was that I needed to get to, just as quickly as I could, and very few of them knew, that I was as young as I was at the time, in-fact the truth is, most of them didn't know that at all.

It certainly wasn't easy though, in-fact it was just the opposite most of the time, but I thought I was out to change the world back then and I was giving it my best shot.

I lied about my age to begin with, so that I could get involved earlier on, changing a six into a four on a piece of paper, which allowed me to join the army at the age of fifteen, instead of seventeen, and I'm pretty sure that I wasn't the only one who did that and besides, I had lied about my age for most of my life anyway, always telling people that I was a couple of years older than what I really was, especially when it came to the fairer sex. Older women, you've got to love em.

Some say I was a natural at it, young, fit, healthy and tough, with a strong will and an ambitious mind that was usually smart as a whip and often just as quick.

But there were others that said, that I was dangerous, quick-tempered, unprepared, gun-ho, often obtuse, and I guess that somehow, all of that added up the fact that I was heading towards an early demise, according to them anyway.

I'd like to think that I was more compassionate than what most people gave me credit for, especially for the work that I did and some of the things that I had to go through back then, always hoping that someday, I'd actually make a difference to this world, in the long run that is. But I was too immature for all of that, and pretty damn naïve with it as well, never quite realizing that the long run, would actually be the rest of my life, and that making any kind of difference to this world or any other world for that matter, would never mean the same thing to anyone else, especially to my older self, whenever I got to it, if I ever got to it that is? Never mind, that's just the way life has been for me, and it don't matter anyway. It never has and it never will.

Once I stepped onto the tarmac, I was immediately confronted by a large group of extraordinarily overbearing people that come at me from out of nowhere? You know the kind I mean, left-wing, liberal, pacifists/tree-hugger types, shouting obscenities from the top of their lungs, on the sidelines of course, like baby-killer, child-rapist, drug-dealer, war–monger, and cold-blooded murderer, amongst other niceties that they were coming out with. Ignorant little pricks, full of self-importance, self-entitlement and self-worth, that didn't know their ass from a hole in the ground and certainly didn't have the brainpower between them to figure it out.

They were the cancel society of the day, which are no different to those around now, over-educated, over-fed, over-pampered and over-paid, if any of them have actually held a job at all, and yet, not a single ounce of decency or common sense between the lot of them.

They threw things at me, while they were stomping on flags, burning them or simply tearing them apart and spitting into the air, trying really hard to hit me with it, and I swear that if I was armed at the time, I would have just shot the lot of them, right there on the spot, for being the pathetic little turncoat traitors, that they appeared to be. I don't suffer fools gladly, that's for sure, especially that kind of fool.

I suppose I'm over that now, after all, it was fifty years ago, and I've been through a lot of life since then, but there are those that I've known, that never did get over it, and there were too many more, that didn't actually survive it all to begin with.

I still feel for them, I hold them in my memories, I still see them in my dreams at times, but that's what a bullshit fucking war does to people. Who would've thought?

In-fact, every war that was ever fought, has turned out to be just as bad. It splits the country down the middle, dividing the North from the south and the east from the west. Pitting brother against brother, and father against son, and it's never the same afterwards, no matter who you are, and no matter where it happens in the first place?

I guess that some people might just call that progress, but I tend to think, it's a step backwards in time. Too many darker days and forgotten periods in our history, where the rich and greedy, take everything from the poor and the needy, then, simply kill the ones that weren't strong enough to object, or survive it all in the first place.

It happens all the time, and it's still happening today. In-fact it's been going on that way for thousands of years, and no-one seems to be able to stop it. But worse than that, is the fact that no-one really cares about it anyway.

It's just the nature of the beast or the devil down inside, or the plain and simple fact, that we as human beings, have that killer instinct, buried deep down inside our own psyche's, waiting to let it loose at the drop of a hat, and it really makes me wonder how in the world, that we as a people, a race, or even a species, have ever survived this long in the first place?

Those so-called citizens; didn't know me from Adam of course. They didn't know who I was, where I'd been or what I was about at all.

Hell, they didn't even know, if I had served in the same war that they were protesting against, but I was wearing a uniform at the time, and that was all it took to set them off, regardless of what had really happened, way back when and to whom. But the worst part about it was the fact that they didn't give a shit about any of it, anyway.

They had their own agendas going on, regardless of what that actually was, or what they thought it was to begin with, and all I really was, was just another dumb, semi-useless, farm animal, that somehow, managed to escape from the slaughter house that people like them, and their self-righteous kind, had actually created in the first place. What a fucking joke?

So there I was, completely worn-out, torn-up and broken down from the life that I'd been living, up to that point in time anyway. In-fact, it had been pretty well, full on, for too long really, but I was undeniably grateful that I was still alive, even though it seemed like I was only hanging on by a thread.

I immediately thought about a place to go for awhile, like a motel or a hotel, because where I had been and what I'd gone through during the past couple of years, was what most people's idea of what "Hell on earth", would look like, and what I needed now, more than anything else, was to try and forget everything that I could, about any of it. I still belonged to the military of course, but I was also a biker with ties, and I planned to reconnect with some of them, just as soon as I could, before my next posting got in the way of that, and to keep things sweet with the club, if nothing else.

I also wanted to scoot, get laid and of course, catch up on all the news that I had missed out on, but most of all, I just wanted out of that damned uniform for awhile, have a nice taste of civy-street and mingle with some of the local yokels, especially the ones of the fairer sex.

I was flown into and processed out of McCord Air Force Base, with a little more time spent at Ft. Lewis, which is just up the road from McCord, but they sent me down to Elliot AFB afterwards and then eventually they shipped me up to Cheyenne Mountain, for a three day debriefing, that was like an inquisition instead of a fact-ending mission, and all of that was before I actually received my official furlough, so getting out of that uniform, had to wait.

Military clearance is a bitch at the best of times, especially if you've ever held any kind of high classification. I was basically on loan to the US for the duration of my contract, which wasn't up for a couple of more years, but still, it had to be done, and that was about all there was to that.

The closest club from there was up the road in Colorado Springs, which is neatly nestled high-up into the mountains, at somewhere just over four-thousand feet or so. It's a little south of Denver and just off to the east side of Interstate twenty-five, roughly midway through the State.

It's basically a religious community, that was started-up during the gold rush days of the eighteen hundreds, filled with Protestants, Mormons, Jo-ho's and Catholics, all battling it out over whose word of God is the real one.

You know the story; it's just another bloody war that's been going on for a couple of thousand years. You'd think that most intelligent people would know better by now. I mean really, if God were to have any kind of religion, it sure as hell wouldn't be mans religion now, would it? And besides that, how many variations do you actually need on ten bloody rules, in the first place?

Of course I'd been there before, several times in-fact; I had stayed in Denver, before I went into the army, and Colorado Springs had always a pit stop along the way, so it was a local club for me, along with the fact that they had only been patched over a year or two before I went in the army, which still made them prospects and probates in my eyes. But before all of that, they were simply known as the Prophets, who would've thought?

Anyway, after a quick call, a few verbal ribs, along with some of laughs and a glad you made it back in one piece my friend, sort of thing, a few of the original Prophets, guys that I knew fairly well, including the "Dude" who ran them all, finally came and picked me up just outside the gates.

It was a warm summers evening with a mild south western wind that was blowing up a light breeze, in and around the area at the time, but to me, it was just what the Doctor ordered, and I was itching to scoot on out of there anyway, no matter what?

Eventually, I spent the night in Colorado Springs, camped out at the clubhouse, in the arms of a gorgeous, little hang-around that was also a full-on stripper at the local titty bar. She was a gift from the "Dude" who was the clubs president back then, and one of four, who had started up the original club in the first place.

I didn't mind at all, because the pair of us had hit it off together, pretty quick like. It was simply lust at first sight and all of that, you might just say. She was a looker though, that's for sure.

We had our fun drinking, laughing, kissing and smoking whatever was on the menu, and then we were simply screwing each other's brains out, in one of the back rooms, long before anyone else had even missed us.

But I needed some hard, cold, down time, in order to be alone with my thoughts, my dreams and all of those bloody nightmares that I could never shake.

So without too much persuasion, I borrowed a bike, and then I headed out of town alone, with my thoughts in tow, early the next morning.

A few short days at the most, is what I figured. I'd have to give the bike back by then anyway, simply because good ole Uncle Sam and her Majesty's Military were still pulling my strings, and they simply wouldn't give me any more time off than that.

It was your typical bureaucratic bullshit really, no matter which way you looked at it, because I had at least a month's furlough coming to me by then, no matter what, but regardless of all of that, they would only dish it out in weekly increments, unless I went back to England of course, because of who I was or where I was, I suppose, no matter who I was with, or what I was actually doing at the time.

Now, don't get me wrong about this, because I had signed up for it all in the first place, but like I've said before, but I really didn't have a choice in the matter.

I had gotten myself into all kinds of trouble in Germany a few years back when I was thirteen. Lying about your age and trying to outsmart the system, doesn't ever do you any good and I ended up in a high security prison cell, right next door to a contract killer known as the "Dutchman" who had worked for some really powerful people back then.

In-fact, I was looking at spending quite a few years next to him in that prison at the time, until he decided to do me a huge favour, by making a few phone calls to one or more of his contacts about me, and my distinct abilities etc.

I guess he figured that he was never getting out of there, but there was still a chance that I could, with his help of course. He was certainly right about that, because they were there in no time at all really and I was freed from that life. However, once that decision had been made, there was no turning back on it and it's not something that you could walk away from neither. Ties that bind, so to speak.

Now, one of the best things about being a biker, is that once you jump on that bike and scoot on down the road, you're back in your own little world again and there's no-one else there, unless you really want them to be that is.

You head out, to where ever you want, whenever you like, and there's no-one to tell you any different. No-one saying that you need to be here, there, or anywhere. No-one saying that you should be doing this or that, no-one at all.

Just you and that motor humming, as you're riding along with the wind, catching the sun, or simply flying down a road that you've never been on before, with the moon high-up above you as well at times. It doesn't matter which one it is, it just feels like heaven either way, and that's about all there is to that.

A lot guys will simply go fishing, or maybe head down to their local pub every night, or even out to the nearest titty bar, or strip joint to relax and unwind, from whatever, whenever. They might even have a boy's night out once or twice a week, or perhaps a week-end hunting trip and camping, etc.

Some of them might even drop a bundle on a horse or two, or a dog race and then spend the next seventy-two hours complaining of their losses and wishing that they had bet on the other one instead.

Some may even save up what few pennies they can earn and do several weeks away at a time, perhaps a few times a year even, but I was never into any of that.

If I wasn't out riding, then all I needed was a roof over my head, with four cold walls and a semi-comfortable bed that I could crawl into at night, but of course, being overseas for as long as I had been, I hadn't had that kind of comfort or luxury, in a helluv a long time.

I was anti-social, or anything of the sort; because I loved having company, especially that stripper, who was a drop-dead gorgeous type of woman in every way, I might add, but it was always a case of time for me, because time itself, was my most valued commodity and I could never get enough of it, if you know what I mean?

Most of us don't, when it gets right down to it, but for me, it was pretty much an all consuming factor at that particular point in my life, because, I've always figured that I was living on borrowed time as it was.

There were just too many instances, that I had seen the end coming and yet I still kept on going, kind of like that bloody rabbit commercial on the TV and I guess that I was either too damn stupid or too damn stubborn, to actually lay down and die, but I also knew that one day I'd have to regardless, just not today. So, it was off to one of those motel/hotel rooms that I headed to next.

Why I left Colorado-Springs in the first place, along with that gorgeous stripper at the clubhouse, and then headed off into the city, like I did, well, I have no idea, apart from the ride itself of course, which, was the thing to do at that particular moment in time, I suppose? Never the less, there I was, pulling into the parking lot of an old, run down, motel/hotel, late in the afternoon.

It was a tall building, somewhere near the city center, with the hustle and bustle of a half a million people at the time, dashing around here, there, and everywhere, along with the constant traffic, that was also polluting up the very air that they all breathed, but I knew it would quieten down after hours and the smog would eventually lift or simply fade away.

That's when the skies would clear again, and for a few brief moments, it would seem like stepping back a hundred years or more, long before any of my troubles began.

Cities are like that, people live their lives out in the suburbs, and then commute to their twenty, forty or even sixty story office buildings, somewhere between the hours of nine to five, five days a week, sometimes six, which is something that I've never been interested in doing, but it is what most of the white collar types do these days.

You know the kind, ones with their five-thousand dollar, three-piece suits, thousand dollar shoes, three-hundred dollar shirts and a hundred and fifty dollar neck-tie, along with their fancy gold watches, wrist-chains and cigarette lighters, as well as their tricked out road cages, that usually cost more than half of their house to begin with.

Anyway, I checked in a little after four pm with no worries and no real problems, cash in hand, saddlebags for a suitcase and with my Desert Eagle strapped to my side. Army issued of course, after a medal and a promotion that I got, just before I came back stateside, and then I went up to my room, which was cosy enough, I suppose?

It had a bed, which was good, an old TV and a shower etc. along with windows that overlooked the parking lot where I could keep an eye out on my borrowed ride, from time to time. Not that I really needed to, after all it was a club bike and it was fully stamped, but still, you can't be too careful about these things. There are idiots everywhere, especially in the city.

Two or three nights of this I thought, and it should do just fine, although I had already paid for five nights in advance and in cash, like I said, which is the way I've always done things, after all, I really needed to relax and sleep, so that's what I did.

I woke up late in the evening after that, fairly hungry, still tired and very, very cold. The room itself was heated of course, but there was frost on the window, so I looked around for the thermostat and turned it up. It wasn't a new building at all, and it definitely wasn't insulated. None of them are, when you think about it, but what the hell I thought, this ain't wintertime yet, so the temperature would probably rise by ten am, regardless.

I certainly hoped so anyway; because I really didn't want to be riding through the snow on my short vacation, even if I was in the middle of the mile high city.

Now, it wasn't long before I made my way out to the streets that night, to check on the bike of course, and then to walk to the nearest restaurant, looking for that proverbial bite to eat.

Fortunately, I found an all-night diner within a few short blocks of the place that I was staying at, and it was one with hardly any other customers in it at that time, so the service was pretty quick and fairly efficient, although the food was a little less than desirable at best.

I was pretty hungry though, so I just assumed that it was edible? I had a cup of coffee with an order of pancakes and a couple of sunny side eggs, along with some rashers of bacon on the side. Not exactly an evening meal, but it would do for now, I thought.

I actually have some simple tastes, when it comes to food these days. A few years of the army life, will usually do that to most people. Not because the C-rations were that bad, you understand, but when you run out of them, you have to make do with whatever you can get and you'd be surprised at what I'd been able to get in my life, both before and after my days in the company of Uncle Sam and her majesty's service.

Anyway, I had just finished eating my meal, when I first noticed the kid.

The girl was too young to be out at that hour of the night and not much to look at, although she was kind of pretty, in the strangest sort of way, but more of a scrawny little thing, that probably didn't weigh more than seventy pounds soaking wet, if that, and she definitely didn't know how to take care of herself yet.

Probably, not a day over twelve or thirteen, I figured, not really sure why I was bothered with it in the first place? And not quite five feet tall either. And the guy that she was sitting with, well, he definitely looked old enough to be her father, although he was a whole lot heavier and at least a foot and half taller than what she was, but fathers don't treat their daughters the way that he was treating her, no sir, they don't do that at all.

I sat there watching them both for awhile, as I drank my coffee; the man had started yelling at the girl to get back to work, saying that she had been taking too many breaks, and that she wasn't making him any money just sitting there on her fat little ass.

I could easily see where that led to pretty quick. This guy was just another low-life, scumbag, a gangster, wannabee pimp type, or what I had always known as a pedo-chicken-hawk, who was hanging onto his prey and this prey was obviously too young to know any better, in-fact, she was probably too damn young to know much about anything at all really.

Now I don't know how or why, but I do know that it's a shame when you realize just how many young women get themselves into that kind of trouble, long before they have a chance in life, but there you go, they do, and that's just about all there is to that. Half the time, I think that it must be that, me, me, me, type of scenario, where they actually think that world owes them something and that it simply revolves around them and nobody else. But the other half, well that can be just about as dark and dangerous, and as pure evil, as evil can get.

Those girls have no chance at all, because of scumbags just like this guy, that are sitting around every bloody corner, just waiting to catch them in the shadows, then casually, carefully, and usually fairly quickly lead them back their lairs. No different than a Spider to a Fly, or a Wolf to a baby Elk.

But, it wasn't any of my business, so I just sat there for awhile, listening to this guy's bullshit, until the girl finally got herself up and left him sitting there, as she quickly stepped outside in the cool night air.

I got up a little while later myself and headed towards the till, to pay my bill. The man just sat there, staring at me, as I walked up to the counter and then he continued staring, when I walked out the door, giving me that cold, hard, say something if you dare asshole, kind of look, catching my eyes more than just once, brazenly staring right back at me, without even a twitch or a flinch. Which is not what the usual citizens of the world do in a situation like that, that's for sure.

I kept an eye on his movements, his breathing and even his heartbeat, with both eyes open behind my back, as I slowly passed him along the way.

I didn't like this guy at all and I knew the guy could feel that about me, because I have a habit of projecting my inner feelings outwards for some reason and I've always known that almost anyone could feel that sensation in a matter of seconds, no matter how hard I'd try to conceal it.

I also figured that this guy was nothing but trouble with a capitol T. from the day that he was born and there was very little doubt about that in my mind. After all, I'd seen a ton of trash, just like him throughout the years and I was bound to see a whole lot more eventually.

I suppose that its human nature as they say, but I really couldn't stand that part about people and I didn't see the point of even trying. Anyway, the guy just sat there, watching me, staring, as I slowly left the building, which was a good thing really, because I wasn't looking for any trouble at the time, I had had my share of that recently, which is another reason of why I checked into that hotel in the first place.

Things had been pretty hectic overseas, for quite awhile, as I've said before, and there were people that I knew, including a couple of my closest friends that had gotten killed along the way. I had come close myself, but I was used to it all by then, hell, I'd been at it for a few years, so I knew what to expect.

Besides that, it was time to rest up for awhile, and try to forget all about that shit, before I had to go back and do it all over again and I was looking forwards to that, resting up that is.

The girl was standing on the corner when I finally got to it, which was no surprise really, after all that's what her chicken-hawk pimp had told her to do, and that's when she asked me point blank, if I wanted a date.

I smiled at her, said "no thanks honey" rather quickly and then as a second thought or perhaps some simple curiosity, I asked her how old she was and of course, she told me that she was eighteen, which I already knew was a lie just by looking at her.

"But, I could be any age you want, the girl said, I love make-believe. Do you like em younger or older?"

I quickly turned her down again by saying that I really wasn't interested, but the girl kept on, walking along with me, asking me a whole slew of questions, like where was I from? Where was I going? And what was I going to do, once I got there? She even asked me if I wanted to get high and then she asked me if I was gay, because I kept on telling her no. I didn't lie to her, but I didn't want her company neither, and no, I certainly wasn't gay.

Then the girl used that old plea-bargaining technique, you know the one, could you please help me out, because I need the money to pay some bills, or her man would start beating her up again.

I told her that the best thing for her was to get back home. Get away from there and that kind of life just as fast as her feet would carry her, but of course she said that she couldn't do that. Her man relied on her to make the money; they were in "Love" and they needed each other in this life, because they didn't have anyone else. Which of course, was just another bullshit lie as well?

That guy wasn't capable of loving anyone but himself, no matter who came along and besides that, he probably had a string of other girls out on every corner, working their little socks off, amongst other things, but maybe she really did love him, who knows? Love is blind, especially when you're too young to know what love really is.

I'd seen it all before, too many times in-fact. Hell, even some of the clubs that I had dealt with in the past, had done the same kind of things, which really disgusted me more than I ever said at the time.

Still, it was their business, not mine and if it aint my business, then staying out of it, is usually the best way to go, unless you simply have no choice in the matter?

But there were times that shit like that had to be sorted out, especially when it was a friend's daughter, which had gotten herself caught up in the mess in the first place.

Fortunately, that only happened a couple of times through the years that I could remember, and usually when the boys found out that the girl was under age, they were quite eager to fix the situation, and make an even quicker retreat from it, typically distancing themselves, just as far away from the problem as they could get and just as fast.

After all, there are some things that you just don't do, even if you're an outlaw, and messing with little kids is definitely one of them.

By then, we had reached the motel/hotel that I was staying at and I simply said goodnight to the girl and then I handed her a twenty dollar bill just for good measure, because I knew that she'd be in a lot of trouble, if she went back empty handed to the guy in the restaurant.

That's the way those chicken-hawks work, and I certainly didn't want her to get into any trouble, for any reason.

The girl smiled at me, thanked me for the note and then went cheerfully on her way, headed back to where we had just come from I'm sure, after all, Buddy the chicken hawk, was probably still sitting there and he'd be waiting for her, with his hands outstretched, along with his cold, dead eyes, no doubt.

Anyway, it was none of my business and that was that as far as I was concerned.

I took the elevator up to the eighth floor, where I turned the key in the lock and then headed straight for the bed. I was way beyond being too tired to think about anything anymore and eventually I slept the entire night away, safe, sound and secure, except for those nightmares of course.

I was up watching the television the following night, when a few soft knocks came to the door. It had been hours since I had gone outside, so I definitely wasn't expecting anyone and I wasn't sure who to expect anyway, but I had a gut feeling that it was going to be the girl again and that would only mean trouble for me.

Sure enough, I opened up the door and straight away I saw that she had been crying. I also saw the bruises on the side of her face and down her neck. One of her eyes was puffy from a fresh hit by the look of things.

A large red welt on her cheek bone, a blood shot eye and some clumped-up hair, which all in all, made her look as if she had been put through some sort of wringer.

"Can you help me?" the girl said, as she entered the room and then quickly took a seat on the big ole easy chair that I had just got up from.

"I'm in trouble again and I really don't know what to do about it? I think he's actually gone crazy this time, because he just beat the hell out me in an alley-way for no reason at all, and I just ran. You were the only one that I could think about. So here I am."

"I told you the other night that this aint no life for a kid, I quickly said, you should have listened to that and got yourself back home, where you belong."

"Home is just as bad, the girl said, my mother's boyfriend used to beat me up all the time as well, unless I gave him what he wanted, that is, which is why I ran away to begin with. He aint nothing but a fucking pervert really and he drinks too much as well. I tried telling my mother that he was all over me when she wasn't around, but she wouldn't listen, so I left. I can't go back there anyway, it's been too long and I really don't know what else to do.

He's going to kill me if he finds me now. I was supposed to meet up with some of the guys that he knows, but I refused to do it, because they like to get it on, all at once, if you know what I mean and that always hurts me, in one way or another.

One of the guys likes to film it while they're doing it as well and he always tells the others what to do, like he's some kind of movie director or something.

They put a knife to my throat one night after they tied me to the bed. And then they brought in a chicken and made me watch as they chopped its head off. They sprayed its blood all over me and filmed me peeing myself, because I was so scared.

I swear that he'd probably kill me if he could, because he's really a fucking asshole and he knows that I don't like him or the kind of things he does. He really scares the hell out me and the others just laugh about it. So my boyfriend started beating me up again, because I wouldn't do what they wanted me to do, in-fact, I don't want anything to do with them. They're just a bunch of sick people, doing some really sick things.

I ran away from him as quick as I could and here I am. I'm really sorry about this; but I just don't know what else to do right now."

"What about calling the cops? I said, won't they help you out? They usually have places that young girl's can go. You know like women's shelters or Halfway houses, or something else? It has to be better than what you've got now."

"They just want to send me back home again she said, and I can't go back there, no way, no how. My mother's boyfriend just makes me want to puke and I know that I'll end up killing him somehow or he'll be killing me, one way or another. So, I can't do that, I just can't."

"Look girl, I said again, it has to be better than a life out on the streets. There are people that can deal with things like this; you just need to get them involved. If your mother's boyfriend is hurting you in anyway, tell them and let them deal with it.

Because it beats getting beat on the street, if you know what I mean? You deserve better than that, infact, everyone does."

It was right about then, that the door came crashing in. Who would've thought?

I should've known that something was about to happen and I actually did, deep down inside, but I didn't know who, what or when for that matter.

Luckily, I'd already been standing at the time, talking to the girl as she was sitting there in the big ole easy chair that I had been sitting in, long before the she ever showed up.

I quickly glanced at the door, making a mental note of the noise and the various broken bits and pieces which were now lying on the carpet and I realized who the guy actually was, that was making his way through it, and then of course, I saw the gun that was held tightly in the guy's left hand.

All I can say after that; is that my basic instincts kicked in and I was all over the guy like a bloody hot rash that one might find on a child with measles.

I don't think he was expecting that, but he should have been, after all, if you're going to kick someone's door in, you better plan for the worst.

Anyway, the gun went off almost immediately during the initial scuffle, then it went off again and just as suddenly as it did, there was a great deal of pain in my right side. Two bloody tours of Nam under my belt at the time and now that I was back in the States, this asshole had just shot me, but that didn't stop me in the slightest, in-fact, it was almost the opposite.

I was fuming as you would imagine, practically seeing red, as they say, while being pumped full adrenaline at the same time, then I was immediately overwhelmed by a considerable amount of self-preservation, which to be honest, had always been there anyway, since I was four years old at least.

I wrestled with guy at first, knocking the gun out of his hand, before I slammed him up against the wall.

I grabbed the top of his jacket and started swinging him around the room with it, punching him in the head a few times and kneeing him in groin, as I was doing it.

I was still reeling from the pain, seeing red, black and just about every other colour that you could imagine, but of course, I didn't stop there. I swung the guy around and punched him a few more times in the face for good measure and then just as the guy was starting to crumble, I let him go and for whatever reasons, I gave him one last kick to his chest.

It was a side kick, up and out, but it was a little too much and definitely a little too late, for him anyway.

To be honest, it was a bit of blur after that, almost surreal. I was so angry at the time, that I couldn't even think straight, but it was also a moment that was instantly filled with regret. A definitive moment, not just for me so much, but it certainly was for him.

Suddenly, there was another loud noise, piercing the air in the room and shattered glass started flying everywhere.

The guy had flown through the bloody window which was definitely not what I had planned, nor what I had even wanted to do at the time, but it was too late to take it back now, it was already done and dusted and there was no changing that.

The guy didn't even have a chance to scream. He just fell through the window, eight floors down and head first straight into a dumpster that had been left there for the garbage. Dead in the middle of a garbage can, wow, how appropriate, I thought, as I looked down on him.

The dumpster was empty, except for that one piece of trash, which had been dropped, pretty much dead in the middle of it, along with the shards of glass from the window that had fallen down right along with him.

Now I can tell you that there's a lot of things that run through your mind pretty quick, when you kill someone.

Most of the time, you might have a good reason for it or you're under orders from someone else, as I had been in the past, but mainly, it's just business as usual and you barely give it a second thought, but this time, well this time it was a little different.

It wasn't much more than an accident really; self-defence at the worst, or perhaps manslaughter, if anyone had cared to push it hard enough. Although I'm quite sure that, that piece of shit deserved every little bit of it, and I certainly wasn't crying over it, that's for sure.

After all, it was him or me, and that guy was just another low-life, scumbag anyway, as far as I was concerned, that had finally left the planet with a little help of course, but the girl was hysterical by then; she didn't know what to do, how to act, what to say, or where to go.

I actually had to slap her, just to get her to calm down. Then I did my best to keep her calm for the next few minutes, by telling her not to worry about anything, that it hadn't really happened and that no-one would ever know about it anyway, because I'd get it all cleaned up, before anyone even suspected that the guy was even gone.

Then I handed her a few hundred bucks that I had stashed in my wallet which she immediately took of course, without any hesitation, I might add.

"Look I said, I just did you a favour and if I were you, I'd take that money and get yourself on a bus heading out of town, real quick like. Head on back home and deal with that asshole boyfriend of your mothers if you have to, and forget about everything else that's happened here tonight, because it never really happened as far as you're concerned and you were never really here to begin with. It was just a crazy dream or a vivid nightmare at the most and it never happened anyway.

It really is as simple as that, trust me Ok? I'll give you a number to call, if you have any more problems, all you have to do is tell them that I gave it to you in the first place. They're some pretty good friends of mine and they understand about these sorts of things.

If you can't straighten out your home life because of your mother's boyfriend, then call the number and they'll be happy to help you out, you have my word on that.

Apart from that, just forget that you ever met me and you'll be fine, ok? So go on now, get the hell out of here and don't come back."

"I'm scared, the girl said, he has a lot of friends out there and if they ever find out that he's been killed, then they'll be looking for me and I don't want that, that's for sure."

"Look I said again, just let me handle this, I'll take you down to the bus station and see you off. No-one will ever know where you went, I promise you that and they won't be able to track you down, no matter what, even if they wanted to.

If they ever did, you'll have that number to call and trust me; my friends are a whole lot different to any of the scum bags that this guy could have ever known.

Once you're out of here, don't come back, it's as simple as that. That piece of shit has just taken a walk and disappeared, that's all. He's done a runner, like they all do eventually, he's simply gone and that's that.

His so-called friends will think that he took off with their money anyway. He'll never be back and he'll never bother you or anyone else again. So just go back home and forget about it, alright?"

She wanted to argue with me some more, but I didn't have the time for that, so I took her by the arm and headed out the door, down the hall to the elevator and finally into the street just as fast as the elevator took to get us down to the ground.

I had already seen that there was another dumpster sitting next to the dumpster that this piece of shit had dropped in, which I also noticed was partially full of used garbage bags. So I quickly tossed several of those bags over to the other one and then I used them to cover up the dead guy's body.

Yeah, I actually checked to make sure that the guy was dead first of course, but that was only too fucking obvious.

There was blood and brain matter, all over the place. His eyes were open and he had a stupid look on his face, but one of his collar bones was sticking out from the wrong side of his neck and there wasn't any blood coming from the open wound, so yeah, he was dead alright. Dead as dead can get.

Once I did that, I went ahead and took the girl down to the bus station on the back of my clubs motorcycle. I also made sure that we weren't being followed by any of the guys that the girl might have been worried about. I took us down different streets and I even circled around the block a few times, before I finally pulled into the bus station.

Then I waited around for the girl's bus to come in and made damn sure that she was on it just as quickly as she could be, which was about thirty minutes later and hopefully with no-one any wiser.

I had already made some calls by then, while we were both waiting around for the bus to leave, even though it was early hours of the morning. I needed some help and of course, I knew exactly who to call for that as usual.

Now, I could have called the spring's club, but this wasn't their problem to begin with, and Uncle Sam never sleeps anyway, so by eight am, the door and the window had been fixed, the mess had been cleaned up and the garbage had been taken away.

Perfect, I thought; out of sight and out of mind, now for some much needed rest.

Of course, the brass wanted to end my furlough right then and there, something about mixing a military jurisdiction with a civilian authority and all that, but I managed to talk them out of that, after all, I only had a couple days left of my leave anyway and I really did want to rest up.

No-one paid attention to the shots that rang out that night or the broken glass that was still laying on the ground after the bin was taken away, or even the fact that people were coming and going long before the sun came up.

If they had seen or even heard any of it to begin with, they certainly didn't say anything about it, but then there's no real surprise there; because cities are like that, especially a city at night, because no-one really cares about what goes on to begin with, unless it affects them personally that is.

The second bullet had hit me in the side, but luckily, it had simply bounced off my hip bone and then crumpled itself onto the inside of the outside wall.

It was eventually found during the clean-up of course, along with the 38 snub-nosed revolver that it came from in the first place. An old Saturday night special, as they called it at the time. And not knowing what crimes had been committed with it, we all made damn sure that it disappeared with the dead guy in the end as well.

I certainly didn't want that coming back to haunt me, or anyone else, for that matter. The first shot, had gone straight through the bottom of the window, leaving a small hole and structural damage to the glass, which is why the guy went through it so easy in the first place I suppose? Was that coincidence, or simply Providence? Who could really say? Maybe it was just his time to go?

A day later and I had rested up enough. It was time to move on, after all, I had things to do, people to see and places to go to etc. And I was finally starting to feel a little more normal again, re-charged, perhaps even ready for business as usual.

The girl called the number I gave to her eventually, telling the guy who answered the phone, to thank me for what I did and she also said, that she had finally worked things out with her mother and that they had both moved down to Florida, without any boyfriends in tow, and if I was ever down that way, to be sure to look her up.

I never heard from her again after that, although Florida was one of my tri-yearly stops for the longest time, which was a good thing really, no matter which way you look at it? I always figured that she had gotten on with whatever she had to do with her life and I wished her well for that.

I hoped that she had finally met herself a nice guy and had settled down eventually, but you never know, because life always has a way of repeating itself, even at the best of times.

I got promoted again after that, who would've thought? And then I finally got stationed where I had actually wanted to be stationed all along, which of course, was almost perfect for me and the club, for a while anyway, but that's just another story that I'll get into later.

Now it's funny sometimes, how this life works out. You think that you have some kind of control over it, at least most of the time, but then you find out that you really don't and you never did. Especially if you're involved with any type of corporate machine, whether it's the military or not, because they always do exactly what they want to do, and you have to comply, whether you want to or not. And even if you think it's all your idea to begin with, you eventually find out that it's nowhere near and it never has been.

Sometimes, it even seems like there's a guiding force that's been pushing you along the way, whether you wanted it or not?

Perhaps it's fate, kismet, or destiny, or maybe it's just plain ole luck? I don't know, but it's always there just the same and I find myself questioning the reasons behind it all, because I know deep inside that it can't all be coincidental, even though others may have gone through the exact same things.

I guess that's the reason for telling this story, because it's not something that I'm proud of, or something that I would ever want to go through again, although I never had a choice in the matter to begin with, because we all do what we have to do, when we have to do it and that's about all there is to that.

****

Postscript

Years later, I read an article in one of the newspapers, about a state Senator who had just gotten married, and then had his wedding ceremony down in the Florida Keys.

The article was filled with pertinent information; probably more than what should have been there in the first place and there were pictures of the wedding, along with most of their guests. I won't tell you their names, but it was quite literally an affair of the century. It was A Triple-A listing, all the way around, rich, lavish, elegant and highly sophisticated.

Of course, the bride was a stunningly beautiful, in-fact she was a drop-dead gorgeous type of woman, in more ways than one. She had grown into an elegant, strong, and almost dazzling kind of woman through the years. She held her head high, she smiled a lot and people were simply awed by her presence.

You could see straight away that she had definitely come up in the world on the right side of life, no-matter what was thrown at her. I was happy about that, after all, it was a long ways away from that night in Denver and I knew that she had made all the right choices after all.

****

12
Another trip to the past

"Bloody rain" I said, walking out of the doors of the casino that night, watching several transparent little droplets, splashing off the top of the tank and then running down to where they gradually pooled, at the indented part of the saddle, which was still firmly attached to the motorcycle, that was strategically parked-up, in a slightly perpendicular manner, not quite in the up-right position, with its short ass-end, hard-up against the concrete curb.

The bike itself was drenched, and it was only too obvious that I was about to be as well. Who would've thought?

It's been the worst weather all year I thought, as I straddled that long, lean, low machine and then quickly sat down in what was left of that puddle, after I had previously swiped it clear, with the back of my already gloved hand.

At the same time, I impatiently hit the start-up button, and listened carefully as the motor coughed a little, watching, as it puffed out a small cloud of bluish/white smoke, just before it finally roared into life and then started to rumble, like only a large V-Twin motor can.

It was pretty obvious that it didn't like the weather much neither.

"If I had wanted wet," I yelled out loud, looking upwards towards the heavens as I said it. "I would have bought a bloody Jet ski, instead of a damn motorcycle." And then I laughed a little, as I noticed that the doorman had over heard me. He was smiling, and shaking his head.

"Well, it's true" I said, smiling back at him, figuring that the guy probably thought that I was either drunk, or just plain crazy, which was the usual kind of response I'd get, from most of the local citizens around my neck of the woods, even the bouncer types, at times. But hey, this wasn't my neck of the woods at the moment, and I really didn't know what to expect? So, I rapidly squeezed the clutch, kicked the stand, cranked the throttle and in less than a blink of your grannies eye, I roared off into the middle of the night, like a madman on some kind of mission, out there doing his thing as usual.

I didn't really mind the rain though, in-fact, I was quite used to it by then, living back in Britain as I did at the time. Typically, it kept me feeling a little more awake and perhaps even more alert than what I usually was.

Sometimes, it even kept me feeling more alive than what I thought I should have been, not that I didn't feel alive most of the time anyway, because I really did and you can bet that I was pretty grateful for that.

It's just that when I rode my bike, there was nothing else in the world that could truly beat that feeling, except for maybe having sex of course, but I usually liked that fairly slow, smooth and easy most of the time, not really fast and furious like I was known to ride.

Oh sure, I'd get down and dirty when I had to, and trust me, I had even wanted to at times, but not that often.

I was more of a let it come to me type of guy, rather than the go out and get it type, and tonight was simply made for riding anyway. In-fact to me, if the truth were known, every night was made for riding, because that's what I've always lived for and that's what I've always done.

What a night though, I thought to myself, as I scooted along those dark, damp and empty streets, noticing just how cold and lonely they actually felt, especially for that time of year and for that time of the morning. Not a soul in sight back then, but never mind, it was the eighties and there was only half the population of what it is today.

My first stop of the night had been Soho, deep in the heart of the big ole smoke that never sleeps.

It was a favourite little hang-out of mine, along with a few others that I knew, not too far from the clubhouse and just up the road from where I was staying.

Then it was due east to South-end on Sea, for a roll of the dice and to drop some coins in a machine. And then finally, it was all the way down south to the Brighton coast, of all places.

Not exactly the greatest road trip in the world, I might add, but hey, it was definitely all right, for a Saturday night.

My custom made chopper had sweetly purred all the way along, as I quickly guided it around every corner and bend that was out there at the time. It was the prettiest machine, that's ever been seen. It was long, it was lean, it was mean and it was green. Who would've thought?

Yeah, that's right it was green. Actually, it was a really shit kind of Green and I've always hated that colour, ever since my army days, in-fact, I swore that if I ever had to see that colour again, it'd be too damn soon, but sure enough, green is what I got, or more to the point, it was an olive-drab type of green, a really shit kind of green when you think about it, and of course, I had to think about it all the time now.

To begin with, I had wanted it two-tone, or perhaps even a flip colour, which was known as Tonic, back in the day.

You probably know exactly what I mean? Blue, grey, silver, or perhaps even black, depending on how the light hits it and the angle that you saw it at.

I even thought about different shades of purple for awhile, which would have been too damn pretty in the long run, but instead of taking it to the man who could paint it up that way, I decided to do it myself, to save a little time and money etc, and sure enough, as luck would have it, it came out green and man was it ever green.

Never mind, it really didn't matter what colour it was in the grande scheme of things, because it was still the best damn ride around and it was all mine. All mine, along with a grubby little bank manager, who thought that I was the scum of the earth that is, and the club that I was involved with of course, but that's just another story that'll have to wait.

Soho was kicking as usual. It's one of "The" places to go, if you want to party hard in London, at any time of the day or night, because the clubs stay open until the early hours of the morning and they're always full of Wine, Whiskey, Women, and Song, or anything else that your heart desires and most of them are simply "waiting for the taking" as they usually say, just as long as you've got the cash to splash and the time to shine, that is.

It was one of those "Women," that had actually started me out on this little road trip, in the first place. She was a tall, slender, well-built, dark-haired, little beauty, with big green, bedroom type eyes, that could've easily sucked any red-blooded man, or woman, right into the center of them, whether they wanted it or not, and when I first drew my own eyes on her, I was lost to them and I couldn't keep myself from looking at her, not for a single minute, right from the get go.

The girl also had a gorgeous set of legs on her that simply wouldn't quit. They were long, thin and shapely, wrapped-up tight, in an old pair of faded blue and grey, denim fashioned jeans that all the girls seemed to be wearing back then, which of course, got a little bit cheeky at the top, in a good way that is. At least that's what I thought anyway.

Needless to say, she was a woman, that had a fine looking ass on her and her hair was simply to die for as well. It too, was long, soft, and flowing, dark, silky and mysterious, you know the kind of woman that I'm talking about, and yes, you could say that she looked a lot like an Angel, but the reality of it all was that she had the Devil wrapped-up inside of her, and he was itching to get out, just as quick as he possibly could.

I'd seen it all before of course, so it was nothing really special to me. Good looking women are a dime a dozen as they say, and most of the time, they really aren't worth the hassle that you know they'll end up putting you through, especially in the long run, but for some reason, I believed that this one, might just be, a little different.

Now most guys would have loved the way that this woman looked and I'd be the first to admit that. After all, I wasn't any different there myself; I've always had an eye for a beautiful woman, what can I say?

But I wasn't looking for anything special that night or any other night to be quite honest. After all, I was already committed to the club and I was living that life to the Hilt.

I used to get my loving on the run, simply because I stayed on the road most of the time. I was more than just a little happy with that, after all, that was my life back then and that's the way it had always been.

Still, we immediately struck up a conversation, that seemed to go on forever, and it didn't really matter what was said, I'd just laugh, and the woman would laugh and then I'd keep on saying it, or something else just as funny or just as stupid, whatever it was? You know how conversations are? And to be honest, this woman, reminded me of someone, that I had known when I was younger, someone that I had met back in my late teenage years, when I was still in the army, during my airborne/recon training days, across the pond, somewhere in North Carolina, probably?

North Carolina is a beautiful state, although Fort Bragg, and the Special Forces, which were known as the Green Berets, at that time, had a lot to be desired, but never mind, it was only one of several bases, that I had trained at over time, and they were all pretty much the same.

Nothing ever happened from that meeting though, the girl was way too young and besides that, I moved around too much. We came from different backgrounds, knew different people, and moved in different circles.

We were the opposite types of people if the truth were known, and I guess that I knew that, even back then, because I was never going to be the suit and tie kind of guy that her father was and the girl was never going to be a world traveller, or even a biker for that matter, but I'll never forget the way that I felt about her at the time and I often wondered, if she had ever thought about me?

I guess everyone has a memory like that, stashed away at the back of their mind. What could've, would've, should've been, but of course it never was.

Anyway, within an hour or so, this woman figured out that she had me wrapped up tight, right around her little finger, for the night anyway, and to tell you the truth, I was pretty happy that she had, because to me, she was a beauty that's for sure, a drop-dead gorgeous type of female, in every aspect of the way and then some.

I was younger back then as well, wild, single and carefree, but I still had my values and my wits about me.

This woman was one of the best looking women, that I had ever laid eyes on at the time and I figured that if I played my cards right, maybe we could make some sort of sweet music together, after all she was raising my blood pressure, that's for sure, and I was aching to get to know her better, to say the least. I was also hoping that the girl was feeling the same way about me.

Now you'd probably have to give her some credit though; because, she had pulled out every trick in the book that she could think of when she first saw me.

She batted both of her sexy eyes and gave me one of the broadest of smiles, that you've ever seen at the time, and she constantly licked her lips, as we stood there talking. She also played the Damsel in distress a few times, getting caught-up on something at the bar, and then once again at the bathroom door. She even slipped over in front of me, so that I actually had to catch her, before she fell to the floor and she was good at sending out all kinds of other body language as well that just didn't seem to quit.

She danced like a professional dancer, grinding herself into me, fast and furious at times and then really slow and easy, at other times.

It was hard for me to concentrate on anything else; I was completely lost in the moment, and I was definitely lost in her.

Then we kissed, and it actually felt as though I'd lose my front teeth, even though they were still firmly attached and all of this happened within the first hour or so of meeting her.

Man, I was feeling like a lucky guy. I was so excited by her, in so many different ways. She made every man's head in the club turn sideways when they saw her, and then she made damn sure that they all knew that she was with me.

Yeah, she was special all right, young, beautiful, elegant, a little sophisticated, and she was all mine, for the night anyway.

It was her idea to go to South-end on Sea to begin with, who would've thought? Of course, she had never been on the back of a motorcycle before, the poor little sheltered thing, that she claimed to be, and I was only too eager, to make her first time out, simply one of the best times, that she'd ever have.

So it didn't take any persuasion at all, to get us both out of the club that night and on to the highway. We practically floated out the door, arm in arm, and then we flew on down the road, like a couple of love birds, looking for an empty nest.

The woman wrapped herself up so tight around me, that it felt like I was wearing an extra jacket at the time, which was a pretty good feeling; I'd happily admit, because the long night air was cool, crisp and clean, without a single drop of rain in sight, I might add.

The throttle was cranked-up, as we listened to the motor purr. It was one of the best sounds in the world, well almost the best sound anyway.

We both enjoyed the night-time ride and when it was over, which is always too soon as far as I was concerned; we were both inside a casino, throwing dice on a cloth covered table, with a lot of signs and numbers on it.

Which was her idea again, of course, having never been to a casino before, at least not in South-end on Sea? And it was just lucky, that I had been paid for a job that I'd just finished the day before, and that I actually had some extra cash to spare that evening, because none of it was cheap that's for sure, but then again, gambling, wine and women, never are.

We quickly moved on to the roulette tables, and then over to the card tables, before we finally hit a few slot machines.

She laughed, I laughed, and we had what seemed to be one of the greatest times of all. It was almost like; we belonged together, like we were even made for each other, hell, it even felt like we were out on our honeymoon at one point in time, or at least something similar.

Everyone noticed us of course, and they especially noticed her, who was simply, the most gorgeous woman that I had ever met at the time.

We were known as the Beauty and the Biker, which was a statement that I overheard the bartender saying as he sorted out our drinks.

"I know, she suddenly said out loud, with a huge smile on her face, just as I lost another twenty-quid, on three reels out of five, that didn't quite line up right, let's go to Brighton."

"Brighton? I said, what the hell's going on in Brighton, of all places?"

"I've got some people down there, she said again, we can spend the night with them and in the morning we can jump into the ocean. You do know how to swim don't you?"

I just laughed and then I said, "We live on an Island don't we love? Of course I know how to swim. Besides that, I spent the first nine months of my fucking life, stuck in a pool of bloody water."

"Good, she replied, laughing at the joke, because you'd be surprised how many people around here don't know how to swim. In-fact, some people have never even been to the ocean before, how sad is that?"

"That's because we live in the North Atlantic, I replied again, and the water around here is too damn cold, even in the summer time.

If we lived in the South Pacific, then everyone would know how to swim" I said, looking back at her with a broad smile.

"What are you, some sort of Geography Teacher now?" The girl asked, laughing again and again, and then she said, "Come on then, let's go to Brighton, it'll be fun."

"Oh, ok I finally said, we'll get out of here."

So off we went for another two and half hour ride, back to the west from where we had already been and then all the way down south to the Brighton sea front, just as fast as the roads would take us.

I wasn't stopping for man or beast, I was on a mission now, and that was all there was to that. It was all done underneath a cool, twilight sky and by the time we got to Brighton, I was a little tired, the woman was a little stiff, we were both a little cold and we both needed to pee. We were also thirsty as hell, a little bit hungry and ready for another smoke.

The pubs were already closed by then, but most of the clubs were still open and the casinos were open twenty-four hours a day anyway, if you knew which ones to go to, that is?

We had several choices of where to go to next, though, and always being amiable, I let her decide, and she chose an out of the way casino, which was down along the sea front, not too far from the pier.

For the next few hours, we danced and drank the night away, laughing, kissing, hugging, and more, basically having a great time in general, but again this little trip was getting pretty damn expensive.

One night out on the town, with this woman, had already set me back a week's wages or more and I was almost out of cash by then, thinking about finding a hole-in-the-wall somewhere, to tap into my savings, which I really didn't want to do.

"What about your friends?" I finally asked her at last, just as the music was starting to wind down a bit and the crowd was thinning out on the dance floor.

"Where do they live and which way do we go to get there from here?"

"Oh, she said, I couldn't get a hold of them, so I just figured that we'd get a hotel room for the night and then try to find them tomorrow, after we go for a swim of course."

Finally, I thought to myself, we'll get a room together, go to bed, have some fun and in the morning maybe even order up some room service. But for whatever reasons and who knows why, I opened up my mouth, and then I stuck my foot, straight into it.

I started saying all the wrong things, at all the wrong times, for all the wrong bloody reasons. I knew what I was saying of course, but it really didn't matter. I just kept on talking, saying all the things that I shouldn't have, when I should have just stopped and kicked myself in the teeth instead, but I didn't. Of course I didn't. Who would've thought?

"Cool babe, I said, I hope that you have some money for all that then, because I'm starting to get a little skint right now, especially after all of this partying tonight and I only just got paid yesterday."

"You're joking, right? The woman said, rather quick and harsh, and without that pretty smile of hers, I might add.

Don't you have enough money left, for a hotel room? It's only for the night and I'm sure that it won't cost anymore than a couple of hundred quid or so, after all, this is Brighton. Come on now; don't be messing around with me like that."

I don't know what it was really, maybe I was just too tired to deal with it, or maybe it was something else, but I certainly didn't like the way that she said what she had just said.

Besides that, it didn't sound very nice. In-fact, it sounded more like a spoilt child, chastising her parents for getting her the wrong bloody doll as a birthday gift, and I could never stand spoilt kids to begin with, I never have and I never would. What more could you say about that?

I turned to her and said, "Well, actually, no my love, I don't have the money any more, shaking my head at the same time, we've blown over a thousand quid tonight, what with all the casinos and all of the drinks that we've had. So, I guess, we'll just have to go home from here then, your place or mine, it doesn't really matter to me which one it is."

"What?" The woman said again, with a voice that was loud enough for all of the others to hear, I can't go home now; my old man would kill me, and besides that, I wasn't supposed to be out tonight, let alone, out with the likes of you."

"What? I said back at her, in total and utter disbelief, Wait a minute here; you're telling me now, that you're married? I thought you already told me that you were single?"

"Yeah right, she said, we're all bloody single. I just happen to have somebody waiting for me at home that's all, and don't start thinking that I'm going home with you neither, because I'm not. I'm definitely not that kind of girl."

I was floored by then, because we had already been together just like that, all night long. Laughing, kissing, hugging, and practically having sex on the bloody dance floor.

The woman had even let her hand drop to my manhood, more than just a few times, during the course of the evening, that's for sure, and I was simply aching to get her into bed; pull her knickers off, slip in-between her legs, then slide my tongue around her little button and deep inside her honey pot, making her scream a little, before I inserted myself and finally exploded in some much needed relief, but now she was saying that she's not that kind of girl? What the fuck is that about?

"What's your problem? I said to her again, in complete, and utter, disbelief? You sure have been acting like that kind of girl, at least for the last six or seven hours now, or more. Are you crazy or what?"

"Screw you biker trash, she said, as she stepped away from me. Screw you and piss right off. I never want to see you again. You're just another greased-up, useless little wanker, that doesn't have a fucking clue, about anything at all, really."

I was completely stunned by then. It was the first time that I had heard the woman swear.

What a waste of space, I thought to myself and what a damn fool I'd been to spend all that money trying to impress her, like I had. Shit! Fuck, damn it all to hell. Oh well, screw her too, it was time for me to scoot on out of there anyway. So, that's when I left her.

The woman just stood there of course, with a drink in her hand which I had already paid for, a horrible scorn on her face, and some pretty sharp and nasty words that were rolling off the tip of her tongue.

She didn't look so appealing to me now though I thought, as I headed out the door, trying to remember where it was that I had parked-up my bike at. Shame really, I bet she would have been pretty lame in bed as well, I thought again, laughing to myself.

Anyway, that's about where we came in with this story to begin with, because that's when the skies opened up, and the rain started to fall, and boy, did it ever come down hard.

Now the rain can be just about as miserable as the weather can get for a biker, unless it turns to into snow and ice that is. It stings you when it hits you in the face, it makes the roads, wet and slippery, and it makes your clothes, feel cold, damp, and sticky, whether they are or not, and then your mind simply goes numb, faster than you can count the minutes ticking by, and that's just on a good day.

Even when the rain isn't falling yet, you can still feel it in the air, and you can taste it at the back of your throat, and let me tell you, it was definitely raining by the time that I had left that crazy woman in the club that night. In-fact, it was more than a little rain; it was torrential and it was coming down in sheets, by the bucketful.

Never mind, I thought as I headed back out through the city, and then straight onto the highway that would eventually lead me up north, towards where I was living at the time.

I figured that it would only take me a good hour and a half or so to get back home, if I hurried, but then again, only if it stopped raining.

Fortunately, by the time I got to the edge of town the rain was easing up. In-fact, by then it was a light rain falling, for the moment anyway, so I was able to get a scoot on, taking the bike up to speed in no time at all.

It wasn't long before I noticed that I was somewhere just south of some services, when the heavens started to open up again. It was another mad downpour, which saw more sheets of water, blowing wildly across the open road.

The wind had come up as well, slowing me and the rest of the traffic down to little more than just a crawl that time, so I pulled off the highway at the main entrance to the services, just as quickly as I could and just in time to hear my headlight pop.

"Shit, I said out loud, well that's just frickin perfect, now I'll be stuck here until daylight." It was already past four in the morning, so I knew that I wouldn't have to wait too long for daylight. Another hour or so and it would be plenty light enough.

I probably had a bulb kicking around somewhere as well, and besides that I was hungry at the time. So, I parked-up at the curb as usual, shook myself off, and then I quickly went inside the restaurant.

Of course, everyone in there stared at me for a minute or two, as I slowly walked passed them un-zipping my jacket at the same time, but they quickly looked the other way, as soon as I caught their eyes in mine.

You could easily see that I wasn't the only traveller on the road that morning; because there were lots of them really, but no bikers at all, except for me of course, and I guess it was kind of typical of regular citizens anyway; because they can't help staring at a biker, even though they usually don't have the balls to look one straight in the eyes.

Never mind though, I probably did look like an overgrown rat at that moment in time anyway. Perhaps one that had just swam its way up from the sewer no doubt.

So, I took off my jacket as soon as I could and then I hung it over the end of the booth, with my colours, tags, and rockers, completely visible for all to see. Then I sat down and ordered up a cup of coffee just as quickly as I could.

I didn't want people thinking that I was out to rob the place, or something else, if you know what I mean?

The waitress was a pretty little thing, young, well dressed, with a good looking build on her and a warm, soft, gorgeous smile, along with an even warmer greeting that I appreciated at the time.

She was short, blonde, fairly thin, and all of about twenty-one or so, I figured. She also had some nice words to go along with her good looks as well, as I soon found out, sitting there, drinking my first cup of coffee, and slowly trying to dry out.

"A bit wet out there, isn't it sweetie? The waitress said, still smiling. Have you been out there for very long?"

"I just rode up from Brighton, I said, smiling back at her, and I'm slowly making my way back home to London now."

"Where's that then?" The waitress said again, still smiling and checking out all of the patches that I had on my jacket at the same time, as well as eyeing up the length of my pony tail?

"Brighton I said with a really big grin, or London?" Then I sipped on some more coffee, watching her, as she looked me up and down.

"I actually live in Brixton," I said to her again. The waitress smiled some more, looking at me, and then she said.

"Oh yeah, Brixton, looking down at my jacket again, of course you do. It seems like everyone's from London these days, so what was going down in Brighton then?" she asked, just as another customer came in and sat down at the counter. I was about to tell her, when she said,

"Listen hon. I'll be back in a minute, do you want anything else? I could always bring you some breakfast, if you like?"

"Yes please, I said, I'd like the full English breakfast if I may, with toast and strawberry jam on the side, thank you."

I watched her walk away. She was a nice girl, I thought, as I stared out the window, watching sheets of water, still blowing across the parking lot. In-fact, she was probably a real warm and genuine type of person, who was into much slower time's maybe, like sipping wine in front of an open fire, with light scented candles burning over the top of a wooden mantel piece, somewhere soft, safe, warm and secure.

She was probably, nothing like the woman that I had gotten hooked up with earlier on. That one was the down and dirty type for sure, a crazy, frigging nut job that I should never have been bothered with in the first place.

After all, I knew better really? I wasn't a bad looking guy at all; tall, dark, and ruggedly handsome, as some people would say, and I had a great sense of humour, most of the time. But that woman, that woman was just too damn good to be true, right from the get-go, too good for me, that's for sure; at least that's what she thought anyway.

Oh well, it was a good job that I got rid of her when I did, because it definitely wouldn't have worked out for either one of us in the long run, after all, we were way too different, and beside that, I wasn't out for anything long term anyway.

She might have been a good looking woman alright, but like my old man always use to say, "if you can't trust em son, then you're better off without them, because they'll get you into a world of trouble quicker than shit otherwise, and you wouldn't want that for anyone, not even your worst enemy."

What a freaking nightmare though. Good riddance to bad rubbish and all of that. Still, I had better things to do with my time.

Right about then, my eyes caught sight of a Red Ferrari, just as it pulled into the parking lot and then parked itself, up next to my chopper.

It was a nice looking car, I thought, although the colour was a bit too bright for my taste, but at least it wasn't green, you'd have to give him credit for that.

Then, before I even realized what was happening, I saw this leggy, dark-haired beauty; quickly get out of the passenger seat and make a mad dash for the restaurants door. She didn't even wait for the driver.

Holy shit, I thought again, as I realized what was going on.

It was her of all people. She must have gotten her old man to come down and get her, or perhaps this was the friend that she couldn't get hold of earlier?

There was nothing that I could do about it though, the woman had already seen my motorcycle as soon as they pulled into the parking lot, so I just sat there watching her, as she stormed into the restaurant like she owned the place, of course, glaring at all of the people that were still sitting there, and then finally, she focused her cold, heartless stare, on yours truly and she didn't even blink, not even once.

"Don't you even talk to me, you bastard," she said, just about as loud as she could, almost stomping over to the table, where she then, just flopped herself down, right in front of me.

"I can't believe that you dumped me like that, you little prick and in Brighton of all places. Do you realize that I could have been killed or maybe robbed and beaten, or even raped?

Maybe, something far worse than that could have happened to me as well and it's all because of you, you leather bound, brainless, little maggot."

I was still watching the Ferrari outside, trying really hard to ignore her, although it wasn't working out too well, because she was starting to sound like my mother and I couldn't stand her, but anyway I could also see this huge, mountain of a man, with arms the size of tree trunks and a neck about the size of both of my upper legs put together, slowly crawl out of the driver's seat.

I kid you not, this guy could have been the incredible Hulks little brother for all I knew. He was built like a brick shithouse and I could only imagine that the rest of his family, were probably built the exact same way, even his mother.

I just sat there and watched as the guy shut the car door, and then rapidly made his way to the entrance. I was just about to say something like, well; it really was your idea to begin with woman, when this big ole boy, quickly lumbered on over to the table as well.

"Do you know this guy then?" the big guy said, with a fairly deep voice, looking down at both of us, but looking at me in particular, with a long, cold, hard, angry, type of stare.

Not quite the friendly little giant that he should've been, I immediately thought, especially so early in the morning.

"Chill out man, I said, just as the guy was about to say something else. I didn't know that she was married and as soon as I found out about it, I split, all right? I ain't looking for any trouble here; I've got enough of that on my plate as it is."

"She's married? The big guy said, almost fuming by then, well, man oh man, that just about takes the piss now, don't it?

She told me, that her "boyfriend" had dumped her off at the club and that her sister was waiting for her to get back home, so that she could watch her kids, before they headed off to school."

I could see that the guy was eyeing up my jacket now, which was still hanging on the backside of the booth drying out, where I had originally put it when I took it off.

His voice was starting to trail off; rather quickly, I might add, as he realized who it was that he was actually talking to.

I was also thinking, that it's Sunday you fool, although, I didn't say anything, because there wasn't any reason to upset the guy, anymore than he already was.

I just figured that I needed to keep him calm really, because at the end of the day, it wasn't his fault that we were all sitting there. I'd jump up and break his nose in a heartbeat if I had to, and then I'd probably take him out at the knees, quicker than he could imagine or even think about, but only if he kicked off first. After all, I didn't actually know him from Adam, so I had no reason to get into it with him, unless he was the one to push it of course.

Then the woman started up again, and the whole damned restaurant seemed to perk-up.

"Ah for fucks sakes, the woman started screaming, now look what you've done, you fucking loser. This guy, is one of the owners of that club, that you left me stranded at, you dumb-assed moron; he's giving me a ride home and you're going to fuck the whole thing up."

And then to everyone's surprise and just as quick as you like, the big guy turned to her and said, "You've got to be joking honey, I'm not giving you a ride home now, that's for sure. You can find your own way home from here and by the way, I never said that I owned that place neither, I just work there, but that doesn't matter anymore, because I don't need any of this shit in my life, especially with someone like you."

Then he turned to me again and quickly said, "I sure hope I didn't get myself into any kind of problem here, friend. I was just trying to help her out really, that's all it was. I certainly don't want any trouble coming from it, especially your kind of trouble."

I could see that the big guy was looking a little worried by then, his eyebrows were starting to sweat, he had a waver in his voice and I swear that he was even starting to shake a little, as if he had just come out of a bathtub full of ice.

Then I watched, as he quickly turned around, and walked right back towards the door that he had just come in from.

"C ya," he said again, as he headed back outside, without a second thought.

The woman and I, along with the rest of the people in the restaurant, just sat there watching in silence, as the big ole guy practically tore open the door of his own car, and then quickly squeezed himself back into the driver's seat, before he finally pulled away, splashing water all over the parking lot and the not so pretty green chopper that was still sitting out there, practically drowning in all of that pouring rain.

Yeah, that's right, my green chopper, of course.

"Oh yeah, that's just fucking great, the woman finally said, practically yelling at me again. How many more times are you going to screw up my life tonight, you idiot, wanker, greaser, loser, biker scum."

The waitress came over right about then, and then she asked me if everything was all right? Then she told the pair of us, to keep the noise level down because everyone in the whole place was listening in.

I agreed with her and then I immediately apologized, before turning my eyes back to the dark-haired woman, who was still sitting there, with me.

"Look woman, I said, it's not my fault that you're screwing around on your old man and as far as I'm concerned, you probably deserve what you get, but don't be yelling at me about it, because it was all your idea to begin with. You're just lucky that I'm a gentleman, otherwise I would've nailed your little ass to the wall by now, if I wasn't."

"Gentleman, she said, in a slightly lower tone of voice, but still high enough for everyone else to hear. You're no fucking gentleman, you're just a screwed up biker, without a pot to piss in. I know what you are and I've known plenty of fools, just like you. I also know that you really want me, because you can't take your eyes off of me, but you can't afford me neither, so keep your damn mouth shut, and leave me the fuck alone, you useless, no good maggot, go on, piss off."

I looked at her again, shaking my head, smiling as broadly as I could and quickly thinking that at least we finally agreed on something. She definitely was high maintenance, that's for sure, and then I laughed out loud and said, "Hey bitch, this is my table, so if you don't like it, then you can be the one to piss off. Go on now, find your own table, or better yet, just get the hell out of here altogether, because I was here first, and I haven't finished my fucking breakfast yet."

The woman started to say something else, but then she just burst into tears instead. "I'm sorry, she said, I really do like you. I was just having some fun tonight, that's all, my old man beats me up all the time and."

"Lookee here woman, I quickly said, cutting her off in the middle of her sentence. I don't want to hear this shit. If you get beat up by your husband, then you probably deserve it. If you don't like it, get a fucking divorce like everyone else does, and quit screwing with people's heads, especially mine.

If you hadn't lied to me in the first place, neither one of us would even be sitting here right now, so it's your own damn fault, not mine."

"All right, all right, she said, smiling back at me now, I get your point, and I'm really sorry, I truly am, I just needed that ride home and now I wish we hadn't stopped here in the first place, but we did.

Then, right out of the blue, she said, "Do you think that you could you buy me a cup of coffee please, and maybe a bite to eat as well, because I didn't realize how hungry I am. Please?"

I looked at her for a moment or two; she really was a beautiful woman. Too bad she was so screwed-up in the head. Too bad she was married and too bad it was still raining, because otherwise, I would have just got up and left the place, leaving her right along with it, but instead I called the waitress back over and asked her nicely to bring the woman a cup of coffee, and a breakfast sandwich, as well as another cup of coffee for myself. After that, we just sat there looking at each other in complete and total silence for quite some time.

The waitress had already brought my breakfast to the table, earlier on and I was digging into it, enjoying the country sausage, mixed in with the strawberry jam, that I had put on my toast as usual. But then I got to thinking again, this woman still looked pretty familiar to me and that had been bugging me all night long, although I couldn't quite place where it was that I'd seen her before, or even if I really had seen her before?

There was feeling though, a feeling that we had known each other briefly, at some point in time, but then someone put Trace Walton's "Black Hearted Woman" on the jukebox and it started playing slightly in the distance.

It was the perfect song, for the perfect moment, at the perfect time I quickly thought, and it totally took my mind off of anything else that I was thinking about.

By then, the sun had started to rise and the rain was finally easing off again. I was still over an hour away from home, but I didn't care much about that, after all, it was Sunday morning and I didn't need to be anywhere, no-where special anyway.

"I don't suppose that you'd give me a ride home now, would you?" The dark-haired woman finally said, after what seemed like an hour and a half or so of complete silence, but in reality it was only a few minutes.

"You've got to be joking, right?" I said, looking at her and wondering if she really was really brain damaged, or maybe it something else.

"I'll pay you of course, she said, as she dug into her purse pulling out a check-book, how about fifty quid?"

"Yeah right, I said, looking back at her, almost laughing at the thought of it, like I could cash that thing anyway? It would probably bounce all the way to the bank and then back again."

"No, no, it's good I promise, I've got the money in my account, she said, I just don't have any credit cards anymore.

Daddy ripped them all apart, just the other day in-fact. He said, that I spend too much money on them."

The waitress made her way over to the table again, "Can I get you anything else Hun?" she asked, looking straight into my eyes and almost ignoring the woman like she wasn't even there.

"Just a taxi for this crazy woman here, I said smiling at her and maybe your phone number as well, which would be really nice."

The waitress, smiled back at me and said, "Sorry love, I'm a happily married woman, showing me the ring on her left hand at the same time, but thanks for asking me anyway.

I'm kind of flattered that you did, because I know that someone like you could have just about any girl out there, and if I wasn't married, I'd love to go out with you sometime I'm sure, but I am married and that's that, so anyway, just let me know when you want that cab and I'll ring it through."

"No wait, the dark-haired woman said, they won't take any checks and that's all that I have, please give me a ride, she said to me again, please. I'll give you my phone number as well."

I started laughing at her for real this time. "Yeah right, I said, like I'd really want to talk to your old man, when he picks up the phone with me on the other end of the line? I'll tell you what though, you write that check out for a Grand and I'll make sure that you get home perfectly safe and sound."

"Ouch," she said, a thousand pounds? I don't think I really deserve that, but how about if I give you, say two-fifty?"

"Two hundred and fifty quid, I said, looking at her still smiling, you really are joking aren't you? And besides that, two-fifty is just taking the piss, you're gonna have to make it out for at least Five Hundred quid, and not a penny less."

"Ok, ok, she said, writing out five hundred pounds on the check, and then handing it to me. Here you go then, but you'll have to fill in your own name on the top of it; because I can't remember for the life of me, what you told me it was."

"Don't you worry about that, I said, as I took the check out of her hand? Just make sure that it doesn't bounce, because your name and address are on it as well, plain as day, and I don't want to have to come back by your house, just to collect my cash at a later date, if you know what I mean? That's just not good business as far as I'm concerned, and this is strictly business now and nothing else."

"Don't worry; it's a good check, honest it is. The money's sitting in the bank already. So, no problems, no worries, she said, you'll get your money, I promise." And then, right out of the blue, like nothing else had happened between us, she said,

"Do you want to do this again next Saturday night? I could always meet you somewhere else? There's a pub around the corner from where I live actually. We could meet up there, and then maybe head out to the country after a few quick drinks of course."

I started laughing again, so hard, that I almost pissed my pants. This woman was a complete and utter lunatic I thought, who was totally off her bloody rocker.

Then I got up and went to the men's room, splashed some water on my face and looked into the mirror. I'm not a bad looking guy really, I thought, so why in the hell, did I have to put up with all of this bullshit tonight?

I dried my hands, and made my way back out to where the woman was still sitting. I sat back down for a minute or two, watching her finish what she was eating and then I started wondering what her father did to control her credit cards and what about her husband?

"So, I quickly said to her, your father tore up your credit cards huh? What's up with that then?"

"Yeah that's true, the girl said, he says that I spend way too much money on them, so he tore them all up. Why do you ask?

"Well, what about your husband, I said quickly, what does he have to say about all of that then?"

"Oh, I see what you're thinking, but it's not like that at all she said. I only got married, so that I could move away from home, while I go to school, you see?

I actually just live with the guy at the moment, although I suppose that's not quite how he sees it, to be honest? But you know, it's only for a little while. He's really more of a friend that I've known since I was a kid, and now we share a flat together, but Daddy pays the rent. He got mad at me for buying the food, and stuff, when my husband couldn't afford too, and I also bought a few new books for his courses as well, which he said, that he'd pay me back for, later on, when he gets a real job I suppose?

That's about all really; except that he's totally gay, my husband of course, not my Daddy, but I imagine, that I spent a little too much on the clothes though, because I always do. I love new clothes, I always have and I always will, probably even more than a little too much, really, but hey I'm a girl, and that's what us girls like.

Then of course, there were the pizzas, and the beers, and the taxi cabs that we get every Friday night, and Sunday afternoon, when we go out to watch movies with our friends. But they're the ones that are already scheduled; I get a bill from them once a month."

"So you really are married then, I said, quickly interrupting her again, before she got into writing a book on the subject, but not really, is that what you're trying to tell me? And he's gay? What the fuck is that? And what was tonight all about then, and while we're at it, how old are you anyway, when you say that you're still going to school and all of that shite?"

"I'm almost twenty-one, she said, but I still have to do, whatever my father wants. He pays the bills for me. He pays my tuition and he pays the rent, what more can I say? I've got one more year of university to go and then I can do what I like.

I'll have my degree and I'll have access to my own trust account that my grandpa set-up before he died. So yeah, things will be fine, eventually.

"Let's just get out of here; I finally said to her, as I got up from the table and put my jacket back on. I'm going to need to get some sleep at some point in time and I'm hoping that that'll be sooner than later, if you know what I mean?

Trace Walton's "She's gone" was playing on the jukebox by then, which was just another great song for the moment, I thought, as I headed for the door.

I bet that guy's been through the wringer, more than just a few times himself, by the sounds of things anyway.

Then I heard the woman say. "I don't suppose that we could stop off and go skinny dipping somewhere along the way, she was grinning from ear to ear when she said it, with a look in her eyes, that anyone would have practically died for. She was so friggin beautiful it was hard to resist.

"Don't push it woman," I said back at her, smiling at the very thought of it. Maybe if I did take her down to the river, I'd get lucky and then she'd leave me alone afterwards, but I thought about that again, figuring that it wasn't such a good idea at all, still smiling though.

I paid the bill and thanked the waitress for her hospitality, by telling her to keep the change from the fifty pound note that I had just handed to her. She smiled really wide and then said, "Thank-you very much honey, you have a great day now you hear and do come back and see us again sometime." Just as the dark-haired woman, grabbed my arm in hers, having us both leave the restaurant looking as if we were an old married couple strolling out after a Sunday brunch.

She was smiling now, and still going on about swimming somewhere, but I wasn't listening to her anymore, or at least I was trying really hard not to listen. I would've liked to have laid her down somewhere just for the hell of it, but I never did married women to begin with, unless of course, I didn't know that they were married at the time that is?

Most married women make me cringe anyway; because you can never trust them especially if they're screwing around on their husbands, then you know that they'd screw around on you and everyone else as well. And besides that, they've always reminded me of those dirty old Cougar types that had fucked around with me when I was just a kid.

They were married too, but they'd just lie through their teeth about it and then kick me out of the bed right before their husbands came home, if I was lucky that is? Definitely not the kind of women that I'd be associated with now that's for sure, and beside that, there's just too many, good looking, honest, single women, out there anyway, and let's face it; no-one could ever get them all, no matter how hard they tried.

Outside, the rain had finally stopped falling and the skies were starting to clear. Soon, we were off and running, out of the parking lot, down the road and completely out of sight, from those that were still sitting in the restaurant wondering what in the hell, that was all about?

It was only a matter of minutes really, until both of us were enjoying the cool, crisp, breeze, which was slowly blowing the fresh air around.

Yeah, it was a lazy Sunday morning alright, with the two of us riding on the wind, a twisted little brain-dead beauty, and a tired worn-out Biker, who would've thought?

I finally pulled up to the corner of the street where the girl lived and quickly noticed that it was an affluent up-market, high-society, type of area, with insanely large, rich and lavish, old houses, that were nestled in close amongst the trees.

Each one had a long drive to the front and then down the side of it, which was pretty nice, if you like that sort of thing?

I watched her walk up to the door, put the key in the lock, and then step inside just as quickly as she could without a seconds thought or hesitation, or even a backwards glance in my direction, as far as that goes.

In-fact, I didn't get a thank-you from her neither come to think of it, but never mind, it would be the last time that we ever crossed paths if I had my way and it wouldn't be soon enough, as far as I was concerned.

I had definitely had enough of her by then, and I just wanted some solitude, if you know what I mean? I looked down at my watch before firing up the bike again. It was a little after eight in the morning, on a clear blue sunny Sunday, with barely a cloud in the sky, or a breeze in the air.

After that, I headed home, for a much needed shower, and a long, peaceful, dreamless, kind of sleep. But the next weekend, I was scooting my way up north on my own this time, with most of my wits about me, along with a full tank of gas and an extra five hundred quid in my pocket.

There was nothing of any real importance on my mind, at that particular point in time, but there was definitely a smile on my face and it was a good ride, it always was.

****

Postscript

When I cashed the check a few days later, I noticed that the name on it was the same last name as the first Commanding Officer that I had been assigned to, during my airborne/recon training days, in the States.

He was also English, spending twelve years in the SAS, before he did another ten years with the U.S. Special Forces. A career Coronel, who was just about as bad assed, as you could get. Well on his way to becoming a General, with all the connections that he had made during his time with her majesty's Military, and then Uncle Sam's Special Forces.

He had very powerful, and extremely influential friends, to say the least, some of them are still living today, but that's neither here nor there.

My point is, that he really liked me, which was good thing, because he made damn sure that I was taught the right way, right from the get-go and as quickly as I could learn, which to be honest, was exactly what I needed back then.

Anyway, I finally remembered, that I had attended a special birthday party; for the Coronel's youngest daughter, right before I was shipped off overseas the first time around. The girl was a few years younger than what I was at the time, probably about twelve or thirteen, I would imagine?

She was living at home with her folks of course, and I guess, she was going to school back then as well. We had spent some quality time together that night, talking amongst ourselves, in-between the other guests that were there about life in general really, voicing our opinions, sharing some of our hopes and dreams, as well as our desires, such as what we wanted out of life and what we hoped was in store for us in the future.

She did most of the talking and she seemed like a really nice girl, quite mature for her age and fairly intelligent with it. She came from a good family, with strong morals, great character and she had the blood of soldiers running through her veins, which of course is always something to be admired. She was also stunningly beautiful, almost perfect in every way or so it appeared to me at the time?

Once the party was over though, I had to leave her with her folks and return to base. And as life would have it, I never saw her again after that.

I also remembered that the girl had sent me a letter once or twice, over the course of my first year out, but it was so long ago now, that I couldn't really remember all that was said in it, and I never wrote back to her anyway. I don't know why really, but I guess that somehow, I just knew that it wasn't right for either one of us, or perhaps I figured that I wouldn't survive the war to begin with, who really knows?

However, I never forgot about her neither, simply because she was one of the prettiest girls that I had ever met at the time and the way that we had gotten along so well in the first place, was pretty hard for me to believe and even that much harder to forget.

The years had flown by pretty fast since then, and I had been through hell too many times to count. I suppose that the rest of it was simply a distant memory somewhere, one that wouldn't quite fade away, stuck at the back of my young and restless mind.

We had grown into adults over time, which made it difficult for either one of us to actually recognize each other, especially after that many years apart and such a short time of being together in the first place, but regardless of that, I knew it was her back then, and that thought alone became one more thing that blew me away about that night. Who would've thought?

Its funny how life is at times, the what could've, would've, should've, been?

Nah, nowhere close, I thought, as I started up my motorcycle again. That was never going to be me in the first place, and I was pretty sure that it never would be.

****

Black-Hearted Woman

I used to think that love was just a game, something that I would never play.
I never realised that I could change, once a woman like you came my way.
You stole my heart and you set it on fire, the flames burned right down through my bones. You took all my love and all my desire, you walked away and left me cold as stone.
But can't you see what it is that you're doing. Don't you know that my hearts been broke in two. How I wish that I'd never started this ole game of love, with a black hearted woman such as you, with a black-hearted woman such as you.
Now, I've learned to play your games girl oh so well, and now it's time I taught you a thing or two. You put me right through a living hell, and now it's time to pay the devil his dues. You stole my heart and you set it on fire, the flames burn right down through my bones. You took all my love and all my desire, and then you walked away and left me cold as stone.
But can't you see what it is that you're doing. Don't you know that my hearts been broke in two. How I wish that I never started, this ole game of love, with a black hearted woman such as you, with a black-hearted woman, such as you.

****

She's Gone

She's gone, my baby's gone, she's gone, my baby's gone, but I don't give a damn no more, no more, I don't give a damn no more. She's gone.

Well I came home drunk again last night and I fell right on the floor and when I turned on the kitchen light, I couldn't find the door, she's gone, my baby's gone, but I don't give a damn no more, no more, I don't give a damn no more, she's gone.

Now she said it's happened too many times, and she can't take no more, she packed up all of her clothes and she ran right out the door, she's gone, my baby's gone, but I don't give a damn no more, no more, I don't give a damn no more. She's gone,

Yeah let me tell you all about it.

Now she took my money and she took my car, she headed for the highway but she didn't get far. Four flat tires and out of gas, well man that woman can kiss my ass.

She's gone, my baby's gone, now I don't give a damn no more, no more, I don't give a damn no more, she's gone, yeah she's gone.

****

13
A different club

There are certain windows of opportunity in everyone's life, that open-up every now and then, but whether we get to see through them, and catch a glimpse of what lies beyond, is usually a different story for most of us.

However, these opportunities do exist and they are frequently found next to, or at the very least, close to doors of perception, which are almost always hidden by a solid brick wall or perhaps it's a very long, dark, veil, that we can never quite see through at the time.

Together, they seem to form part of a house, the house of life if you like, where each one of us will journey through, at one point or another.

Inside the house there are many large rooms, with dark, hidden passages, nooks and crannies, stairways and corridors, which lead us through and keep us coming back for more. Each room has its own space for storage, filled with memories, treasures, trinkets and baggage and every room has its own way in and out, whether that's the same way or not, it doesn't really matter.

What we find inside these rooms, is not always what we want, or even what we're looking for, but very often, it is exactly what we need, so choosing the right door, at the right time is the real trick of it all, because the doors of perception are constantly revolving and the windows of opportunity open and close very quickly indeed.

I've spent most of my life, working various contract jobs, like roofing, construction and demolition, which to be honest, has always been a mainstay of mine, ever since I was a kid. I'm a hard worker and I always have been. But there are a few other things that I've had to put my hands to as well, including club business, personal protection, the odd bounty hunting, playing guitar and working on motorcycles of course.

Most of it was usually for little money at the end of the day, money that I could never seem to keep hold of anyway, no matter how hard I tried. It didn't matter what I did and it didn't matter how much I actually got paid for doing it, or even when it was that I got paid, because it was never enough.

There was always something that I'd have to spend the money on. There was always something that I needed, wanted or simply had to have. Simple things in life really, like food, shelter, transportation, and clothing, etc. You know the score.

Now some of those years were definitely better than others, in fact some of those years, I could actually afford to eat steak rather than hamburger, fresh halibut rather than tinned tuna, but then there were those other years, where I could hardly afford to eat at all, and in the grande scheme of things there were way too many of those times along the way, but never mind, that's just the way life is.

I always had the club to fall back on when I was younger though, but through the years I tried to distance myself from all of the bullshit, politics, wars and trouble that they seem to be involved with.

I loved the life, but the rest of it has really changed over time, especially as I grow older and perhaps, a little bit wiser than what I used to be.

I knew that I could count on the club to help me out of a sticky situation though, but the cost was usually too high and I was getting too old to be bothered with any of that now. These days, I just wanted to be left in peace and then hopefully enjoy the good times I may have left in life.

I spent years defining the nature of the club to begin with; working my way up from being a probate to finally becoming a President and then of course, starting my own chapter as well as another club altogether, but that was never what I wanted to do in the first place. It was never my intentions or what my ultimate goal in life should have been, although when I did it, I did it extremely well, better than any others in-fact, if the truth were told?

Now, a lot of things had gone under the bridge during that time. There were years of club policies, new recruits, enforced rules and in house fighting, along with territorial disputes and expansions, faster than you could shake a stick at.

The club had grown from hundreds of members to literally thousands overnight. It had gone from Northern California to a worldwide organization, faster than anyone could see it happen and through it all, there were brothers, cousins, friends of friends and acquaintances that became lost, found and then lost again.

Nothing stayed the same, it never does, times change, people change and the world changed; but unfortunately, I was still me, regardless.

I was back on my own, living life as a simple Nomad, with no real ties, no club dues and no enforced boundaries, just as I had started out all those years ago.

I still had my place, don't get me wrong. My integrity remained in-tacked and my loyalty never waivers, but life was a lot easier, to say the least.

I was my own man again, although I've always been that in the first place, but no one could tell me any different, even if they tried. I was fortunate in that aspect of things, because very few people get to walk from that kind of life, and I know that only too well.

So when a job came up, regardless of what the job was, I could either do it or not. Take it or leave it, it was up to me, it was my call and my decision, unless of course, it was club business.

If that was the case and they wanted me to do it, then I had no choice in the matter, I'd have to do it regardless, after all, old bikers like me, don't get to say no, because they can never retire, not from the club anyway, which is always something to consider before you ever prospect for one. If you were ever that way inclined?

Now this one job was a job like any other job really. All I had to do was get in, get it done and get out. Then I could carry on with my life like it had never happened, hopefully without mistakes, compromise or repercussions, if it all went well that is. If not, I might be on the run for the rest of my life, always looking back over my shoulder, waiting for that long, red dot with a hammer behind it, to finally drop me in my tracks.

I was a man that had always met his obligations in the past. My word has always been my bond, and everyone knew that. But there's no pleasing all of the people, all of the time. Mistakes are made and because of that, there's always a consequence to be dealt with. I knew that only too well. I had made my mistakes over the years, and more than one of them, had cost me a friendship.

This particular situation had gotten out of hand right from the start. I knew that these guys played rough, but I figured that I was still strong enough to deal with it. It was just business after all, it was my business and I was good at it. It should never have gone so far in the first place, but somehow, it did and now I was beginning to realize that I had been set up to take a fall, right from the start.

I should have seen it coming, I should have known it all along, but I didn't and I had no choices left in the matter, it was truly a do or die situation, and I wasn't about to lay down and die just yet. However, there was someone else that was supposed to do, exactly that.

I sat there looking at the picture for awhile. I knew the person well. I had looked up to him from time to time, asked him for his opinions, taken his advice. I had even spent some quality time with him over at his house on various occasions.

I knew his family; I knew his wife and kids, hell, I even knew his mother before she died. I had known him for years by that time and now, I was supposed to kill him.

Don't get me wrong here; things like this were not my normal routine. But if the situation called for it, then I wasn't that opposed to it either. At the end of the day, business is business and on this day, it was all mine.

Now, it doesn't matter what you do in this life. Where you go, who you are or who you even think you are? There's always someone else that's ready, able and willing to take your place in the space of a heartbeat.

Even a homeless person living on the streets, in the middle of nowhere, gets replaced by another homeless person, sooner or later. It's the law of the jungle and it's the way of the world that we all live in. You can't fight it you just have to go with the flow and then hopefully realize that it's never been under your control to begin with.

I could have refused the job of course, but then someone else would have done it for them, and I would have been added to their list of eventual kills. After all, a witness in a hearsay matter or some other similar situation can become a threat, if push came to shove.

Oh sure, I still had my status, my history, my reputation and a ton of wherewithal etc. After all, I was an original member of my own club, and a Nomad of the highest calibre, but all of that was slowly fading away, as life itself usually does and it was a new generation that was coming up now, one that didn't think much of the old school ways to begin with.

They weren't into a slow burn; they wanted to go out fast, with a bang and the bigger that was, the better they liked it. They wouldn't have stopped with just me either; my whole family would have been on that list, if I didn't do exactly what they wanted me to do.

That's just the way it was and like I said, it wasn't really the norm, but it was the cost of doing business, this time around anyway.

Now, apparently the guy in the picture had somehow siphoned off a whole lot of money from the boys in the club. Money that was ill gotten gains to begin with; at least that's what certain people have said, but it didn't matter if it was true or not, because you just don't steal from the boys and expect to live long enough to tell the tale. It doesn't happen and it never has.

Drugs, prostitution, strong arm tactics etc. All cash under the table and pennies on the dollar stuff really, but those pennies soon add up over the years and they grow into dollars faster than you can blink an eye. Of course, none of that was really here or there to me anymore. After all, the boys aren't a bunch of dumb assed cub-scouts, playing after school games in the local woods, everyone knows that.

They're one the largest motorcycle clubs in the world, and they have eyes and ears everywhere, with friends of friends, and acquaintances of acquaintances, from every walk of life that you could imagine.

You don't mess with them and you certainly don't cross them, even if you were one of their own to begin with. And if you're an accountant that's been hired by the club, then you had best be keeping track of every one of those pennies that they make, otherwise you're quite likely to piss some people off and you definitely don't want to do that, no, not at all.

Now, the fact that this particular accountant, was also my business accountant, may have added fuel to the fire so to speak. After all, I was the one that had brought him into the club to begin with.

The boys needed a new accountant and I already had one for my own business, so it should have been fairly simple really, if the guy hadn't of been such a thief that is?

How was I to know what this guy was all about? He had never taken anything from me, at least nothing that I knew of anyway. He seemed to be legit, on the up and up, so to speak. So, what could possibly go wrong?

I brought him in when I was asked to, simple as that. I set him up with the boy's and then went about my own business like I always had.

I never gave the guy a second thought after that, I was too busy with my own thing and besides that, the guy worked out well for me over the last two or three years and I never had any problems. He just did what he was supposed to do and that was about all there was to that.

I've had to deal with lots of people in my time, from all walks of life and I suppose that I always will. You know what I mean, like bikers and bankers, doctors and lawyers, cops and judges etc. It didn't matter who they were or what they were about, because business is business, and one man's money is as good as any other.

I always treated the boy's pretty much the same way, but maybe that was a mistake, when you think about it.

Most of the time if you're in business, and you get screwed-up for whatever reasons, you can usually justify it, simplify it, and then change directions, effectively saving yourself from losing whatever may be at risk at the time, and if it all gets too serious, then it's usually the business itself that takes the fall, not you personally.

However with the boy's, their business is you, no matter what happens. If your employee screws something up, it's up to you to get it fixed. If you hire on another business to help do the work and they screw it up, it's still up to you to fix it, and if you have a partner that takes a hike with all of the working capital, that was in the business accounts, leaving you high and dry, then it's still up to you to find the money to carry on with, because when it comes to the boy's, their business is you. Whether you know it or not?

I'd been doing just fine before that, business was booming, money was going into the accounts, jobs were being completed and workers were getting paid on time, with the right amounts. Creditors were in kept in check and the banks were happy, but right out of the blue, my partner did a disappearing act, along with all of the company cash, which was my company cash to begin with and the so-called partner, was never to be seen again, alive anyway.

Now, I know what you're thinking and yeah I should've hunted him down myself, right quick like, but I didn't. And you would also think that I might have had a contingency plan, for whatever mess that I got myself into, but that just wasn't on the cards this time around either. I simply never guessed that any of this would have happened in a hundred years. It wasn't something that I had even thought about, let alone planned for.

Maybe that's what age does to you, dulls your senses. It would never have happened in my younger day, that's for sure.

Now, the boys were cool with it at first, "You need some cash bro, they said, no problem, just tell us how much you need, where and when, and we'll be there for you, you can always rely on us."

It was way too easy really, but that's how they do it; they make it easy, to begin with.

I did have a need for the cash though and I couldn't see any other way around it.

I needed the money that my partner had taken off with, because even if the cops found him before I could, he would have spent it all, and there wouldn't be enough left to do what I needed to do with it and it would take far too long going through the system before I could get the cash back anyway.

I had work to do and I had a limited amount of time to do it in.

The banks wouldn't help me, they were going through their own problems at the time and I didn't have any rich relatives that I could call, nor was I any good at winning the lottery, so I saw it as a total necessity, to go ahead and take the money from the boys, as and when they offered.

Just a short term loan, you understand and it should have been as simple as that, but nothings ever quite that simple.

I needed a Hundred and fifty thousand pounds sterling, to make everything work out the way it should. That was thirty grand shy of what his ex-partner had disappeared with, but that was all right, because the extra thirty thousand, was company profit anyway, give or take a grand or two.

The boys were only too happy to come up with that kind of money. A hundred and fifty grand was nothing to them. Not even the cost of one of their show bikes. But the interest was high; twenty-five grand for ninety days, then it would double for the next ninety days and so on.

If I still owed them the money after a year, the bill would be the original one hundred and fifty grand, plus another two hundred grand on top. That adds up to Three Hundred and fifty Thousand Pounds Sterling at the end of a year.

The interest doubles up every ninety days. But hey, I only needed the money for ninety days to begin with, so I wasn't too worried.

Now, you might just say that I was a little foolish for not folding the game to begin with. After all that's what my partner did and it seems that he got away with it, along with all the cash as well.

It wasn't that I wanted to continue on neither; it just seemed that I had little choice in the matter. A lot of people were counting on me to do the right thing, and that meant that I had to be there for them. So I went ahead and borrowed the money from the club, bought up the materials that I needed and arranged for them to be delivered.

Then I scheduled the people in to do the work and arranged with the clients to get the money back as quickly as the work progressed, and eventually my business was headed back to normal, for a short while anyway.

However, I was still missing a partner and unknown to me at the time, was the fact that my partner had also absconded with all of the small tools and equipment that was necessary to do the work in the first place. In fact, my partner had cleaned me out of almost everything that was involved with the business to begin with, including the paperwork for the last three years. He also took all of the customer databases and every single computer and laptop in the office that the business was being run from.

Fortunately, I kept my own laptop with a lot of the pertinent information stored on it, but it would take some time to sift through it all, just to see if it was complete or not. Oh well, another little set back in the great game of entrepreneurial life.

The work went well though and time passed by fairly quickly. By the eighty-fifth day of the loan, I had a hundred and fifty thousand pounds sitting there, ready to pay the boys back with. In five more days, I was looking at another thirty eight thousand coming in, plenty enough to pay off the loan and then have a little left over to start up some more business later on. Of course, I wouldn't go so far overboard this time, maybe fifteen grand's worth of business, rather than a hundred grand like before.

Things didn't quite work out to plan though, they never do. Ninety days were up and I was still eight grand short of the full hundred and seventy five thousand.

I had called everyone that I could think of, eight grand wasn't a lot of money, but it could end up costing me a lot more than what I figured, because if I couldn't find the rest of the cash by the end of the afternoon, the boys would hold me for another ninety days on the loan. This time the interest would be fifty grand instead of twenty-five.

By four thirty that afternoon I had narrowed it down to being four grand short, but that still wasn't enough. If I didn't have it all, I may as well not have any of it.

I needed the full hundred and seventy-five thousand, not just a hundred and seventy-one.

I finally called my accountant as a last straw. I figured that he wouldn't have the money, but maybe he could advise me on where to get that last four grand.

"Four Grand, he said, is that all you need? I'll lend it to you myself, I'll bring it over later on tonight; shall we say around seven-thirty then?"

"How about five-thirty, I quickly said on the phone back to him, could you make here with the money by then? You'll have it back in a couple of days no problem, I just have to wrap up what's left of the work that I have at the moment, you know how it is."

"Yeah, yeah, that's ok, I'll be there in an hour or less, you sure all you need is four grand?"

"Yeah, that's great man, thanks for that, I'll see you soon then" and I hung up the phone.

Now everything should have been fine at that point. I had the money to pay the boys off and I could get on with my life again, maybe even take some time out to hunt down my missing partner and then wring his freaking neck for putting me in this situation to begin with, but luck wasn't with me that day at all.

The accountant showed up at five o'clock on the dot, with four thousand pounds in a paper bag. I invited him in and offered him a beer straight away, which he happily accepted. We were starting to enjoy another one, when the doorbell rang.

Thinking that it was the boys showing up a little bit early; I got up and answered the door. What a surprise that was, who would have thought? It was the police. A whole bunch of them actually, and I was now in one hell of a spot.

You see the boys don't do cops at all, and if I didn't get rid of them fast, like within the next ten minutes or so, then all of my hard work was going to be wasted.

The boys would never show up with the cops there. They would simply just drive on by and then charge me for another ninety days on the big.

This couldn't be happening, I thought, why oh why, did they pick today of all days?

"Hello officers, what can I do for you gentlemen today then?" I quickly said.

"We have a warrant to search the premises sir, the big and tall officer said, looking down at me, is there anyone else in the house at the present time?"

"Well yeah, there's my accountant, but the rest of my family are away at the moment so," I was cut off in mid sentence.

"Please have them all come to the door now," the tall cop said.

"Yeah ok, I said, as I called out to the accountant, what this all about then?"

"We're going to need to take you down town for questioning sir, the cop said, along with your friend here and anyone else who may be in the house, so please go with this officer now. We need to search the house."

The two of us were led to the back of a van and then driven down to the station.

I could see two of the boys on their bikes coming around the corner just as we passed them by. It was then that I realized that I had left the money for them, sitting out on the dining room table.

It didn't take the cops long to search the place and it took them even less time to get the two of us down to the station, where we were placed into separate holding cells.

The boys on the bikes had seen what was going on and simply just drove on by the house like it meant nothing to them; however they were more than just a little concerned for not knowing about what had become of their investment.

They took the news of the whole ordeal back to the clubhouse and let everyone there know what went down. It was already after six pm and there was another twenty five grand put on the big. They were now looking to collect two hundred grand within the next ninety days, although they didn't know how that would be possible, especially if I was kept inside.

The big and tall cop came into the room about an hour after I arrived. Looking at me as he sat down on a chair opposite of where I was already sitting.

"So, he said, do you want to talk about it now or should we wait for a lawyer?"

"I don't understand, I said, what's going on? What is it that you want from me?"

The cop started laughing. "Oh please, he said, grinning from ear to ear, don't play the innocent man with me, we know you did it, we know how and we know why, we just need you to confess and then we can wrap all of this up real quick like.

Hell, no-one liked the guy anyway, so you might get away with a lighter sentence, if you play your cards right that is, less than ten years maybe?"

"What, I said, what the hell are you talking about? Ten years? Ten years for what?"

"For killing your partner of course, the big cop said, you're not planning on an insanity thing are you?"

"Wait a minute, I said again, Insanity? You're the one that's insane my friend, my partner took off with all of the assets of our business and then split the scene, I didn't kill him, I don't know where he went just yet, but when I find him, I probably will kill him, especially after all of this."

"Oh yeah, how much assets are we talking about then?" a few grand, ten grand, a hundred grand or what?"

"You know perfectly well how much it was, because it's in the report that I had to fill out the day after he disappeared. It was a hundred and eighty thousand pounds sterling."

"I see, said the cop, so it wasn't a hundred and seventy-one thousand like we have here in this bag then?" He raised it from the floor to show me.

"No, that's my receivables for all of the work that I've done during the last three months and I can prove it." I quickly said to him as I started sweating bullets. I knew this wasn't good, but I really didn't kill the guy.

"That's good sir; I really hope that you can prove ownership, the cop said again, and what about the other four thousand pounds that we found in the house as well then?"

"Money borrowed from my accountant, just ask him, he's in here too somewhere, as you well know."

"Yes indeed he is, and that's exactly what he say's as well. So, I can let him have his money back, but I'm afraid I'll have to hold on to yours for a little while. You won't need it for anything just yet, will you?

"You see, the cop said as he carried on talking, we found your partner laid out on a motorway with a bullet in the back of his head and no sign of the money that he was supposed to have had. Now we have an ongoing murder investigation and you my friend, is our only suspect at the moment. So, we'll keep this bag here under lock and key for the time being, until we can finish up our investigation, make sure that this here money is truly accountable, and of course, solve the mystery that has presented itself to us."

"I'm not sure I'm following you here, I said, are you charging me or letting me go?"

"Oh, you're free to go alright, but don't plan any on any holidays for a while.

We may need to reach you fairly quickly, if you know what I mean. Have a good day sir." And with that he was up and out of the door in a heartbeat, taking my bag of cash with him of course.

I didn't really understand. First of all, how could they just keep my money like that? And secondly, who was it that had killed my partner and where was the money that my partner had taken from the business to begin with?

The accountant opened up the door next and at that point he said, "Hey man, we're free to go, let's get out of here, I've called for a cab already and it should be waiting for us on the outside, oh yeah, don't worry, I got the four grand back as well, so you're not skint, but you can pay for the ride home my friend."

Cool I thought, not everything was lost as of yet, but my mind was racing on the way home. What was I going to tell the boys? How could I possibly come up with another twenty five grand as interest on money that I no longer had and what would happen if I didn't get the money back from the cops? I knew that I was in some serious trouble now and I just couldn't see a way out of it.

The boys were waiting for me when I got back home; one of their prospects had been posted at the cop shop while I was in there, so he knew that I had been released when I had. Fortunately I had dropped the accountant off along the way as well. He said that he would pick his car up later on, or perhaps sometime in the morning.

All the boys who were waiting for me came inside the house, except one of course, as I unlocked the door. The place was mess; it looked as though a bomb had hit it. The cops had gone through everything, leaving nothing untouched.

"So where's our money mate?" "The One" said, as the rest of the boys sat down in the living room, while a few of them ransacked my kitchen looking for beers.

"Well, there's a little problem here, I said, I don't have it at the moment."

"Oh dear, that's not so good and its going to cost you another twenty-five grand, I hope you know that right?" "The One" said, nonchalantly, we only hope that you can afford that, we certainly don't want to see you getting into any trouble, now do we? So, how soon do you expect to have the money for us then?"

I went through everything that had happened that day. I told him that the cops had found my partner and that they were keeping my money as evidence. They figured me for their prime suspect at the moment and there was very little that I could do about that.

I was sure that they would find the killer quick enough though, and then return my money in due course, but when any of that would happen, was just another question that was one that I simply couldn't answer. I could also see that "The One" wasn't too pleased about any of it.

"That could take year's mate, "The One" said, as I finished up my story. We don't have years to wait, and you can't afford the points, (meaning the interest on the money.)

The big is a hundred fifty grand and you're in to us for fifty more already. I think you need to come up with a different plan mate. You need a plan that will get you out of this mess. In-fact, you need a plan that will keep these boys of mine from busting you up, if you know what I mean? But there is an alternative though, "The One" said again, as he took hold of my arm and led me through to the kitchen, grabbing a couple of beers out of the fridge.

We have a contract that needs to be filled and you could be the one to fill it for us. We could maybe drop the points that you have now and possibly some of the big as well, if you decide to do it. It's a pretty good contract mate, but then you'll only owe us, say a hundred and fifty thousand pounds instead of the two-hundred thousand, that you don't seem to be able to pay back right now anyway.

If you like the work, a couple of more jobs and you could be free and clear with us and maybe even have some extra cash in your pockets as well. Hell, you might even decide that it's the kind of career that you've always been looking for, one that's right up your alley to begin with and perhaps you'll even carry on doing it for several years to come, after all, people like us don't really get to retire now, do they?

Besides that, I don't see that you have much choice at the moment, and my boys are waiting patiently, so what do you think?"

"Yeah right, I said, so who do I have to kill for that kind of payday?" hoping that it wouldn't be as serious as all of that, but knowing full well that these bikers wouldn't give away money for nothing, especially that kind of money.

"Good man, "The One" said, I knew that we could count on you. Here's a picture of your prey, so to speak, you already know him, so it won't be too difficult to track him down. Shall we say, a week or so for you to sort it all out? I'll tell you what, let's make it two weeks, it'll give you a little time to think about how to do it etc. Because, it needs to look like an accident of course, open and shut if you know what I mean?

All right then, we'll leave you in peace brother. Have a great evening. I see your family is out of town at the moment, aren't they?" Gone to Devon yeah?

I didn't reply to that, but I got the message loud and clear, these boys weren't playing around, they knew who I was, what I did, and where I'd be at all times, and they knew my family as well. I was a rat in a trap and there was no way out.

They were out of the house, on their bikes and down the road before I could say "holy shit, again."

What had I got myself into now, murder for hire, what a fucking mess? I looked at the picture for a minute, yeah I knew him all right. The guy had just tried to help me out of the jam that I was in earlier that day.

Man, it just goes from bad to worse doesn't it? What the hell was I going to do now?

I had just finished straightening up the place when a knock came on the door. It was late and I figured that it was the accountant, come back to pick up his car up, but it wasn't. It was the big and tall detective that had talked with me earlier downtown. Great, I thought, just when things couldn't get any worse than they were.

The detective wanted to ask me a few more questions, he said, I almost said no, come back tomorrow, but I didn't. Instead, I brought him in to the living room and offered him a drink.

"I don't drink when I'm on duty, he said, but I sure do make up for it when I'm off duty, so maybe you'll see me out there sometime, and we'll have a drink together then."

"Oh, I see, I said, so does this mean that you no longer think that I killed my partner then?"

"I never did think that, to tell you the truth, the detective said; I just figured that if you admitted to the murder, you might have a better chance of staying alive inside the prison that is."

"What, I said, are you crazy or something? I'm not following this at all."

"It's a long story here my friend, so sit back, keep quiet and I'll fill you in on all the details. Ok?"

I sat there listening to what ended up being a story that I could never have imagined in my wildest dreams. The cops already knew everything that had happened to me, even before the last three months.

The story actually went back for the last three years when my partner and I, had started up this particular business to begin with. The cops knew all about it back then as well; in-fact they were in on it.

My partner was actually an undercover cop that was working on a case that had been pending for some time. The case was about an accountant, who was involved with swindling money from a certain known bike club.

The accountant had turned state's evidence, he was put into the witness protection program, where things should have been well and good, but, he up and disappeared one day and that was that. But the thing was, he had a brother, who was also an accountant. The first accountant had put the money away into some offshore bank accounts that couldn't be traced.

With him out of sight and out of mind, so to speak, the second accountant, his brother, was the natural choice for the cops to get to infiltrate the bikers, assuming that he didn't have anything to do with the first accountant's disappearance to begin with that is.

Now the story gets out of hand, when the first accountant disappears, because he ends up having his face altered with plastic surgery and looks like a new man.

He then somehow manages to take on the identity of a dead cop that came from way up north. Then, claiming to be alive, which of course he was, he gets himself transferred as a cop down here, where he eventually became my partner. It wasn't until after they found him dead the second time around that the truth finally came out.

Why he took my money and all of the paperwork, along with the computers etc. was left to be seen, but somehow the bikers had found out who he was and they took him out, taking the hundred and eighty thousand pounds that he had on him at the same time. The money they assumed was theirs to begin with.

The thing is that he had swindled millions of pounds from the bikers in the first place. He certainly didn't need the hundred and eighty thousand now; unless he had somehow lost the other money somewhere along the line or perhaps someone had stolen it from him?

So, now all the cops could do was play the game out. They needed me to find out who had the money, the real money, not just the money from my company.

Was it the bikers as they suspected at first, or was it actually the brother of the first accountant, the same one that the bikers wanted dead now?

In order to do all of this, I would have to appear to go ahead and kill the second brother and then see what the next step was for the bikers? I didn't have any other choice. I was already in way over my head no matter what direction I took. So, together, the big cop and I set up the scenario for the accountant's demise.

The plan was simple enough, call up the brother, get him to meet me on an old deserted highway near the coast, have the cops drag him off to a safe house, and then put the body of his brother which was still on ice in the county morgue, in the car, set it on fire and chuck it over the cliff.

Easy stuff really, and it would look like an accident or maybe even suicide, but definitely not murder. Of course some surgery on the corpse would be in order, just to hide the bullet wound if nothing else; that he still had in the back of his head, but that was easy enough to do for the right guy. And the cops had the right guy in mind.

I couldn't believe my luck, because if I did this right; then I'd get the bikers and the cops off my ass and in the process, I'd get all of my money and equipment back as well. The gods were smiling down on me and I didn't even have to kill anyone. Thank goodness for that, and just as long as it worked out right, no one would ever be the wiser.

It seemed like the perfect plan and it actually went off without a hitch; the bikers were only too happy to drop my points and they gave me fifty grand off the big, just like "The One" had said they'd do.

Then they told me, that they would be back in contact with him, sometime in the future and not to worry about the money anymore. I still owed them a hundred grand, but they had stopped the clock on it and decided that two more jobs, like the one that I had just done, would have it paid off. They knew that I could be trusted; after all I had just committed a murder for them.

Meanwhile the cops found out that the brother of the first accountant had all of the computers stashed at his place. He had taken them from my office, because he knew that the bikers were on to his brother and that the offshore accounts were buried in the information that was on them.

His brother had taken my money to buy himself a little more time from the bikers, because the off shore accounts were not quite up and running yet. They had the money in them, but there was some kind of waiting period before any of the funds could be released. Kind of like a five year bond or something similar, I guess?

The object of the whole thing to begin with, before it all went crazy, was simply to capitalize on the interest of the new offshore accounts, and then put the money back into the old accounts before the bikers ever found out about it.

Bankers and money men do it all the time, but they never let on and they seldom get caught out.

The bikers just had poor timing really. They found out that the money was missing and then put a hit out on the original accountant before he had time to tell them what he had done. So, he went to the cops and then he disappeared before any charges were actually made. He had to become a cop in order to get close to his brother without drawing any attention and he needed his brother to get close to the bikers to get their account numbers again, so that he could eventually put the money back into them.

I was just the guy that could put it all together, because I was well known to "The One," the President of that particular chapter of the bike club.

It was rotten luck all the way around to begin with really, on my part anyway, but still, what can you do, you have to play the game with the cards you're dealt with. Things finally worked out all right though and I eventually came up with a hand full of aces.

Three men sat at the bar that night, when everything was finally said and done. They had smiles on their faces and they were laughing and joking out loud.

"You know, I always thought that I'd be a rich man some day, I said, I just didn't know how it was going to happen?

Then I laughed. Yeah right, if only that was the fucking case, oh well, who would have thought?" The other two guys started laughing again,

"It sucks to be you, "The One" said, laughing even harder. You just handed me back a hundred grand, which is money that you would never have had if it hadn't of been for me to begin with, who would have known that this cop was actually going to give you back your money, now eh? They never did find the killer of that guy did they?"

"What guy was that? The big and tall guy said, laughing out loud as he ordered three more beers. It was an accident anyway and besides that, we can't even find the body anymore, let alone whoever killed him, if someone actually did? I guess it just wasn't meant to be."

"Yeah, I'll drink to that, "The One" said, as he finished off his beer and reached for another, still, if you ever need money again my friend, you know who to call don't you?"

"Yeah, I do indeed, I said, still smiling. I do indeed." That'll be my new partner here, I quickly thought to myself, looking over at the big and tall ex-cop that was sitting across the table from me. You never know though, because life sure has a way of repeating itself from time to time, whether you realize it not, and that's just a fact.

****

14
The Emerald City

Follow the yellow brick road out of L.A, take a sharp turn to the left and then head north into the valley of the damned, which is often referred to as the valley of the dead and dying. It's a long trip, filled with all kinds of twists and turns, so you're going to want to bring enough water with you, coffee, wine, beer or whatever else you'd want to drink, because this journey will definitely take some time to complete and it'll make you extremely thirsty.

When you gaze upon a painted desert that's filled with ten foot tall, three branched cacti's without their sombreros on top, you'll need to start your climb up and over the slow rolling hills and high mountain passes, that you'll find along the way, with their large, lush, rich fertile field's of barley, corn, grain and wheat, who's multiple root systems reach way down into ancient glassy sands, along with soft virgin snow-capped mountain peaks, that are covered with some sort of strange and mysterious, other-worldly signs?

Signs that were once brightly painted on prehistoric, cobbled stone bridges, gigantic monoliths, and towering spires, that seem to reach-up high into the midnight skies, like the fingers of a sleeping giant, all set out in a line that runs over long, cool, crisp and clear, underground fresh-water river-systems, which were undoubtedly carved into and out of this magical land, long before the beginning of man and perhaps, even the dawn of time.

Still heading North, you'll make your way out past the ancient Redwood forests that always stand-up straight and tall, out towards the tattered and slightly twisted Sycamore trees, and the strangely coloured, silver birch ladies, whom, while standing there in their numbers, seem to have had their bark completely stripped from the lower regions, forever scarred in the scratches of the great brown or black-bear's nails, in some sort of weird and sadistically, unanimated fashion, and then you'll head into the midst of the high, but much younger pine forest, that's gently clothed in lichen, surrounded by a dense thicket, wild mushrooms, dark-skinned bluebells and so much more, that no-one could really describe it, or even start to contemplate it all.

Eventually, you'll find yourself beyond the shadows of Mother Nature's last true rainbow. Caught-up between the wilds of the North Pacific Ocean and those massive eagles nests, that have been carefully built-upon the not so extinct volcanoes, that were once set-out in a ring of fire eons ago, most likely with the help of some long forgotten Deity or Demi-god, whom according to most legends, rode around perched on the back of a strange but colourful demon, or flew up high on the wings of a giant pterodactyl, eventually becoming the father of children, born to those luscious, red-blooded, dark-haired, beautifully fit, young, healthy, and hugely voluptuous, half-human women, that he had always adored and lusted after, from a great distance, of course, but could no longer resist when they began to settle into the area, long before the dawn of time and way before the time of man itself, humankind that is, One-point-fucking-zero, or maybe less?

Perhaps then, if you're truly lucky, you'll eventually come to what's known as the real Emerald City, but don't ever expect to find the Wizard there or Dorothy for that matter and all of those little Munchkins, along with the Wicked Witch of the West, either died off, or more than likely, killed off years ago.

Of course, if you haven't seen the movie by now, then you probably have no idea of what I'm talking about here and the words that I've just written, will mean nothing to you at all. But if you have seen it, then you already know that it's a story about a young girl named Dorothy, who bangs her head during a tornado one afternoon while the rest of her family runs for the buried shelter that's dug-out in the bottom of their garden. And as she lays there, completely unconscious, she's rapidly transported into a mystical, far-away land called Oz, where her best friends end up to be her faithful dog named Toto, whom she somehow manages to bring with her, a strange looking, animated scarecrow, that walks, talks and tells her that he's been searching for a brain. A tall and rusty tin-man with an axe, who tells her that he's been looking for a heart and a not so fearsome, cowardly type of weird and scruffy assed lion that walks upright his hind-quarters talking to birds, who's apparently been trying to find his courage for the last several years.

Together, they travel the yellow brick road towards the Emerald City, hoping to find a mysterious Wizard, whom they believe, has the power to get the girl safely back home and then give the rest of the group what it is that they truly desire, but first of all, they have to deal with weird and wonderful, yet sometimes dangerous scenarios along the way, including the Wicked Witch of the West who simply wants to kill them all for no particular reason, along with some of her many minions, who seem only too happy, to do the same.

There's other character's in the movie as well, such as the Good Witch and her crew, along with all of the people that actually live in the Emerald City in the first place, but our girl Dorothy, really doesn't know what to make of them all, because they certainly aren't like any of the other people that she's ever met or known before.

Anyway, the girl does eventually return to the land of the living, after saving the day in a variety of Holly-weird ways of course, which include the accidental murder of the Wicked-Witch of the West, along with some of her faithful followers, then she rapidly discovers that all of the characters that were in that far-away place to begin with, were actually real people, living right where she was from in the first place, including the Wicked Witch of the West, her dog Toto, the tin man, the scarecrow and of course that cowardly assed lion.

At the end of it all, she decides that there's no place like home and never sets foot out of the house again, so-to-speak, probably severely traumatized for the rest of her life, for having to go through such an awful experience in the first place.

Still, it's suppose to be one of Hollyweird's greatest movies that was ever made, with record breaking crowds of people, standing in a queue for literally hours at a time, just to get into the movie theatres to see it. But it wasn't for the story that was being told, or even the acting that was done. It was simply because, it was the first movie made in Technicolor, which was a feast for the human eyes back then, especially when everything else appeared to be plain ole black and white, high upon that silver screen anyway and I suppose that you could almost say, that we've come a helluva long ways ever since that time, but to tell you the truth, I've often wondered if that's really the case?

****

Now the night-time skies above Seattle, which has always been known as the real Emerald City, long before that movie ever came about, have got to be some of the most stunningly beautiful, vividly spacious, wildly intense and entirely picturesque, that anyone could truly imagine, especially on a warm summers evening, when this medium-sized, high-tech, modern type of super-city, springs into life, with a different view, of what living that life, is all about.

The light pollution doesn't actually allow for star-gazing though, but it is those very lights, that create a certain kind of glow around the city, that shines like no other city in the world, except for maybe Hong Kong, once upon a time, on a cool, bright, crystal clear night, and I suppose that you could almost say, it really is quite magical, wonderful, strange and perhaps, even somewhat ethereal at certain moments in time, especially when you see it all from a distance.

On a clear day, when you're standing in the right place, you can look west, across a large inland-sea, that's commonly referred to as the Puget Sound and you can gaze upon the snow capped, mountain peaks of the Olympics, that stretch out, off in the distance as they lightly shimmer and glisten with the setting sun and yet, in a slightly different location, you could also look to the south and then slowly to the east of the city, where once again, you can gaze upon an inactive volcano, that's called Mount Rainier, which looms larger than life, in what looks to be almost, the exact same distance.

Looking directly east, you'll be able to catch a glimpse of the Rocky Mountains, which actually start-out somewhere south of Mexico City, literally thousands of miles away from Seattle, where they're known as the Sierra Madre and it's from there that they gradually swoop up north, through New Mexico, Colorado, Nevada, Wyoming, Idaho and Montana with their foothills steadily rolling all the way up the west coast, on into British Columbia and Alberta Canada and then finally ending up in the Yukon and the northern tip of Alaska, somewhere near the Bering Strait. But let's get back to Seattle, before we move on to Alaska.

Who could ever forget the Space needle, with its rotating restaurant, high above the land that it was built on? A tall, but simple reminder of the 1962 world's fair that it was originally created for, although it has also become the standard build, for many other towers, that have been designed and constructed in much the same way.

Then there's Gasworks Park, Queen Anne hill, and the University district, which has often been the home of students, artists, doctors and lawyers, along with so many talented teachers, and musicians, that have made their mark upon the world, in one way or another, including Kurt Cobain, Jimi Hendricks, and the Wilson sisters, to name a few.

Off to the west, there's Pikes Place Market, with the smell of freshly caught fish, that lingers through the air, twenty-four seven and three-sixty-five, and just north of that, the mono-rail system, that runs high above your head, both day and night, no matter what the weather is, or for that matter, any of the multi-storied, air-craft carriers, that usually sit out, on the harbour, always accompanied by a mad array of billion dollar plus, supersized yachts, and some pretty slick, ocean going liners, with their young and gorgeous, bikini clad crews?

On the east side of the city there's Lake Washington, one the longest, deepest and possibly, the coldest, fresh-water lake on the entire west-coast, crossed by two floating bridges that support super-highways, one of which is interstate 90, which will eventually lead you to Snoqualmie Pass and then, on into New York City, some three thousand miles away.

In the north of the city, you'll cross-over the Ballard Bridge, and enter into the Freemont district, or you can travel along the King's highway, which is often called the Pacific Highway, in the south, or the King George's Highway up north, which will eventually lead you into Canada, if you drive far enough, that is.

If you're in a hurry though, there's always the west-coast corridor that parallels the kings highway, from L.A. all the way up to Vancouver B.C., which is known, simply as I-5, or Interstate Five, and it is often the most preferred route to travel, for those who don't like travelling alone, or for those, that actually spend their lives travelling alone, transporting goods and equipment, from point A to point B.

In the south of the city, there's Sea/Tac airport where most people fly in to, and then leave from, if they're that way inclined, but there's also a private airport, known as Boeing Field, for the much more sensitive, influential, or extremely rich and elite traveller, which has always been the better way to go, if you could truly afford it, that is. It's been the host of Kings and Queens, along with certain dignitaries, including Senators, and Presidents, which is why it's so special, in its own kind of way. That and the simple fact, that the Boeing Airplane Company, actually own it all, although a lot the land and space, is leased out to the military, and speaking of military, further south of Seattle, you'll find a city called Tacoma, and just south of that, there's McCord Air Force base, which has now been combined with Fort Lewis, one of the largest Army bases in the entire country.

It was the home of the 9th Infantry Division and the 272nd Armour division, which could have easily overseen, a million troops, during the Viet-Nam war, and west of that, there's a large, Trident nuclear submarine base, called Bangor, near a town they call Bremerton, out on the Kitsap Peninsula, and of course, there's also a massive Coast Guard, National Guard, TSA, FBI and Military Police presence in the area as well.

Interesting enough, there's also a six-thousand, three-hundred square mile Island, that's a permanent home to over fifteen-hundred incarcerated prisoners, as we speak, most of whom are paedophiles, murderers, rapists and thieves, called McNeil Island, which had its prison system built sometime during the mid 1800's, only to become the largest Island prison, in the nation. Apparently, it also housed Japanese/American citizens, during the Second World War as well, along with all of their families and possible friends, jailed for being a different race and colour, so to speak.

So, if you think about it long enough, you'll begin to realize, that this particular area, is one of the most protected areas in the world, with over ten million people, spread out, north to south and east to west, all living out their daily lives, while going about their businesses and that doesn't count the other half of the state in the east, which hosts one of the largest military firing ranges in the world, and a Nuclear storage facility called Hanford, further on up the road near the Tri-cities..

And then there's the 405, which is a highway that does a soft, semi-circle, around the eastern side, of the Emerald City area altogether, for those that don't really fancy stopping in town or for the ones that are more comfortable or simply in a bigger hurry to get past all the hustle and bustle, that a big city brings.

It'll take you through a little town called Tukwila, which is famous for its "South Center Mall", one of the largest shopping malls in the area, of course, and then on into Renton, which is another little town, located, just north of the mall.

From there you'll drive into Renton and then Bellevue, where massive computer corporations like Micro-soft and Egghead software or even Amazon, have practically taken over with giant factories, huge parking lots, and towering high-rise apartment buildings, specifically built to trap, house and contain thousands of their employees, working on the latest computer technologies and so-called state-of-the-art programs, that they're always trying their best to make us believe, that we can no longer live without, which is typical consumerism at its finest, if you ask me?

Eventually the 405 joins with Interstate five again in the north and you can then carry on all the way to the Canadian border, passing through one of the country's largest and most colourful poppy fields that has ever been created this side of Afghanistan, located in one of the longest valleys ever known to man, that was fashioned by an ancient ice-sheet, which suddenly melted for mysterious reasons, between twelve and thirteen-thousand years ago, or at least that's what they say?

All in all, there's a lifetime of scenery in this area, that no-one could ever cover, no matter which road they took, or how long they travelled it.

From the mountains, to the forests, from the rivers, to the seas, and all of those little Islands, and back-roads, that lie scattered in-between. It is possibly the most beautiful and diverse state in the Union, barring Alaska of course.

Now the entire country is basically riddled with Interstates and their side-roads, just like these, happily making their way from the east to the west and north to south, criss-crossing through, to one place or another, as if they were part of an interlaced concrete web that was laid out by a gigantic construction spider, all those years ago.

They supply the needs of a great nation, spanning from sea to shining sea, as the song says, climbing the highest mountains and then dropping down into the lowest valleys, in every part of the country that you could imagine, and they are without a doubt, a network of exterior-skeletons that hold the very backbone of this country together.

So this is where this part of the story begins, out there on one of those highways, that's not too far from the Emerald City, the Pacific Ocean and Mount Rainier of course, but it aint about Dorothy, or her dog Toto, and it's a helluva long ways away from Kansas.

****

Intermission

It usually takes about seventeen hours to drive down to L.A., from the Emerald City, if you're in a hurry that is? It's a trip I've made many times, for one reason or another, but when I wasn't in a hurry, I'd always take the scenic route, and casually glide down the coastal highway on a large V-twin motor that was usually strapped to one of the best rides around, at least as far as I was concerned anyway, and it also gave me some of the finest views that anyone could have ever seen, or even started to imagine. It also left me prone to the weather, but I didn't mind.

It's known as highway one, or 101 in some spots, and it's also known as the Pacific Highway, depending on what part you're on at the time, and if you get the chance to do the same thing sometime, I would recommend the journey whole heartedly, because honestly, you'll be able to see some of the most beautiful sights in the world, or at least some of the most beautiful sites on the West Coast of America, that is.

Now L.A. will always be what it is and some folks really like that, while other folks don't. Personally, I've always wanted to get through L.A. just as quickly as I could, although there were times when I had to stick around for weeks on end doing one thing or another, and when I did that, I'd usually end up in Las

Vegas as well, which is just a quick three and half hour journey on up the road, on a good day that is.

There's a lovely place by the river, near a town that's called Blythe, California, just south of the border of Nevada that I always used to stop at.

It's about halfway from L.A. to Vegas. A great little place to cool off for awhile, and then swim in the river, relaxing, while trying to get rid of the dust and grime that you're bound to have accumulated along the way.

It used to have some of the best dark skies as well, back in the day, where you could see the Milky Way just as clear as you could see the moon, which was always huge and bright back then.

You could park up along the river, spread out your raggedy ole bedroll, and after counting the stars for awhile, you'd have a great night's sleep, and usually with no-one else around, and in the morning, the birds would wake you up at the crack of dawn, with their soulful songs. So yeah, it was pretty magical; I'd have to admit that, maybe even mystical at times?

There were other times when I'd head down to Tijuana or out through the Painted Desert on my way to Phoenix and then over to El-Paso before I'd start back up north again. Of course, there were times, when I'd go the northern route, straight on up to Chicago and maybe from there, head east to New York City, or even cross the border into Winnipeg,

Manitoba, before I'd finally made my way back to the Seattle area, passing through Calgary and Vancouver along the way, with a lot of other beautiful places in-between.

It was the life that I loved, travelling from here to there, and back again, just as often as I could, and meeting so many different people along the way, from so many different walks of life, at so many different times, that I could never really remember them all, but I always knew that I was a lucky man, even back then, in-fact, I knew it only too well.

I've spent a lot of time in Texas through the years as well, but then again, who hasn't? If you've ever travelled anywhere in the lower mainland, then you're bound to have gone through Texas, at least once or twice, after all, it is the biggest little country in the U.S of A. Except for Alaska of course, but that doesn't really count, because Alaska's not exactly attached to the rest of the States, and it's still regarded as a territory by some, especially those that live their lives out there.

Anyway, Texas has things going on, no matter where you are, or who you're with, day or night, it doesn't matter, because you can always find something to do in Texas. Places like Dallas or Fort Worth, Houston, Sweetwater, Brownsville and Texarkana. Then there's Austin, Orange, El-Paso, Amarillo, Port Arthur, Lubbock, Plano, and Justin, just to name a few more, and no matter where you go, you'll always find it full of polite and extremely well-mannered people, that will usually say, "Sir" or "Ma'am," and "Ya'll come back now, ya hear."

Of course, they'll all be wearing a side arm at the time, like a nine millimetre glock, or a colt-45 perhaps, or even a .357 magnum, tucked-up in their belts and they may even have a few rifles hanging in the back of their pick-up truck, ready for that proverbial Armageddon, social unrest, or another bloody civil war, but on the whole, you couldn't find a nicer bunch of people anywhere else in the States. I know, I've been to them all.

Now, that doesn't mean that there aren't some very nice people everywhere else in the US of A, because there are and that's truly a fact.

It's just that the southern states are usually the best states to be in. They seem to have that natural, southern hospitality that everyone hears about, and they aren't afraid of sharing it with anyone else, no matter who you are?

Everyone is courteous, agreeable and smiling a lot, and most of them are pretty laid back in their lives in general, after all, there really is no sense in hurrying about anything down south, because you already know that whatever needs to be done, will always need to be done, until it finally gets done, that is.

It's a good way to live, and a better way to be. It's a lot less stressful than life in Chicago or New York City for instance.

Now, apart from having some really distant relatives, that own one of the largest chains of retail stores in the world, and a few others that got their money from that black gold, or Texas tea, that was conveniently found oozing up out of their front yards, which were inherited lands originally stolen from the Indians, way back when, you'd probably think that I would have just stayed in Texas, for the rest of my days, but the truth of the matter is, I was adopted and I'm half Indian, so I was never really part of their world to begin with.

It may be the case though, that my particular relatives who seem to spend most of their time living on a houseboat just south of Dallas, when they aren't travelling the country in a high-end, forty-foot motor home, with an extremely fancy sports car parked-up underneath its belly, may actually think about me from time to time and they may even decide to leave me a little something in their wills, but that's highly unlikely. After all, I was never regarded as one their own in the first place, and if the truth were really known, I probably never will be, because to their way of thinking, just like most of the folks that live in Texas, if it aint Texas, then it aint shit, and that's about all there is to that.

Never mind, I certainly won't be holding my breath over that one, and I'll always love the State regardless, even if I aint really Texan, so to speak. I will also most sincerely, wish those people the very best that I can, no matter where they are or what they're doing with their lives. But if that houseboat ever sinks, or if that motor home ever crashes, then you can be pretty sure that I'll be wondering, if they ever thought about me, sometime and somewhere, along the way?

Probably not a snowballs chance in hell though and I'm pretty sure about that, but hey, I could be wrong.

Anyway, this next story, actually happened in Texas and I hope that you enjoy it, because there's definitely worse places to be in the world, and I guess that if I ever did inherit some sort of finances or property, from a rich and distant relative, or perhaps, they'd even throw me a bone once in awhile just for good measure, then I'd probably have to go back there for a visit, if only to see how much things have really changed, but then again, maybe not? Anyway, enjoy.

****

15
A strange kind of Wickedness

It was another long, drawn-out summer afternoon in West Texas, without a cloud in the sky and barely a breeze in the air. I'd been standing there alone, looking up and down that long, empty stretch of public highway, for what seemed to be hours at the time, waiting patiently for someone to come along and give me a ride.

It wasn't something that I was used to, and it certainly wasn't anything that I had planned for, because usually I'd be flying down the road under my own steam, riding hard so to speak, like a man on a mission, keeping it upright and in between the lines just as fast as the road ahead would take me. But this time things had turned out a little different. This time, things had gone from bad to worse in a New York minute and I wasn't anywhere near fucking New York. Who would've thought?

The back tire of my custom made chopper, that I had been riding for days and even weeks on end, had suddenly frayed, popped and splintered, quickly going flat, with a very loud bang, which of course effectively rendered my modern day horse of custom steel, bright, shiny chrome and totally tricked out paint, completely useless, leaving yours truly, high and dry at the same friggin time.

Typical luck I thought, as I stood there silently, stuck out in the middle of that Texas no-where, sweating profusely like some fat pig at a rinky-dink rodeo, utterly parched, chafed and dry, waiting patiently for someone to come along and help me out, someone that would have to come my way eventually.

Patience had never been high on my list of virtues though, and today wasn't going to be, any different. The truth of the matter is that I was a long ways away from where I needed to be and now I was starting to realize, that I probably should have left a whole lot earlier than what I actually did. Oh well, nothing ventured, nothing gained, they say?

I looked at the empty span of desert which stretched out for literally miles in all directions. Of all the places that I could have broken down, this one was just about the worst one that I could think of. There wasn't a single tree in sight. There wasn't a bridge, or a house, or even a barn close enough to walk to. All there was was that bloody desert, and there was literally too many miles of that.

Suddenly, I felt an uneasy feeling slowly creeping up from the pit of my stomach, as I stood there reeling from the heat of the day.

A strange kind of wickedness, had swept across the middle portion of my back and then up and down both of my sides, while at the same time, a cold, damp tingle, slowly rippled itself, all the way up and back down my spine, settling once again at a point, somewhere near the base of it.

There was also a deep knotted feeling, growing in the pit of my stomach as well, and then just as suddenly, for no real reason at all, I felt like throwing up, dry heaving for almost a minute or more, while I was standing there, waiting for someone to come along.

Afterwards, I needed a drink; and there was no doubt about that in my mind. Perhaps even a bite to eat as well, but there wasn't much hope of that either, I certainly hadn't planned on having a picnic out there and I always travel light, so any food that I may have needed at the time, was simply nonexistent.

Suddenly, there was a sense of insane desperation, that completely overwhelmed me for a few brief moments in time and it seemed to have a touch of déjà vu thrown in with it for good measure, or at least something that seemed to be a whole lot like it to me, because as I stood there, looking around, I started feeling like I must have been down this road before and yet I was pretty sure, that wasn't really possible, or was it?

"Where's a frigging ride, when you need it the most?" I said out loud, with a natural, nervous irritation, trying to convince myself that this feeling was just plain stupid, while casually wiping the sweat away that was dripping off the tip of my brow.

I watched slightly amused, as a flock of birds flew out of the clutter of bushes that were gathered together on the other side of the road from where I was standing.

I carried on watching, as those same birds quickly flew upwards and onwards, until they were completely out of my sight. Then, I turned around and tripped on a large rock that was laying there on the side of the road, twisting my ankle at the same time and wincing from the pain of it all.

No-one had answered my question of course; there was no one there to answer me. I was totally alone.

"Now that really was stupid," I thought to myself, as I stood there kicking out at one of the loose stones that was laying on the ground around me, looking back towards where I had just come from and then turning around again to look at where it was that I should be going to.

The ankle hurt, but it wasn't serious, it was just another twist to the day in the grande scheme of things. I knew that eventually someone would have to come along, they always did. I had never gotten myself into a jam that I couldn't get out of and this wasn't going to be the first one. It would take a little time maybe, but that's all, just a little time.

That heat of the summer sun was directly over my head now, beating down on me like a giant halide lamp without a hood, like you might find in the corner of a grow room, or in one of those sleazy saunas, that you read about in the girly magazines.

It was brutal, relentless and it was beginning to affect the way that I was breathing.

I was only able to manage short, shallow breaths before the actual heat of the air, started to irritate the inside of my lungs.

I swear it has to be at least ninety degrees out here, maybe even more, I thought to myself again, as I stood there dripping those precious little droplets onto the ground around me. Then I stared listlessly, as a big ole desert rabbit, jumped up and darted across the road in front of me, running into the field and then quickly slipping itself into a deep, dark, empty hole.

Now that's a pretty good idea, I thought again, as I looked around, but there was nowhere that I could go. There was nowhere for me to get any shade at all, I just had to stand there and wait, and then finally, I had to wait some more.

How long had it been now, an hour or maybe two? The sun still hadn't moved. It was as if that infernal globe was stuck in the same damn spot, constantly shining down on me like some giant torch, sitting high in the sky, getting hotter and hotter all of time.

I had taken my jacket off, just as soon as I stopped the bike, right after blowing out the back tire. Then I took my shirt off a little while later and then finally, I took off my under shirt and tied it around my head. My skin was already too hot; it was also turning red in the heat and probably starting to blister, but I didn't have any choice in the matter really, I just had to stand there and wait for some help to arrive.

It was a good job that I had brought some water with me though; I thought to myself, as I reached into my saddlebags. Uh oh, where had I put it? Ah there it is, I thought again, as I finally found it. It was only a little bottle, maybe half a pint at the most, but it should be enough to get me through the mess that I was in.

I took a few sips from the bottle before I realized that the water was about as warm as piss and probably even hotter than that, so I just swirled it around in my mouth and then I spat it back out towards a small lizard that I noticed was sunning itself in the desert sand, close to my feet. It didn't even move, as my spit almost hit it.

Never mind I thought, as I placed the cap back on the bottle, and then put the bottle back into deepest part of my saddle bags, right next to the hammerless .357 that I always carried with me, one way or another. After all, you never know when some fool will try to rob you or something even worse.

I usually carried it strapped to my upper left side, but I had removed it just as quick as I could when the tire blew out. It was simply too hot and too heavy, to be carrying it there, in this heat anyway.

I looked back down the highway, from where I had just come from, once again, but there was still nothing, not a single car or truck in sight.

I turned around and looked the other way, but it was just the same, mile after mile, of empty space, with nothing moving at all. Not even a bird or tumbleweed or even a damn coyote.

It was about then that I realized how much I really hated West Texas highways. They are without a doubt, the longest, loneliest roads in the world and as straight as an arrow for mile after every loving mile.

They're endless, I thought, eventually spanning across the entire nation, coast to coast, connecting with other roads that go from state to state and border to border.

They cross over everything that gets in their way and once in a while, they'll go under something, like a bridge, or a mountain or even a skyscraper or two.

There's at least one two-lane highway, a little further west, that actually goes through the center of a tree, somewhere in Arizona or California? Which is pretty cool when you think about it? I actually rode through it myself once, just for a jolly, and it was pretty amazing to say the least.

Texas roads were always a great ride though, once you got away from the cities and all those little towns. There's very little traffic on them and even less cops, especially if you were used to being stuck inside a city like New York, Boston, Los Angeles or Chicago or any other well built concrete jungle for that matter, and I knew them all, only too well.

There's not a city in the nation that I haven't been to at one time or another, from Fairbanks, Alaska up in the northwest, to Key Lagos, down south in Florida, and all points in between.

New York to L.A. was a pretty consistent trip for a couple of times a year and then there was Boston to Seattle and Vancouver to Toronto which sometimes stretched on into Halifax, Nova Scotia, or St. John's, Newfoundland, depending on what time of year it was, and what the weather was doing of course, along with who needed what, when, and where. Supply on demand, was the game back then.

Getting stuck in a blizzard on a scoot wasn't a lot of fun though, but it could be done, that's for sure, just not a preference of mine, more like a real pain in the back side. Not to mention the damn cold which I could always do without. Except for today maybe?

I'd been through all of that before though and the cities that went with it. As far as I was concerned, you could keep every last one of them; I much preferred the open roads of the country, along with less travelled highways, every time, except for in a blizzard of course. That was the only time that a city was better than the country side.

You could crank up the throttle and catch the wind, for hours in the country, if you really wanted to and most of the time that was exactly what I wanted to do. I loved to ride; in-fact I lived to ride and when you think about it, it's the next best thing to flying. It's quiet and peaceful, with only the sound of the wind rushing by your ears and the sun's rays on your back, and that awesome purr, of the engine running between 4 and 6000 rpm's, or maybe more, when you push it.

It really is something special, scooting down the road like that, right up until you have to stop, that is. That's when you want a place to pull into, that actually has some air-conditioning or perhaps a heater in the wintertime, along with some great food, good people and lots of pleasant conversation.

A place with comfortable furnishings and of course plenty of beers to wash away the dust and grime that you've managed to accumulate at the back of your throat, simply from being out there for hours on end to begin with.

A great looking barkeep and a waitress with a big smile, long legs and a healthy personality, never hurts either and if she has a twin sister or even a friend that looks pretty much the same, then you might just find yourself thinking about staying for a little while. You know what I'm saying. Life on the road can be pretty damn sweet at the best of times, even for a biker.

Anyway, there I was on my way to El Paso to put my super-charged iron horse into a national bike show. I was hoping to take that "Twenty Thousand Dollar" first prize that was up for grabs. It would help me to re-coup some of the money that I had spent on building the damn thing to begin with and of course, I could always use the cash for other things as well, because let's face it, I was never a rich man by any means and money had always been pretty hard to come by, let alone keep, and like anyone else in this world that wasn't born with a silver spoon in their mouth, I could always find a good use for mine, always. Who couldn't really? I just had to get there in time and win that bloody contest.

Now, Sonny Barnett, who is not to be confused with any of the other Sonny's that we all know and love, owned one of the largest Harley Davidson motorcycle shops in the world. It was located just outside of old El Paso and he always put on a bike show at least once a year and sometimes even twice, if the mood took him?

This year, I was bound and determined to take that prize money if I could only get there in time, but somehow, at this particular moment, it didn't look as if I'd make it there at all.

"Where in the hell is all the traffic, especially when you really need them the most?" I thought again. "You'd think that at least one car, truck or even another motorcycle would have caught up with me by now? I can't be the only one heading towards the border. What about all those people that live around here? Don't they go anywhere?

It was about then that I looked down at my watch, what time is it? I quickly thought, as I noticed that it had stopped working.

"Oh yeah, that's just great" I said out loud, watching the second hand sitting there doing absolutely nothing? I shook it a few times and then I shook it some more. It still didn't move and it looked like it wasn't ever going to move again.

I was growing more and more impatient by then and my temper was starting to flare, right along with my temperature that was already way too high.

"Ah to hell with this," I said out loud, as I took the watch off of my wrist and then shook it some more.

"And yeah, that's just what I need right now," I yelled out again, instinctively throwing the watch upwards and outwards, just as far as I could throw it, far into the empty desert span that was spread out in front of me.

"Now I don't know what time it is," I said, still talking to myself louder than usual. I don't know what time it is and I'm stuck in the middle of a desert, in the middle of the day, with no one else around. Damn it all, I thought, this really is getting on my fucking tits and then I realized just what I had done?

I was starting to lose the plot. My brain was beginning to fry and I was acting like a captain going down with his ship, only it was into a fiery pit, instead of the deep blue ocean.

That watch had been a gift from a good friend of mine, a brother from another mother type of friend. I couldn't just throw it away like that. It didn't matter whether it worked or not, I still needed to keep it, for the sake of our friendship, if nothing else. So, I quickly walked towards the direction of where I felt the watch should be laying and then I started looking around for it. It had to be there somewhere? It couldn't have just disappeared like that, now could it?

I kept searching, in ever expanding circles, growing frantic by the minute. I was becoming obsessed, with finding it. It had quite suddenly become an all or nothing situation for me, a manic type of compulsion that was completely consuming my every thought and desire.

I had to have that watch back again, right now, no matter what it took and yet I didn't really know why? It wasn't like it was an expensive watch to begin with and I knew that I could always buy another one, just like it, practically anywhere, at any time. Anytime, except for right now that is, and although it really was a gift from a good friend of mine, he'd be none the wiser, if I had to buy another one to replace it.

No-one would know the difference anyway, especially my friend and I was pretty sure that he wouldn't really mind anyway, even if he did know. Hell, he'd probably just laugh about it, and then tell me that it was just another cheap, crappy watch, to begin with, hardly worth the bother. But somehow, for some unknown and truly insane reason, it had become more than just a principal now, it had suddenly become an all out obsession, a belief in the fact that I needed to find that watch, no matter what it took, even if I had had to search for it, for the rest of my life, which in this heat, probably wouldn't be too long anyway. I had to find it and that was all there was to that. I had to get it back and I was determined that I would, eventually.

Then, as luck would have it, as I was senselessly searching for it, getting further and further, out into the field, I turned my head around just in time to see a car that had slowed down by my bike, alongside of the road that it was sitting on.

The only car, that I had seen for literally hours now, the only car, that was on the road in either direction, the only car, that could have actually stopped and helped me out of the situation that I was in and I had turned my head around just in the nick of time to watch it, simply speed up and drive away.

"No, no, no," I said, running towards the highway just as fast as I could go, but it was completely pointless by then, the car was already gone. It was clean out of sight by the time I got back to my bike.

"Damn it", I said out loud again and again, panting and puffing, almost entirely out of breath, how stupid can a man get? That flipping watch has got to be some sort of a jinx."

Then, I just happened to glance down at the side of the road close to where I was standing at the time and I saw something laying there, something that was shining right back up at me, almost smiling at me, like that proverbial grin on the Cheshire cat that was in the movie of Alice in Wonderland.

Naturally, I walked straight on over to it and picked it up. Would you believe it, it was my watch.

Whoa, that's way too frickin weird; I thought as I quickly bent over to get it. I could have sworn that I had chucked this thing far out into the desert. So how in the hell did it get back here?

I quickly put it inside one of my jeans pockets, planning to never lose it again. Then I looked up at the sun one more time. It still hadn't moved, although it seemed like it had grown to almost double its size.

In-fact I was sure that it was larger than I had ever seen it before, but I didn't know if that was really the case, or not, because my head was spinning around and I was feeling sick to my stomach again, I needed to sit down for a while; because I was seriously beginning to overheat.

If only the sun would hurry up and make its way across the sky or perhaps a few clouds could form and the wind could pick up a little, then maybe I could sit down in the shade of my motorcycle for a while and cool off. But the sun wasn't moving. It just stayed there, hovering high overhead and the more I looked at it, the dizzier I felt. I finally sat down on the side of the road for a quick rest.

My head was spinning pretty fast by then and even with my shades on, the light was becoming completely unbearable. It was hurting more than just my eyes, so I layed back for a few minutes, closing them tight, pulling the t-shirt down over them and enjoyed my rest, especially from my recent, insanely mad dash around that opened field. I was exhausted from the heat as it was, so I wasn't really sure how long I stayed like that. It could have been a minute or two, or maybe even five or ten, but it wasn't too long until I suddenly opened up my eyes again and was scrambling to get to my feet as I did.

Something had stung me and then another one and another one. Ahhh I screamed, feeling the pain and the burning sensations that were beginning to work their way all over my body as I jumped to my feet again, stomping on the earth and gravel, circling around myself again and again, stamping more and more and then jumping up and down on an already bruised ankle.

I figured that I must have looked like a half-crazed Indian at the time, doing a bloody rain dance or something even stranger, but then I finally realized what was going on. The road was crawling with red ants and a few of them had decided to check out my legs, ass and back, looking for their breakfast, lunch or dinner.

I practically ripped my trousers off in one sheer swoop, standing there all but buck-naked, except for the riders on my feet, my socks of course, and the T-shirt around my head, carefully inspecting them all for anymore of those pesky little assassins that were out to do me in.

"Great! I yelled out loud, just frickin great, what else could possibly go wrong now? Damn it all, this is definitely not what I needed right now, especially when I'm stuck out in the middle of nowhere."

I quickly put my trousers back on as soon as the inspection was over, but I knew that I only had about twenty minutes left to get to a hospital and get myself a massive shot of adrenaline and anti-histamine, along with whatever anti-bug bite serum I could find, if there even was such a thing, before I finally keeled over.

You see, I was highly allergic to bug bites, bees, wasps, spiders, and especially ants. I had been that way all of my life, ever since I was kid, so I knew that I was pretty screwed up now, for sure.

What I needed was some pure antihistamines, along with a shot of adrenaline and a whole lot of drinking water as well, but of course, I didn't have anything like that with me at the time.

Now, you'd think that I would have, knowing what would happen if I ever got stung, but to be honest, it was probably the last thing on my mind when I left the hotel that morning. It was just too nice of a day and all I was thinking about was getting to the bike show. I never dreamt that I'd be stuck out on the highway for any reason, let alone a flat tire.

Anyway, that's what I needed sure enough. It was that or maybe some kind of anti-venom injection, straight into my veins, but that wasn't about to happen anywhere near to where I was at the time, so I looked back down the road again. Still not a car in sight and now, it seemed that time for me anyway, was definitely running out.

What in the hell am I going to do now, I thought?

I only had one choice left really. I had to jump back on my bike and hobble it down the road, flat tire or not. I had to try. So, I stood there thinking about it, for a minute or two.

The wheel on the rear of my motorcycle had cost me well over three thousand dollars to put together at the time. It was specifically made as wide as I could possibly get it and the rim was made out of pure cast, cut and polished, solid aluminium. Three-thousand-dollars, was a lot of money to me at the time, but it was either that, or else take a chance on losing the rest of my life completely, by doing nothing at all.

Suddenly, three-thousand-dollars seemed pretty damn cheap, especially considering the alternative. So I jumped up on the bike, kicked the stand and pushed the button. Nothing happened. What in the hell? I thought to myself quickly, what's going on now? I tried the starter button again. Still nothing happened. Everything was dead, not even the tail light was working.

"Oh man, I said, it just doesn't get any better than this. Now I've got a dead battery, stuck out in the middle of a desert, in the middle of the day and it just happens to be the middle of the bloody week as well. Who would have thought?"

I was fuming. I could feel my heart picking up its beat, racing towards that final pump, the very last one that I'll ever have in this life, if I didn't get help fast.

My heart usually runs steady at about sixty-seven beats a minute or so, but it was probably up to a hundred and ten by now and it wasn't going to slow down any time soon.

There had been a few other times, when I had come close to dying from a bug bite. One in particular, was when I was bitten by a spider, on my lower leg, in the middle of the night.

When I woke up, apart from the searing pain and the black-hole that it created, I also watched, as a thin red line, travelled up my leg, past my groin area, on to my lower stomach and from there, it went all the way up my chest towards my heart.

Fortunately, I managed to get to a hospital just in time, and I was immediately put on an I.V. drip and fed other medication, for literally days afterwards, but there was no chance of that happening now, even if someone had stopped in time to help me out.

So, you have to know, that I really figured that I was dying out there and there was no doubt about it in my mind. A bad situation had just gone to the worst situation that I could have possibly got myself into no matter what, and all in matter of minutes really and there was simply nothing that I could do about it.

Most people would have thought about pulling their pistol out of the saddle bags and putting a bullet in their own head at that point in time, which I was seriously contemplating, because to honest, dying from anaphylactic shock, or any kind of fast acting, blood poisoning in the middle of a desert, in the middle of a day or not, certainly isn't the best or even the easiest way to go out in this life.

So, I thought about it all right, I thought about it real hard, but I wasn't going to be beaten yet. I wasn't going to be the victim here, if I could help it, that is? I wasn't going to be some sort of statistic, that someone else finds out about days or even weeks later, that's for sure.

"The devil could go straight back down to hell," I yelled out as loud as I could.

You see, when the truth is known, I've always been a stubborn son of bitch, when I wanted to be and apart from that, I figured that no matter what, it just wasn't my time to die yet, and that was about as plain and as simple, as it gets.

Then all of sudden, completely out of the blue, standing in the middle of nowhere, half-way to nothing and coming from out of nowhere to begin with, I suddenly heard a voice.

"Is that a fact now?" The old man said, standing there, right next to me and my bike. Leaning on an old black, walking stick that had a white stone skull carefully carved into the top of it.

"What makes you think that anything like that could ever be your choice to begin with?"

"What the hell," I said, startled all to shit, "Who are you and where on God's green earth, did you come from?" I looked up and down the road real quick for the old man's car, but I couldn't see it anywhere.

"Exactly, he said again, Now answer my question."

"What? What question are you on about?" I said, still searching for the old man's car, but it just wasn't there, in fact, there was nothing to be seen at all, not even an old donkey, or a tired ass mule, like they had in the movies that those old prospectors used to ride away on, back in the day.

"There aint no car here Gypsy, the old man said, so just answer my question or it'll be the last one that I ask."

"Ok, ok, I said, what question was that? I don't remember you asking me any questions to begin with?"

"I said the old man spoke quite firmly again, what makes you think, that it could be your choice, to begin with?"

"I still don't get it I said, How could you even begin to know what I was thinking about, and how in the hell do you know my name?"

"Just answer the bloody question, already." The old man said, rather sternly, looking at me, with a slight smile on his face, but there was a distinct chill in his eyes, and they were cold, dark, and piercing, as well as the weirdest looking blue that anyone has ever seen.

You certainly didn't trust him, no matter who he was, or where it was, that he actually came from.

"All right, all right, I said, it's my life, and I'll end it, when I feel like it, or when it's my slated time? But that won't be for the devil to decide, or anyone else, for that matter. It'll be my decision, and mine alone."

"All right then, the old man said, what makes you think that it's not your slated time right now then?"

"I'm too young to die," I said again, with a smile on my face and a fire burning inside my own piercing hazel/green eyes.

"Younger people than you have died before, the old man said; you know it happens all the time."

"Well then, I guess I'm just too tough," I said again, clenching my fists, preparing myself for whatever was about to come my way, but nothing did. The old man just stood there with an even bigger grin on his face, as though he was really enjoying the moment.

"Tougher men than you have died, the old man said, smiling back at me, and you know that, as well as I do. Hell, you've even been with some of them at the time."

"Okay, okay, I quickly said, I'm just too damn stubborn to die, and I'll never give up, I never have, and I never will."

"Yeah, you're right about that, but you're not too clever now, are you my friend, especially by putting yourself out in the middle of the desert like this to begin with.

Shame on you, and shame on you again, for tempting an old man like me," he said, laughing right out loud.

I was beginning to get pretty irritated with this old fool and his stupid assed sense of humour by then, so I finally said,

"Look, just piss off old man, I don't know who you think you are, but I'm sure that I don't owe you anything, and I don't need you hanging around here, messing with my head like this. I certainly don't want you here, that's for sure, and I'm pretty sure, that I'm not going anywhere with you either, if that's what you have in mind, so go on now, piss off and leave me alone."

"Actually, I think you really do need me Gypsy, the old man said, as he reached out to touch my chest. Your heart is racing faster than you can count, just like a raging bull, and if you don't slow it down soon, it'll pop just like that tire of yours did, back down there on the highway, and then I'm afraid, you'll be mine forever, with no hope in hell, if you get my pun," he said again, laughing almost hysterically.

"Do you have a shot of something in your pocket old man? Because that's just what I need to slow this ole ticker down, that and some really good frickin luck for a change," I said, barely catching my breath.

My heart was pounding so hard now, that the sweat was rolling off the top of my forehead, down into my eyes, and then continuing down to the tip of my nose, before it dripped off, onto the ground.

"Well I'd like to help you out if I could, I really would, the old man said, but as you can see, I'm not actually here, not in the physical sense anyway, if you know what I mean? However, if you walk on out to that cactus, way over yonder, you could jab one of its quills into your chest and that just might help you out for a little while.

In-fact, it would probably help you out quite a bit, if you were to think about. You never know, it might be, just what the doctor ordered."

"Yeah right," I said to him again, like I'm really going to fall for that one, yeah?"

I looked around and the old man was gone. Vanished into thin air and now I figured that I really was losing it. I was definitely dying for sure and I had just been talking to some fictitious entity, in the middle of the desert, arguing with him about some cactus plant that I could barely see, not to mention the fact that it was way off in the distance, and it would take a lot of time and effort, to get to.

So yeah, I felt that it wouldn't be too long now for sure, because even if a ride did come by right now, at this very moment, it wouldn't get me to the hospital on time.

I may as well have put that bullet into the side of my head, just as I figured that I would have to do, all the way along.

I looked at my chopper that was still sitting there, as I got off of it again. It had cost me over three year's salary to finally put it all together. It was beautiful, it was long, low and mean looking, with that special kind of paint, chrome and a back tire that was never meant to fail, but it certainly wasn't worth any of the effort or the blood, sweat and tears that I had lost over it. In-fact, it may as well have been just another piece of twisted steel, sitting there at the side of the road, because that's what it was starting to look like now, to me anyway.

It was probably just the heat of the day I thought, that and the bug bites, but I looked up at the sun again, and saw that it still hadn't moved.

What in the hell? Is it ever going to get across that damn sky? Shit, I thought again, as I suddenly felt a very painful jolt, making its way into the center of my chest.

My heart was definitely racing now, boom, boom, boom, boom, boom, boom.

Maybe this cactus thing, is a good idea, I thought again, I certainly didn't have anything to lose, because if I stood there much longer, I'd die anyway.

"To hell with it," I said out loud, as I headed back out into the desert field. It never occurred to me that if I actually dropped dead out there, they might never find my body. Still what choice did I have?

It took me at least ten minutes to get to that plant or so it seemed at the time. It was a lot further away than I originally thought. My legs had swelled up and my lips were chapped and dry, even cracking by the time I got there.

A trickle of blood was oozing out of my left nostril and my head was pounding like a jack hammer. I was so dizzy, that when I finally got to that plant, I just fell to my knees at the foot of it.

Ahhh, another sharp pain across my chest and then upwards into my head. Ahhh, there it was again, this time it knocked me all the way to the ground. This is it, I quickly thought, as I struggled to keep myself from passing out. I'll be seeing that old man again real soon, I guess? Then I swore that I heard him laughing at me again.

"I thought you told me that you weren't a quitter, the old man said, smiling down at me. I thought you said, that it wasn't your time to go, that you were too damn young to die and way too tough. I guess you must have been talking about somebody else then because that person certainly doesn't look like you now, does he?"

"You again," I said, coughing my lungs out after the words that I practically spat out, you can't wait until I finally kick it, can you old man? What's your problem? I told you that I aint ready to die yet and I aint, so you can go fly yourself a kite upside Devil, because you're just wasting your time up here with me, that's for sure."

"I don't know about that," the old man said, just look at all those buzzards circling around up there; they always know where to get a good meal, don't they?"

"Yeah, well it aint going to be me old man, not today anyway, I said, pulling myself over to the cactus, I'll stick two or three of these things inside of me, if it'll help.

I reached up and broke off a hand full of quills.

"You better hurry now, the old man said, time marches on and it sure aint waiting for no-one now, let alone you."

I took the quills and stabbed myself in the chest with them, they were long and thin but they were full of cactus juice and they hurt like hell when I did it. It was even worse than the bloody bug bites to begin with, and I was sure, that I heard that old man, screeching out hysterically when I did it again and again.

I had to be sure that I had put enough of that shit into my system didn't I? And then I heard the old man say,

"I'll see you later my boy, you have yourself a real good rest now you hear because you're definitely going to need it."

I finally dropped back down to the ground, while my head spun around several more times and then I just simply passed out.

When I woke up, I didn't know how long I had actually laid there, but the buzzards had come swooping down on me in my dreams; they pecked around for a bit, trying to get at my eyeballs and all the other shit that was caked up inside of my nostrils, but then they finally left me alone. I wasn't going to be a meal for them today they thought, perhaps they'd come back tomorrow or maybe they'd leave me to cook in that desert sun for another day or two first.

When I finally opened up my eyes again, the first thing I saw was that damned old fire ball in the sky. It still hadn't moved, not anywhere, not at all and it was just as big and just as hot, and just as bloody powerful, as it had been all day long.

"This is way too fucking much," I thought, looking up at it again, it was still directly over my head. Still beating down on me like an oversized heat lamp.

I struggled to get to my feet feeling pretty weak and feeble at first. I certainly wasn't used to feeling that way, that's for sure. Ordinarily I was as strong as an ox. Years of riding, had put a lot of muscle, in all the right places and it had also kept the fat off. Besides that, I was still a young man at the time.

I was also, pretty dizzy still but I noticed that my head wasn't pounding nearly as hard now as it had been, and in fact, it was barely pounding at all.

Damn, I thought again, that old man was right on the money, those cactus quills had done some sort of magic on me. I felt all over my legs, they were still pretty puffy and sore, especially around the bite marks, but the swelling was going down and they didn't sting half as bad as they had before. That's good I thought, because it was time to get back to my bike. So, I got up on my feet, steadied myself and took a good, long, look around. I didn't like what I saw.

"Damn it all to hell again" I said, which way is it? I can't even see the road from here, damn it, damn it and damn it some more." Then I heard the old man's laughter again, as I quickly turned around to face him.

"You'll still be mine by the time this day is over Gypsy, the old man said with a chuckle, unless you're smarter than you look right now. I guess those Army days didn't teach you much of anything, did they? The old man just kept on talking without waiting for an answer. Special Forces wasn't it? Airborne Rangers, Forward Recon and all of that hard assed shit that you went through back in the day, yeah, you can shoot a gun for fun my boy and you're even better when people are shooting back at you, but you really can't tell which way is up most of the time, especially these days, now can you?"

"Go back down to hell old man, I said; don't you know that they're called weapons in the Army? Guns are for fun, or for girls and I aint never been one of those, talk about me not knowing anything?"

"Now, now, be nice boy, because what I really know is that you can't see the road from here, and I also know that you only have four ways that you could go and three of them will lead you straight back to me no matter what.

The fourth one, will get you back to the road and back to your pretty little motorcycle eventually but I'll bet, that you don't take that one, so what do you think about those odds Gypsy? Do they scare you?" The old man said, laughing right out loud.

"I'd say those odds as you just called em, are in my favour, you old devil, smiling as I said it, don't you know that Army brats have always been rated as the underdog."

"Yeah, that's right, poor little ole you, the old man said, let me see if I have a hanky to wipe away those tears you're about to cry, hmm, here's one right now just blowing in the wind."

I turned around just in time to see a small piece of blue cloth blow right on by me. I thought for a moment about the situation that I was in and how I might be able to turn this around to my advantage, if I could only use my head.

"I'll tell you what old man, I said with a smile, If I can't walk out of here and find my bike, I'll be happy to go with you to where ever it is that you want me to go, without a fuss or even an argument, but if I can walk out of here and I do find my bike, then I want you to put it back together for me, back into its original shape, so that I can get on it and get the hell out of this God forsaken desert, away from that screwed up sun, that seems like its stuck out there in the middle of the sky, and even further away from you old man. How does that sound to you?"

"Are you trying to make a deal with me boy? Don't you know that I could just wait for you to completely fry yourself out here? Don't you know that I could just walk away in a heartbeat and simply wait my time, the old man said; because sooner or later you'll be with me anyway? What does it matter to me when or where that is, I've got all the time in the world and then some."

"What's the matter old man, I said, aren't those odds good enough for you? We're talking a Seventy-five percent chance, that you'll win anyway, what do you say old man, take the bet and prove to me who it is that you think you are, otherwise I'll just say that you're full of shit; you've got no power over me, and never will have. You're just a figment of my imagination and that's all there is to that."

The old man just stood there for a few moments, looking at me and smiling as he always seemed to do. You could see that he was thinking about it though and I knew that whatever he had on his mind wouldn't be too good for me anyway, but then the old man said.

"You put that hanky over your eyes Gypsy boy and I'll take that bet," just as the piece of blue cloth, flew around again and back into my face, "put it over your eyes and spin yourself around ten times. It'll be a bet then, fair and square."

"Yeah right, I said, fair bet my ass. If you want to throw in the hanky to blindfold me, then, I want you to throw in some cash as well, in-fact I want you to fill my saddle bags with it and I want nothing less than One hundred dollar bills, and just as many as those bags will carry."

The old man laughed out loud, cackling again, as he had before.

"You know that you can't win in this situation, no one ever beats the Devil, he said, but all right then, if you really do win. One Hundred dollar bills it is." He spat in his hand and held it out for me to shake.

Of course that didn't happen, it was gone when I reached for it and so was the old man, but a bet was a bet regardless, and I was bound and determined to win this one, hands down.

His voice was still there though, lingering in mid-air. It said, look down Gypsy, your money is sitting there waiting for you, just dig it up.

What? I thought as I looked down at the ground around me and sure enough, I caught sight of some thin plastic material, stuck in the desert sand, so I tried pulling on it and then I started scooping up the sand around it.

It was a plastic bag full of one hundred dollar bills. Wow, I thought, what the fuck? Had somebody stashed this money out here all along, or was this old man for real?

I didn't know for sure, but I had a lot of cash now and all I needed to do was get the hell out of there, before someone saw me with it.

I didn't know if I was going insane or not, but I figured that I still had a bet to win regardless. So I fed the plastic through my belt and tied it up tight. I looked around for a moment, noting where the cactus was, and then I put the cloth over my eyes and tied it tight as well. I spun myself around ten times, just like the old man had asked and then I fell to the ground again.

When I rose up I started walking with my arms stretched out wide, after a few steps I turned and walked a few more and then I turned again. Finally after another turn I ran into the cactus once more. I felt around it and found just what I was looking for, the moist bleeding scar of where I had pulled the quills out of its side earlier on.

Then, I turned myself around again and quickly strolled straight on out of there, just as fast as my feet could carry me.

It took about fifteen minutes to get to the gravel on the side of the road I reckon. What a wonderful sound that was.

The old man knew he had lost his bet, and I reckon that he wasn't smiling anymore as he watched me reach the edge of the road. He could have told me to keep the cloth on right up until I found my motorcycle, but for some strange reason he didn't, thank God.

As soon as I heard the gravel, I took it off. I knew that I was out of the field by then and onto the road. The old man was there right in front me, he started laughing again. He said that he was only playing with me this time around; preparing me for the inevitable that was yet to come, I suppose? But I really hoped there wouldn't be another time, especially anytime soon.

"Next time I'll have you *Gypsy* and trust me, there will always be a next time for sure" he said, with a bit of a throaty growl, as he quickly disappeared again.

"Next Time" echoed through the air like before, lingering for the rest of those few moments as I looked up the road towards where my bike was sitting and then I started laughing. I practically ran the rest of the way up to it and then I jumped on it and started it up in a heartbeat. The back tire was hard again and the motor was running smooth as ever.

There was a low-loader tractor/trailer, sitting there as well, just ahead of where my bike was parked-up; it was the first vehicle that I had seen in sometime.

The driver just happened to be a really nice looking woman, who quickly asked me if I needed a ride and if I wanted to load my bike on the back of her trailer, which I gladly accepted, even though I didn't really need it now, but I was thinking just how fortuitist this all was, and within a half an hour or so, the bike was loaded up and tied down securely, and then we were off down the road with the air-conditioning turned on full. Oh the joys of a cage at times.

Before we left, I looked back out across the desert from where I had just been. I could barely see the cactus tree that was still shining in the distance; it was the only thing that looked like a piece of twisted steel in that hot desert sun now.

I looked up again, flipped my middle finger at the ball of fire in the sky, put my shirt and jacket back on and then I quickly jumped into the passenger seat of that red, dog nosed, Kenilworth, that she was driving.

A storm was approaching; I could smell it in the air and I could feel it on my breath. I still had a long ways to go but at least the air that I was breathing now, was quickly cooling off, and wouldn't you know it, the bloody traffic had finally picked up again, who would've thought?

Now, never being too shy about the fairer sex, I introduced myself as quickly as I could to the driver and eventually, I bought her a cup of coffee and some lunch when we finally got to a truck stop, further on up the road. Sharing her table and some light conversation, as you do, I eventually told her my entire story about being stuck out in the middle of that desert, as we casually sat there eating.

I probably shouldn't have done that, but she didn't seem to mind, in fact, as luck would have it, she was on her way to El Paso as well, with a little time on her hands and of course, I had lots of that myself with money to burn and nowhere in particular to be.

****

16
Outside El Paso

There's a lot of things about El Paso that people really loved back in the day, perhaps even more than the weather, which is usually always hot, clear, and dry, and if you ride a motorcycle, that's exactly what you want, clear blue skies, long, hot, lazy roads and the ability to catch the wind for literally hours at a time. But the best thing about El Paso is the simple fact that it's one of the gateways to Mexico. Juarez to be specific, just across the street really, which for me and so many others that I had known along the way, was the one thing that they had all cherished the most, simply because you could buy things south of the border, a whole lot cheaper than you could buy them anywhere else, unless of course, you jumped on a plane and went to the Far East, like Thailand or Singapore.

What was even better than that though, was the fact that you could always get things across the border, that might be considered illegal, or even outlawed in the U.S at the time, but not necessarily illegal in Juarez or anywhere else in Mexico for that matter and it was always easy enough, just to pop across the border for a day or two, get what you wanted and then pop on back again, just as quickly as you liked and if you knew what you wanted to begin with and where to get it, it didn't take much time at all, but it's definitely not that simple now and I suppose that if the Republicans actually get their way, it'll be practically impossible.

These days, it's just a bloody hassle right from the get go, no matter which border it actually is and you can guarantee, that it'll take you hours to get through customs whether you're coming or going and believe you me when I say that the boys in Texas, definitely don't want you bringing things back with you anymore.

No, no, that's just un-American, there's no patriotism in that after all and way down here in El Paso, Texas, you can bet that they are definitely into their patriotism, big time. They have a saying down here that basically goes like this, "If it aint Texas, then it aint shit, and if it aint shit, then it aint worth nothing, nothing at all."

You can ask any of the good ole boys that live around here, and they'll all tell you the same. Texans are a pretty proud lot when it comes to that, after all Texas is the biggest little country in the whole of the US of A, and that's just the way they think about it. To them, it's a country not a state.

If you even look like you might have something that you shouldn't have, you're going get hassled one way or another, and us bikers always look that way, at least to them that is. The border patrol, the customs agents, the TSA, the local yokels and of course, the good ole boys that run everything down here anyway.

The list just goes on and on and everybody wants their piece of the pie so to speak, they always have.

It's a shame really, because it used to be a pretty good way of making some extra cash for those that would actually take the time and the risk, but nowadays that risk is pretty damn high and most people can't be bothered with it anymore.

Besides that, it's pretty much run by the Mexican Mafia, and some of their lackeys on both sides of the law and on both sides of the border, and they'll be the first to feed an outsider up to the law, especially a biker every now and then, just for good measure. But, never mind, times change, people change, and the law, everyone knows that the "Law" is always changing.

Motorcycle clubs get their money from variety of different revenues, as we all know. Most of their members are simply hard working, middle class types, that are more than happy to pay their dues once or twice a month for the chance to be part of something bigger than what they are alone, but the club is actually a business run by its members, from a President at the top, right down to its soldiers, wannabees, and hanger-ons at the bottom.

At least that's the way it used to be, but nowadays, clubs have a couple of dozen bloody board members and trustees as well, along with other officers of the so-called corporation. OG's (old gangsters), bosses and associates and of course way too many investors that probably don't even ride a motorcycle to begin with, let alone put on a leather jacket and yet they still call the shots, whether you know it or not, and they want their dues. Money talks, bullshit walks, and it's always been about as simple as that.

Clubs grow into Corporations, and Corporations simply absorb other Corporations. It's the way of the jungle but in this case, it's a concrete jungle that we're talking about here and it's slowly dying a hideous death.

Combine all of that with the new laws that are being passed every other week, along with the cost of doing business in the first place like taxes, license fees and all that insurance money and it makes you wonder why anyone would want to be a biker to begin with?

Still, if they're smart enough, they stay ahead of the law, and invest what little they have into legal venues like dance and fitness clubs, or bars, restaurants and road houses, security companies, strip joints and of course anything that deals with motorcycles and their parts, amongst many other things.

Any business that makes money is an opportunity for a motorcycle club, whether they actually own a piece of it or not, doesn't matter in the grande scheme of things.

Having the largest motorcycle shop in the world aint a bad idea neither, but bike clubs are bigger than that, they always were and they're always hungry for more.

Now, a lot of clubs don't care about the law and they go about their business trying to break it, every chance they get. To them, it's just a game really; after all, laws change all the time. What was legal yesterday won't be legal tomorrow, and most bikers know that, so they get in and take what they can, while they can, before the law finally catches up to them.

When that happens a few bikers get arrested and the club spends a little money on lawyer's fees, bail bonds and care packages etc, without even skipping a beat in the real world.

Some of its members may even do a little prison time for whatever, whenever and then when they finally get out, they usually have one hell of story to tell, an extra tag on their jacket and an even a better party to go to, right before they start the same ole game all over again.

Of course, some of its members never do get out, for whatever reasons, but they all know the stakes and they're all used to working the odds and some of them will even get rich doing it along the way or they'll just simply die trying.

You might just say that that's the reason they're called "Outlaws" to begin with, even though most of clubs are usually owned, operated and registered, as legal businesses in every state, province, and country around the world that you can find them in.

They pay their taxes, workman's comp, business insurance, and any other dues, in the same way as anyone else that's in business does, and yet they're labelled as "Outlaw" bike clubs, and their members are known as "outlaw bikers."

Unless you're down under, then they're called Bikies, for whatever reasons? Still 1%ers, are one-percenters, whether they're truly outlaws or not.

What people don't really know is just how many bike clubs there are in today's society, or just how many members each club has. Another thing that people don't know, is who those members really are, because they're not all gypsies, tramps and thieves, as the law, the news or the government, tries to make you believe and they don't all wear rockers on their backs, or even a leather jacket for that matter.

Some of those bikers are actually doctors, lawyers, and judges believe it or not and there are too many cops and ex-cops that are active patch-holding members of every so-called, outlaw motorcycle association out there.

Firemen, paramedics, soldiers and the odd banker or two, are high on the list as well and you probably know some of the millionaires or even billionaires that ride with a patch on their back, as well as politicians, actors and musicians, that call themselves bikers.

All of those people that are well known to be full-time patch-holders in the world of entertainment, high finance and government, are at the very least, part-time members of many of the world's most renowned motorcycle clubs, that everyone knows about today.

Almost anyone that's ever had an interest in motorcycles, can name the most famous bikers in the world and everyone knows the name of the club that runs in their own neighbourhoods, but for every club that gets a mention, there are literally thousands that most people will never know about and every one of those, usually has at least fifty to a hundred members, if not more. After all, strength is in the numbers. So the bigger you are, the badder you are and the hungrier you'll get.

These numbers are pretty staggering when you think about it, with well over three and half million, one percent bikers, in the United States alone, not to mention Canada, Mexico and the rest of the world.

Add all of that with the simple joy rider clubs, solo riders, backwoods, cross country, and serious road racers and you will double or even triple that amount.

These people live and breathe motorcycles every single day of their lives and they have friends and family that do the same thing. Think about that for a moment. Think about all of that revenue; think about all of that insurance money that keeps going up and up. Hell, just think about all of those motorcycles and the cost of buying a new one in today's economy.

Just one percent of the world's population, equals out to over Eight hundred million bikers worldwide, which is not quite as big as China's army, which is said to be over a billion people strong, but it is pretty big none the less and it's growing all the time. Who knows, maybe China's army is full of bikers as well?

Imagine if they all got together to change the world into a better place. Imagine if every club member, joined forces with every other club member out there and then they all became members of one large, single, super club?

Think about all the good things that they could do for the world around them; think about what they could accomplish? What they could actually own and control?

A complete, united society of motorcycle enthusiasts, at least Eight hundred million strong, simply called the "S.M.E," or the Society of Motorcycle Enthusiasts.

Now we're definitely not talking about going down the same routes that two or three largest motorcycle clubs in the world, have gone down before. Nor are we talking about some sleazy, low-life, gang banger, ball breaker type of scenario, which would only be in it for the anarchy and the money of course and to hell with the little guys and all the rest of those that just want to ride around occasionally and rightly deserve to be able to do that as well. After all, money is only good for what it is and it takes a lot more than money to heal the world from all of its problems, that's for sure.

What it really takes is a dream, a dream big enough to turn it all into a reality and a vision strong enough to get all of those bikers together at the same time, for exactly the same reasons.

Think about that for a moment, it might be a dream, but it's a dream that many bikers would have liked to have seen come true at one point in time, especially when the world was a younger place and the whole concept of motorcycles was fairly new.

I wasn't alone with those thoughts though; there were a lot of others, dreaming the same dream as well. I just happened to be an offspring of the one that came up with the name to begin with, the "S.M.E. ™"

Maybe it never happened though, maybe there were always way too many barriers to overcome and far too many disputes to settle and the real bottom line was the fact that there was way too much greed and corruption on both sides of the law, and especially in the ones that started up all of those little clubs to begin with.

Maybe they could never get it together, because they were being torn apart every chance they got and eventually, they all just started fighting each other, first, in their own inner cities and counties and then moving on to complete provinces or States, until finally, they were at it all over the world, after all, every single club wants to be the biggest, the baddest and the ugliest club on the planet, or at least, in their own territories.

They became no different than some of the punk assed, street gangs that ran amuck right along with them or even the ones that were there years before them.

Honour, Integrity, loyalty and trust as well as any kind of brotherhood, were words that every biker had tattooed in their minds and on their bodies at one time or another, but now, they're just signs of the past, "Old School shit" is what most of the younger ones say and it's all down to greed when you think about it, simply because enough is just never enough.

It didn't used be that way when I was younger; you could always trust your brothers back then and they always had your back no matter what, even if it meant going to prison or facing certain death.

You knew that you were a part of something that was so big, so special and so unique, that it could never be broken and it would never die. But as usual, things change, just as they always have and they always will.

I could see it coming though. I always had a knack for that sort of thing, especially, back then. Maybe that's why I finally stopped being a patch-holder and went back out on my own to begin with.

I could be anywhere I needed to be, when it was necessary and then I could be on my way again, and I wouldn't have to answer to anyone afterwards.

I didn't have to worry about who said what, when or where and I didn't have to stick around for the politics or answer to any club members. I just did what I needed to do, no matter what that meant?

Get in and get out just as quickly as I could, because that's what I was known for anyway, and that's what I had always been good at doing. I had learned those skills in the army as a "Reconnaissance Specialist", spending my time getting in and out of enemy territory, doing black ops, TDY's, skirmishes, and sorties etc. without being noticed and without getting caught, so it was the perfect road to travel down with the S.M.E. as well.

But then again, maybe that's not really the case; maybe there is no S.M.E at all. I'll just leave you with that thought for the moment and we'll get on with the next story.

Five days later, that woman truck driver that I had hooked up with after my last time out in the desert, was up with the sun and gone with the wind so to speak, as the song says and so was my money. I never did get to the bike show; instead I wasted myself and most of my time on a good looking female truck driver, with lots of party favours and a fancy hotel room that I'll never see again.

Yeah, it had been a lot of fun for sure, she was a beauty for her age, and she certainly knew how to party. She was damn good at it as well, but the fun never lasts that long, and when reality sets in, it can bite you pretty hard at the best of times.

So, I woke up alone, wondering why in the hell I was still inside that hotel room to begin with? Where was the woman that I had been with the nights before and more to the point, where was all my money?

Typical frigging luck I thought, just another stupid plan that didn't quite work out right. You'd think a guy like me, would have known better than to trust a woman with anything, but I had always been a sucker for a pretty face and that certainly hadn't changed much over the years, regardless of what they'd put me through.

They may have more lines under their eyes these days, a softer body and a few extra pounds that they shouldn't have, but I was still a sucker for em, just the same. I couldn't help that. I loved women, I always had, and always will and I guess it really is, as simple as that.

At least I had my wits about me to begin with. I had put the bike in the shop straight away and it was checked out in no time and then I had gone to the bank, as soon as I could get there. I walked in with my saddle bags strung over my shoulder and then I dropped forty-grand on the counter in a heartbeat.

The staff simply looked at me, as if I had robbed another bank somewhere, with their eyes almost popping out of their sockets and their jaws hanging open, but I stood my ground, counting the money for them, dressed in my tattered jeans, tee-shirt and black leather jacket.

I didn't care what they thought? But I swear that they didn't know what to do with me at first. Whether to call the cops or not?

It all turned out fine by the end of it though and I was certainly smiling a lot when I finally got the receipt and then walked back out the same door that I came in through.

That old man had done me well, there was actually fifty grand inside that black plastic bag when I left the desert that day, fifty grand was more than a couple of years' salary for most people back then and ten grand more than I would've got if I had won first prize at the bike show, but I had just blown five of it in five days, half of that was what I knew I spent, but the other half, was what the woman had left with, except for a lonely, hundred dollar bill that was lying on the table with a quick note saying that breakfast, lunch and dinner was on her.

She also said that she had to get back to work, really missed her kids and was sending most of the money out to her old man so that he could get his rig back on the road and then hopefully meet-up with him in L.A.

She thanked me for it all of course and then as a post script, she said that she'd pay me back some day, but I definitely wasn't holding my breath over that one and I certainly didn't remember giving her any of the money to begin with.

Never mind, it was a done deal now anyway and it was time for me to scoot on down the road, so I put some music on my pocket radio and cranked up the throttle to both, the radio and my bike. It was going to be a good day and that was for sure.

Now one of the problems about being a biker is that you always have to travel in the weather.

If it's raining, you're gonna get wet. If the sun shines, you'll definitely feel it and sometimes it'll even burn you, and if the wind's up, that affects the way you ride and it often blows you off course time after time.

If you run into a storm, then you have to look for the nearest overpass, underpass, tree, farmyard or barnyard door, that's been left open, just to wait it out in, but on a great day, when the weather is fine, you can reach right up and touch the sky, like the song says and that's when you feel like you're riding somewhere in-between heaven and hell and there's no doubt about it my friend, all in all, it aint a bad way to travel, but then you can never count on the weather now, can you?

Take that morning for instance; I decided to give myself eighteen hours to get back to Tulsa, even though I knew that I could probably make it back in twelve, if I pushed it. It was about eight-hundred miles and pushing it would mean cranking the throttle wide-open for most of the way.

I didn't like riding that way anymore, which is why I rode a chopper to begin with, and not a crotch-rocket or a road-racer, or whatever else you want to call those bloody death machines.

I've seen too many riders go down on those, and usually for their own stupid mistakes, like going too damn fast to begin with, but don't get me wrong, I still like to fly and I love speed, but I aint going to do that for twelve hours straight anymore, those days are long gone and besides that, who can afford the extra gas that you use, not to mention the wear and tear on the motor and the risk of losing your license.

I used to have about a dozen of those at one point in time, one for every state that I travelled through on a regular basis, Texas, Oklahoma, Arkansas and Mississippi, in one direction, and Colorado, Nevada, California, Oregon and Washington, in the other, and there were the three Canadians and a Mexican license that I had as well.

It was just the thing to do back then and to be honest, it was a lot cheaper to buy a license than it was to pay for any speeding tickets, but that all changed with personal computers.

Licenses went national and then international, so it didn't matter anymore where you were, they could see what tickets you had from any State or Province and they could also read up on your entire life story and access the other details as well, like how many times you've been arrested for whatever reasons and when or wherever that was.

Yeah, those times had changed that's for sure, but that was then and this was now, so I just figured that it was such a nice day with blue skies and high temps, I could easily cruise for hours and the sun would be with me most of the way back, but little did I know, although there was that gut feeling again, somewhere deep-down inside of me.

First of all there was an accident on the freeway just up ahead. It involved three cars and a jack-knifed rig that had no business being out there in the first place.

Now, I know what you're thinking, and no, it wasn't her.

I wouldn't wish that on anyone anyway, not even another thief just like her, but it had certainly killed a few people and then it had mangled up a few more just for good measure, you might say.

Apparently, the driver had been drinking and popping Mexican Christmas trees, like they were going out of style. He also had some pink ladies, purple hearts and a very large bottle of black beauties on him as well, which was more than enough speed to keep him awake for at least a month at a time, if he hadn't mixed it with that bottle of Johnny Walker, which they found at the scene.

Who knows how long he had actually been up, or even how long it took him to cross the border in the first place?

They said he was headed up to New York City, which was a solid four or five day drive for a big rig like that, if not longer, so it was bound to happen sooner or later and maybe this was better than what could've, would've, should've been. You just never know?

Anyway, they closed the highway in all directions because of that and even though I was on a bike, I couldn't get passed the cops that had it all blocked off.

So for the next two hours I had to sit there in traffic, patiently waiting it out, with the sun shining up above me again, which eventually crept up over my head. Oh well, at least it was moving this time.

Then, when the way was finally cleared those bloody cops decided to hold me back for a little while longer to run a make on my bike they said, and to do a safety check on it as well. Of course they also decided to run my name through their computers while they were at it, just for good measure. So, it was another hour and half wasted after all that.

I should have turned back right then and there. I should have gone back to that hotel room and found another woman to spend some time with or at least hit a few bars and a good restaurant, but I had already decided that I had to go on regardless, I had people to see, places to go and things to do, you know how it is.

So, there I was finally cruising at about seventy five miles an hour or more when I saw this dark ominous cloud coming up over the horizon. Yeah, that's right, I was heading into a thunderstorm and it was looking pretty grim but then, as my luck would have it, all of a sudden, it just got worse.

A long tail in the clouds started developing and I could see that it would probably drop right down on top of me if I wasn't careful. I was heading north at the time and I knew that turning around was out of the question.

What I really needed was to get passed it all somehow or at least find somewhere safe to wait for awhile, until the worst of it was over, like an overpass or underpass, if possible.

Now, I'm not talking about a little Texas twister here, no, this was a full blown, category three or four tornado and it was coming right at me.

A little rain and some bad weather wouldn't hurt anyone, too much, but this thing could get deadly for hundreds of people, if it came down the right way or even the wrong way, it doesn't really matter and believe you me when I say that it looked as if it was about to come down right on top of me.

I was back in the desert by then, with nowhere to run and nowhere to hide. I didn't have a choice really, it was find another direction to go like turning east or west, or simply ride on through it. Unfortunately, there wasn't any other road to take and out running it wasn't going to be an option, because it never is.

These things can travel up to three hundred miles an hour at times and they can lay a path of destruction for mile after mile depending on how long they touch down.

Some people say that they can tear up fifty miles or more around them. But I sure as hell wasn't waiting to find out.

So, I cranked up my throttle from seventy five to eighty, eighty to ninety and then ninety to one twenty. Was I crazy or what? I was riding like a bat out hell, heading straight for it and sure enough I was right on the money.

The damn thing was touching down in front of me, ripping the bushes apart along the side of the road and throwing up dirt and debris all over the place, including me, but I wasn't stopping for no one, I was going to ride right on through it; at least that's what I thought I'd do.

Now, I'm going to tell you that it's hard for me to know exactly what happened next, simply because it all became too surreal. Did I crash, or did I pull over to wait it out?

I honestly don't remember, but what I do remember, is that everything seemed to be slowing down at the time and then somehow, it all just completely stopped, as if I'd been trapped in a time warp, or something else that was just as strange and as twisted as you could ever imagine.

The worst thing about it, was the fear that I had lost my hearing through it all, because one minute, the sound was louder than a freight train smashing itself into the side of a mountain and the next minute, well, it was completely silent, as if someone had simply reached-up and pulled out both of my eardrums at the same time.

I was still on my bike though, at least that's what I thought, but the road wasn't there anymore. In fact, nothing was there anymore; it was simply another world, as if I had just been beamed up by some freaky alien in a spaceship, like the ones you see in a bad Star Trek movie.

I finally realized, that my bike wasn't even running and that I wasn't moving. Not up, down or sideways, not straight ahead or backwards, in fact nothing was moving, there wasn't anything there left to move.

I didn't know what to do so I just got off the bike and found out that I was standing on thin air only I couldn't see it and my bike was standing there by itself as well, without the aid of its kick stand.

I quickly decided that I must have died and that all of this was some sort of limbo like purgatory or nirvana and that's when I heard that old familiar voice calling out to me again, somewhere in the darkness and not too far off.

"Hello *Gypsy*" the voice said, but I couldn't see a thing standing there, so eventually I just yelled out.

"Here I am old man, what do you want with me this time and where in the hell are you?"

Of course, I immediately knew, that it was that crazy old man again, after all, who else would it have been? You know the one I'm talking about, the one that I had met in the desert a few days before.

He was probably the devil in all reality, he simply had to be, but he looked like any other old man, to me.

"Well here you are again, the old man said; fancy meeting up here like this. You've gone and done it good and proper this time, haven't you? You should have turned off when you had the chance, instead of heading straight for me."

"I guess so, old man; I said, rather quick and impatiently, so what now? Where do we go from here?"

"That all depends on you my boy, the old man said, where do you want to go?"

"Well, I was heading to Tulsa and that's where I really want to go, but surely you already know that?"

"Oh yeah, he said, I actually do know that and to Tulsa you shall go eventually, but first I want you to do something for me?"

"Why me? I asked, what could I possibly do for you old man?"

"Oh, you'll see soon enough my boy; the old man said, laughing with that stupid eerie laugh that he's always had.

You see, you're one of my "Angels now and I have a need for all of my Angels at this moment in time. There's a war going on and I need all the help that I can get."

"Wait a minute I said, you know I've already done my time fighting for the cause, I don't need any more of that bullshit and besides I'm too old for all of that now, so why don't you go and get yourself a younger man, you know the type, one with no brains, no worries and no doubts and maybe a ton of muscle, if you're really lucky. I'm sure that you could find a few of those out here easy enough."

"Ha, ha, the old man said, and here I thought you were the hero type. Don't worry about it *Gypsy* just do it. I'll be here to hold your hand if necessary, he said, still laughing."

"Don't get me wrong here old man, I don't need any ones hand to hold thank you very much, but I sure as hell don't appreciate being shanghaied either. So let's just get on with the business, so I can get back to my life and away from you for good.

This sort of inconvenience just pisses me off and I'm about fed up with being pissed off lately, if you know what I mean, particularly by you."

"That's the spirit my boy, the old man said, I knew that you wouldn't let me down, especially after I saved your life only a few days ago."

"Oh yeah, go ahead and take the credit for that will you, I said, after all it was you that put me in the middle of that mess in the first place. I spent a lot of money on that bike just to have you screw it up like you did."

"Yeah well, I gave it all back to you and then some, if you remember right, so don't come complaining to me about it *Gypsy* boy and by the way, how was that sweet looking truck-driver anyway, she certainly was a pretty little thing wasn't she?" he said, smiling even bigger than what he normally did.

"Speaking of money, I said, quickly, changing the subject, what's a gig like this going to be worth to me then? I figure that it has to be worth quite a lot, especially, if I have to kill all the bad guys and save the frigging world etc."

"Here we go again, the old man said, always looking for that almighty dollar. It's not as if I couldn't do this without you now is it? You would think that you'd just want to do it for the shear hell of it, if you get the pun, after all, it's not every day that you get to go to where we're going and then come back from it all, now is it?"

"So I have to agree to this then, right? I quickly said, otherwise you can't force me to do anything, can you?"

"Well, I could just keep you where you're at right now, with no problems, the old man said, and you would never get back to Tulsa, or anywhere else for that matter. Life could become pretty boring just hanging around here all by yourself."

"Ok, ok, I get the picture, but I still want the money, it's not like it's off your back or something, all you have to do is conger it up like you did before and then all I have to do is spend it," I said, with a really big smile on my own face.

"Hahaha, the old man said, that's not a problem *Gypsy*, when it's all finished you'll be a rich man for a little while and you have my word on that."

Then, we went through the motions of shaking hands again, only this time it was all too real. I could actually feel the old man's hand this time around, and it didn't feel so good to me. It was kind of cold and clammy, almost like shaking hands with a corpse. It sent a shiver down my spine and I immediately wiped my hand on my jeans afterwards. I also realised that I should have stated just how much money was involved to begin with, but I didn't. Oh well, it was done deal by then, I figured.

The next thing that I knew, I was being sucked into the very depths of the earth itself, somewhere into a deep, dark pit like place, filled with absolutely nothing and there I was all of a sudden, sweating my nuts off again, trying to make sense of it all and also trying to plug my ears from the God awful sounds that I was hearing which were agonizing screams of utter misery, that surrounded us, no matter which way we turned.

The place was more than you could imagine, let alone hope to write about. It was horrible, indescribably horrible in-fact. The only thing that lit the place up, were fires burning everywhere, especially the ones burning everyone inside of them.

Some of them, were up in the air, suspended on their own somehow, floating around in the ether, while on fire, at the same time, it was kind of like staring at stars, only not quite so good.

The closest that you could come to a complete description of it all, would be like a gigantic cave buried somewhere near the centre of the earth, or perhaps a different dimension altogether?

You could see for what seemed like miles in every direction though, and mile after mile, there were the fires, along with completely indescribable beings, living or half living, or completely dead, I didn't know which, but all of them were being tossed and turned every which way I looked, in what seemed to be pure agony in one way, shape or another.

And then there was the smell of it all, an overwhelming putrid stench, the smell of certain death that filled my nostrils and lungs to the point of suffocation.

It was definitely not the place that you would book a holiday to, that's for sure, and I wanted to leave it as soon as I got there, but naturally I knew that it wouldn't be an option for me. So I had to ride it out, no matter what it took.

I finally said, as we walked along, "what is it that I'm supposed to do down here old man? What is it that you really want from me?"

"Well, the old man said, now that you're here; let me tell you what you'll really need to know. So listen up now, because I don't want to have to repeat myself.

Today, you are the chosen one, thanks to yours truly that is. Every power that you'll ever need is at your finger tips. In-fact, all of the powers of the universe are deep down inside of you right now at this very moment in time, as we speak.

You are everything that I am, perhaps even more and before you, out there in the emptiness, lie's the battle ground, along with an army of such immensity, intensity and mass, that no one has ever seen the likes of it before, no one at all, you can take my word for that and it all waits there for you and you alone.

It's the perfect killing machine *Gypsy*, of all the ages, with warriors that will never die, no matter how many times they get shot, stabbed or blown into little bits and pieces. After all, you can't kill something that's already dead and believe me when I say that they are all dead, they are beyond dead, they are as dead as dead can be, and all you have to do is take control of it, take control of them and then make it all work for you, make it do your bidding, as you desire."

And then the old man said, "The object of it all is of course to win the war, the war that will be waged here in no time at all."

"So, who are we fighting?" I quickly said, as if I didn't already know the answer.

"What you and your kind have always referred to as God of course, the old man said, as he laughed out loud again, it's always God and it always has been."

"Well isn't that just a little bit strange then, I said again, because if you're always fighting God and he's the one that actually made you to begin with, along with everything else that there ever was, then how in the world could you ever expect to win a war against him?"

"I don't expect to win *Gypsy*, I expect you to win, the old man said, still laughing, it's down to you now, and you're just the man for the job, trust me, I'm never wrong about these things."

"I still don't get it, I said, how could I ever expect to beat God? From what I understand he's the beginning of everything that I know, and the end of everything else, and there's nothing that anyone could ever do to change that, because if they did, it would simply put an end to all that there is, and we wouldn't have anything to fight about anyway, because we just wouldn't exist. We would be nothing, nothing at all without God, simple as that. You should know this old man, what's the matter with you? Where's your head at?"

"You mean to tell me, that a big ole bad assed biker like yourself actually believes in all that bullshit then? You mean to say that you're really afraid of God?" the old man said, pointing his finger at me and shaking it.

"No old man, I'm not saying that at all. I'm not afraid of God; I'm not afraid of dying either, and I'm certainly not afraid of you. It's just that I have respect for God and for what he is, just as I have respect for you and for what you are, along with everything else, for what it is as well.

To me, there's simply no point in going to war against the one that created "War" to begin with, the one that created everything that there ever was, and everything that there ever will be and in-fact, the only being that truly exists. To me, a war with God, is a war against myself, because without God, there wouldn't be any me to begin with, now would there?"

The old man started laughing again, only this time it wasn't his usual laugh, this time it was a whole lot softer and slightly sweeter than it usually was.

Then he started to fade from my sight, disappearing slowly, right in front of my eyes, while the fires of hell that were burning all around us to begin with, suddenly started going out one by one, and the cave that we were in, simply opened up to the heavens above and a great star, brighter than any that I had ever seen before, sat there high above it all.

I turned to the old man again and saw that somehow, he had changed his appearance. He was a lot younger, more agile, taller and much thinner. He also had long flowing white hair, a clear complexion and no scars on his face anymore.

It was almost like looking into a mirror with a reflection of my father, or myself, if that makes any sense, looking right back at me, except for the fact, that he was all dressed up in white and had something around him that glowed, shimmering like the stars above.

"You seem to have become a pretty wise old man in your younger years, *Gypsy*, the old man standing next to me said, and it seems that you may have finally seen the truth of things, and now all I can do is expect you to go back into the world and tell that truth to whomever may listen.

When you've finished telling all that you can tell, then we'll meet again and you will become part of me again, as you truly are now, for I am you and you are me and we are all that there ever was and all that there will ever be. Because without you there is no me and without me, there is no you.

So, go now my son and rest assured that your troubles are over for awhile. Find your peace in the world of the living and try to live a good life; try to keep up with good will towards all of mankind, for they are within you as well, as they are within me. We are all one with everything and everything is always one with us."

It was a pretty profound moment to say the least, as I stood there and suddenly realized the meaning behind it all, finding myself in awe by this supernatural beings presence, along with his mannerisms and his mild tone of voice.

I also realized that at that very moment in time, I was completely and utterly at peace with myself in such a way, that I had never experienced before. I knew right then and there, that what this old man was saying was one of the greatest truths that I had ever heard before, and I also knew, that I had finally come home and that I never wanted to leave home again, but then, I didn't have a choice in the matter, just like any other time and I know now that I still don't.

Suddenly, I found myself sitting on my bike again along side of the highway that I had been travelling down earlier, before the tornado had actually hit me. The younger old man was standing there with me.

"Close your eyes *Gypsy*, the old man said; imagine yourself floating back through space and time, which really doesn't exist. All of your yesterdays are gone; all of your teenage years, your childhood years and even your infancy.

Close your eyes and see yourself before you were brought into this life. Before you were in your mother's womb, before you were even a twinkle in your father's eye. Then see yourself, a hundred years before that, as another person that once walked this earth, as you do today.

Then quickly go back to a thousand years ago and then go back to a million, until finally you will see yourself as part of that great abyss that has always been there and will always be there.

Relax now, and take all of that in, because this is where we have all started. This is where we come from. This is the beginning of all that there ever was, and at the same time, it is also the end of all that will ever be.

In the beginning there was the word and the word was with God. Now this isn't about Christianity *Gypsy*, Christ himself found out these same answers long before they nailed him to the cross. And since that time, billions of people on this planet have read it, or they have been told about it, for thousands of years or more, and still, they don't have a single clue, as to its true meaning."

Nevertheless we all have a beginning and to that beginning we shall go to next. Relax and come with me, it won't take us long."

I just sat there on my bike listening intently to what the old man was saying. I had never been religious before and I certainly wasn't going to change my ways now, but what this old man was saying was making perfect sense to me, and besides that, it wasn't about religion, in any way, shape or form, it was about something that was far beyond all of that. It was the secret to life itself.

I could only hope that I was making some sense of it all to begin with, but perhaps it was beyond my comprehension, so I can only write what I remember; and trust that I've got it right?

"In the beginning there was the Emptiness, the old man said, a cold, distant, dark and lonely place, completely void of any light, sound, sense or reason. No shape, no substance, nothing at all, but a big black hole, caught up in the deep, dark recesses of a nonexistence. Then for whatever reasons, out of the emptiness, there came a single thought." "I am"

"Once that happened, I am, started thinking other thoughts, which somehow, quite miraculously even, just seemed to flow out of "I am" at that single moment in time."

"Some would say that it was a sudden sense of awareness of the self, but that's all debatable? Anyway, "I am" then realized that he/she/it was, and it was as simple as that; therefore "I am" said to itself, I am and I shall always be everything that I am.

Eventually and always thinking, "I am" realized that there was more to think about, and so much more to do than "I am" could ever do alone and soon "I am" decided not to be alone, ever again. So "I am" split itself into two parts, and these two parts became "We." We are, therefore we shall always be all that we can be, because "We are."

For awhile, millions, or even billions of years, or perhaps, it was only a few seconds in the grande scheme of things, this was the way things were. "We are", therefore we will be, but "We are", also realized that there was more to be achieved, and so much more to be done as well, so the second part of "I am" "We are" split itself again and the three parts became known as "they."

"The two had become three. They are and therefore, they shall always be, we are and so we shall always be, I am and I will always be. Not long after that, the two parts that split split again and they became them."

"I am" we are, they are, them, and then it was you.

You, them, they, we, "I am" All that ever was, is and will always be, multiples of "I am." It's as simple as that my boy and I do hope that you're following all of this because there's a lot more to it than that.

Long before life came to this planet; there was already life in the outer regions of what we now call space and time.

The heavens were full of life, but it wasn't quite like the life that we know now and obviously, it wasn't anything like it is today. An accurate description of what that life was, at that particular moment in time, would be almost impossible to put into words, but I believe that the time has come for you to try and understand it.

The thought was pure and simple. "I am," it was neither a question nor an answer, but simply a statement.

"I am" became "We are", multiples of itself, by splitting itself into two. This in turn was multiplied again and it became they are, over and over and over again.

There really isn't any, "they" or "we", for truly all there is, is "I am." You are I am. They are I am. We are I am. I am, I am. Everything that ever was, has always been and will always be, "I am."

Now let me tell you what you already know *Gypsy*, because you've forgotten about it through the years and the lives that you've lived before. I am the father, the grand-father and the great-grandfather of Quicksilver, whose multiple legions were of the planet Mars.

I have lived a thousand lifetimes and many more, and I will continue to live until the end of all that there ever was. I've taken many shapes and many forms over the centuries, and I've been known by many different names. I am on this earth, as I have been for thousands of years waiting for the time that has finally come.

Hear me speak and mark my words well, because the world that you know is finally changing and what it is today will soon be no longer. And what it was before will ultimately be again.

I am a being of light; I am the first and the last of the multiples of my kind. "I am". "We are". "They are" etc, etc.

My kind rules the heavens and the earth, the planets and the stars, and everything that truly lies in-between. They have brought everything into existence. We have brought everything into existence. I brought everything into existence."

Now hear these words, my son and hear them well.

When this earth was formed long ago, a great canopy was placed around it. We called that canopy the misty-ring and it surrounded the earth much as the Ozone layers do today. However, the misty ring was miles thick and yet it was still quite transparent and it gave all below it, complete protection, from all of everything that was above it. Not much different to a mother's womb, it nurtured everything in it. Plants grew in great abundance and everything flourished. Animals fed extremely well which in turn allowed them to grow into incredible sizes and every man, woman and child, that walked this earth started out living, just as long as they wanted to or wished for.

There was no death, no sickness, no such thing as disease, and no need for war, and there was never any famine.

There wasn't an ageing population either, people grew up, but they never grew old. A thousand years was simply like twenty or thirty years today, as far as body growth goes. Everyone was fit and healthy, and all was good here, in-fact, all was very well in the gardens of "Pangaea" or this Earth, as it's known today.

The legions of light, (multiples of "I am") had split the darkness in the heavens for all time, sitting Pangaea along with eleven other planets in the middle of a space that circled a great star that you earthlings now call the sun. The sun gave up its light and reigned down its energy, to all of the planets, and it was good for a very long time. Everything was, as it came to be until finally, the thought wars in the heavens started. That's when the legions of the sky grew restless, through the millenniums of time.

The thought was that it wasn't any good to exist anymore, without being able to actually feel that existence, and the multiples had no feelings. They were beings of light, made from pure energy, with no earthly form, or any real shape. They had no bodies, no solid mind to speak of, and no kind of soul to nurture; they were just pure light, pure energy, and pure thought."

So it came to pass, that some of them, had seen humankind develop on Pangaea and had decided that it would be pretty good to live like man, and to take on man's daughters for wives of their own, and to create their own offspring. But in order to do this, they would have to become the same as man, because, a being of Pangaea, could never become a being of the sky, nor of the heavens.

The two were completely incompatible with each other, as they have always been and of course they will always be.

Mankind has been made of the earth, and of the earth is where they will always remain.

So, the beings of light who chose to ground, would have to sacrifice everything that they were in the heavens, for who or what it was, that they wanted to be here on earth. It was known as the great sacrifice, but in the long run, it was also a very foolish one.

Eventually the thought was completely erased from the minds of those that chose to ground. Causing them to forget where it was that they actually came from to begin with.

Most of them were happy enough to do so anyway, except that it was no longer meant for them to live forever in one simple existence, now they had to exist time after time.

In doing this, we also changed the course of humankind as well, because now man could no longer exist forever neither, they had to die, in order for us to die.

At first that life span was well over a thousand years.

A thousand years was plenty enough time us to experience what we wanted or needed to experience during that lifetime, but soon that became old hat and new experiences were needed.

More and more of the multiples wanted to experience this existence as well, until finally all of humankind, was basically possessed by all of the multiples that were left in the heavens.

Now, I'll tell you a little secret Gypsy, before I leave you again, the old man said, You won't remember the rest of what I said anyway, because it's locked-up so deep inside of your subconscious mind, that it simply won't ever come out, and in the long run it doesn't really matter anyway, because you are, who you are, and you will do what you do, regardless.

I hope that you remember this, because it's the most important thing to remember in this life, and probably the most important thing that I could ever tell you.

Everything we go through in life, affects us. Everyone we meet, everyone we even think about, everyone we wish for and desire, has an effect on us from birth, right up until death, and all of the time in-between."

"Grandparents, parents, uncles and aunts, friends, relatives, strangers, siblings and grandchildren, are all continuations of the life that we live, as we are in the lives that they live as well.

Whether we know those people or not, whether they are even real or not, they are still a part of us. What we are to them, and what they are to us, is what truly what makes us who we are, and there's so much more.

Water, earth, wind, fire, and the sky, the Sun and the Moon, plants, animals, insects, the stars and the planets themselves, all affect us in one way or another, whether we can see it, or even feel it, doesn't matter, it's always been that way, right from the beginning of time.

However, what truly makes us completely individual, set apart from everyone and everything else in this world, is our own ability to reason, pro-create and perceive the absolute truth behind all of that thought.

Perception is everything, alongside our own emotions. Love, hate, envy, happiness, despair, sadness, loneliness etc, these are all the things that make us truly unique, because no-one has our specific thought patterns and feelings, although some people may share those thoughts and feelings with us, from time to time, but in reality, they are yours and theirs alone.

What you like or dislike, what you find funny or sad, can be found in others, don't get me wrong, it's just that how funny, is funny to you? And how sad, is sad to them? Or vice versa, and it gets better than this.

When it all gets down to it, in the end, it is really plain and simple perception. What we perceive, is what we think reality really is, and the truth of that matter is that we all have separate reality's, every single one of us, from the beginning of our lives, up until the end of it, and of course, every second of that life in-between."

How is it all possible, that's really quite simple as well? There is no such thing as life for a being of light.

We exist and have always existed, and by living when we take on earthly forms. However, life is a thought and the perception of that thought, made by us to explain something that has yet to be explained.

Now, you're probably lost to what it was that I've just said, after all, how could that be, when we are all living, breathing creatures, you might just ask?"

So, let me explain it to you as simply as I can. We exist as we always have, from the beginning to the end, but the perception of that existence changes as we allow it to and others have the will to change it as well.

What we're all going through is a continuation of our own existence. A perception that we have created to allow us to feel our own emotions which in truth, is necessary for the benefit of that existence.

We can change our perception, as we often do and we can allow others to change it for us, which is more often the case, but in order to change it completely, we have to go back to the beginning, when that first perception, first came into our existence, in other words, when thought, first became thought.

That, my friend, is what is known as Shamaiya. (Our initial thought) Knowing that we exist, knowing what that existence is and knowing how to change it all at will.

This then becomes Shamaiya as well (only it's the way that we exist.) Shamaiya is our existence, our way of life and when you finally arrive at or into the final stages of Shamaiya, (which is Death, for want of a better word) then all of the answers, to all of the questions, that have ever been asked, will be yours to do as you wish.

That's known, as the Ultimate Shamaiyan experience, a complete awareness of the beginning and of the end of all that there ever was, all that was ever perceived, and all that there has ever been.

You are Shamaiyan Gypsy, from the beginning of it all, up until the end of it all. Shamaiyans are the true multiples of "I am" Shamaiya, is simply the beginning and the end of that absolute truth.

The old man cackled again, just as he had so many times before. His appearance was back to his older self, the one that I had met in the desert to begin with.

"It's time that I got back to it my boy, you won't remember half of what I told you anyway and time is waiting for no one. You've got all that you need for awhile and we will eventually meet up again, there's no doubt about that.

You have yourself a great trip back to Tulsa; I really don't think that there will be too many problems ahead of you for awhile, but do keep it upright and in-between the lines this time, because you never know what's around the corner." and with that, the old man was gone.

The sun was shining, the grass was green, and the skies were crystal blue and clear.

I looked down at my saddle bags once again and saw that they were stuffed full of cash, one hundred dollar bills, just like before.

What a great day, I thought, as I started up my motorcycle.

Then I sniffed the air and took a good look around, I liked what I saw and with that, I scooted off just like a man on a mission, one more time.

****

Postscript

Now, I don't want anyone to think that I'm trying to convert them into some kind of religion here, or that I'm trying to install a thought process that they really have no idea about and could care less about anyway. Because I'm definitely not, you can trust me on that.

After all, I'm just a biker and bikers don't do religion, as I've said before. So what I've written in the last two stories, are only words and that's what they should be regarded as. What you believe or what I believe, will always be two different things, no matter what? But what I will say here, is this.

Yes, I was out there in that Texas desert and yes, I got bit several times by some fire ants and yes, I was picked up by a woman truck driver and spent almost a week with her in a hotel room and most of all, I had some strange experiences that I can't really explain, that happened to me on the way back to Tulsa, but you believe whatever you want to believe, after all, I'm only writing a book here, trying to keep you entertained and hoping that you won't shoot the messenger, as they say.

So with that said, I'd like to give you another view of where my life has been before we get to the final story, that will eventually lead you on to the next book, if you've stuck it out this far that is, and if you like the way I write of course.

Add me to your Facebook page, and tell all of your friends to buy a copy of this book and write a great review on it, or at least give it a five star rating if nothing else? That would be great, because every little bit helps and feed-back is essential to all writers.

You know what they say about telling two friends, who will also tell two friends etc. We all know that that really works, so please don't be shy about it, because the best advertising in the world is always by word of mouth.

Anyway, thanks for hanging in here, because if nothing else, it's been an amazing journey and I've loved every minute of it, at least the ones that I didn't hate.

****

17
Twenty-six minutes

A biker drops in to see his doctor one afternoon, hoping for quick check-up and a serious conversation, about the state of his health in general, when the Dr. eventually says to him, "Look, I've got some good news and I've got some bad news as well, so which one would you like me to give to you first?"

The biker says, "Go ahead and give me the bad news first, if you would please."

So the Dr. says, "I'm afraid that you've got terminal cancer, with less than a year left to live."

"Holly shit the biker says, so what's the good news then?"

The Dr says, "You've got the onset of Alzheimer's or Dementia, so you'll probably forget all about the cancer in a week or two." Then he goes on to say, "I'm really sorry about this, but there's not a lot more that I can tell you right now, except that this is the third time this month, that you've been in here to see me, and your bike, is still parked-up where you left it the first time around."

****

Sometimes life gets pretty screwed up, in-fact, sometimes it seems like there really is no rhyme or reason, for every little thing that happens to any one of us, at any given moment in time, it just happens and that's about all there is to that.

One minute you might be standing on the top of the world, right next to the most beautiful person that's ever been born, feeling like a king or a queen, high above all the others, and then in the very next moment of time, in less than a flick of an eyelid, you find yourself drowning in a sea of deep, dark, despair, gasping for the very air that you breathe, and watching the rest of your life, being sucked out of you, in some major way, shape or form, never even knowing, what that particular person's name was, that you were so infatuated with, or where it was that they came from or indeed, where in the hell they actually went?

So yeah, sometimes, nothing makes any sense at all, but then again, there are those other times, when everything around you, suddenly becomes, way too fucking clear.

Take this one morning for instance, I got up early, made some breakfast, did some of my daily routines and then it was out the door, across the yard, into the garage and on to the saddle of my deeply loved, American made motorcycle, just like any other day of the week.

In less than a few beats of my heart, I was straddling my machine; pulling it up-right and pointing it outwards, like a modern day horseman, that was heading out to the range, as I quickly slipped the key into its specified slot, and then turned it forwards to the on position.

I gripped the handlebars, kicked the stand, pointed it out the door and pushed the button all at the same time.

The button that should have made the machine come to life, but nothing happened. Not even a cough or a splutter. Not even a clickety-click. The bike wouldn't start. Who would have thought?

It was only two years old, a pretty little custom chop, with less than ten thousand miles on the clock, and I had just bought it a new battery less than a week ago. I did that, not because the old one wasn't any good anymore, or because it was worn out, or even because it had leaked all over the place.

No, I bought it because when I put the bike in for a service, my wrench told me that I would probably need a new battery to get me through the next winter.

So I took his word for it and then I went ahead and spent the extra cash having a new one fitted, just to be on the safe side. I was only trying to be smart really, I figured that I didn't want to be stuck anywhere because of a dead battery, especially out on my own driveway, but there I was anyway, straddled across the chop, without a hope in hell of going anywhere, and that's where I sat for twenty-six minutes.

Now twenty-six minutes, aint a lot of time really? It takes less time to cook a steak, drink a beer, pay your taxes, smoke a cigarette or even have an orgasm, if you're in the mood that is? In-fact, you could do all of that in twenty-six minutes if you put your mind to it, but still, twenty-six minutes could be a lifetime for some people, and for me, it was definitely too damn long.

Usually, I'm up and running, moving down the road in seconds.

I'd be gone with the wind, so to speak and loving every minute of it. It's what I did every day of the week and it had never let me down before.

Monday to Friday it was off to the day job, like every other working stiff that's out there, but then Saturday and Sunday was my time and I was usually off on a tour of pure un-adulterated, ride it like the wind, and don't give a damn about anything, motorcycling adventure and of course, a lot of sheer pleasure to go along with it.

It doesn't matter what the weather's like, how early or late it is, or who needs what, when and where. I lived to ride and I rode to live.

To me they just go hand in hand, they always have and they always will, but this morning? Well, this morning was just not going to be one of my best mornings at all.

"Now it's a good job it's Saturday," I thought, otherwise, I would have been late for work by now and the boss would have flipped me shit about it.

Not that I'd care too much about that anyway, because let's face it, the boss and I never really got along as it was, but I would have lost a little money for being late and that means a lot less miles to travel in the overall scheme of things.

Instead it was Saturday and I was headed out to the café, to join in on a charity run with some of the boys, "Toys for Tots" or something similar. It didn't matter what it was, it was all about the same to me. One charity is as good as any other I figured? Still, I was ready to go, but that ole bike of mine, must have thought a little different at the time.

I had put the key in the lock, turned the fuel on, even put the gearbox into neutral for a change, but when I pushed the button, nothing happened, absolutely nothing at all.

Naturally, I had checked all the bits and pieces that I could think of to check, wires, connections, battery terminals etc, but it didn't help, my iron horse was truly and unmistakably, dead to the world.

So, I sat there watching the world spin, as other riders rode by on their own trusty metal steeds. Some of them had even looked in my direction as they passed my driveway, but none of them had stopped. None of them even waved. They all just seemed to ignore me, even my own brothers of the club that I was involved with.

I tried again and again to start up my bike, but it was all to no avail, instead I just sat there and sat there, and then I sat there some more. Much like that proverbial "lump on a log" that we all hear about from time to time.

Twenty-six minutes of just sitting there, twenty-six minutes of wondering what to do next.

It was a great day for a ride though, the sun was shining high-up and bright, the weather was warm and the skies were clear and blue, and there was simply nowhere else on this planet that I would have rather been, except for the fact of sitting on my own driveway of course, on top of my own dead horse that is, watching the sun slowly crawl its way across that crystal blue sky.

Now, I thought about calling up my wrench, several times in fact, because usually the guy could get to my place within an a hour or so and if he actually did that today, then I could probably still make the start of the charity run, if all I needed to get the bike started, was just a boost that is.

I even thought about jump-starting it myself, but then I realized that I lived on the flat, without a single bump or hill in sight. I could probably dig up a rope from somewhere and get somebody to tow me up the road a ways, but I changed my mind on that pretty quick like, after all, this was an awesome chopper, one of the best that I had ever owned.

It wasn't a crotch-rocket that's for sure, not a rice burner or a conversion kit. It was a real live one of kind, custom made motorcycle, with a more chrome on it than a Rolls Royce has on its front grill.

It was made right here in the south of England and the last thing that it needed was a rope around its neck, besides that, knowing my kind of luck, it would get damaged somehow and I certainly didn't want that to happen.

So I just sat there for awhile, watching a half dozen more bikers ride past me, feeling like some kind of wannabe man-child, stuck in the house on detention, looking out the bedroom window, hoping that someone, somewhere, would come and rescue me. But they all just scooted past, like I wasn't even there.

I may as well have a cup of tea while I wait for the wrench, I finally thought to myself again, just as the last of the other bikers, disappeared around the corner.

Then for some reason, I looked down at my watch again and noticed that twenty-six minutes had gone by since I had first gone outside and sat down on my leather saddle.

What the hell, I thought, I may as well try this thing one more time, as my thumb reached for the button and wouldn't you know it, just like that, the bike started up in an instant, like it was always supposed to. Putt, putt, Putt, putt, it purred.

What in the land of Harleys? I thought, as I quickly revved it up, what on earth is going on here? It was as dead as dead could be, only minutes ago.

Oh well, it's running now, I can forget about that tea though, because it was definitely time to scoot on out of there.

I quickly threw on my jacket and then reluctantly put my helmet back on. I've always hated helmets; to me they just get in the way. Still, in a few more heartbeats I was up and gone, riding into the wind, roaring down the highway without a care in the world, at least that's what should've happened.

Instead, I came across the traffic that was backed up from the main intersection, to over a mile or so, further on up the road from where I had just come from.

I weaved my way through the stalled traffic just as far as I could get, until I finally reached some of the other bikers that were stuck waiting there as well. "Hey, what's going on?" I asked, as I pulled up to one of them.

"I'm not too sure the woman said, looking back at me through a darkened face shield, I think there was an accident."

"Oh, shit, that's too bad, I hope no one was hurt" I said, looking at the woman again thinking about how good her body looked in those tight-assed, black leather trousers that she was wearing at the time, and then naturally wondering who she was and where it was that she came from?

"Listen, there's a few side streets up ahead that we could take if you like? Are you headed to the café as well?" I said, still gazing at the woman's beauty.

"Yes the woman said, there's a run on for charity this morning and I was planning on being in it, what about you?"

"Same here exactly, I said, maybe we could ride together, team up so to speak, if that would be alright with you?"

"I don't see why not, the woman said, as long as we can make it there on time?"

"Follow me then I said, I know the back streets around here pretty well and there's quite a few shortcuts that we can take.

We should still make it there in time, without any more problems that is?" I said again rather quickly, gunning my throttle and then easing off on the clutch.

The roads were full of traffic being diverted away from the accident of course, but the two of us weaved our way through it all and made it out to the café with plenty of time to spare. Twenty-six minutes to be exact.

We parked-up on the outskirts of the parking lot, got off the machines and then I turned to the woman and said, "So what's your name?" as I watched her take off her helmet and then realized once again, what a beautiful woman she truly was, as she shook her long hair all around.

"Misty, the woman said with a smile, short for Mystique, after my great, great-grandmother's name."

"Wow, that's really a great name I said, mine's DeWalt, T.S. DeWalt."

"I know Misty said, I've seen you around before and I really like your bike, it must have cost you a small fortune to buy it, or did you build it yourself?"

"No, I bought it this way and yeah, it cost me a few quid, I said right back at her, but then that twelve hundred sporty that you're riding wasn't cheap was it?"

"I wouldn't really know, Misty said, I only borrowed it for the day, I usually fly a different way, except for charity runs of course."

"Oh I see, I said, not taking my eyes off of her, that's cool, is it your boyfriend's bike then?"

"No no, more like my boss's bike actually, Misty said with a smile, but it suits its purpose."

"Well lucky me, I said again, it's not every day that I get to ride with such a beautiful woman, especially one that rides so well and looks pretty much like an angel."

"Ah, Misty said laughing, you've gone and guessed my secret now and it seems as though you're pretty good at it as well. That's my last name of course, Angel. Mary Mystique Angel, at your service. But you can just call me Misty, like I said before."

"Wow, I said again, that's another cool name, your parents must have been into the whole sixties thing, sex, drugs and rock and roll, yeah?"

"Well, not really, Misty said, but they were into various types of religion from time to time, that's for sure, of course I didn't bother too much with that back then, I always had my own things to do."

"Ouch, I said, that's something that us bikers don't usually do. It's right up there with politics, world peace and saving the bloody whales etc."

"And what's wrong with saving the bloody whales?" Misty said, laughing with her hair blowing in the breeze. She almost had a glow about her, or at least it seemed that way to me, kind of like a strong aura or something else; it was strange to say the least, but really quite pretty and surreal, all at the same time.

"Hey, nothing at all, I said quickly, whatever floats your boat or whatever finally sinks it."

Misty just laughed some more and then she told me to stay put, she said that she'd take care of this as I watched her walk into the café and then disappear.

I just stood there like she had told me to, like some puppy dog I guess, not really knowing why? But for some reason, it just seemed like the right thing to do.

A few guys that I knew passed me by, but they didn't stop to chat, they seemed to be in a hurry and I was the last thing on their minds, but then almost out of nowhere, Misty was back again, holding two sets of tickets for the run.

"It was the least that I could do," she said, as she handed me mine, we were just in time thanks to you; it's a good job that you know your way around here "*Gypsy*" Misty said again, or we wouldn't have made it otherwise."

She must have heard some of the boys talking about me while she was inside, because I was sure that I hadn't told her my road name at all, but she had just called me by that very same name anyway.

"*Gypsy*" It was a name that the boys had given me when I joined the club, all those years ago, a name that I wore well and with a lot of pride. I guess everybody knew it; I just didn't know that Misty did?

"So what is it that you do Misty? I said to her, as we sat there waiting for the start of the run to finally happen. What kind of work are you into? Real Estate, Banking, or perhaps it's modelling?" The woman just laughed at that.

"That's really funny she said, so do you think that I'm pretty enough to be a model then? I actually wanted to be a banker once upon a time though, but that was a long time ago. Now, I'm just into collecting things instead."

"Oh, I said, what is it that you collect then? Art, Jewellery, antiques, motorcycles?"

"Oh no, nothing like that Misty said, what I collect is a little more precious than all of that, but I can't really tell you what it is just yet, so you'll have to wait and see."

"Ah ha I said, so your name really does suit you then, Mystique, the mysterious one of course. How long will I have to wait then?"

"That depends on you, *Gypsy*" she said, as she put her helmet back on and then fired up her sporty. You'll see.

The run started off without a hitch, with well over two-hundred bikers chomping at the bit so to speak and raring to go. It was like a horse race really, but no one wanted to take the lead of course and no one really wanted to win, after all, it was just a day out for charity and the sheer joy of riding on top of it all.

Misty and I were all the way at the back, in fact, we were the very last ones on the ride, stragglers to the end, as they say, but it was more than fine for the moment.

I usually rode up front when I was on a club run. That's what happens when you're the President of a local chapter; it just wouldn't do to ride anywhere else, would it?

So this ride was a little different, quite a bit actually, but I didn't mind, I figured that I was in good company anyway.

I was a little more than a bit surprised that none of the other riders had even bothered to usher us up to the front lines though, in-fact, it was almost like they were ignoring us completely, but I quickly forgot all about that as the two of us rode through the course, taking in the sites, as we passed by each one along the way.

It was a great day, I thought, beautiful weather, with hardly a cloud in the sky, warm and sunny, just the way I liked it. It was truly one of the best days that I had seen in a long time and then of course, there was Misty, which was just another very pleasant surprise, because, not only did she look good, but the girl could ride as well, which for any biker, is always a pretty damn good bonus.

It wasn't long before we chose to stay back even further than where we were at, at the start of it all. We started taking short-cuts and detours through different places, at different moments along the way, and some of the scenery seemed almost enchanted and quite surreal, almost like I had stepped off the planet for awhile.

I couldn't describe it, but I guess I hadn't been down those roads before, at least I didn't remember them, and yet, all the while, the two of us were riding in perfect harmony and it seemed like we were communicating almost telepathically at times.

It was pretty strange to say the least, but somehow it felt like we had made this trip before and yet at the same time, it was like we had to wait for the experience to catch us up. It almost seemed like time itself, was way out of sync and I was starting to feel ill because of it, sort of like a sick feeling that's way down in the pit of your stomach, about to explode all the way back up into your mouth, but then, that quickly faded away, thankfully, and we kept on riding.

We finally pulled into the first checkpoint, we were the last in the pack, but we were still in the run regardless and again it wasn't really like a race anyway, so none of that mattered.

"Stay here and I'll do this, Misty said, as she got off her bike again and walked over to the roadside stand that had been specifically set up for the event.

I became a little preoccupied, watching a few of the boys from my club pulling away again, I waved at them, but it was too late, they were already halfway down the road by that time.

Oh well, I thought, we'll just have to catch up with them later.

"Here we go again, Misty said, as she got back to her bike, everything is sorted, we've got twenty miles to the next check point and it's all out in the country."

"Cool, I said, maybe we could pick up the pace a bit and catch up to some of my home boys that are up ahead of us?"

"Don't you like riding along with me then? Misty said, as she started her bike up again and kicked into gear. I know I'm just a girl, but I ride well enough don't I?"

"Yeah, yeah it's cool, we can catch up with them later" I said, with a big smile on my face and was immediately thinking just how stupid I was for even suggesting what I had, to begin with.

After all, I had the best looking rider of the bunch riding right next to me, why blow it by having any others around. I should keep her all to myself, after all, I was a single man and I could only hope that Misty was single as well.

We were into the wind, with exceptional speed after that. Misty set the pace and I simply followed in behind her, down the road like a little schoolboy with a crush.

She rode us up and down those country roads with the precision of a guided missile, until finally pulling over at a rest area in the middle of nowhere, without another soul in sight. It was truly a beautiful spot to stop, peaceful, serene and calm. In-fact it was almost heavenly.

I watched her as she got off her bike, took off her helmet and her jacket and then shook out her long, dark hair again.

"I like it here *Gypsy* she said, it's a place where time truly stands still. It's also a place where a person can stand up and think back upon their lives and perhaps, even look at what they might have wanted to change along the way, and if they're really lucky and maybe just smart enough, they might even do that. Change their lives I mean. Do you know what I'm saying to you?"

"Well no, not really, I said, but it is a great place, that's for sure. It's actually quite beautiful here; calm and serene, but I can't say that I've ever been here before."

"You haven't *Gypsy*, not in this lifetime anyway. It wasn't your time until now."

"Hmm, I said, looking at Misty with a little curiosity that didn't quite sit right in my mind now, "This is all starting to sound a little too heavy for me, I said, I was actually hoping that we'd get into some lighter conversation, perhaps even get to know each other better?"

Misty just laughed, "I'm not who you think I am *Gypsy* she said, still laughing, in fact I'm really someone that you would never want to get to know too well and the reason that I know that, is because I already know you and I've always known you."

"I don't really understand Misty, I said, I've never seen you before in my life, so how could you know me at all?"

"You still don't get it do you *Gypsy*? She said, smiling away, but you will soon enough, I can promise you that."

"I think that maybe we should just ride out of here Misty, I said, as I jumped back onto my bike. I think you may have me mixed-up with someone else, or maybe you're a little crazy in the head, because I don't know what it is that you're talking about."

Then I pushed the starter button and quickly found out that the bike wouldn't start. I tried it again and again to no avail.

Misty didn't move, she stood there watching me, smiling away. She was a crazy woman and there was no doubt about it in my mind, but so damn good-looking, I couldn't take my eyes off of her.

"I'm not crazy," Misty said, as I tried to start my bike up for a third time. This is your time *Gypsy*; this is what your life has been about. This is your crossroads to heaven or hell, so to speak. This is where you make it or break it, do you understand me now?"

"No woman, I really don't understand you at all" I said, still frustrated with the damn bike that wouldn't start. What are you on about? Tell me in plain English or just ride on out of here and leave me the fuck alone."

"Forget the bike *Gypsy*, it doesn't exist anymore" and with that she waved her hand in the air and I immediately found myself sitting on the ground. My bike wasn't there anymore neither. It had simply disappeared.

"What the hell?" I said, as I got up and dusted my backside off; looking at the scenery around us that seemed to be violently changing into different shades of purple and grey, in a matter of seconds.

"What in the hell is going on here?" I said again quickly and rather lamely at the same time. It was all getting way too weird for me and I was feeling something that I had never felt before in my entire life. Not since I was a kid anyway.

It was something that I just wasn't used to anymore; something that I thought was long dead inside. It was a feeling that I had shed years ago; it was a feeling of being afraid. In fact, I was starting to feel scared to death.

"Don't worry about that now Misty said, you're already dead, you just don't know it yet. Once you realize that, then all those feelings will slowly pass you by and you'll be right as rain again, trust me.

Now, do you remember when you asked me what I do for a living *Gypsy*? She carried on talking, and I told you that I collect precious things.

Well that's what I do *Gypsy*; I collect some very precious things, in fact I collect souls, Human souls that is."

"Get the hell out of here, I said, you've got to be mad as a hatter, even though you're very beautiful with it, but I aint ready to go nowhere, I like living the life I live and besides that, this is all bullshit, I aint dead, I just rode fifty miles or so, down these bloody back roads just to be with you. So who's put you up to this shit, Springer? Snake or was it Crocket?"

I looked around again and saw the sky was almost pitch black now and the ground was glowing dark orange and mauve in colour. Misty's hair was blowing violently in the wind, only there wasn't any wind, in-fact, there wasn't anything at all, just the two of us standing there, wherever there was?

"It's like this *Gypsy*, she said, you got up this morning, jumped on your bike and rode on up the road, just in time to be hit by a bloody truck. That's what the accident was all about, you remember that don't you?

I couldn't make it to you in time, so I had to have you wait for me and the best place to wait, was in your own back yard. I just figured that it would be easier that way, easier than having you wait at the scene of your own accident, wondering what to do next?"

"What? I said, no, that ain't right lady, my bike wouldn't start this morning that's for sure, that's why

I missed that accident, that's when I met you, don't you remember that?"

"But your bike starts every time *Gypsy*, you know that, she said waving her hand in a circular motion again, try it now."

I looked around and there it was again, sitting there like I had just parked it up. So I quickly jumped on it, hit the starter button and of course, it roared into life quicker than ever.

"Try it again," Misty said, as it stopped all by itself. I did, and it started up again in no time at all.

"It's a new battery," Misty said, it's good for a couple of years and it starts every time."

"Shit, I said, that's it. I'm out of here," kicking the bike into gear and popping the clutch like a man on a mission, but then I suddenly found myself, flat-assed on the ground again and the bike had simply disappeared, like it had never been there in the first place.

Mystique gave me a hand-up this time and quietly watched as I dusted myself off again.

"Alright, alright, so what am I supposed to do now?" I finally said: in-fact, what does anyone ever do when they're dead?

"Well, that really depends on you now *Gypsy*, Misty said, you can come with me or you can stay here for a little while and think about your life. Could you have changed it? Would you have wanted to? Would you still want to? Think about it, take some time and think real hard, because you might not ever get this chance again.

"Ok, ok, I get it, I said, I think I'll just stick around here for awhile, then what?

Misty smiled at me again and then she finally said, "You'll see *Gypsy*, eventually, everyone does sooner or later" and with that she was gone.

It was early Saturday morning, and the sun was shining so bright that it was hurting my eyes. The sky was a gorgeous deep, dark blue colour and the weather was simply to die for.

What a great day for a ride I thought? Then all of a sudden there was a loud siren ringing in both of my ears, and I slowly opened up my eyes again. I looked around and all I saw was that I was in the back of an ambulance, heading towards the nearest hospital, at least I hoped it was the hospital we were headed to, and not to the county morgue.

Then I heard a familiar voice and quickly saw the vision of an Angel, sitting there beside me, holding my hand in hers. Mary Mystique Angel that is?

"Welcome back *Gypsy*, she said with a smile, we thought we had lost you there for awhile, but now it appears that you're gonna make it after all."

I looked down at my watch; my eyes were burning, watery and slightly blurry, but I could see that it was actually twenty-six minutes after the time that I had finally left my house that morning. Twenty-six minutes, who would have thought?

****

18
The big sky

I had just stepped down from that trusted metal steed that I had been riding for several hours now, parked it up somewhere near the middle of the high street and then I took a long, slow, look around.

The sun was low on the horizon, and there was a warm, soft, southern breeze blowing through the town, raising-up strange dust devils, which appeared to be dancing around in the distance, like little fairies next to an open fire.

What a weird and wonderful little place this is, I thought, rather facetiously, as I brushed off the dirt and grime, that had tried to cover me from head to toe during my ride. Then, I spat out the final remnants, of the last little critter, that had accumulated at the back of my throat, which I had all but consumed at the same time, extra protein and all of that. Yuk.

A single blink of your grannies eye and you'd probably miss this entire village, I thought again, as I stood there still looking around.

It was pretty strange though, because I was quite sure that this place was a whole lot bigger than what it seemed to be now that I was here again, and that the streets were essentially paved before as well. After all, who actually does dirt roads in this day and age?

It was a strange thing to see, to say the least, but it didn't matter that much to me at the time, after all, I was there now and that was about all there was to that.

It really was a pretty weird looking town though, I thought again, as I stood by my motorcycle and looked around to see if I could see any of the other bikes that should have been there by now.

Where is everyone? I quickly thought as I looked down at my watch. It was half passed four in the afternoon already and the streets were completely empty? What's that about?

I had left my last stop, way behind the other riders, about an hour after them or maybe more, so where could they be now? They should have all been here by this time, surely?

I looked up and down the street again, but there was no one in sight, no one at all. The streets were completely empty.

They've got to be in the bar already, I thought again, as I started walking, but where was that? And where did they park their bikes?

I kept walking and I kept looking, but things just didn't appear to be right to me at all. What is this place I quickly thought again?

It was such a strange little town and it seemed to be getting stranger by the minute. The stores that I passed along the street didn't seem to have any of the usual suspects in them. In fact, there didn't seem to be any "usual" type of people around here at all, anywhere.

The ones that I actually saw were more than just a little bit odd to say the least, although there was nothing that you could really pinpoint, but they were a little strange and none of them were people that I knew or even recognized.

"What's up with all of this then, I said to myself out loud, and where's the boys at?"

There was a slight echo drifting past my words, almost as soon as they left my mouth, as if he was standing in a hallway somewhere, instead of in the middle of a high street. No one answered me of course; no one was there to listen to me.

I kept on walking, looking around and walking some more. None of this was making any sense to me, but I finally found the bar that I was looking for and of course, I quickly went inside.

No-one was in there though, not even the barkeep or his waitress or even the town drunk passed out in the corner. Who would have thought?

Everything was getting stranger by the minute, I quickly thought again, as I called out for some service, but of course, no-one answered me, no-one was there to answer. The place was completely empty and I was left totally alone.

I finally poured myself a drink, from a very odd looking whiskey bottle that was sitting on the counter right in front of me. In-fact, I poured myself a double and then I went and sat down at a table near the back wall, taking that odd looking bottle with me of course.

Someone will show up eventually, he thought, as he put his feet up and kicked back in the chair. Someone has to.

The day had been pleasant enough, a regular meeting in the morning at my local club house, although I didn't remember what the meeting was about, but that was nothing new for me.

Church was usually just routine anyway, roll call and going through the motions etc. and then afterwards, it was a poker run for some charity event in the afternoon.

The run itself had covered a whole lot of miles, several different stops, and the little village that I was in now, which was the last stop on the list. It was usually quite a bubbly little town, full of life and lots of people, as far as I remembered, but today for some reason it was just, really strange and almost empty and I didn't know why? Oh well, not to worry, someone will turn up sooner or later, they always do.

I sat there for about an hour, thinking about the run, the weather and the waitress that I had left at the last stop. No, not that tall dykey looking one with tattoos on her neck, different coloured eyes, short dyed hair and arms bigger than what my legs were, but the shorter one, an almost sweet sounding blonde looking woman, that looked so much better. She was a real cutie and she had a nice personality to go along with it.

It was supposed to rain that morning, but it didn't do that. In fact the big sky had remained rather stormy looking, all the way along.

It'll probably chuck it down later as I head for home, I figured, knowing my luck anyway. Then I finally looked at my watch again and poured myself another drink.

That was going down a treat at least, I quietly thought as I sat there contemplating what to do next.

I was starting to get a little hungry though, so I went back over to the bar to help myself to some crisps, peanuts and a couple of pickled eggs if I could find them, but there wasn't any, in fact there wasn't any food anywhere that I could see.

I looked outside again, up and down the street and even up into the air. Nothing, not a soul in sight, but then I noticed that a crowd of people had gathered around my motorcycle that was still parked up at the curb, near the middle of the street.

It seemed like a bunch of weirdo's really, wearing really tall black hats, long dresses and old fashioned two piece suits.

Probably some sort of religious group, I quickly thought as I headed out the door and back down the street towards them, just to see what was what?

That's about the time that I heard that unmistakable click of a set of twin hammers from a double-barrelled shotgun, being slowly pulled back into their firing position, right behind my back.

"You need to pay for your drinks there mister, a voice said behind me, we don't do charity in this town, especially for the likes of you."

I quickly raised my hands and then I slowly turned around.

"Not a problem Sir, I said, I just didn't know who to give the money to" and that was about the time when everything went black.

When I woke up, I found myself locked up in a steel cage. The back of my head was about as sore as I had ever felt it and the rest of my head was pounding out of control. Whatever it was that had hit me had been pretty damn hard and if my skull wasn't cracked, then I was more than just a little lucky, that's for sure.

I looked around and saw that there was another cage right next to me. It was empty and there was another cage just like that one, on the other side of me as well, which was just as empty.

I soon realized then that I was actually in some type of old jail house or maybe even an animal facility of some sort, like a vets office or farmyard hospital building.

I called out for several minutes, but no one answered me of course and then I started to lose my cool more and more, especially as the time went on.

"Where in the hell are all of the people in this town, I yelled out just as loud as I could and where in the hell are all of my friends?"

No one answered me though; again, no one was there to answer me.

I looked down at my watch again; it was nine thirty at night. Damn, I thought, I've been knocked out and locked up in here for hours now.

The facts were becoming pretty clear by then and they also seemed to be quite simple really.

While I was on my way to this stinking little shithole, happily putt, putt, putting down the road on my trusted metal steed, without a single care in the world, the entire country and perhaps even the whole damn world, must have been invaded by aliens from another planet.

It had to have been a massive operation; happening all over the place at the very same moment in time and one that only lasted for a few brief minutes at most.

These aliens, were of course, so far advanced from any of us here on earth, in everything that there is and everything that they do, they simply wiped out the entire planets population in a heartbeat and no-one even knew what hit them.

I had been travelling through a mountain tunnel at the time, the tunnel took me exactly four minutes to pass through and that must have been at the very same moment in time that the aliens did what they did?

Whatever they had used to make everyone disappear had an added benefit to me of course. It prolonged my life. It kept me from aging and it even made me some kind of super-human, but it also got me locked up in this cell.

No, no, wait a minute, none of that's right at all, I thought again, as I put my imagination back into check. Someone or something had locked him up in here.

Someone or something had hit me over the fucking head and put me into this cage to begin with, someone or something that still had to be here, somewhere?

So, it was pretty obvious that my theory didn't hold water in the least, but if it wasn't aliens, what about those people that I saw outside on the street, they were really weird looking and what about that guy with the shotgun?

He was pretty strange as well and he talked kind of funny, maybe with a lisp or something.

Never mind, all I wanted to do now was get the hell out of there, but that wasn't about to happen, not just yet anyway, so I finally decided to lay back down on the floor where I had already been laying and that's when I went back to sleep.

When I eventually woke up again, I was sitting in the chair, back at the barroom that I had previously left before all of the commotion in the street. The glass and that weird looking little bottle, was still sitting in the same place as they were before and as I looked around the room, I noticed that I wasn't quite alone anymore.

There was in-fact an extremely large, jet black, Arctic wolf, sitting by the doorway and it looked as if it was ready to eat me up along with just about anything else in the bar that it could sink its teeth into, in a heartbeat.

Great, I thought, just another thing that I needed at that particular moment in time.

I looked at the wolf and then quietly watched as it looked right back at me. Its long and pointed tongue, was hanging out of one side of its mouth and it was licking at its extremely large pure white teeth quite sporadically.

It's cold, dark, hungry looking eyes, were staring right across the room at me and they seemed to be looking right through me at times, down into the very depths of my troubled and completely tortured soul and I just knew that if I even moved, it would indeed jump-up and devour me for its dinner.

It was about then that I saw the sign sitting on the table next to him. PLEASE WALK THE DOG? Thank-you, very much, it said in big, bold, brash letters.

Is this some kind of joke? I thought? Walk the fucking dog?

I reckon that animal would be walking me if I even tried to move. Oh well, I thought again rather quickly, I couldn't just sit there anymore now, could I?

I got up, shaking from my head to my toes and then slowly but oh so carefully, walked over to the animal and said, "Hello boy, just as I reached it and then I said, would you like to go for a walk then?"

"Well, I thought you'd never ask," the wolf replied in a very posh British accent, acting as if it were just as human as I was.

Naturally, I was floored by that and didn't quite know what to say or do next. I mean, what in the hell was going on here?

I was in a strange town, with strange people and now I was talking to a strange looking mutt that was talking right back at me.

"Let me introduce myself, the wolf said, I am of course, a purebred arctic wolf; I can assure you of that" it said, as it got up from the floor, stretching out its legs and arching its back at the same time.

"My name is Clifton Lloyd James the seventh and my pedigree spans the ages. My grandfathers, grandfathers, father, was none other than "The" Clifton Lloyd James, that was the first of course, but I'm sure that you must have heard of him, yes?"

"Well actually, I said, in complete and utter disbelief, I must admit that I haven't been into the wolf culture too much lately, not that I ever was in the first place, you do understand?

Is there some sort of agenda for all of this, in this life, or is this the first time that you've actually done this sort of thing?"

"I'm not sure that I know what you mean exactly, the wolf said, I usually do go for a walk about this time of day, if that's what you're referring to, simply to stretch out my legs you see and to get some sort of exercise as well etc."

"I'm sure that you do, I said, however that wasn't what I meant at all. What I really meant was..........." The wolf interrupted me at that very moment.

"Quickly now, we must get going now, time is of the very essence here." The wolf said, as it nudged me towards the door and then outside again.

Outside, the sun was shining, the grass was green, the sky was blue and that fucking town that I had arrived in that very afternoon was no longer there.

I looked around as I walked along by the side of the wolf. It was then that I realized that we were actually walking through a meadow, filled to the brim with buttercups and daisies and all of that, and we were following along some sort of ancient, manmade footpath, with coloured and completely manicured, cobbled stones.

"Where is this place? I said, as we walked along, admiring the scenery that was spread out before us. What happened to the town that I was in? And where is it that we are going to?"

"You'll see soon enough *Gypsy*," the wolf said, as we carried on walking through the flowers and then finally into the trees.

Uh, oh, woods, I quickly thought, oh yeah, that's just great. So who's afraid of the big bad wolf then? I thought, as I looked around again and noticed that I was deeper in the woods now, completely alone and feeling quite overwhelmed by it all and totally lost which I never get, ever since I was a child of seven years old.

The wolf had apparently just abandoned me to my little misfortune and my utterly insane confusion as well. Oh well, at least I wasn't locked up in that cage anymore and nowhere near the town that was so strange to me in the first place.

However, I didn't have my motorcycle with me anymore either and that was of course, a very major problem. That bike had cost me several years of savings and I'd be damned if I was about to lose it, that's for sure. So I had to find my way back to that town, no matter what it took.

But then, something suddenly moved out of the corner of my eye, I looked down at it, in total disbelief; it was a little man no more than two feet tall, dressed up with a top hat on his head and long tails running down his back. The hat was almost as tall as he was and the tails were actually dragging on the ground.

This is impossible; I said to myself, as if a talking wolf wasn't? This simply can't be happening to me. This man isn't any bigger than the bottom half of the tire on the back of my bike and certainly not nearly as wide. What the hell is going on here?

"Oh, there you are" the little man said in a squeaky voice, waving his arms up at me, trying to get my attention.

"I was beginning to think that you weren't coming at all. Hurry up now, walk this way, time is of the very essence. We've got places to go and people to see. Hurry up now or we'll be late and that just won't do, no, no, no that just won't do at all."

"What's going on here, I quickly said to the little man, where am I and what is this place?"

I looked around again and saw that I was now standing in the middle of a rather large white room without any windows or doors.

Where had all of the woods gone to? I quickly wondered just as the little man started to speak.

"This is a place called Shamaiya, the little man said, it's that place between what you refer to as heaven and hell.

You've been here before my friend and you'll probably be here again, you do know this, don't you? You do remember this, right?"

"No, I actually don't think that I do, I said, still looking around. What is it that you want with me and how exactly, did I end up in here?"

"You had another accident, you silly boy, you smashed-up your head, good and proper this time, the little man said, don't you remember that?"

"No, I said, I don't remember that at all and none of this can be true anyway, because I was sitting in a bar waiting for my friends to show up when all of this started to happen to me.

I had already parked-up my bike and people were standing around it…………..I was cut off in mid sentence again.

"Yeah, yeah, yeah, what is it with you people? The little man said, you never seem to get it right. It's like you cling on to that miserable existence that you all call life and nothing is ever as good as what it was before, or the way you thought it should be. What's up with that?

We sit around here watching you guys all the time, helping you to get through whatever it is that you need to get through and then when it's all over, you simply don't want to come back here. Its only life for crying out loud and there's so much more to experience in the grand scheme of things. So much more, that you could never experience it all anyway and still, all you want to do is go back to that same old humdrum, that same old fucking existence, that you've already had. What is that and why is that? And more to the point, how do we actually change that?"

"Wait a minute I said, are you telling me that I'm dead then? Are you saying that I can't have my life back, that I've lost my friends and family and now I'm actually standing here as some sort of spirit in the nether world, caught-up in between heaven and hell without a clue of what's going on."

"Bingo, the little man said, the hammer drops, the bell rings and the light finally fucking goes on. Wow, so you do still know how to use that brain of yours then?"

"I don't get it, I said, I don't remember any accident and the only thing that I do remember is getting my head thumped by someone out on the street of that little town back there, where ever that actually was."

"Yeah, yeah the little man said, it's all part of the process you know, just to ease you into the situation so to speak. You were hit by a truck at exactly twenty-six minutes past the time that you left your house this morning. You were taken to the hospital and operated on, but you never recovered. Sorry about that. Your body's still there, but I'm afraid that you're here now and there aint no going back."

It was beginning to make sense to me now, unfortunately.

I remembered it all, the charity run that I never made it to, the Angel that rode along with me, taking me to that strange little place, out there in the middle of nowhere and at the same time she was the one that was in the back of the ambulance?

I realized that I was in way over my head now and I didn't know how to get out of it or what it was that I should actually do next?

"Right then, the little man said, pulling open a drawer that was part of the desk that he was now sitting down at and taking out a folder that was just inside of it.

"Take a seat and we'll see what's going on now, shall we?" he said, just as I realized that there was also a chair directly behind me.

I flopped down into it, basically stunned, feeling stoned and stupid as the realization of my situation was starting to unfold.

Oh boy, this is definitely not good, I thought as I sat there waiting for this little man that suddenly seemed to have grown bigger and bigger right before my eyes.

He wasn't so little now, I thought, in fact he seemed just a tad bit too large to me, rather obese and a little more than just enormous. The man had grown from a little munchkin into a gigantic being, within a few precious heartbeats of who knows what kind of time?

"So, you leave relatives and friends in your wake, boomed the fat man, looking down at me now, with the largest pair of reading glasses, that you've ever seen anyone wear in your entire life, let's just see what they thought of you then."

"Wait a minute, I said; almost screaming the words out, I don't want to hear all of that shit. I don't even want to be here. I just want my life back. I don't care what it is that I can do now or where it is that I can go. I just want to get back to the life that I had, I want to get back to the life that I know.

The fat man started laughing and laughing and then he laughed some more. All of a sudden, he laughed so much that he simply exploded in front of my eyes, sending bits of his gooey shit, down all over the place and of course, scattering the white walls that surrounded us as well.

I was stunned again, ducking my head just as some of the bits and pieces hit and then trickled down my face. I was immediately repulsed by it all and quite violently sick; in fact, I suddenly threw up all over the floor.

"Sorry about that," a voice said to me somewhere, out there in the darkness again, as I felt a hand wiping my face off with a warm towel or something similar, and then I noticed that there was the strangest smell in the air, a smell like that of ether or possibly some sort of disinfectant.

"We'll have you stitched up here in a moment, the voice went on to say, it looks like you're going to make it after all. It was touch and go there for awhile, but you've come through the worst of it now and you're on the mend."

Bingo, I thought, I'm back at the hospital now and I guess I'll make it through to another day and that devil can surely wait. Then I drifted backwards into the darkness once again. Only this time I didn't care too much about that, I just figured that I needed the rest.

"Fetch the stick junior, I said to the wolf, as I threw it out just as far as I possibly could, watching it fly into the field of bright coloured flowers and dark green clover that stood there before us.

The sun was shining, the air was warm and smelling sweet and I actually felt at peace with myself, which was something that I hadn't felt in a really long time.

"Yeah right, the wolf said, arching his back and licking his lips at the same moment, fetch it yourself, I'm out of here.

****

19
TIME

I knew it wouldn't be easy, because nothing ever is, but the plan was simple enough, I just needed to finish building the one machine that would take me back through space and time, rescue the love of my life from an early grave, kill all the bad guys that I could find along the way, and then take over the entire world.

It was a simple plan really, if you were some kind of a Superman, or a seventh son of a seventh son maybe, or even an alien from another planet? But I on the other hand, well I was just another biker that had been in the wrong place at the wrong time, and evidently, with the wrong bunch of people.

Yeah ok, so taking over the world wasn't really on my mind, and it never had been, in-fact that would be the last thing that I'd want to do, the world was going to hell in a bucket, and there was nothing that I could do about that. But getting back at all those people that caused this mess to begin with, well, that certainly would be an appealing prospect, that's for sure.

Some of those people were so called "Government officials", and it was at a "World Peace Conference" of all places, where they, whomever "they" really were, had been discussing the shape of things to come and yes, it was perfectly true, that I had helped my wife rally up support for them, and that I had also helped her to set up the booth in that specific spot, not knowing what I knew now though, for surely if I had of known, then none of this would have happened in the first place and I wouldn't be telling this tale. But, it did happen though; just as sure as you're sitting here reading about it, it did happen, I swear it did.

Now, it hasn't always been that way for me. I really was just another biker that loved to ride his bike. I bought my first chopper when I was fourteen years old and I've bought, built, salvaged and pieced together about thirty more since then, but I was also a family man and a bit of a mad scientist if the truth were known, with a PhD. in Quantum physics.

I had also worked for the government in the aerospace industry, along with computer technology and rocket engineering, amongst other things that I've done, and some of those things were quite experimental and highly classified, especially when it came to the many "Time Continuum" theories that were always floating around through the years. People just love that kind of stuff, especially the big-wigs.

I can't tell you much about that right now, except that it was my job to come up with some pretty hefty answers for some of those bigwigs at the time. Simple little things really, like, does "Time" have any range to it? Does it have any depth? Does it have a field of energy that surrounds it, like so many people speculate? Does it have any width, length or perhaps some sort of shifting variety?

And the ultimate question was always, whether it could be controlled, or not, especially by certain individuals of course.

There were so many questions, that too many people wanted to find the answers to, especially the people at the top, high up in the government, like Presidents and Prime ministers.

Now, you've heard of the G-8 people right? Well, this is one biker that usually got sent a personal postcard from most of those guys, every Christmas, like clockwork.

I was a top consultant of theirs for years, and I was pretty good at being what I was. Apart from that, it was a fairly good paying job and even better than that at times.

It made me enough money to pay off all of my bills and then some, take my wife on holidays, raise the kids, send them off to good universities and buy our house almost outright, along with all the toys that I could have ever wanted, especially my bikes, which was what I was mostly concerned about, anyway.

I wasn't into that world peace bullshit to begin with, saving the planet or anything political like that at all. I didn't even keep up with football on the telly, but I sure did like my bikes and I always loved to ride them, every chance that I could get.

It was on a Friday afternoon, like any other Friday afternoon, when my wife told me about the rally and the conference that was going on in London over the weekend. She was a teacher by profession and her school was going to represent the whole of the southeast of England in this two-day event.

I had just got home from work at the time and she had already arranged everything, prior to letting me know of course, which is usually just power for the cause in our marital life. I quit arguing with her about anything, a long time ago, now I just did what she wanted me to, when she wanted me to do it, and that was pretty much the way it was. A perfect relationship some would say, but the rest of the time was all mine and it was used it well.

I rode-up on the coach with her that evening. It was full of kids and other teachers of course and it was also one of a dozen other coaches, that were heading up to London at the same time, for the same thing, but I didn't mind, I just stuck my nose into a book and then I quickly fell asleep, in no time at all.

Once we arrived in London, we checked into a hotel, just up the road from where the conference was being held, just so it would be an easy walk in the morning. It was actually quite nice to get away from home for a change. After all, everybody likes to have a break at some point in time, even if it is somewhere inside the city limits.

We relaxed and took in a minor play later on that evening, and we had a great supper about an hour or so before hand. Although I was never a suit and tie type of guy to begin with, I wore it well and I made my wife proud to be with me as usual, and that was about all that mattered to me anyway. She was the love of my life and there was no doubt about that. I loved her completely. In fact, it seemed as if I had been in love with her forever. Back during our school days, and throughout university. Then every year that followed. In-fact, I was more in love with her now, than I had ever been before. Every day with her was a total treasure for me, and I had envisioned our final moment's together on this earth, arm in arm and side by side.

It was a pretty good life that we made together, full of love, laughter and light and very little heartache or pain along the way. So, who could ask or even want, anything more than that?

Saturday, went off without a hitch. We were at the booth by eight o'clock in the morning and eventually we stayed until half-past nine that night. It was a very long and tiring day and we saw thousands of people and eventually handed out even more than that in flyers, pamphlets, and plastic parking tokens, full of information about what we were trying to do and what we were trying to achieve etc.

Of course, I got to wander around to all of the other booths that had been set up as well, but I always stayed fairly close to my wife, which is the way I am. It's in my nature to be protective, especially when it came to her. That's why I went along with her to begin with; otherwise I would have spent most of the weekend, simply riding around on my bike.

It was later on in the evening, while we were in bed together, that my wife told me about the strange man that she had seen, while I had been checking out some of the other booths.

She said that this guy was a biker type, with dark-hair, dark-eyes and dark-clothes, and that he carried a dark helmet with him as well. Who would have thought?

The man had told my wife in not too uncertain terms, that she shouldn't be there tomorrow if she wanted to stay alive that is? At first, she just thought that he was joking about it all and she tried to shrug it off. But he kept pestering her, becoming more and more persistent as the time went on. She almost mistook him for her own husband, when he walked up to her to begin with. He did look a lot like me, she said, but of course I was walking around the convention in a suit and tie, not with any of my leathers on. Anyway, this guy kept coming back to her, to tell her the same things over and over again. She finally reported him to one of the guards at the center and then she just figured that the guard must have run him off, because she didn't see the biker again after that.

He was probably just another crazy conspiracy type of guy, she had thought at the time, but it had made her feel pretty damn uncomfortable, because there really was something strange about the way the guy was acting, almost like they had met before or perhaps she knew him from somewhere, but she simply put that down to the fact that he looked a whole lot like me.

"Well, that's it then, I said, when she finally told me the story. We'll just pack up and go home tomorrow and be done with all of this. We'll leave here first thing in the morning, get the bike out when we get back home and then we'll head down to the beach, or just go on a road trip for the day, yeah?"

"I can't do that Hun, she said, they all expect me to stay and finish the job, and I really do have to make sure that the kids get back home safely as well. Don't worry about it. That guy was just a crackpot, some crazy dude with a scary story to tell that's all; I'm not going to let it bother me. Everything will be fine I'm sure."

However, everything wasn't fine.

We were out there by about ten to nine the next morning, and people from all over the world were wandering around by eleven o'clock. By noon we had the largest turnout that we'd had yet. Everything was going well and the place was completely packed.

I had just gone to get us both a bite to eat from the food wagon that was out on the high street, forgetting all about what my wife had said the night before, when the bomb went off, suddenly exploding everything around me, into a million pieces.

I was probably more than a thousand feet away from her at the time, but the blast still knocked me over and threw me up against a wall. The only good thing about it was that she hadn't felt a thing. The bomb had been planted right underneath our booth. It had created a huge blast that took out all of the windows and kicked out all of the doors, for at least two blocks in every direction. One hundred and fifty people were instantly killed in one single, terrible moment of time, and over five hundred people were injured, due to the flying glass, body parts and other debris.

I was lucky that I hadn't been hurt at all, but my wife was dead. My entire life had been shattered in mere seconds and the only thing that I had left on my mind, at that particular moment in time, was strictly revenge.

To hell with the Bush Dynasty, and their bloody war machines, to hell with Tony Blair and Gordon Brown and their brown-nosing, back-stabbing, ass-kissing, piss ant ways that they tried to ruin this country with. To hell with France, Germany, the U.S. and the rest of the Neo-Nazi, pro-Zionist establishment, that has taken on the world up to this point in time, oh yea, and to hell with Iran and Israel too, they sure haven't learned anything worthwhile in the last five thousand years and it looks as if they don't have another five thousand years to waste.

I said to hell with them all. It was time to change the world and make things right, but the question now, was how could I ever do that?

I've studied time-travel theories all of my life, starting with H.G. Wells's "Time machine" and Michael Angelo's drawings when I was just a kid. I've always figured that it just might be possible to do, at least in theory anyway.

The laboratories that I've worked in, along with many of the colleagues that I've worked with, had already developed a machine that was almost complete. In fact, it had been tested numerous times on inanimate objects with more than a few positive results, but it hadn't had any animal testing done yet, or any human testing for that matter. In-fact it was still experimental in every aspect of the word, but I figured that it was the only way to get my life back to where it was.

It was the only way to get my wife back, and I didn't have a choice in the matter.

I had to finish making the machine work and then try it out for myself.

I dropped everything and rushed back home, the train ride was gruelling, but there wasn't much time. I grabbed some tools and headed straight for the lab as soon as I could. It was Sunday evening, and no-one else would be around until at least six o'clock the next morning. So I had about fourteen hours to finish whatever I needed to finish; otherwise I'd never be able to pull it off in time.

I raced around the factory like a mad man. Bit after bit was strategically placed in specific order, until finally at about four-thirty A.M.; I had completed the machine to the best of my abilities.

I stepped back and looked at it. It was perfect. All I had to do was take a seat, set the controls and let the machine do the rest. I didn't care about the consequences, I didn't care about the dangers, and I didn't care about the fact that if it worked, I would alter the course of history, almost as soon as I turned it on. Making what was, something that might have been and might not be anymore, but I didn't care about any of that; I just wanted the love of my life back.

Finally, I stepped in, sat down and turned the dials as I pushed the button. Whoosh. The machine started and stopped all in the same motion, and at the same time.

I looked around. It was pitch black and I couldn't see a thing.

Fortunately, I had a torch with me and I shone the light into the darkness, but there was nothing, in fact the light just stopped at the edge of the machine. I had gone back in time sure enough, but it appeared that time itself had just gone forward. It was no longer there to go back to. There was nothing to see, nothing to do. Time no longer existed in the past; it was now in the future. Well that's just really great I thought, so much for my plan to save my wife and kill all the bad guys.

I thought about it all again, for a few more moments. Ah, yeah, I said as I reset the controls. Whoosh. The machine did its thing.

This time I was in the future instead of the past. Damn it, I said again, it's still dark and the flashlight still doesn't shine past the edge of the machine. Time hasn't got here yet. Damn it all.

I set the controls again. Whoosh. The clock on the wall said four thirty five. Five minutes had gone by. Five minutes. I thought as I set the controls again. Five minutes into the past and whoosh. The clock on the wall said four thirty again. Cool I thought again, so it does work to some degree. I set the controls and Whoosh. The clock now said six o'clock and people were walking in to the building to go to work.

No, they'll see me; I can't let them do that, so I hit the controls a few more times.

Finally, after travelling backwards and forwards, and then forwards and backwards again and again, I found out that "time" had a twenty-four hour hold on the world and it seemed that after that or before, there was no time at all.

The "Time continuum" so to speak was only twenty-four hours long. Twelve hours into the future and twelve hours into the past and that, was simply all that I could get, that was it.

I wasn't going to be able to save my wife after all. She was gone and there was nothing that I could do about it. My heart ached and I sobbed as I sat there. Simply put, I needed more time.

My thoughts raced as I checked and double-checked all of my calculations and ran through the theories one more time, at least, all of the theories that I could remember anyway and all of the ones that I could find on the computer.

I began finding way too many inconsistencies for it all to make much sense. I found that if I skipped forwards for twelve hours, I actually lost twelve hours of time. I wasn't there for those twelve hours, so anything that I should have done or would have done during that time, didn't get done at all. Everything else moved forwards in time as it usually does including me, my body and the machine.

I also found that if I jumped twelve hours into the future and shaved right before I went; once I was in the future, I needed to shave again. However, when I went backwards, I no longer needed to shave. So in essence going back in time made me younger, but I could only go back twelve hours.

Another thing was that as long as I was travelling through time, time never stopped like I thought it would. So if I spent an hour at six o'clock in the morning travelling through time, I could go forward to six o'clock in the evening and backwards to six o'clock in the morning, but as the hour passed, I could no longer reach six o'clock in the morning, it was seven, then eight, then nine o'clock. Because time didn't stand still, it just kept going forwards, apparently in hourly increments.

I could get a glimpse of twelve hours into the future, but that was actually twelve hours without me. Twelve hours that I hadn't lived, so no matter what I saw in the future, it all changed as I lived it, because if I wasn't in the future, I was living the moment and when I was, I simply wasn't, if you can understand that one?

I began to realize that there isn't any such thing, as time at all, really. Time didn't exist, and if time didn't exist, then time was just a way that someone had discovered or invented to measure the here and now. Yesterday was really today, which is also tomorrow, which is really just the day before and the day before that. The past is the present and the future; the future is the present and the past, only time lies in between, but there aint no such thing as time, and there sure is hell, no real way to get back to it.

Bullshit, I said, I had to try. I had to think outside the box, there must be something that I was overlooking, something that I had actually missed along the way.

The machine was a simple device really. Apart from a few classified bits and pieces, it was virtually run by a laptop computer and a small electronic motor. There was no getting around the computer; it was the best in the world, connected by remote to a new super computer that was recently built in the United States, and then fired up on a secondary or duplicate model, somewhere in the deepest, darkest part of Yorkshire.

It was a computer that was capable of handling billions upon billions of different commands and calculations, in Nano seconds. It was indeed an awesome machine, some say it was even powered by a form of A. I. (artificial intelligence) which isn't surprising, especially as fast as it worked.

Anyway, the motor on the time machine however, was just your average everyday electronic motor that had been in existence for over fifty years. It certainly wasn't anything special, it could run a variety of objects, from washing machines down to hairdryers; it was that small and powerful.

I thought about it though. Perhaps the "Time continuum" could be extended with a bigger, more powerful motor than the little one that's being used right now and I knew just where to find another one, in fact there were dozens of them in the ceiling fans around the place.

So I quickly got into one of them and replaced the machines motor with the larger ceiling fan motor and swoosh, I was off again.

Yes, by God, it worked. Thirty-six hours into the past. It was all that I needed. I could get on my bike and reach London in a couple of hours, warn his wife and then stop the bomber in his tracks.

The plan was made and it was perfect, or so I thought, but nothing is ever perfect, never has been and never will be.

It was Saturday morning again and the weather outside was miserable as usual. It had been raining all night long and it didn't look like it was going to stop anytime soon.

I was on his full dresser, doing about seventy five on the road to London, driving like a man on a mission. I knew where I was going and I knew what I had to do. The traffic was crazy, but I had plenty of time, you see there was a convention going on and that's where me and thousands of other people were headed, the only thing was, my wife was already there.

Once I arrived, I found a spot to park up my hog and then I quickly headed into the building. I knew exactly where I wanted to go, but the place was already crowded and it took me some time to get there. When I finally did get there, I stopped dead in my tracks.

"Damn it, I said, I can't be in two places at the same time, I'll have to wait until he leaves, I mean, when I leave. Then I can tell her to get the hell out of here."

I waited and watched as my other self in a fancy suit, finally walked away from her and then I quickly made my way over to the table.

"I have to tell you something honey I said to her, as I reached the table, you have to leave here and not come back at all tomorrow or you'll be killed."

She looked at me strangely, almost as if I was a ghost or something, and then she turned to another person who was also standing there.

"Maybe you didn't hear me, I said again, you have to leave here today and don't come back." I looked around, damn it again, I thought; it was him coming back already. I would have to try this later.

I walked away frustrated that she hadn't listened to me. I stood in the distance, watching and waiting. An hour or so passed when I finally saw myself leave again. I made my way back over to her booth and tried telling her once again.

"Listen to me, you have to leave here, do you understand? You'll die if you don't." I said to her again and again, but she wouldn't listen, she kept ignoring me, then finally she called a security guard over and pointed me out.

Uh, oh, I thought, as I finally realized what was going on, I was the guy that she saw, I was the guy that had told her all about all of this to begin with and I was the guy that the guards ran off. Damn it all. Why didn't I figure that one out to begin with?

I didn't have any choice at that particular moment in time. I was completely surrounded by several different guards. They tackled me to the ground as I tried leaving the building to escape. They tied my hands and feet together behind my back and then threw me into the back of an old van.

When the doors opened again, there were people in white suits waiting for me. Finally, in the end, it was a simple padded cell, with a single bed and a needle in my arm.

I tried to explain it all to them of course, but no one listened, I was just another crackpot, like so many others that they dealt with on a daily basis. Hell, they even had the real Jules Vern, sitting in a cell right next to me and they had been taking care of him for years.

Twenty hours later though, I simply disappeared from that padded cell like I had never been there to begin with. I vanished from both the sight and most of the minds of everyone there, but no one really cared what happened to me anyway, you see a bomb had gone off in London that day, killing a hundred and fifty people.

I was back on the train, heading back home, with a great plan of revenge.

The people at the hospital had told the cops that they had a guy, who had told them that it would all happen, at least that's what they thought he had said, but then he had just disappeared somehow and quite frankly, no one had really taken him too serious anyway. After all, he was just a crazy biker, talking about weird shit, that doesn't really exist.

"Time travel; yeah right. We all know better than that now, don't we? Sorry I have to go so soon, but this is my stop you see, just remember, whatever you do, don't go into London tomorrow, now will you?"

****

20
My Last Fall

A man falls through a fragile roof hitting the concrete floor that was layed-out far below him, with a sudden, tragic, life ending crunch.

The voice of an Angel, who actually sounded as if she had been a lover from his past, quickly came to him and said, "Are you ready to go now?"

The man says "Yes, I'm always ready, but I can't leave my wife."

"Ok the voice says, I'll see you next time then, and the man simply fades to black, waking up in hospital, several days later.

The first thing he sees is a woman that's sitting in a chair next to his bed, wiping away the tears, that had been slowly dripping down her face.

So he quickly says to her, "Who are you, and why are you crying?"

"I'm your wife," she answered, in a mild state of panic and confusion, worried about why he would even ask such a question in the first place?

"Oh shit, the man says, I guess it's too late to change my mind?"

****

I had an accident like this a few years back, and I can tell you there was definitely a clear and distinctive, yet familiar voice that came to me, saying pretty much the same thing. But regardless of that, I could never tell you how much I've hesitated to write about it, or even include it in this book, especially right here and now.

However, it is one of the reasons that I'm writing in the first place, and I think that it's important to let you know where I'm at, as a writer, a musician, a poet, or a story teller for that matter. But please, don't get me wrong here, I'm not looking for any pity over this and I really don't want to give that impression neither, because I'm still the same person that I used to be, I just have to do things a little differently now, and of course, there are some things that I can't do at all anymore, at all, but I'll write about them from time to time, and I hope that you'll appreciate the way that I do.

I also hope that some of the things that I write about, will help others along the way, by letting them know, that they're not alone in this world, and that whatever they're having to go through in life, can usually be overcome, with a little bit of time, a lot of patience, and lots of luck. Having true friends and loved ones around, usually helps out as well.

Meanwhile, misfortune can and will be thrown upon anyone, at any given moment in time, no matter who, where, when, how or what, they think they are? You wouldn't wish it on anyone, but it happens and you can take that to the bank, so please, tread lightly, watch your step and keep those that you love close to you, because this life is more precious than what anyone will ever know?

With all of that in mind, this is what happened not long ago, as far as I remember anyway. It was before lock-down that much I'll say.

While working in London, I fell through a warehouse roof, hitting the concrete floor that was spread out far below me, with a quick, sudden stop, and an extremely hard, painful and utterly sickening, bone crunching thud.

Life, as I had known it, had suddenly come to an end.

The height of the fall was almost fifteen meters, or just under fifty-feet. Not quite five stories, but it certainly felt like it was, especially to me at the time and the entire ordeal, may have only taken a couple of seconds to accomplish, but the damage that was done, is something that I'll have to live with for the rest of my life.

Naturally, an ambulance was called and a helicopter was dispatched, if only to ensure that my trip to the emergency room would be as quick as they could possibly make it.

I was lucky that I wasn't too far away from the hospital to begin with. I was also lucky that I hadn't been working in a third world country at the time, but most of all, I was really lucky, that a Doctor had been flown out to me, instead of having to wait, until I reached the hospital to start the lifesaving procedures, that he started, right there on the spot.

There's no doubt, that the Dr. and his flying machine, saved my life that day, and you can bet that I'll always be grateful to him, along with the other members of his team and the hospital staff, for doing just that.

They said that it was touch and go for me at the time. That my life was truly hanging on the brink of the here and there, for literally days afterwards, but I wasn't aware of that. In-fact, I was oblivious to those facts by then, because I was in a coma, not knowing anything about what was going on for several weeks to come.

My wife had been immediately notified of course, and she was told that the two hour journey for her and our youngest daughter, who would also accompany her on the trip, would probably not be enough time to actually reach me alive, but regardless of that, they jumped into the car as quickly as they could, and drove up to be with me anyway.

No-one could imagine the horrors that must have been running through both of their minds at the time as they travelled up the motor-way. What happens now? What will happen later? Would he survive long enough for the pair of us to say our goodbyes?

Nor could they imagine the anguish and the trauma that they must have felt, when they saw me lying there, hooked-up to those machines, watching strange people that were swarmed around me at the time, like bee's to a hive and then realizing just how badly damaged I was, unconscious, physically-broken, battered, bruised, shattered, helpless, and swelled-up, out of all proportion, far beyond any recognition, even to them.

I had suddenly been thrown back into an abyss, much like the one that I had found out there on that highway all those years ago, only I wasn't slip-sliding at the edge of it this time, I was being sucked into the middle of it, deeper than what anyone had ever been before, at least as far as I could tell anyway, and I was also dragging my loved ones down right along with me, which to my way of thinking, wouldn't do at all. They didn't deserve that.

They were good people, full of love, hope, laughter, and light. In-fact, they were the ones, that had helped me to escape from the clutches of that empty pit in the first place, but there they were anyway, just as helpless as I was, and even though I was completely unconscious, the thought of what they were going through, really pissed me off, more than anything else that had ever pissed me off before in-fact, or at the very least, more than anything else that had pissed me off in a very long period of time.

I can't explain how or why I felt that way, but I certainly did, and I didn't like it one bit. I had been thrown back into the depths of an emptiness that I couldn't even begin to describe, let alone conceive, but my loved ones, had been thrown forwards, into a world that was full of chaos, madness, panic and confusion, anxiety and despair, along with loneliness, depression, sadness and a great deal of regret.

It was a world full of unknowns, where each passing minute, seemed to take literally hours to complete.

It was a world full of strangers, talking in foreign tongues, who had their own lives to live of course, that went about doing what they did, without a single thought or care, for anyone else that might have been around them at the time, let alone, concerned about how that person felt, or what they were going through themselves.

It was also a world full of hard, cold, calculated facts, combined with long drawn-out, medical terms and curious, little, clinical expressions, that most people, without a doctorate in medicine, would simply struggle to appreciate, let alone, comprehend.

It was in-fact, a far cry from their usual existence, which had almost always been the exact opposite, up to that point in time anyway, that it quickly became, quite a severe and lengthy shock to their entire nervous systems, which would eventually take them decades to recover from, and all the while, there was simply nothing that I could do about it, because I didn't know that they were there to begin with, and yet somehow, I could feel them around me. Somehow, I could sense their pain and sorrow, right along with their anguish, and I'd almost bet my life, that that's what really pissed me off the most, because memories like that will never fade, not just for me, but for those around me as well.

Memories that I alone, have to bear the responsibility of creating in the first place, although I know that I had no way of preventing them from happening and I certainly had no choice in the matter what-so-ever. They happened for whatever reason, and that was that.

Now they sit here and fester at the back of my mind, collecting cobwebs along the way, attaching themselves, to any number of painfully agonizing moments that are continuously set up and slowly played out over the course of both space and time.

They build themselves upwards, outwards and onwards, throughout each of our individual lives, whether we want them to or not, and even though we try our best, to forget all about them, they stubbornly remain hidden somewhere, deep-down inside the dark recesses, of our painfully shattered existence, forever haunting our thoughts, dreams and desires, up to a point of where they physically manifest themselves in one way or another, in the middle of the deepest, darkest night, or perhaps, even during the brightest of all bright days, if only for a few brief seconds of time, and if only at the back of our own sub-conscious minds, and they continuously alter our existence, regardless of what it is, or what it was?

They change our attitudes, our perceptions, our frame of mind and even the very way that our own thought processes work.

You can't help that, and you can't fight it, you just have to live with it, and then realize what it truly is and what it's doing to you, because if you don't, it will either kill you, or turn you into a much colder, darker, distant, insular type of person, than you ever were before.

Like a fucking Vampire, that drains the life from within you, quicker than you've ever been drained before, and it's not pleasant let me tell you. In-fact, it's quite horrifying, to say the least.

Both my wife and daughter, crawled inside themselves, for literally years afterwards, completely changed from being the strong, vibrant, bright, beautiful, healthy, happy, extroverted, types of people, that they once were, to an almost, secluded introverts, not quite as strong, nor as bright and nowhere near as bouncy.

They became damaged, sad, lonely and emotionally stunted, by this incident, as well as all of the other incidents and tragedies, that life had brought them along the way, while our oldest daughter, who was living up in Scotland at the time, became filled with a sense of fear and longing, sadness and regret, for simply not jumping on the first plane back home to be with her family.

These women were the loves of my life. They were the ones that I lived for in-fact, they were my entire world, and having to see them go through such pain and agony, sorrow and despair, was too much for any husband and father to bear, but life goes on regardless, and they are slowly recovering from this ordeal, as am I.

However "Slowly" is the significant word here, because everything has taken its time and what has taken the longest is adjusting to the life that we now live, a life that's completely different to what it was before.

Regrettably, they have to cope with other tragedies that have come their way since that moment as well, but I'd like to think that they're becoming a lot stronger, with each passing event, that affects them now.

Of course, I've tried to give them all of the love and support that I can, but I'll always wonder if that's been good enough and I can only guess that time will tell. Who would've thought?

Anyway, here's the truly boring part of all of this. They eventually found out that I had broken my neck and my back, in six different places, including my coccyx and sacrum, which snapped, tilted, twisted and turned, moving slightly to the left.

I blew out three bottom disks, which were located in-between the broken vertebrae and along with my shattered spine, I broke most of the ribs on the left hand side of my body, as well as, a few more on the right hand side, just for good measure.

I banged my head on the way down, cracked some teeth and pierced a lung when I hit the ground. I also dislocated my left collar bone, lost a couple of pints of blood and stopped my heart from beating for a few brief seconds as well, which I suppose was when I was asked if I was ready to go?

I had even managed to damage some of the major nerves on the left hand side of my body, down my arm, hand and leg, which has left me with a very uneven, dizzy and fairly weak feeling, not to mention the pins and needles, which still lingers on, to this day. Of course, I've had a lot of problems to overcome; I was in a coma to start with, bedridden, high on large doses of morphine, blood thinners, and other medications, with tubes stuck inside both of my lungs, through my nostrils, down my throat and a few other places that I don't need to mention.

I was flat on my back for almost two years, because of the broken vertebrae in my spine, two of which, had collapsed, before I had even left the hospital, pinching off even more nerves on my left side etc.

Eighteen months of that time, I was stuck in a body-brace twenty-four-seven. It was also eighteen months of drug induced sleep, twenty hours a day and eighteen months of virtually forgetting everything and everyone that I had ever known before, except for a close-knit family, along with friends of course, which I barely see anymore, because I spend most of my time, trying to write all of these things down.

My mind and it's thought processes, were so badly damaged, that I didn't even know which way was up, and my body, just didn't want to function properly anymore, no matter how hard I tried to make it and to this day, I'm still having certain brain-malfunctions and cognitive problems, like short-term memory lapses and slurred speech, especially when I get weak or tired, or when I'm simply not feeling that well to begin with, which has left me with a complete lack of words, along with an inherent inability, to start up a sentence properly, or to actually think things through, as quickly, and efficiently, as I'm almost positive, that I was once able to do.

There are those other things as well, like the remote control, or a laptop computer, or even a micro-wave oven, that can be confounding, or confusing to me at times and of course, walking, sitting too long, or standing anywhere, for any length of time, is still out of the question and will probably remain so for the rest of my life.

I suffer depression, sleeplessness, hyper-tension and mood-swings, amongst other idiosyncrasies that have popped up over this time of healing as well?

I guess that's what happens, when you fall almost five stories through a roof to the concrete floor below, breaking your neck and back in a half-a-dozen places.

Banging your head, popping a lung and stopping your heart, at the same time, never knowing, whether you're dead or alive, for months on end, and then after all of that, having to pick up the pieces of what was the only life you've known, for literally years afterwards. But hey, I survived it and I suppose that's what really counts in the long run? It's not the first major accident that I've had.

Now, large crowds have made me uneasy in the past and I'll freely admit that, but now every stranger puts me on edge, even the ones that are simply walking by in the distance.

Loud noises, bumps and groans in the middle of the night and cold, damp, weather conditions, bother me and I'm always nervous, anxious and depressed, yet I know that whatever I'm worried about, is strictly in my head and there's nothing that I can do about it anyway, because whatever will be, will be, and that's all there is to it. I also know that I'll have to deal with these issues for the rest of my life, in-fact, I've been told that these things will eventually deteriorate over time, as I age, which is of course, something to look forwards to for sure; not just for me, but for those around me as well.

The in-between times of all of that, were filled-up with ambulance rides, to and from the hospital in London, for more ex-rays, specialist treatments, general check-ups and finally, a relatively minor operation that actually got me back on my feet again, walking with the aid of crutches anyway.

But the best thing about it all was finally getting out of that damn brace and getting close enough to cuddle-up with my wife again.

However, they also told me that the operation, may not last that long, and that it will probably have to be repeated at some point, in the near future, which is something else that I can look forwards to, I suppose?

It's been a few years now and I've recovered as best as I can, but I definitely don't have the abilities that I used to have. I'm nowhere near as strong as I used to be, not as heavy or as muscled as I once was, and I certainly don't breathe the same way either. In-fact now they tell me that I have C.O.P.D which will do me in, if nothing else does?

I can't walk far because of the pain in my back, which sometimes shoots down my leg and foot. I can't bend easy, sit or even stand for too long, and I don't sleep for anymore than a couple of hours at a time. Leg cramps, stomach-aches, pins, needles, little twitches, brain malfunctions, shooting pains and all those bloody nightmares, are fairly common occurrences now, with some of them being pretty damn vivid, extremely intense and always within an hour or two of trying to sleep.

Needless to say, I'm exhausted most of the time but I'm not complaining at all, trust me, I know just how lucky I am and I really do appreciate everything that I still have in this life, including my wife and family and of course, what's left of my friends.

I know that I'm not alone with my problems, and that they could also be a helluva lot worse, and I know that there are others that are going through worse things in their lives as well, because we all have our own trials and tribulations to go through and that's just a fact.

My life has been no different to anyone else's and I'm sure of that, but here I sit anyway, trying to write about it, while wondering if any of this information is even worth remembering in the first place, let alone writing it down?

Now, every one of us takes what we're given in this life and runs with it for as long as we can, doing whatever it is that we have to do, in order to survive. But in the end, we'll all end-up in the same place, wondering if we actually did anything worthwhile to begin with and I reckon, that there's no escaping that.

Some of us will have it easy, but most of us will struggle every day of the week, hoping for something better and trying to get ahead in life, one way or another.

It's the nature of the beast or the luck of the draw, or is it simply the hand that we've been dealt? Whatever it is, there's no changing it and there's definitely no going back on it neither.

I sit here every morning with my memories, feeling some of the pain and frustration that I've tried to forget, curiously wondering about the friendships, love, laughter and light, that I've lost through the years.

Or perhaps, one of the many sorrows and heartaches, which I've had to endure and then bury somewhere, deep-down inside, the back of a slightly damaged, somewhat disturbed, and yet, still a highly inquisitive mind.

Whatever it is, I know that when I'm alone, listening to my own thoughts, feelings and desires, as intently as I can, then that's when the magic starts to appear, flowing through me, like a river into a sea, or at least, a small trickle into a stream, some of the time anyway, and songs, poems, little phrases and finally, the words of this book, begin to materialise into something that's incredible, something that I'm sure that I must have had some help with, right from the beginning, from something or someone else along the way. I'm very thankful for that.

I've always wondered if that's truly inspiration. Or is it simply, some kind of strange, twisted, spontaneous connection to the nether world, or perhaps the universe around us?

Do any of us write the songs we sing, or are they simply, some sort of subliminal messages, that have been handed down to us, from ancestors, ancient spirits, God, or perhaps, even the Angels up above?

It doesn't matter what you believe, or what anyone else tells you to believe, as far as that goes, because we all know in time, that we're only here to do, what we can do, when we can do it.

I've always preferred to think, that it's the latter, because I've never thought myself, intelligent, imaginative, or anywhere near creative in the first place, but hopefully that's changing a little bit now. Hopefully I've become what I was meant to become?

Maybe we all go through that kind of thinking in the long run, or something similar, but for me, I'm still trying to get on with things as well as I can and I also try to write them down, just as often, which is one of the reasons, of why I started writing this book to begin with.

However, things do change, sooner or later, just as long as we're alive and kicking that is, and it seems to me that what I started out to write in this book, well over seven years ago now, has truly become a whole lot more than what I could have ever imagined it to be and I suppose that I'm left wondering, whether that's really me, or has it been something else that's been driving me along to write the words that I've written?

I don't really know, but I am hoping that time, will tell.

****

Postscript

So I guess that's where I'm going to leave this book for now. It is only the beginning of what I'd like to write about and the stories that I want to tell you from here on out will be about others as well, simply because I get bored with my own voice more than anything and I'm sure that there's some of you, who didn't appreciate what was written here, or even liked the way I wrote it, but I thank you for coming this far anyway.

I apologise if you didn't get anything out of this, but I'm quite sure that others will, otherwise it would be a waste of time, and I really don't want to be accused of wasting peoples time. So, Please be kind when you rate this work regardless.

Now, most of what's been written here is as accurate as it gets, however names have been changed, along with places, times and events etc. After all, I'm still a fairly private individual, and I hope to remain that way, even though I'm basically writing some of my memoirs. I just hope that you can appreciate and understand that.

They say that only 3% of those that set out to write a book in the first place will actually finish it, and less than 1% of those, will actually publish it. So I guess I'm doing alright in that department, considering everything?

Anyway, be on the lookout for Biker Tales, Black Book Files Two, sometime near mid to late summer hopefully, and we'll meet again….cheers for now and thank-you so much for you time and support in all of this, it is very much appreciated, as always. Cheers for now.

To be continued

T.S. DeWalt

****

Printed in Great Britain
by Amazon